A Life for a Life

Dinah Maria Craik

A life for a life

By

Dinah Craik

1859

A Life for a Life

Chapter 1

HER STORY

Yes, I hate soldiers.

I can't help writing it—it relieves my mind. All morning have we been driving about that horrid region into which our beautiful, desolate moor has been transmogrified; round and round, up and down, in at the south camp and out at the north camp; directed hither and thither by muddle-headed privates; stared at by puppyish young officers; choked with chimney-smoke; jolted over roads laid with ashes—or no roads at all—and pestered everywhere with the sight of lounging, lazy, red groups,—that colour is becoming to me a perfect eyesore! What a treat it is to get home and lock myself in my own room—the tiniest and safest nook in all Rockmount—and spurt out my wrath in the blackest of ink with the boldest of pens! Bless you! (query: who can I be blessing, for nobody will ever read this?) what does it matter? And after all, I repeat, it relieves my mind.

I do hate soldiers. I always did, from my youth up, till the war in the East startled everybody like a thunder-clap. What a time it was—this time two years ago! How the actual romance of each day, as set down in the newspapers, made my old romances read like mere balderdash: how the present, in its infinite piteousness, its tangible horror, and the awfulness of what they called its "glory," cast the tame past altogether into shade! Who read history then, or novels, or poetry? Who read anything but that fearful *Times*?

And now it is all gone by—we have peace again; and this 20th of September, 1856, I begin with my birthday a new journal (capital one, too, with a first-rate lock and key, saved out of my summer bonnet, which I didn't buy). Nor need I spoil the day—as once—by crying over those who, two years since,

"Went up
Red Alma's heights to glory."

Conscience, tender over dead heroes, feels not the smallest compunction in writing the angry initiatory line, when she thinks of that odious camp which has been established near us, for the education of the military mind and the hardening of the military body. Whence red-coats swarm out over the pretty neighbourhood like lady-birds over the hop-gardens— harmless, it is true, yet for ever flying in one's face in the most unpleasant manner, making inroads through one's parlour windows, and crawling over one's tea-table. Wretched red insects! except that the act would be murder, I often wish I could put half-a-dozen of them—swords, epaulets, moustaches, and all—under the heel of my shoe.

Perhaps this is obstinacy, or the love of contradiction. No wonder. Do I hear of anything but soldiers from morning till night? At visits or dinner-parties can I speak to a soul—and 'tisn't much I do speak to anybody—but that *she*—I use the pronoun advisedly—is sure to bring in with her second sentence something about "the camp"?

I'm sick of the camp. Would that my sisters were! For Lisabel, young and handsome, there is some excuse, but Penelope—she ought to know better.

Papa is determined to go with us to the Grantons' ball to-night. I wish there were no necessity for it; and have suggested as strongly as I could that we should stay at home. But what of that? Nobody minds me; nobody ever did that I ever remember. So poor papa is to be dragged out from his cosy arm-chair, jogged and tumbled across these wintry moors, and stuck up solemn in a corner of the drawing-room—being kept carefully out of the card-room because he happens to be a clergyman. And all the while he will wear his politest and most immovable of smiles, just as if he liked it. Oh, why cannot people say what they mean and do as they wish! Why must they hold themselves tied and bound with horrible chains of etiquette even at the age of seventy! Why cannot he say, "Girls"—no, of course he would say "young ladies"—"I had far rather stay at home—go you and enjoy yourselves;" or, better still, "go, two of you—but I want Dora."

No, he never will say that. He never did want any of us much; me less than any. I am neither eldest nor youngest, neither Miss Johnston nor Miss Lisabel—only Miss Dora— Theodora—" the gift of God," as my little bit of Greek taught me. A gift—what for, and to whom? I declare, since I was a baby, since I was a little solitary ugly child, wondering if ever I had a mother like other children, since even I have been a woman grown, I never have been able to find out.

A Life for a Life

Well, I suppose it is no use to try to alter things. Papa will go his own way, and the girls theirs. They think the grand climax of existence is "society"; he thinks the same—at least for young women, properly introduced, escorted, and protected there. So, as the three Misses Johnston—sweet fluttering doves!—have no other chaperon, or protector, he makes a martyr of himself on the shrine of paternal duty, *alias* respectability, and goes.

The girls here called me down to admire them. Yes, they looked extremely well:—Lisabel, majestic, slow, and fair; I doubt if anything in this world would disturb the equanimity of her sleepy blue eyes and soft-tempered mouth—a large, mild, beautiful animal, like a white Brahmin cow. Very much admired is our Lisabel, and no wonder. That white barége will kill half the officers in the camp. She was going to put on her pink one, but I suggested how ill pink would look against scarlet; and so, after a series of titters, Miss Lisa took my advice. She is evidently bent upon looking her best to-night.

Penelope, also; but I wish Penelope would not wear such airy dresses, and such a quantity of artificial flowers, while her curls are so thin, and her cheeks so sharp. She used to have very pretty hair, ten years ago. I remember being exceedingly shocked and fierce about a curl of hers that I saw stolen in the summer-house by Francis Charteris, before we found out that they were engaged.

She rather expected him to-night, I fancy. Mrs. Granton was sure to have invited him with us; but, of course, he has not come. He never did come, in my recollection, when he said he would.

I ought to go and dress; but I can do it in ten minutes, and it is not worth while wasting more time. Those two girls—what a capital foil each makes to the other!—little, dark, lively—not to say satirical; large, amiable, and fair. Papa ought to be proud of them;—I suppose he is.

Heigho! 'Tis a good thing to be good-looking. And next best, perhaps, is downright ugliness,—nice, interesting, attractive ugliness—such as I have seen in some women: nay, I have somewhere read that ugly women have often been loved best.

But to be just ordinary; of ordinary height, ordinary figure, and, oh me! let me lift up my head from the desk to the looking-glass and take a good stare at an undeniably ordinary face. 'Tis not pleasant. Well; I am as I was made. Let me not undervalue myself, if only out of reverence for Him who made me.

Surely—Captain Treherne's voice below. Does that young man expect to be taken to the ball in our fly? Truly, he is making himself one of the family already. There is papa calling us. What will papa say?

Why, he said nothing; and Lisabel, as she swept slowly down the staircase with a little silver lamp in her right hand, likewise said nothing; but she looked—"Everybody is lovely to somebody," says the proverb.

Query: if somebody I could name should live to the age of Methuselah, will *she* ever be lovely to anybody?

What nonsense! Bravo! thou wert in the right of it, jolly miller of Dee!

> "I care for nobody, no, not I;
> And nobody cares for me."

So let me lock up my desk, and dress for the ball.

Really, not a bad ball; even now—when looked at in the light of next day's quiet—with the leaves stirring lazily in the fir-tree by my window, and the broad sunshine brightening the moorlands far away.

Not a bad ball, even to me, who usually am stoically contemptuous of such senseless amusements. Doubtless, from the mean motive that I like dancing, and am rarely asked to dance; that I am just five-and-twenty, and get no more attention than if I were five-and-forty. Of course, I protest continually that I don't care a pin for this fact (*mem.*, mean again). For I do care—at the very bottom of my heart, I do. Many a time have I leaned my head here—good old desk, you will tell no tales!—and cried, actually cried, with the pain of being neither pretty, agreeable, nor young.

Moralists say it is in every woman's power to be, in measure, all three: that when she is not liked or admired—by some few at least—it is a sign that she is neither likeable nor admirable. Therefore, I suppose I am neither. Probably very disagreeable. Penelope often says so, in her sharp, and Lisabel in her lazy way. Lis would apply the same expression to a gnat on her wrist, or a dagger pointed at her heart. A "thoroughly amiable woman!" Now, I never was—never shall be—an amiable woman.

To return to the ball—and really I would not mind returning to it and having it all over again, which is more than one can say of many hours in our lives, especially of those which roll on, rapidly as hours seem to roll, after five-and-twenty. It was exceedingly amusing. Large, well-lit rooms, filled with well-dressed people; we do not often make such a goodly show in our country entertainments; but then the Grantons know everybody, and invite everybody. Nobody could do that but dear old Mrs. Granton, and "my Colin," who, if he has not three pennyworth of brains, has the kindest heart and the heaviest purse in the whole neighbourhood.

I am sure Mrs. Granton must have felt proud of her handsome suite of rooms—quite a perambulatory parterre, boasting all the hues of the rainbow, subdued by the proper complement of inevitable black. By-and-by, as the evening advanced, dot after dot of the adored scarlet made its appearance round the doors, and circulating gradually round the room, completed the colouring of the scene.

They were most effective when viewed at a distance—these scarlet dots. Some of them were very young and very small: wore their short hair—regulation cut—exceedingly straight, and did not seem quite comfortable in their clothes.

"Militia, of course," I overheard a lady observe, who apparently knew all about it. "None of our officers wear uniform when they can avoid it."

But these young lads seemed uncommonly proud of theirs, and strutted and sidled about the door, very valorous and magnificent, until caught and dragged to their destiny—in the shape of some fair partner—when they immediately relapsed into shyness and awkwardness. Nay, I might add—stupidity; but were they not the hopeful defenders of their country, and did not their noble swords lie idle at this moment on that safest resting-place—Mrs. Granton's billiard-table?

A Life for a Life

I watched the scene out of my corner, in a state of dreamy amusement; mingled with a vague curiosity as to how long I should be left to sit solitary there, and whether it would be very dull, if "with gazing fed"—including a trifle of supper—I thus had to spend the entire evening.

Mrs. Granton came bustling up.

"My dear girl—are you not dancing?"

"Apparently not," said I, laughing, and trying to catch her, and make room for her. Vain attempt! Mrs. Granton never will sit down while there is anything that she thinks can be done for anybody. In a moment she would have been buzzing all round the room like an amiable bee, in search of some unfortunate youth upon whom to inflict me as a partner—but not even my desire of dancing would allow me to sink so low as that.

For safety, I ran after and attacked the good old lady on one of her weak points. Luckily she caught the bait, and we were soon safely landed on the great blanket, beef, and anti-beer distribution question, now shaking our parish to its very foundations. I am ashamed to say, though the rector's daughter, it is very little I know about our parish. And though at first I rather repented of my ruse, seeing that Mrs. Granton's deafness made both her remarks and my answers most unpleasantly public, gradually I became so interested in what she was telling me, that we must have kept on talking nearly twenty minutes, when some one called the old lady away.

"Sorry to leave you, Miss Dora; but I leave you in good company," she said, nodding and smiling to some people behind the sofa, with whom she probably thought I was acquainted. But I was not, nor had the slightest ambition for that honour: strangers at a ball have rarely anything to say worth saying or hearing. So I never turned my head, and let Mrs. Granton trot away.

My mind and eyes followed her with a half sigh; considering whether at sixty I shall have half the activity, or cheerfulness, or kindliness, of her dear old self.

No one broke in upon my meditations. Papa's white head was visible in a distant doorway; for the girls, they had long since

A Life for a Life

vanished in the whirligig. I caught at times a glimpse of Penelope's rose-clouds of tarlatan, her pale face and ever-smiling white teeth, that contrast ill with her restless black eyes—it is always rather painful to me to watch my eldest sister at parties. And now and then Miss Lisabel came floating, moon-like, through the room, almost obscuring young slender Captain Treherne, who yet appeared quite content in his occultation. He also seemed to be of my opinion that scarlet and white were the best mixture of colours, for I did not see him make the slightest attempt to dance with any lady but Lisabel.

Several people, I noticed, looked at them and smiled; and one lady whispered something about "poor clergyman's daughter," and "Sir William Treherne."

I felt hot to my very temples. Oh, if we were all in Paradise, or a nunnery, or some place where there was neither thinking nor making of marriages!

I determined to catch Lisa when the waltz was done. She waltzes well, even gracefully, for a tall woman—but I wished, I wished— My wish was cut short by a collision which made me start up with an idea of rushing to the rescue; however, the next moment Treherne and she had recovered their balance and were spinning on again. Of course I sat down immediately.

But my looks must be terrible tell-tales, for some one behind me said, as plain as if in answer to my thoughts— "Pray be satisfied; the lady could not have been in the least hurt."

I was surprised; for though the voice was polite, even kind, people do not—at least in our country society—address one another without an introduction. I answered civilly, of course, but it must have been with some stiffness of manner, for the gentleman said—"Pardon me; I concluded it was your sister who slipped, and that you were uneasy about her," bowed, and immediately moved away.

I felt uncomfortable; uncertain whether to take any more notice of him or not; wondering who it was that had used the unwonted liberty of speaking to me, a stranger, and whether it would have been committing myself in any way to venture more than a bow or a "Thank you."

A Life for a Life

At last common-sense settled the matter.

"Dora Johnston," thought I, "do not be a simpleton. Do you consider yourself so much better than your fellow-creatures that you hesitate at returning a civil answer to a civil remark—meant kindly, too—because you, forsooth, like the French gentleman who was entreated to save another gentleman from drowning, 'should have been most happy, but have never been introduced.' What, girl, is this your scorn of conventionality—your grand habit of thinking and judging for yourself—your noble independence of all the follies of society? Fie! fie!"

To punish myself for my cowardice, I determined to turn round and look at the gentleman.

The punishment was not severe. He had a good face, brown and dark: a thin, spare, wiry figure, an air somewhat formal. His eyes were grave, yet not without a lurking spirit of humour, which seemed to have clearly penetrated, and been rather amused by, my foolish embarrassment and ridiculous indecision. This vexed me for the moment: then I smiled—we both smiled: and began to talk.

Of course, it would have been different had he been a young man; but he was not. I should think he was nearly forty.

At this moment Mrs. Granton came up, with her usual pleased look when she thinks other people are pleased with one another, and said in that friendly manner that makes everybody else feel friendly together also—"A partner, I see. That's right, Miss Dora. You shall have a quadrille in a minute, Doctor."

Doctor! I felt relieved. He might have been worse—perhaps, from his beard, even a camp officer.

"Our friend takes things too much for granted," he said, smiling. "I believe I must introduce myself. My name is Urquhart."

"Doctor Urquhart?"

"Yes."

Here the quadrille began to form, and I to button my gloves not discontentedly. He said—

"I fear I am assuming a right on false pretences, for I never danced in my life. You do, I see. I must not detain you from another partner." And, once again, my unknown friend, who seemed to have such extreme penetration into my motives and intentions moved aside.

Of course I got no partner—I never do. When the doctor reappeared, I was unfeignedly glad to see him. He took no notice whatever of my humiliating state of solitude, but sat down in one of the dancers' vacated places, and resumed the thread of our conversation, as if it had never been broken.

Often in a crowd, two people not much interested therein, fall upon subjects perfectly extraneous, which at once make them feel interested in these and in each other. Thus, it seems quite odd this morning to think of the multiplicity of heterogeneous topics which Dr. Urquhart discussed last night. I gained from him much various information. He must have been a great traveller, and observer too; and for me, I marvel now to recollect how freely I spoke my mind on many things which I usually keep to myself, partly from shyness, partly because nobody here at home cares one straw about them. Among others, came the universal theme—the war.

I said I thought the three much laughed-at Quakers, who went to advise peace to the Czar Nicholas, were much nearer the truth than many of their mockers. War seemed to me so utterly opposed to Christianity that I did not see how any Christian man could ever become a soldier.

At this, Dr. Urquhart leaned his elbow on the arm of the sofa, and looked me steadily in the face.

"Do you mean that a Christian man is not to defend his own life or liberty, or that of others, under any circumstances?—or is he to wear a red coat peacefully while peace lasts, and at his first battle throw down his musket, shoulder his Testament, and walk away?"

These words, though of a freer tone than I was used to, were not spoken in any irreverence. They puzzled me. I felt as if I had been playing the oracle upon a subject whereon I had not the least grounds to form an opinion at all. Yet I would not yield.

"Doctor Urquhart, if you recollect, I said '*become* a soldier.' How, being already a soldier, a Christian man should act, I am not wise enough to judge. But I do think, other professions being open, for him to choose voluntarily the profession of arms, and to receive wages for taking away life, is at best a monstrous anomaly. Nay, however it may be glossed over and refined away, surely, in face of the plain command, '*Thou shalt not kill,*' military glory seems little better than a picturesque form of murder."

I spoke strongly—more strongly, perhaps, than a young woman, whose opinions are more instincts and emotions than matured principles, ought to speak. If so, Dr. Urquhart gave me a fitting rebuke by his total silence.

Nor did he, for some time, even so much as look at me, but bent his head down till I could only catch the fore-shortened profile of forehead, nose, and curly beard. Certainly, though a moustache is mean, puppyish, intolerable, and whiskers not much better, there is something fine and manly in a regular Oriental beard.

Dr. Urquhart spoke at last; "So, as I overheard you say to Mrs. Granton, you 'hate soldiers.' 'Hate' is a strong word—for a Christian woman."

My own weapons turned upon me.

"Yes, I hate soldiers because my principles, instincts, observations, confirm me in the justice of my dislike. In peace, they are idle, useless, extravagant, cumberers of the country—the mere butterflies of society; in war—you know what they are."

"Do I?" with a slight smile.

I grew rather angry.

"In truth, had I ever had a spark of military ardour, it would have been quenched within the last year. I never see a thing—we'll not say a man—with a red coat on, who does not make himself thoroughly contempt—"

A Life for a Life

The word stuck in the middle. For lo there passed slowly by, my sister Lisabel, leaning on the arm of Captain Treherne, looking as I never saw Lisabel look before. It suddenly rushed across me what might happen—perhaps had happened. Suppose, in thus passionately venting my prejudices, I should be tacitly condemning my—what an odd idea!—my brother-in-law? Pride, if no better feeling, caused me to hesitate.

Dr. Urquhart said, quietly enough, "I should tell you— indeed I ought to have told you before—that I am myself in the Army."

I am sure I looked—as I felt—like a downright fool. This comes, I thought, of speaking one's mind, especially to strangers. Oh! should I ever learn to hold my tongue, or gabble pretty harmless nonsense as other girls? Why should I have talked seriously to this man at all? I knew nothing of him, and had no business to be interested in him, or even to have listened to him—my sister would say—until he had been "properly introduced";—until I knew where he lived, and who were his father and mother, and what was his profession, and how much income he had a year.

Still, I did feel interested, and could not help it. Something it seemed that I was bound to say; I wished it to be civil, if possible.

"But you are Doctor Urquhart. An Army-surgeon is scarcely like a soldier: his business is to save life rather than to destroy it. Surely you never could have killed anybody?"

The moment I had put the question, I saw how childish and uncalled-for, in fact, how actually impertinent it was. Covered with confusion, I drew back, and looked another way. It was the greatest relief imaginable when just then Lisabel saw me, and came up with Captain Treherne, all smiles, to say, was it not the pleasantest party imaginable? and who had I been dancing with?

"Nobody."

"Nay, I saw you myself, talking to some strange gentleman. Who was he? A rather odd-looking person, and—"

"Hush, please. It was a Doctor Urquhart."

"Urquhart of ours?" cried young Treherne. "Why, he told me he should not come, or should not stay ten minutes if he came. Much too solid for this kind of thing—eh, you see? Yet a capital fellow. The best fellow in all the world. Where is he?"

But the "best fellow in all the world" had entirely disappeared.

I enjoyed the rest of the evening extremely—that is, pretty well. Not altogether, now I come to think of it, for though I danced to my heart's content, Captain Treherne seeming eager to bring up his whole regiment, successively, for my patronage and Penelope's (N.B. *not* Lisabel's), whenever I caught a distant glimpse of Dr. Urquhart's brown beard, conscience stung me for my folly and want of tact. Dear me! what a thing it is that one can so seldom utter an honest opinion without offending somebody.

Was he really offended? He must have seen that I did not mean any harm; nor does he look like one of those touchy people who are always wincing as if they trod on the tails of imaginary adders. Yet he made no attempt to come and talk to me again; for which I was sorry; partly because I would have liked to make him some amends, and partly because he seemed the only man present worth talking to.

I do wonder more and more what my sisters can find in the young men they dance and chatter with. To me they are inane, conceited, absolutely unendurable. Yet there may be good in some of them. May? Nay, there *must* be good in every human being. Alas, me! Well might Dr. Urquhart say last night that there are no judgments so harsh as those of the erring, the inexperienced, and the young.

I ought to add that when we were wearily waiting for our fly to draw up to tie hall-door, Dr. Urquhart suddenly appeared. Papa had Penelope on his arm, Lisabel was whispering with Captain Treherne. Yes, depend upon it, that young man will be my brother-in-law: I stood by myself, in the doorway, looking out on he pitch-dark night, when some one behind me said—

"Pray stand within shelter. You young ladies are never half careful enough o your health. Allow me."

And with a grave professional air, my medical friend wrapped me closely up in my shawl.

"A plaid, I see. That is sensible. There is nothing for warmth like a good plaid," he said, with a smile, which, even had it not been Or his name, and a slight strengthening and broadening of his English, scarcely amounting to an accent, would have pretty well showed what part of the kingdom Dr. Urquhart came from. I was going, in my bluntness, to put the direct question, but felt as if I had committed myself quite enough for one right.

Just then was shouted out "Mr. Johnson's"—oh dear, shall we never get the aristocratic *t* into our plebeian name!— "carriage," and I was hurried into the fly. Not by the doctor, though; he stood like a bear on the doorstep, and never attempted to stir.

That's all.

A Life for a Life

Chapter 2

HIS STORY

Hospital Memoranda, Sept. 21st. — Private William Carter, æt. 24; admitted a week to-day. Gastric fever—typhoid form—slight delirium—bad case. Asked me to write to his mother—did not say where. *Mem.* To inquire among his division if anything is known about his friends.

Corporal Thomas Hardman, æt. 50. Delirium tremens — mending. Knew him in the Crimea, when he was a perfectly sober fellow, with constitution of iron. "Trench work did it," he says, "and last winter's idleness." *Mem.* To send for him after his discharge from hospital, and see what can be done; also to see that decent body his wife, after my rounds to-morrow.

M.U.—Max Urquhart.—Max Urquhart, M.D., M.R.C.S.

—Who keeps scribbling his name up and down this page like a silly school-boy, just for want of something to do.

Something to do! Never for these twenty years and more have I been so totally without occupation.

What a place this camp is! worse than ours in the Crimea, by far. To-day especially. Rain pouring, wind howling, mud ankle-deep; nothing on earth for me to be, to do, or to suffer, except—yes! there is something to suffer—Treherne's eternal flute.

Faith, I must be very hard up for occupation when I thus continue this journal of my cases into a personal diary of the worst patient I have to deal with—the most thankless, unsatisfactory, and unkindly. Physician, heal thyself! But how?

I shall tear out this page—Or stay, I'll keep it as a remarkable literary and psychological fact—and go on with my article on Gunshot Wounds.

In the which, two hours after, I find I have written exactly ten lines.

A Life for a Life

These must be the sort of circumstances under which people commit journals. For some do—and heartily as I have always contemned the proceeding, as we are prone to contemn peculiarities and idiosyncrasies quite foreign to our own, I begin to-day dimly to understand the state of mind in which such a thing might be possible.

Diary of a Physician, shall I call it?—did not some one write a book with that title? I picked it up on shipboard—a story-book or some such thing—but I scarcely ever read what is called "light literature." I have never had time. Besides, all fictions grow tame compared to the realities of daily life, the horrible episodes of crime, the pitiful bits of hopeless misery that I meet with in my profession. Talk of romance!

Was I ever romantic? Once perhaps—or at least I might have been.

My profession—truly there is nothing like it for me. Therein I find incessant work, interest, hope. Daily do I thank Heaven that I had courage to seize on it and go through with it, in order—according to the phrase I heard used last night—"to save life instead of destroying it."

Poor little girl—she meant nothing—she had no idea what she was saying.

Is it that which makes me so unsettled to-day?

Perhaps it would be wiser never to go into society. A hospital-ward is far more natural to me than a ball-room. There, is work to be done, pain to be alleviated, evil of all kinds to be met and overcome—here, nothing but pleasure, nothing to do but to enjoy.

Yet some people can enjoy—and actually do so; I am sure that girl did. Several times during the evening she looked quite happy. I do not often see people looking happy.

Is suffering, then, our normal and natural state? Is to exist synonymous with to endure? Can this be the law of a beneficent Providence? Or are such results allowed—to happen in certain exceptional cases, utterly irremediable and irretrievable—like——

A Life for a Life

What am I writing?—what am I daring to write?

Physician, heal thyself. And surely that is one of a physician's first duties. A disease struck inwards—the merest tyro knows how fatal is treatment which results in that. It may be I have gone on the wrong track altogether—at least since my return to England.

The present only is a man's possession: the past is gone out of his hand—wholly, irrevocably. He may suffer from it, learn from it—in degree, perhaps, expiate it; but to brood over it is utter madness.

Now, I have had many cases of insanity—both physical and moral, so to speak; I call moral insanity that kind of disease which is superinduced on comparatively healthy minds by dwelling incessantly on one idea; the sort of disease which you find in women who have fallen into melancholy from love-disappointments; or in men for overweening ambition, hatred, or egotism—which latter, carried to a high pitch, invariably becomes a kind of insanity. All these forms of monomania, as distinguished from physical mania, disease of the structure of the brain, I have studied with considerable interest and corresponding success. My secret was simple enough; one which Nature herself often tries and rarely fails in—the law of substitution; the slow eradication of any fixed idea, by supplying others, under the influence of which the original idea is—at all events temporarily—laid to sleep.

Why cannot I try this plan? why not do for myself what I have so many times prescribed and done for others?

It was with some notion of the kind that I went to this ball—after getting up a vague sort of curiosity in Treherne's anonymous beauty, about whom he has so long been raving to me—boy-like. Ay, with all his folly, the lad is an honest lad. I should not like him to come to any harm.

The tall one must have been the lady; and the smaller, the plainer, though the pleasanter to my mind, was no doubt her sister. And of course her name, too, was *Johnson*.

What a name to startle a man so—to cause him to stand like a fool at that hall-door, with his heart dead still, and all his nerves quivering! To make him now, in the mere writing of it, pause and compel

A Life for a Life

himself into common-sense by rational argument—by meeting the thing, be it chimerical or not, face to face, as a man ought to do. Yet as cowardly, in as base a paroxysm of terror, as if likewise face to face, in my hut corner, stood— Here I stopped. Shortly afterwards I was summoned to the hospital, where I have been ever since. William Carter is dead. He will not want his mother now. What a small matter life or death seems when one comes to think of it. What an easy exchange!

Is it I who am writing thus, and on the same leaf which, closed up in haste when I was fetched to the hospital, I have just bad such an anxious search for, that it might be instantly burnt. Yet, I find there is nothing in it that I need have feared—nothing that could, in any way, have signified to anybody—unless, perhaps, the writing of that one name.

Shall I never get over this absurd folly—this absolute monomania?—when there are hundreds of the same name to be met with every day—when, after all, it is not exactly *the* name!

Yet this is what it cost me. Let me write it down, that the confession in plain English of such utter insanity may in degree have the same effect as when I have sat down and desired a patient to recount to me, one by one, each and all of his delusions, in order that, in the mere telling of them, they might perhaps vanish.

I went away from that hall-door at once. Never asking— nor do I think for my life I could ask—the simple question that would have set all doubt at rest. I walked across country, up and down, along road or woodland, I hardly knew whither, for miles, following the moon-rise. She seemed to rise just as she did nineteen years ago—nineteen years, ten months, all but two days—my arithmetic is correct, no fear! She lifted herself like a ghost over those long level waves of moor, till she sat, blood-red, upon the horizon, with a stare which there was nothing to break, nothing to hide from—nothing between her and me, but the plain and the sky—just as it was that night.

What am I writing? Is the old horror coming back again. It cannot. It *must* be kept at bay.

A Life for a Life

A knock—ah, I see; it is the sergeant of poor Carter's company. I must return to daily work, and labour is life—to me.

Chapter 3

HIS STORY

Sept. 30th.—Not a case to set down to-day. This high moorland is your best sanatorium. My "occupation's gone."

I have every satisfaction in that fact, or in the cause of it; which, cynics might say, a member of my profession would easily manage to prevent, were he a city physician instead of a regimental surgeon. Still, idleness is insupportable to me. I have tried going about among the few villages hard by, but their worst disease is one to which this said regimental surgeon, with nothing but his pay, can apply but small remedy—poverty.

To-day I have paced the long, straight lines of the camp; from the hospital to the bridge, and back again to the hospital—have tried to take a vivid interest in the loungers, the football players, and the wretched, awkward squad turned out in never-ending parade. With each hour of the quiet autumn afternoon have I watched the sentinel mount the little stockaded hillock, and startle the camp with the old familiar boom of the great Sebastopol bell. Then, I have shut my hut-door, taken to my books, and studied till my head warned me to stop.

The evening post—but only business letters. I rarely have any other. I have no one to write to me—no one to write to.

Sometimes I have been driven to wish I had; some one friend with whom it would be possible to talk in pen and ink, on other matters than business. Yet, *cui bono?* To no friend should I or could I let out my real self; the only thing in the letter that was truly and absolutely me would be the great grim signature—"Max Urquhart."

Were it otherwise—were there any human being to whom I could lay open my whole heart, trust with my whole history;— but no, that were utterly impossible now.

No more of this.

A Life for a Life

No more, until the end. That end, which at once solves all difficulties, every year brings nearer. Nearly forty, and a doctor's life is usually shorter than most men's. I shall be an old man soon, even if there come none of those sudden chances against which I have of course provided.

The end. How and in what manner it is to be done, I am not yet clear. But it shall be done, before my death or after.

"Max Urquhart, M.D."

I go on signing my name mechanically, with those two business-like letters after it, and thinking how odd it would be to sign it in any other fashion. How strange,—did any one care to look at my signature in any way except thus, with the two professional letters after it—a commonplace signature of business. Equally strange, perhaps, that such a thought as this last should have entered my head, or that I should have taken the trouble, and yielded to the weakness of writing it down. It all springs from idleness—sheer idleness; the very same cause that makes Treherne, whom I have known do duty cheerily for twenty-four hours in the trenches, lounge, smoke, yawn, and play the flute. There—it has stopped. I heard the postman rapping at his hut-door—the young simpleton has got a letter.

Suppose, just to pass away the time, I, Max Urquhart, reduced to this lowest ebb of inanity by a paternal government, which has stranded my regiment here, high and dry, but as dreary as Noah on Ararat— were to enliven my solitude, drive away blue devils, by manufacturing for myself an imaginary correspondent? So be it.

To begin then at once in the received epistolary form:—

"My dear——"

My dear—what? "Sir?"—No—not for this once. I wanted a change. "Madam?"—that is formal. Shall I invent a name?

When I think of it, how strange it would feel to me to be writing "my dear" before any christian name. Orphaned early, my only brother long dead, drifting about from land to land till I have almost forgotten my own, which has quite forgotten me—I had not considered it before, but really I do not believe there is a human being living whom I have a right to call by his or her christian name, or who would ever think of calling me by mine. "Max"—I have not heard the sound of it for years.

Dear, a pleasant adjective—my, a pronoun of possession, implying that the being spoken of is one's very own—one's sole, sacred, personal property, as with natural selfishness one would wish to hold the thing most precious. *My dear;*—a satisfactory total. I rather object to *"dearest"* as a word implying comparison, and therefore never to be used where comparison should not and could not exist. Witness, "dearest mother," or "dearest wife," as if a man had a plurality of mothers and wives, out of whom he chose the one he loved best. And, as a general rule, I dislike all ultra expressions of affection set down in ink. I once knew an honest gentleman—blessed with one of the tenderest hearts that ever man had, and which in all his life was only given to one woman; he, his wife told me, had never, even in their courtship days, written to her otherwise than as "My dear Anne,"—ending merely with "Yours faithfully," or "Yours truly." Faithful—true—what could he write, or she desire more?

If my pen wanders to lovers and sweethearts, and moralises over simple sentences in this maundering way, blame not me dear imaginary correspondent, to whom no name shall be given at all—but blame my friend—as friends go in this world— Captain Augustus Treherne. Because, happily, that young fellow's life was saved at Balaklava, does he intend to invest me with the responsibility of it, with all its scrapes and follies, now and for evermore? Is my clean, sober hut to be fumigated with tobacco and poisoned with brandy-and-water, that a lovesick youth may unburden himself of his sentimental tale? Heaven knows why I listen to it! Probably because telling me keeps the lad out of mischief; also because he is honest, though an ass, and I always had a greater leaning to fools than to knaves. But let me not pretend reasons which make me out more generous than I really am, for the fellow and his love-affair bore me exceedingly sometimes, and would be quite unendurable anywhere but in this dull camp. I do it from a certain abstract pleasure which I have always taken in dissecting character, constituting myself an amateur demonstrator of spiritual anatomy.

An amusing study is, not only the swain, but the goddess. For I found her out, spelled her over satisfactorily, even in that one evening. Treherne little guessed it—he took care never to introduce me—he does not even mention her name, or suspect I know it. Vast precautions against nothing! Does he fear lest Mentor should put in a claim to his Eucharis? You know better, dear Imaginary Correspondent.

Even were I among the list of "marrying men," this adorable she would never be my choice, would never attract me for an instant. Little as I know about women, I know enough to feel certain that there is a very small residuum of depth, feeling, or originality, in that large handsome physique of hers. Yet she looks good-natured, good-tempered; almost as much so as Treherne himself.

"Speak o' the de'il," there he comes. Far away down the lines I can catch his eternal "Donna é mobile"—how I detest that song! No doubt he has been taking to the post his answer to one of those abominably-scented notes that he always drops out of his waistcoat by the merest accident, and glances round to see if I am looking— which I never am. What a young puppy it is! Yet it hangs after one kindly, like a puppy; after me too, who am not the pleasantest fellow in the world. And as it is but young, it *may* mend, if it falls into no worse company than the present.

I have known what it is to be without a friend when one is very inexperienced, reckless, and young.

Evening.

"To what base uses may we come at last."

It seems perfectly ridiculous to see the use this memorandum-book has come to. Cases forsooth! The few pages of them may as well be torn out, in favour of the new specimens of moral disease which I am driven to study. For instance:—

No. 1—Better omit that.

No. 2—Augustus Treherne, æt. 22: intermittent fever, verging upon yellow fever occasionally, as to-day. Pulse, very high; tongue, rather foul, especially in speaking of Mr. Cohn Granton; countenance, pale, inclining to livid. A very bad case altogether.

Patient enters, whistling like a steam-engine, as furious and as shrill, with a corresponding puff of smoke. I point to the obnoxious vapour.

"Beg pardon, Doctor; I always forget. What a tyrant you are!"

"Very likely; but there is one thing I never will allow—smoking in my hut. I did not, you know, even in the Crimea."

The lad sat down, sighing like a furnace.

"Heigho, Doctor, I wish I were you."

"Do you?"

"You always seem so uncommonly comfortable; never want a cigar or anything to quiet your nerves and keep you in good humour. You never get into a scrape of any sort; have neither a mother to lecture you, nor an old governor to bully you."

"Stop there."

"I will then; you need not take me up so sharp. He's a trump, after all. You know that, so I don't mind a word or two against him. Just read there."

He threw over one of Sir William's ultra-prosy moral essays—which no doubt the worthy old gentleman flatters himself are, in another line, the very copy of Lord Chesterfield's letters to his son. I might have smiled at it had I been alone—or laughed at it were I young enough to sympathise with the modern system of transposing into "the Governor," the ancient reverend name of "Father."

"You see what an opinion he has of you. 'Pon my life, if I were not the meekest fellow imaginable, always ready to be led by a straw into Virtue's ways, I should have cut your acquaintance long ago. 'Invariably follow the advice of Dr. Urquhart,'—'I wish, my dear son, that your character more resembled that of your friend, Dr. Urquhart. I should be more concerned about your many follies, were you not in the same regiment as Dr. Urquhart. Dr. Urquhart is one of the wisest men I ever knew,' and so on, and so on. What say you?"

A Life for a Life

I said nothing; and I now write down this, as I shall write anything of the kind which enters into the plain relation of facts or conversations which daily occur. God knows how vain such words are to me at the best of times—mere sounding brass and tinkling cymbal—as the like must be to most men well acquainted with themselves. At some times, and under certain states of mind, they become to my ear the most refined and exquisite torture that my bitterest enemy could desire to inflict. There is no need, therefore, to apologise for them. Apologise to whom, indeed? Having resolved to write this, it were folly to make it an imperfect statement. A journal should be fresh, complete, and correct—the man's entire life, or nothing. Since, if he sets it down at all, it must necessarily be for his own sole benefit—it would be the most contemptible form of egotistic humbug to arrange and modify it as if it were meant for the eye of any other person.

Dear, unknown, imaginary eye—which never was and never will be—yet which I like to fancy shining somewhere in the clouds, out of Jupiter, Venus, or the Georgium Sidus, upon this solitary me—the foregoing sentence bears no reference to you.

"Treherne," I said, "whatever good opinion your father is pleased to hold as to my wisdom, I certainly do not share in one juvenile folly—that, being a very well-meaning fellow on the whole, I take the greatest pains to make myself out a scamp."

The youth coloured.

"That's me, of course."

"Wear the cap if it feels comfortable. And now, will you have some tea?"

"Anything—I feel as thirsty as when you found me dragging myself to the brink of the Tchernaya. Hey, Doctor, it would have saved me a deal of bother if you had never found me at all. Except that it would vex the old governor to end the name and have the property all going to the dogs—that is, to Cousin Charteris; who would not care how soon I was dead and buried."

"*Were* dead and buried, if you please."

"Confound it, to stop a man about his grammar when he is in my state of mind! Kept from his cigar, too! Doctor, you never were in love, or you never were a smoker."

"How do you know?"

"Because you never could have given up the one or the other; a fellow can't; 'tis an impossibility."

"Is it? I once smoked six cigars a day, for two years."

"Eh, what? And you never let that out before? You are so close! Possibly, the other fact will peep out in time. Mrs. Urquhart and half-a-dozen brats may be living in some out-of-the-way nook—Cornwall, or Jersey, or the centre of Salisbury Plain. Why, what?—nay, I beg your pardon, Doctor."

What a horrible thing it is that by no physical effort, added to years of mental self-control, can I so harden my nerves that certain words, names, suggestions, shall not startle me—make me quiver as if under the knife. Doubtless, Treherne will henceforth retain—so far as his easy mind can retain anything—the idea that I have a wife and family hidden somewhere! Ludicrous idea, if it were not connected with other ideas from which, however, this one will serve to turn his mind.

To explain it away was of course impossible. I had only power to slip from the subject with a laugh, and bring him back to the tobacco question.

"Yes; I smoked six cigars a day for at least two years."

"And gave it up? Wonderful!"

"Not very, when a man has a will of his own, and a few strong reasons to back it."

"Out with them—not that they will benefit me, however—I'm quite incorrigible."

"Doubtless. First, I was a poor medical student, and six cigars per diem cost fourteen shillings a week—thirty-one pounds eight shillings a year. A good sum to give for an artificial want—enough to have fed and clothed a child."

"You're weak on the point of brats, Urquhart. Do you remember the little Russ we picked up in the cellar at Sebastopol? I do believe you'd have adopted and brought it home with you if it had not died."

Should I? But as Treherne said, it died.

"Secondly, thirty-one pounds eight shillings per annum was a good deal to give for a purely selfish enjoyment, annoying to almost everybody except the smoker, and at the time of smoking—especially when to the said smoker it is sure to grow from a mere accidental enjoyment into an irresistible necessity—a habit to which he becomes the most utter slave. Now, a man is only half a man who allows himself to become the slave of any habit whatsoever."

"Bravo, Doctor—all this should go into the *Lancet*."

"No; for it does not touch the question on the medical side, but the general and practical one—namely, that to create an unnecessary luxury, which is a nuisance to everybody else, and to himself of very doubtful benefit—is—excuse me—the very silliest thing a young man can do. A thing, which, from my own experience, I'll not aid and abet any young man in doing. There, lecture's over, and kettle boiled—unless you prefer tobacco and the open air."

He did not: and we sat down—"four feet upon a fender," as the proverb says.

"Heigho! but the proverb doesn't mean four feet in men's boots," said Treherne, dolefully. "I wish I was dead and buried."

I suggested that the light moustache he curled so fondly, the elegant hair, and the aristocratic outline of phiz, would look exceedingly well—in a coffin.

"Faugh! how unpleasant you are."

And I myself repented the speech: for it ill becomes a man under any provocation to make a jest of Death. But that this young fellow, so full of life, with every attraction that it can offer—health, wealth, kindred, friends—should sit croaking there, with such a used-up, lackadaisical air—truly it irritated me.

"What's the matter—that you wish to rid the world of your valuable presence? Has the young lady expressed a similar desire?"

"She?—Hang her! I won't think any more about her," said the lad sullenly. And then, out poured the grand despair, the unendurable climax of mortal woe. "She cantered through the north camp this afternoon, with Granton—Colin Granton, and upon Granton's own brown mare."

"Ha!—horrible vision! And you?—you

> 'Watched them go: one horse was blind;
> The tails of both hung down behind.
> Their shoes were on their feet'—"

"Doctor!"

I stopped—there seemed more reality in his feelings than I had been aware of; and it is scarcely right to make a mock of even the fire-and-smoke, dust-and-ashes passion of a boy.

"I beg your pardon; not knowing the affair had gone so far. Still, it isn't worth being dead and buried for."

"What business has she to go riding with that big clod-hopping lout? And what right has he to lend her his brown mare?" chafed Treherne, with a great deal more which I did not much attend to. At last, weary of playing Friar Lawrence to such a very uninteresting Romeo, I hinted, that if he disapproved of the young lady's behaviour, he ought to appeal to her own good sense, to her father, or somebody—or, since women understand one another best, get Lady Augusta Treherne to do it.

"My mother! She never even heard of her. Why, you speak as seriously as if I were actually intending to marry her!"

A Life for a Life

Here I could not help rousing myself a trifle.

"Excuse me—it never struck me that a gentleman could discuss a young lady among his acquaintance, make a public show of his admiration for her, interfere with her proceedings or her conduct towards any other gentleman, and *not* intend to marry her. Suppose we choose another subject of conversation."

Treherne grew hot to the ears, but he took the hint and spared me his sentimental maunderings.

Wd had afterwards some interesting conversation about a few cases of mine in the neighbourhood, not on the regular list of regimental patients, which have lately been to me a curious study. If I were inclined to quit the Army, I believe the branch of my profession which I should take up would be that of sanitary reform—the study of health rather than of disease, of prevention rather than cure. It often seems to me, that we of the healing art have began at the wrong end—that the energy we devote to the alleviation of irremediable disease would be better spent in the study and practice of means to preserve health.

Thus, I tried to explain to Treherne—who will have plenty of money and influence, and whom, therefore, it is worth while taking pains to inoculate with a few useful facts and ideas—that one-half of our mortality in the Crimea was owing, not to the accidents of war, but to the results of zymotic diseases, all of which might have been prevented by common sense and common knowledge of the laws of health, as the statistics of our sanitary commission have abundantly proved.

And, as I told him, it saddens me, almost as much as doing my duty on a battle-field, or at Scutari, or Renkioi, to take these amateur rounds in safe England, among what poets and politicians call the noble British peasantry, and see the frightful sacrifice of life—and worse than life—from causes perfectly remediable.

Take, for instance, these cases, as set down in my note-book. Amos Fell, 40, or thereabouts, down with fever for ten days; wife and five sons; occupy one room of a cottage on the Moor, which holds two other families; says, would be glad to live in a better place, but cannot get it; landlord will not allow more cottages to be built.

A Life for a Life

Would build himself a peat hut, but doubts if that would be permitted; so just goes on as well as he can.

Peck family, fever also, living at the filthiest end of the village; themselves about the dirtiest in it; with a stream rushing by fresh enough to wash and cleanse a whole town.

Widow Haynes, rheumatism, from field-work, and living in a damp room with earthen floor, half underground; decent woman, gets half-a-crown a week from the parish, but will not be able to earn anything for months; and what is to become of all the children?

Treherne settled that question, and one or two more. Poor fellow, his purse is as open as his heart just now; but among his other luxuries he may as well taste the luxury of giving. 'Tis good for him; he will be Sir Augustus one of these days. Is his goddess aware of that fact, I wonder?

What! is cynicism growing to be one of my vices? and against a woman too? One of whom I absolutely know nothing, except watching her for a few moments at a ball. She seems to be one of the usual sort of officers' belles in country quarters. Yet there may be something good in her. There was, I feel sure, in that large-eyed sister of hers. But let me not judge—I have never had any opportunity of understanding women.

This subject was not revived, till, the tobacco-hunger proving too strong for him, my friend Romeo began to fidget, and finally rose.

"I say, Doctor, you won't tell the governor—it would put him in an awful fume?"

"What do you mean?"

"Oh—about Miss you know. I've been a great ass, I suppose; but when a girl is so civil to one—a fine girl, too— you saw her, did you not, dancing with me? Now isn't she an uncommonly fine girl?"

I assented.

"And that Granton should get her, confound him! a great logger-headed country clown."

"Who is an honest man, and will make her a kind husband. Any other honest man who does not mean to offer himself as her husband, had much better avoid her acquaintance."

Treherne coloured again; I saw he understood me, though he turned it off with a laugh.

"You're preaching matrimony, Doctor, surely. What an idea! to tie myself up at my age. I shan't do the ungentlemanly thing either. So good-night, old fellow."

He lounged out, with that lazy, self-satisfied air which is misnamed aristocratic. Yet I have seen many a one of these conceited, effeminate-looking, drawing-room darlings, a curled and scented modern Alcibiades, fight—*like* Alcibiades; and die—as no Greek ever could die—like a Briton.

"Ungentlemanly,"—what a word it is with most men, especially in the military profession. Gentlemanly,—the root and apex of all honour; ungentlemanly,—the lowest term of degradation. Such is our code of morals in the Army; and, more or less, probably everywhere.

An officer I knew—who, for all I ever heard or noticed, was himself as true a gentleman as ever breathed; polished, kindly, manly, and brave—gave me once, in an argument on duelling, his definition of the word: "A *gentleman*—one who never does anything he is ashamed of, or that would compromise his honour."

Worldly honour, this colonel must have meant, for he considered it would have been compromised by a man's refusing to accept a challenge. That "honour" surely was a little lower thing than virtue; a little less pure than the Christianity which all of us profess, and so few believe. Yet there was something at once touching and heroic about it, and in the way this man of the world upheld it. The best of our British chivalry—as chivalry goes—is made up of materials such as these.

But is there not a higher morality—a diviner honour? And if so, who is he that can find it?

Chapter 4

HER STORY

'Tis over—the weary dinner-party. I can lock myself in here, take off my dress, pull down my hair, clasp my two bare arms one on each shoulder—such a comfortable attitude!—and stare into the fire.

There is something peculiar about our fires. Most likely the quantity of firewood we use for this region gives them that curious aromatic smell. How I love fir-trees of any sort in any season of the year! How I used to delight myself in our pine-woods, strolling in and out among the boles of the trees so straight, strong, and unchangeable—grave in summer, and green in winter! How I have stood listening to the wind in their tops, and looking for the fir-cones, wonderful treasures! which they had dropped on the soft dry mossy ground. What glorious fun it was to fill my pinafore—or in more dignified days my black silk apron— with fir-cones; to heap a surreptitious store of them in a corner of the school-room, and burn them, one by one, on the top of the fire. How they did blaze!

I think I should almost like to go hunting for fir-cones now. It would be a great deal more amusing than dinner-parties.

Why did we give this dinner, which cost so much time, trouble, and money, and was so very dull? At least I thought so. Why should we always be obliged to have a dinner-party when Francis is here? As if he could not exist a week at Rockmount without other people's company than ours! It used not to be so. When I was a child, I remember he never wanted to go anywhere, or have anybody coming here. After study was over (and papa did not keep him very close either), he cared for nothing except to saunter about with Penelope. What a nuisance those two used to be to us younger ones: always sending us out of the room on some pretence, or taking us long walks and losing us, and then—cruellest of all—keeping us waiting indefinitely for dinner. Always making so much of one another, and taking no notice of us; having little squabbles with one another, and then snubbing us. The great bore of our lives was that love-affair of Francis and Penelope; and the only consolation we had, Lisabel and I, was to plan the wedding, she to settle the bridesmaids' dresses, and I thinking how grand it would be when all is over, and I took the head of the table, the warm place in the room, permanently, as Miss Johnston.

Poor Penelope! She is Miss Johnston still, and likely to be, for all that I can see. I should not wonder if, after all, it happened in ours as in many families, that the youngest is married first.

Lisabel vexed me much to-day; more than usual. People will surely begin to talk about her—not that I care a pin for any gossip, but it's wrong—wrong A girl can't like two gentlemen so equally that she treats them exactly in the same manner—unless it chances to be the manner of benevolent indifference. But Lisabel's is not that. Every day I watch her, and say to myself, "She's surely fond of that young man." Which always happens to be the young man nearest to her, whether Captain Treherne or "my Colin," as his mother calls him. What a lot of "beaux" our Lisa has had ever since she was fourteen, yet not one "lover"—that I ever heard of; as, of course, I should, together with her half-dozen very particular friends. No one can accuse Lis of being of a secretive disposition.

What, am I growing ill-natured, and to my own sister? a good-tempered, harmless girl, who makes herself agreeable to everybody, and whom everybody likes a vast deal better than they do me.

Sometimes, sitting over this fire, with the fir-twigs crackling and the turpentine blazing—it may be an odd taste, but I have a real pleasure in the smell of turpentine—I take myself into serious, sad consideration.

Theodora Johnston, aged twenty-five; medium looks, medium talents, medium temper; in every way the essence of mediocrity. This is what I have gradually discovered myself to be; I did not think so always.

Theodora Johnston, aged fifteen. What a different creature that was! I can bring it back now, with its long curls and its short frocks—by Penelope's orders, preserved as late as possible;—running wild over the moors, or hiding itself in the garden with a book,—or curling up in a corner of this attic, then unfurnished, with a pencil and the back of a letter, writing its silly poetry. Thinking, planning, dreaming, looking forward to such a wonderful, impossible life: quite satisfied with itself and all it was to do therein, since

> "The world was all before it where to choose:
> Reason its guard, and Providence its guide."

And what has it done? Nothing. What is it now? The aforesaid Theodora Johnston, aged twenty-five.

Moralists tell us, self-examination is a great virtue, an indispensable duty. I don't believe it. Generally, it is utterly useless, hopeless, and unprofitable. Much of it springs from the very egotism it pretends to cure. There are not more conceited hypocrites on earth than many of your "miserable sinners."

If I cannot think of something or somebody better than myself; I will just give up thinking altogether; will pass entirely to the uppermost of my two lives, which I have now made to tally so successfully that they seem of one material: like our girls' new cloaks, which everybody imagines sober grey, till a lifting of the arms shows the other side of the cloth to be scarlet.

That reminds me in what a blaze of scarlet Captain Treherne appeared at our modest dinner-table. He was engaged to a full-dress party at the Camp, he said, and must leave immediately after dinner—which he didn't. Was his company much missed, I wonder? Two here could well have spared it—Cohn Granton and Francis Charteris.

How odd that until to-night Captain Treherne should have had no notion that his cousin was engaged to our Penelope, or even visited at Rockmount. Odd too, that other people never told him. But it is such an old affair, and we were not likely to make the solemn communication ourselves; besides, we never knew much about the youth, except that he was one of Francis's fine relations. Yet to think that Francis all these years should never have even hinted to these said fine relations that he was engaged to our Penelope!

If I were Penelope—but I have no business to judge other people. I never was in love, they say.

To see the meeting between these two was quite dramatic, and as funny as a farce, Francis sitting on the sofa by Penelope, talking to Mrs. Granton and her friend Miss Emery, and doing a little bit of lazy love-making between whiles. When enters, late and hurried,

Captain Treherne. He walks straight up to papa, specially attentive; then bows to Lisabel, specially distant and unattentive (I thought, though, at sight of her he grew as hot as if his regimental collar were choking him); then hastens to pay his respects to Miss Johnston, when lo! he beholds Mr. Francis Charteris.

"Charteris! what the—what a very unexpected pleasure!"

Francis shook hands in what we call his usual fascinating manner.

"Miss Johnston!"—in his surprise Captain Treherne had quite forgotten her—"I really beg your pardon. I had not the slightest idea you were acquainted with my cousin." Nor did the young man seem particularly pleased with the discovery.

Penelope glanced sharply at Francis, and then said—how did she manage to say it so carelessly and composedly—

"Oh yes, we have known Mr. Charteris for a good many years. Can you find room for your cousin on the sofa, Francis?"

At the "Francis," Captain Treherne stared, and made some remarks in an abstract and abstracted manner, At length, when lie had placed himself right between Francis and Penelope, and was actually going to take Penelope down to dinner, a light seemed to break upon him. He laughed—gave way to his cousin—and condescended to bestow his scarlet elbow upon me, saying as we went across the hail—

"I'm afraid I was near making a blunder there.—But who would have thought it?"

"I beg your pardon?"

"About those, there. I knew your sister was engaged to somebody—but Charteris! Who would have thought of Charteris going to be married. What a ridiculous idea!"

I said, that the fact had ceased to appear so to me, having been aware of it for the last ten years.

"Ten years! You don't say so!" And then his slow perception catching the extreme incivility of this great astonishment, my scarlet friend offered lame congratulations, fell to his dinner, and conversed no more.

Perhaps he forgot the matter altogether—for Lisabel sat opposite, beside Cohn Granton; and what between love and hate my cavalier's attention was very much distracted. Truly, Lisabel and her unfortunate swains reminded me of a passage in Thomson's *Seasons*, describing two young bulls fighting in a meadow:—

> "While the fair heifer balmy-breathing near,
> Stands kindling up their rage."

I blush to set it down. I blush almost to have such a thought, and concerning my own sister; yet it is so, and I have seen the like often and often. Surely it must be wrong; such sacred things as women's beauty and women's love were not made to set men mad at one another like brute beasts. Surely the woman could help it if she chose. Men may be jealous, and cross, and wretched; but they do not absolutely hate one another on a woman's account unless she has been in some degree to blame. While free, and showing no preference, no one can well fight about her, for all have an equal chance; when she has a preference, though she might not openly show it towards its object, she certainly would never think of showing it towards anybody else. At least, that is my theory.

However, I am taking the thing too seriously, and it is no affair of mine. I have given up interfering long ago. Lisabel must "gang her ain gate," as they say in Scotland. By-the-bye, Captain Treherne asked if we came from Scotland, or were of the celebrated clan Johnstone?

Time was, when in spite of the additional *t*, we all grumbled at our plebeian name, hoping earnestly to change it for something more aristocratic—and oh, how proud we were of Charteris! How fine to put into the village post letters addressed, "Francis Charteris, Esq.," and to speak of our brother-in-law elect as having "an office under Government!" We firmly believed that office under Government would end in the Premiership and a peerage.

It has not, though. Francis still says he cannot afford to marry. I was asking Penelope yesterday if she knew what papa and his first wife, not our own mamma, married upon? Much less income, I believe, than what Francis has now. But my sister said I did not understand: "The cases were widely different." Probably.

She is very fond of Francis. Last week, preparing for him, she looked quite a different woman; quite young and rosy again; and though it did not last, though after he was really come, she grew sharp and cross often—to us, never to him, of course, she much enjoys his being here. They do not make so much fuss over one another as they did ten years ago, which indeed would be ridiculous in lovers over thirty. Still, I should hardly like my lover, at any age, to sit reading a novel half the evening, and spend the other half in the sweet company of his cigar. Not that he need be always hankering after me, and "paying me attention." I should hate that. For what is the good of people being fond of one another, if they can't be content simply in one another's company, or, without it even, in one another's love? letting each go on their own several ways, and do their several work in the best manner they can. Good sooth! I should be the most convenient and least troublesome sweetheart that ever a young man was ever blessed with; for I am sure I should sit all evening quite happy—he at one end of the room and I at the other, if only I knew he was happy, and caught now and then a look and a smile—provided the look and the smile were my own personal property, nobody else's.

What nonsense am I writing? And not a word about the dinner-party. Has it left so little impression on my mind?

No wonder! It was just the usual thing. Papa as host, grave, clerical, and slightly wearying of it all. Penelope hostess. Francis playing "friend of the family," as handsome and well-dressed as ever—what an exquisitely embroidered shirt-front, and what an aerial cambric kerchief! which must have taken him half-an-hour to tie! Lisabel—but I have told about her; and myself. Everybody else looking as everybody hereabouts always does look at dinner-parties—*ex uno disce omnes*—to muster a bit of the Latin for which, in old times, Francis used to call me a "juvenile prig."

Was there, in the whole evening, anything worth remembering? Yes, thanks to his fit of jealousy, I did get a little sensible conversation out of Captain Treherne. He looked so dull, so annoyed, that I felt sorry for the youth, and tried to make him talk; so, lighting on the first subject at hand, asked him if he had seen his friend, Dr. Urquhart, lately?

"Eh—who? I beg your pardon."

His eyes had wandered where Lisabel, with one of her white elbows on the table, sat coquetting with a bunch of grapes, listening with downcast eyes to "my Colin."

"Doctor Urquhart, whom I met at the Cedars last week. You said he was a friend of yours."

"So he is; the best I ever had," and it was refreshing to see how the young fellow brightened up. "He saved my life. But (or him I should assuredly be lying with a cross over my head, inside that melancholy stone wall round the top of Cathcart's Hill."

"You mean the cemetery there. What sort of a place is it?"

"Just as I said—the bare top of a hill, with a wall round it, and stones of various sorts, crosses, monuments, and so on. All our officers were buried there."

"And the men?"

"Oh, anywhere. It didn't matter."

It did not, I thought; but not exactly from Captain Treherne's point of view. However, he was scarcely the man with whom to have started an abstract argument. I might, had he been Dr. Urquhart.

"Was Doctor Urquhart in the Crimea the whole time?"

"To be sure. He went through all the campaign, from Varna to Sebastopol; at first unattached, and then was appointed to our regiment. Well for me that! What a three months I had after Inkerman! Shall I ever forget the day I first crawled out and sat on the benches in front of the hospital, on Balaklava Heights, looking down over the Black Sea?"

I had never seen him serious before. My heart inclined even to Captain Treherne.

"Was he ever hurt—Doctor Urquhart, I mean?"

"Once or twice, slightly, while looking after his wounded on the field. But he made no fuss about it, and always got well directly. You see, he is such an extremely temperate man in all things—such a quiet temper—has himself in such thorough control—that he has twice the chance of keeping in health that most men have—especially our fellows there, who, he declares, died quite as much of eating, drinking, and smoking as they did of Russian bullets."

"Your friend must be a remarkable man."

"He's a—a brick! Excuse the word—in ladies' society I ought not to use it."

"If you ought to use it at all, you may do so in ladies' society."

The youth looked puzzled.

"Well, then, Miss Dora, he really is a downright *brick*—since you know what that means. Though an odd sort of fellow too; a tough customer to deal with—never lets go the rein; holds one in as tight as if he were one's father. I say, Charteris, did you ever hear the governor speak of Doctor Urquhart, of ours?"

If Sir William had named, such a person, Mr. Charteris had, unfortunately, quite forgotten it. Stay—he fancied he had heard the name at his club, but it was really impossible to remember all the names one knew, or the men.

"You wouldn't have forgotten that man in a hurry, Miss Dora, I assure you. He's worth a dozen of—but I beg your pardon."

If it was for the look which he cast upon his cousin, I was not implacable. Francis always annoys me when he assumes that languid manner. For some things, I prefer Captain Treherne's open silliness—nothing being in his head, nothing can come out of it—to the lazy superciliousness of Francis Charteris, who, we know, has a great deal more in him than he ever condescends to let out, at least

A Life for a Life

for our benefit. I should like to see if he behaves any better at his aforesaid club, or at Lady This's and the Countess of That's, of whom I heard him speak to Miss Emery.

I was thinking thus—vaguely contrasting his smooth, handsome face with that sharp one of Penelope's—how much faster she grows old than he does, though they are exactly of an age!—when the ladies rose.

Captain Treherne and Cohn rushed to open the door—Francis did not take that trouble—and Lisabel, passing, smiled equally on both her adorers. Cohn made some stupid compliment; and the other, silent, looked her full in the face. If any man so dared to look at me, I would like to grind him to powder.

Oh! I'm sick of love and lovers—or the mockery of them—sick to the core of my heart!

In the drawing-room I curled myself up in a corner beside Mrs. Granton, whom it is always pleasant to talk to. We revived the great blanket, beef, and anti-beer question, in which she said she had found an unexpected ally.

"One who argues, even more strongly than your father and I, my dear—as I was telling Mr. Johnston to-day at dinner, and wishing they were acquainted—argues *against* the beer."

This was a question of whether or not our poor people should have beer with their Christmas dinner. Papa, who holds strong opinions against the use of intoxicating drinks, and never tastes them himself, being, every year, rather in ill odour on the subject. I asked who was this valuable ally?

"None of our neighbours, you may be sure. A gentleman from the Camp—you may have met him at my house—a Doctor Urquhart."

I could not help smiling, and said it was curious how I was perpetually hearing of Dr. Urquhart.

"Even in our quiet neighbourhood, such a man is sure to be talked about. Not in society perhaps—it was quite a marvel for Cohn to get

A Life for a Life

him to our ball; but because he does so many things while we humdrum folk are only thinking about them."

I asked what sort of things? In his profession?

"Chiefly, but he makes professional business include so much. Imagine his coming to Cohn as ground-landlord of Bourne hamlet, to beg him to see to the clearing of the village pool? or writing to the lord of the manor, saying that twenty new cottages built on the moor would do more moral good than the new county reformatory? He is one of the very few men who are not ashamed to say what they think—and makes people listen to it too, as they rarely do to those not long settled in the neighbourhood, and about whom they know little or nothing."

I asked if nothing were known about Dr. Urquhart? Had he any relations? Was he married?

"Oh no, surely not married. I never inquired, but took it for granted. However, probably my son knows. Shall I find out, and speak a good word for you, Miss Dora?"

"No, thank you," said I, laughing. "You know I hate soldiers."

'Tis Mrs. Granton's only fault—her annoying jests after this fashion. Otherwise, I would have liked to have asked a few more questions about Dr. Urquhart. I wonder if I shall ever meet him again? The regiments rarely stay long at the Camp, so that it is not probable.

I went over to where my two sisters and Miss Emery were sitting over the fire. Miss Emery was talking very fast, and Penelope listening with a slightly scornful lip; she protests that ladies, middle-aged ladies particularly, are such very stupid company. Lisabel wore her good-natured smile, always the same to everybody.

"I was quite pleased," Miss Emery was saying, "to notice how cordially Captain Treherne and Mr. Charteris met: I always understood there was a sort of a—a coolness, in short. Very natural. As his nephew, and next heir, after the Captain, Sir William might have done more than he did for Mr. Charteris. So people said, at least. He has a splendid property, and only that one son. You have been to Treherne Court, Miss Johnston?"

A Life for a Life

Penelope abruptly answered, "No;" and Lisabel added amiably, that we seldom went from home—papa liked to have us at Rockmount all the year round.

I said wilfully, wickedly—maybe, lest Miss Emery's long tongue should carry back to London what was by implication not true—that we did not even know where Treherne Court was, and that we had only met Captain Treherne accidentally among the camp-officers who visited at the Cedars.

Lis pinched me: Penelope looked annoyed. Was it a highly virtuous act thus to have vexed both my sisters? Alack! I feel myself growing more unamiable every day. What will be the end of it?

"First come, first served," must have been Lisabel's motto for the evening, since, Captain Treherne reappearing, scarlet beat plain black clear out of the field. I was again obliged to follow, as Charity, pouring the oil and wine of my agreeable conversation into the wounds made by my sister's bright eyes, and receiving as gratitude such an amount of information on turnips, moor-lands, and the true art of sheep-feeding, as will make me look with respect and hesitation on every leg of mutton that comes to our table for the next six months.

> "O, Colin, dear Colin, my Colin, my dear,
> Who wont the wild mountains to trace without fear,
> O, where are thy flocks that so swiftly rebound,
> And fly o'er the heath without touching the ground?"

A remarkable fact in natural history, which much impressed me in my childhood. What is the rest?

> "Where the birch-tree hangs weeping o'er fountain so clear,
> At noon I shall meet him, my Colin, my dear."

What a shame to laugh at Mrs. Grant of Laggan's nice old song, at the pretty Highland tune which ere now I have hummed over the moor for miles! Since, when we were children, I myself was in love with Colin! a love which found vent in much petting of his mother, and in shy presents to himself of nuts and blackberries: until, stung by indifference, my affection

"Shrunk
Into itself, and was missing ever after."

Do we forget our childish loves? I think not. The objects change, of course, but the feeling, when it has been true and unselfish, keeps its character still, and is always pleasant to remember. It was very silly, no doubt, but I question if now I could hove anybody in a fonder, humbler, faithfuller way than I adored that great, merry, good-natured schoolboy. And though I know he has not an ounce of brains, is the exact opposite of anybody I could fall in love with now—still, to this day, I look kindly on the round, rosy face of "Colin, my dear."

I wonder if he ever will marry our Lisa. As far as I notice, people do not often marry their childish companions; they much prefer strangers. Possibly, from mere novelty and variety; or else from the fact that as kin are sometimes "less than kind," so one's familiar associates are often the furthest from one's sympathies, interests, or heart.

With this highly moral and amiable sentiment—a fit conclusion for a social evening, I will lock my desk.

Lucky I did! What if Lisabel had found me writing at—-one in the morning! How she would have teased me—even under the circumstances of last night, which seem to have affected her mighty little, considering.

I heard her at my door, from without, grumble at it being bolted. She came in and sat down by my fire. Quite a picture, in a blue flannel dressing-gown, with her light hair dropping down in two wavy streams, and her eyes as bright as if it were any hour rather than 1.30 A.M., as I showed her by my watch.

"Nonsense! I shall not go to bed yet. I want to talk a bit, Dora; you ought to feel flattered by my coming to tell you, first of anybody. Guess now—what has happened?"

Nothing ill, certainly—for she held her head up, laughing a little, looking very handsome and pleased.

"You never will guess, for you never believed it would come to pass, but it has. Treherne proposed to me to-night."

The news quite took my breath away, and then I questioned its accuracy. "He has only been giving you a few more of his silly speeches—he means nothing. Why don't you put a stop to it all?"

Lisabel was not vexed—she never is—she only laughed.

"I tell you, Dora, it is perfectly true. You may believe or not—I don't care—but he really did it."

"How, when, and where, pray?"

"In the conservatory; beside the biggest orange-tree; a few minutes before he left."

I said, since she was so very matter-of-fact, perhaps she would have no objection to tell me the precise words in which he "did it."

"Oh, dear, no; not the smallest objection. We were joking about a bit of orange-blossom Colin had given me, and Treherne wanted me to throw away; but I said 'No, I liked the scent, and meant to wear a wreath of natural orange-flowers when I was married.' Upon which he grew quite furious, and said it would drive him mad if I ever married any man but him. Then he got hold of my hand, and—the usual thing, you know." She blushed a little. "It ended by my telling him he had better speak to papa, and he said he should, to-morrow. That's all."

"All!"

"Well?" said Lisabel, expectantly.

It certainly was a singular way in which to receive one's sister's announcement of her intended marriage; but, for worlds, I could not have spoken a syllable. I felt a weight on my chest—a sense of hot indignation, which settled down into inconceivable melancholy.

Was this indeed all? A silly flirtation—a young lad's passion—a young girl's cool, business-like reception of the same—the formal "speaking to papa," and the thing was over! Was *that* love?

"Haven't you a word to say, Dora? I had better have told Penelope. But she was tired, and scolded me out of her room. Besides she might not exactly like this, for some reasons. It's rather hard; such an important thing to happen, and not a soul to congratulate one upon it."

I asked, why might Penelope dislike it?

"Can't you see? Captain Treherne roving about the world, and Captain Treherne married and settled at home, make a considerable difference to Francis's prospects. No, I don't mean anything mean or murderous—you need not look so shocked— it is merely my practical way of regarding things. But what harm? If I did not have Treherne, somebody else would, and it would be none the better for Francis and Penelope."

"You are very prudent and far-sighted: such an idea would never have entered my mind."

"I daresay not. Just give me that brush, will you, child?"

She proceeded methodically to damp her long hair, and plait it up in those countless tails which gave Miss Lisabel Johnston's locks such a beautiful wave. Passing the glass, she looked into it, smiled, sighed.

"Poor fellow. I do believe he is very fond of me."

"And you?"

"Oh, I like him—like him excessively. If I didn't, what should I marry him for?"

"What, indeed!"

"There is one objection papa may have: his being younger than I—I forget how much, but it is very little. How surprised papa will be when he gets the letter to-morrow!"

"Does Sir William know?"

"Not yet; but that will be soon settled, he tells me. He can persuade his mother, and she, his father. Besides, they can have no possible objection to me."

She looked again in the mirror as she said this. Yes, that "me" was not a daughter-in-law likely to be objected to, even at Treherne Court.

"I hope it will not vex Penelope," she continued. "It may be all the better for her, since, when I am married, I shall have so much influence. We may make the old gentleman do something handsome for Francis, and get a richer living for papa, if he will consent to leave Rockmount. And I'd find a nice husband for you, eh, Dora?"

"Thank you; I don't want one. I hate the very mention of the thing. I wish, instead of marrying, we could all be dead and buried."

And, whether from weariness, or excitement, or a sudden, unutterable pang at seeing my sister, my playfellow, my handsome Lisa, sitting there, talking as she talked, and acting as she acted, I could bear up no longer. I burst out sobbing.

She was very much astonished, and somewhat touched, I suppose, for she cried too, a little, and we kissed one another several times, which we are not much in the habit of doing.—Till, suddenly, I recollected Treherne, the orange-tree, and "the usual thing." Her lips seemed to burn me.

"Oh, Lisa, I wish you wouldn't—I do wish you wouldn't."

"Wouldn't what? Don't you want me to be engaged and married, child?"

"Not in that way."

"In what way, then?"

I could not tell. I did not know.

A Life for a Life

"After the fashion of Francis and Penelope, perhaps? Falling in love like a couple of babies, before they knew their own minds, and then being tied together, and keeping the thing on in a stupid, meaningless, tiresome way, till she is growing into an elderly woman, and he—no, thank you; I have seen quite enough of early loves and long engagements. I always meant to have somebody whom I could marry at once, and be done with it."

There was a half-truth in what she said, though I could not then find the other half to fit into it, and prove that her satisfactory circle of reasoning was partly formed of absolute, untenable falsehood, for false I am sure it was. Though I cannot argue it, can hardly understand it, I *feel it*. There must be a truth somewhere. Love cannot be all a lie.

My sister and I talked a few minutes longer, and then she rose and said she must go to bed.

"Will you not wish me happiness? 'Tis very unkind of you."

I told her outright that I did not think as she thought on these matters, but that she had made her choice, and I hoped it would be a happy one.

"I am sure of it. Now go to bed, and don't cry any more, there's a good girl, for there really is nothing to cry about. You shall have the very prettiest bridesmaid's dress I can afford, and Treherne Court will be such a nice house for you to visit at. Good night, Dora."

Strange, altogether strange!

And writing it all down this morning, I feel it stranger than ever, still.

Chapter 5

HIS STORY

I will set down, if only to get rid of them, a few incidents of this day.

Trivial they are—ludicrously so—to any one but me: yet they have left me sitting with my head in my hands, stupid and idle, starting, each hour, at the boom of the bell we took at Sebastopol—starting and shivering like a nervous child.

Strange! there, in the Crimea, in the midst of danger, hardship, and misery of all kinds I was at peace, even happy: happier than for many years. I seemed to have lived down, and nearly obliterated from thought, that one day, one hour, one moment—which was but a moment. Can it, or ought it, to weigh against a whole existence? or, as some religionists would tell us, against an eternity? Yet, what is time, what is eternity? And what is man, measuring himself, his atom of good or ill, either done or suffered, against God?

These are vain speculations, which I have gone over and over again, till every link in the chain of reasoning is painfully familiar. I had better give it up, and turn to ordinary things. Dear imaginary correspondent, shall I tell you the story of my day?

It began peacefully. I always rest on a Sunday, if I can. I believe, even had Heaven not hallowed one day in the seven—Saturday or Sunday matters not; let Jews and Christians battle it out!—there would still be needful a day of rest; and that day would still be a blessed day. Instinct, old habit, and later conviction always incline me to "keep the Sabbath"—not, indeed, after the strict fashion of my forefathers, but as a happy, cheerful, holy time, a resting-place between week and week, in which to enjoy specially all righteous pleasures and earthly repose, and to look forward to that rest which, we are told, "remaineth for the people of God." The people of God. No other people ever do rest, even in this world.

Treherne passed my hut soon after breakfast, and popped his head in, not over welcomely, I confess, for I was giving myself the rare treat of a bit of unprofessional reading. I had not seen him for two or three days—not since we appointed to go together to the General's dinner, and he never appeared all the evening.

"I say, Doctor, will you go to church?"

Now, I do usually attend our airy military chapel—all doors and windows—open to every kind of air, except airs from heaven, of which, I am afraid, our chaplain does not bring with him a large quantity. He leaves us to fatten upon Hebrew roots, without throwing us a crumb of Christianity; prefers Moses and the prophets to the New Testament; no wonder, as some few doctrines there, "Do unto others as ye would they should do unto you," "He that taketh the sword shall perish by the sword!" would sound particularly odd in a military chapel, especially with his elucidation of them, for he is the very poorest preacher I ever heard. Yet a worthy man, a most sincere man: did a world of good out in the Crimea; used to spend hours daily in teaching our men to read and write, got personally acquainted with every fellow in the regiment, knew all their private histories, wrote their letters home, sought them out in the battle-field and in the hospital, read to them, cheered them, comforted them, and closed their eyes. There was not an officer in the regiment more deservedly beloved than our chaplain. He is an admirable fellow—everywhere but in the pulpit.

Nevertheless, I attend his chapel, as I have always been in the habit of attending some Christian worship somewhere, because it is the simplest way of showing that I am not ashamed of my Master before men.

Therefore, I would not smile at Treherne's astonishing fit of piety, but simply assented; at which he evidently was disappointed.

"You see, I'm turning respectable, and going to church. I wonder such an exceedingly respectable and religious fellow as you, Urquhart, has not tried to make me go sooner."

"If you go against your will, and because it's respectable, you had better stop away."

"Thank you; but suppose I have my own reasons for going?"

He is not a deep fellow; there is no deceit in the lad. All his faults are uppermost, which makes them bearable.

"Come, out with it. Better make a clean breast to me. It will not be the first time."

"Well, then—ahem!" twisting his sash and looking down with most extraordinary modesty,—"the fact is, *she* wished it."

"Who?"

"The lady you know of. In truth, I may as well tell you, for I want you to speak up for me to her father, and also to break it to my governor. I've taken your advice and been and gone and done for myself."

"Married!" for his manner was so queer that I should not have wondered at even that catastrophe.

"Not quite, but next door to it. Popped and been accepted. Yes, since Friday I have been an engaged man, Doctor."

Behind his foolishness was some natural feeling, mixed with a rather comical awe of his own position.

For me, I was a good deal surprised; yet he might have come to a worse end. To a rich young fellow of twenty-one, the world is full of many more dangerous pitfalls than matrimony. So I expressed myself in the customary congratulations, adding that I concluded the lady was the one I had seen?

Treherne nodded.

"Sir William knows it?"

"Not yet. Didn't I tell you I wanted you to break it to him? Though he will consent, of course. Her father is quite respectable—a clergyman, you are aware; and she is such a handsome girl—would do credit to any man's taste. Also, she likes me—a trifle!"

And he pulled his moustache with a satisfied recognition of his great felicity.

I saw no reason to question it, such as it was. He was a well-looking fellow, likely to please women; and this one, though there was not much in her, appeared kindly and agreeable. The other sister, whom I talked with, was something more. They were, no doubt, a perfectly unobjectionable family; nor did I think that Sir William, who was anxious for his son to marry early, would refuse consent to any creditable choice. But, decidedly, he ought to be told at once—ought indeed to have been consulted beforehand. I said so.

"Can't help that. It happened unexpectedly. I had, when I entered Rockmount, no more idea of such a thing than—than your cat, Doctor. Upon my soul, 'tis the fact! Well, well, marriage is a man's fate. He can no more help himself in the matter than a stone can help rolling down a hill All's over, and I'm glad of it. So, will you write and tell my father?"

"Certainly not. Do it yourself, and you had better do it now. 'No time like the present,' always."

I pushed towards him pens, ink, and paper, and returned to my book again; but it was not quite absorbing; and occasional glimpses of Treherne's troubled and puzzled face amused me, as well as made me thoughtful.

It was natural that having been in some slight way concerned in it, this matter, foreign as it was to the general tenor of my busy life, should interest me a little. Though I viewed it, not from the younger, but from the elder side. I myself never knew either father or mother; they died when I was a child; but I think, whether or not we possess it in youth, we rarely come to my time of life without having a strong instinctive feeling of the rights of parents—being worthy parents. Rights, of course modified in their extent by the higher claims of the Father of all, but second to none other; except, perhaps, those which He has Himself made superior—the rights of husband and wife.

I felt, when I came to consider it, exceedingly sorry that Treherne had made a proposal of marriage without consulting his father. But it was no concern of mine. Even his "taking my advice" was, he knew well, his own exaggeration of an abstract remark which I could not but make; otherwise, I had not meddled in his courting, which, in my opinion, no third party has a right to do.

So I washed my hands of the whole affair, except consenting to Treherne's earnest request that I would go with him, this morning, to the little village church of which the young lady's father was the clergyman, and be introduced.

"A tough old gentleman, too; as sharp as a needle, as hard as a rock—walking into his study, yesterday morning, was no joke, I assure you."

"But you said he had consented?"

"Ah, yes, all's right. That is, it will be when I hear from the governor."

All this while, by a curious amatory eccentricity, he had never mentioned the lady's name. Nor had I asked, because I knew it. Also, because that surname, common as it is, is still extremely painful to me, either to utter or to hear.

We came late into church, and sat by the door. It was a pleasant September forenoon; there was sunshine within and sunshine outside, far away across the moors. I had never been to this village before; it seemed a pretty one, and the church old and picturesque. The congregation consisted almost entirely of poor people, except one family, which I concluded to be the clergyman's. He was in the reading-desk.

"That's her father," whispered Treherne.

"Oh, indeed." But I did not look at him for a minute or so; I could not. Such moments will come, despite of reasoning, belief, conviction, when I see a person bearing any name resembling *that* name.

At last I lifted my head to observe him.

A calm, hard, regular face; well-shaped features; high, narrow forehead, aquiline nose—a totally different type from one which I so well remember that any accidental likeness thereto impresses me as startlingly and vividly as, I have heard, men of tenacious, fervent memory will have impressed on them, through life, as their favourite type of beauty, the countenance of their first love.

I could sit down now, at ease, and listen to this gentleman's reading of the prayers. His reading was what might have been expected from his face—classical, accurate, intelligent, gentlemanly. And the congregation listened with respect, as to a clever exposition of things quite beyond their comprehension. Except the gabble-gabble of the Sunday-school, and the clerk's loud "A-a-men!" the minister had the service entirely to himself.

A beautiful service—as I, though in heart a Presbyterian still, must avow. Especially, when heard as I have heard it— at sea, in hospital, at the camp. Not this camp, but ours in the Crimea, where, all through the prayers, guns kept booming, and shells kept flying, sometimes within a short distance of the chapel itself. I mind of one Sunday, little more than a year ago, for it must have been on the ninth of September, when I stopped on my way from Balaklava hospital, to hear service read in the open air, on a hillside. It was a cloudy day, I remember; below, brown with long drought, stretched the Balaklava plains; opposite, grey and still, rose the high mountains on the other side of the Tchernaya; while, far away to the right, towards our camp, one could just trace the white tents of the Highland regiments; and to the left, hidden by the Col de Balaklava, a dull, perpetual rumble, and clouds of smoke hanging in the air, showed where, six miles off was being enacted the fall of Sebastopol.

Though at the time we did not know; we, this little congregation, mustered just outside a hospital tent, where I remember, not a stone's-throw from where we, the living, knelt, lay a row of those straight, still, formless forms, the more awful because, from familiarity, they had ceased to be felt as such—each sewn up in the blanket, its only coffin, waiting for burial—waiting also, we believe and hope, for the resurrection from the dead.

What a sermon our chaplain might have preached! what words I, or any man, could surely have found to say at such a time, on such a spot! Yet what we did hear were the merest platitudes—so utterly trivial and out of place, that I do not now recall a single sentence. Strange, that people—good Christian men, as I knew that man to be—should go on droning out "words, words, words," when bodies and souls perish in thousands round them; or splitting theological hairs to poor fellows, who, except in an oath, are ignorant even of the Divine Name,—or thundering anathemas at them for going down to the pit of perdition, without even so much as pointing out to them the bright but narrow way.

I was sitting thus, absorbed in the heavy thoughts that often come to me when thus quiet in church, hearing some man, who is supposed to be one of the Church's teachers, delivering the message of the Church's Great Head—when looking up, I saw two eyes fixed on me.

It was one of the clergyman's three daughters; the youngest, probably, for her seat was in the most uncomfortable corner of the pew. Apparently the same I had talked with at Mrs. Granton's, though I was not sure—ladies look so different in their bonnets. Hers was close, I noticed, and decently covering the head, not dropping off on her shoulders like those I see ladies wearing, which will assuredly multiply ophthalmic cases, with all sorts of head and face complaints, as the winter winds come on. Such exposure must be very painful, too, these blinding sunny days. How can women stand the torments they have to undergo in matters of dress? If I had any womankind belonging to me—pshaw! what an idle speculation.

Those two eyes, steadfastly inquiring, with a touch of compassion in them, startled me. Many a pair of eager eyes have I had to meet, but it was always their own fate, or that of some one dear to them, which they were anxious to learn: they never sought to know anything of me or mine. Now, these did.

I am nervously sensitive of even kindly scrutiny. Involuntarily, I moved so that one of the pillars came between me and those eyes. When we stood up to sing, she kept them steadily upon her hymn-book, nor did they wander again during church-time, either towards me or in any other direction.

The face being just opposite, in the line of the pulpit, I could not help seeing it during the whole of the discourse, which was, as I expected, classical, laboured, elegant, and interesting—after the pattern of the preacher's countenance.

His daughter is not like him. In repose, her features are ordinary; nor did they for one moment recall to me the flashing, youthful face, full of action and energy, which had amused me that night at the Cedars. Some faces catch the reflection of the moment so vividly that you never see them twice alike. Others, solidly and composedly handsome, scarcely vary at all, and I think it is of these last that one would soonest weary. Irregular features have generally most character. The Venus di Medici would have made a very stupid fireside companion, nor would I venture to enter for Oxford honours a son who had the profile of the Apollo Belvidere.

Treherne is evidently of a different opinion. He sat beaming out admiration upon that large, fair, statuesque woman, who had turned so that her pure Greek profile was distinctly visible against the red cloth of the high pew. She might have known what a pretty picture she was making. She will please Sir William, who admires beauty, and she seems refined enough even for Lady Augusta Treherne. I thought to myself, the lad might have gone farther and fared worse. His marriage was sure to have been one of pure accident: he is not a young man either to have had the decision to choose, or the firmness to win and keep.

Service ended, he asked me what I thought of her; and I said much as I have written here. He appeared satisfied.

"You must stay and be introduced to the family: the father remains in church. I shall walk home with them. Ah, she sees us."

The lad was all eagerness and excitement. He must be considerably in earnest.

"Now, Doctor, come—nay, pray do."

For I hesitated.

Hesitation was too late, however: the introduction took place: Treherne hurried it over; though I listened acutely, I could not be certain of the name. It seemed to be, as I already believed, *Johnson*.

Treherne's beauty met him, all smiles, and he marched off by her side in a most determined manner, the eldest sister following and joining the pair, doubtless to the displeasure of one, or both. She, whom I did not remember seeing before, is a little sharp-speaking woman, pretty, but faded-looking, with very black eyes.

The other sister, left behind, fell in with me. We walked side by side through the churchyard, and into the road. As I held the wicket-gate open for her to pass, she looked up, smiled, and said—

"I suppose you do not remember me, Doctor Urquhart?"

I replied, "Yes I did": that she was the young lady who "hated soldiers."

She blushed extremely, glanced at Treherne, and said, not without dignity—

"It would be a pity to remember all the foolish things I have uttered, especially on that evening."

"I was not aware they were foolish; the impression left on me was that we had had a very pleasant conversation, which included far more sensible topics than are usually discussed at balls."

"You do not often go to balls?"

"No."

"Do you dislike them?"

"Not always."

"Do you think they are wrong?"

I smiled at her cross-questioning, which had something fresh and unsophisticated about it, like the inquisitiveness of a child.

"Really, I have never very deeply considered the question; my going, or not going, is purely a matter of individual choice. I went to the Cedars that night because Mrs. Granton was so kind as to wish it, and I was only too happy to please her. I like her extremely, and owe her much."

"She is a very good woman," was the earnest answer. "And Colin has the kindest heart in the world."

I assented, though amused at the superlatives in which very young people delight; but, in this case, not so far away from truth as ordinarily happens.

"You know Cohn Granton;—have you seen him lately—yesterday I mean? Did Captain Treherne see him yesterday?"

The anxiety with which the question was put reminded me of something Treherne had mentioned, which implied his rivalry with Granton; perhaps this kind-hearted damsel thought there would be a single-handed combat on our parade-ground, between the accepted and rejected swains. I allayed her fears by observing, that to my certain knowledge, Mr. Granton had gone up to London on Saturday morning, and would not return till Tuesday. Then, our eyes meeting, we both looked conscious; but, of course, neither the young lady nor myself made any allusion to present circumstances.

I said, generally, that Granton was a fine young fellow, not over sentimental, nor likely to feel anything very deeply; but gifted with great good sense, sufficient to make an admirable country squire, and one of the best landlords in the county, if only he could be brought to feel the importance of his position.

"How do you mean?"

"His responsibility, as a man of fortune, to make the most of his wealth."

"But how?—what is there for him to do?"

"Plenty, if he could only be got to do it."

"Could you not get him to do it?" with another look of the eager eyes.

"I?—I know so very little of the young man."

"But you have so much influence, I hear, over everybody— that is, Mrs. Granton says.—We have known the Grantons ever since I was a child."

From her blush, which seemed incessantly to come, sudden and sensitive as a child's, I imagined that time was not so very long ago—until she said something about "my youngest sister," which proved I had been mistaken in her age.

It was easier to talk to a young girl sitting forlorn by herself in a ball-room, than to a grown-up lady, walking in broad daylight, accompanied by two other ladies, who, though a clergyman's daughters, are as stylish fashionables as ever irritated my sober vision. She did not, I must confess; she seemed to be the plain one of the family: unnoticed—one might almost guess, neglected. Nor was there any flightiness or coquettishness in her manner, which, though abrupt and original, was quiet even to demureness.

Pursuing my hobby of anatomising character, I studied her a good deal during the pauses of conversation, of which there were not a few. Compared with Treherne, whom I heard in advance, laughing and talking with his usual light-heartedness, she must have found me uncommonly sombre and dull.

Yet it was pleasant to be strolling leisurely along, one's feet dropping softly down through rustling dead leaves into the dry, sandy mould which is peculiar to this neighbourhood: you may walk in it, ankle-deep, for miles, across moors and under pine-woods, without soiling a shoe. Pleasant to see the sunshine striking the boughs of the trees, and lying in broad, bright rifts on the ground here and there, wherever there was an opening in the dense green tops of those fine Scotch firs, the like of which I have never beheld out of my own country, nor there since I was quite a boy. Also, the absence of other forest trees, the high elevation, the wide spaces of moorland, and the sandy soil, give to the atmosphere here a rarity and freshness which exhilarates, mentally and bodily, in no small degree.

I thank God I have never lost my love of nature; never ceased to feel an almost boyish thrill of delight in the mere sunshine and fresh air.

For miles I could have walked on, thus luxuriating, without wishing to disturb my enjoyment by a word, but it was necessary to converse a little, so I made the valuable and original remark "that this neighbourhood would be very pretty in the spring."

My companion replied with a vivacity of indignation most unlike a grown young lady, and exceedingly like a child —

"Pretty? It is beautiful! You never can have seen it, I am sure."

I said, "My regiment did not come home till May; I had spent this spring in the Crimea."

"Ah! the spring flowers there, I have heard, are remarkably beautiful, much more so than ours."

"Yes;" and as she seemed fond of flowers, I told her of the great abundance which in the peaceful spring that followed the war, we had noticed, carpeting with a mass of colour those dreary plains; the large Crimean snowdrops, the jonquils, and blue hyacinths, growing in myriads about Balaklava and on the banks of the Tchernaya; while on every rocky dingle, and dipping into every tiny brook, hung bushes of the delicate yellow jasmine.

"How lovely! But I would not exchange England for it. You should see how the primroses grew all along that bank; and a little beyond, outside the wood, is a hedge-side, which will be one mass of bluebells."

"I shall look for them. I have often found bluebells till the end of October."

"Nonsense!" What a laugh it was, with such a merry ring. "I beg your pardon, Doctor Urquhart — but, really, blue-bells in October! Who ever heard of such a thing?"

"I assure you I have found them myself, in sheltered places, both the larger and smaller species; the one that grows from a single stem, and that which produces two or three bells from the same stalk — the campanula. Shall I give you its botanical name?"

"Oh, I know what you mean — *harebell*."

"Bluebell; the real bluebell of Scotland. What you call bluebells are wild hyacinths."

A Life for a Life

She shook her head with a pretty persistence.

"No, no; I have always called them bluebells, and I always shall. Many a scolding have I got about them when I used, on cold March days, to steal a basket and a kitchen knife, to dig them up before the buds were formed, so as to transplant them safely in time to flower in my garden. Many's the knife I broke over that vain quest. Do you know how difficult it is to get at the bulb of a bluebell?"

"Wild hyacinth, if you please."

"A bluebell," she laughingly persisted. "I have sometimes picked out a fine one, growing in some easy soft mould, and undermined him, and worked round him, ten inches deep, fancying I had got to the root of him at last, when slip went the knife; and all was over. Many a time I have sat with the cut-off stalk in my hand, the long, white, slender stalk, ending in two delicate green leaves, with a tiny bud between—you know it—and actually cried, not only for vexation over lost labour, but because it seemed such a pity to have destroyed what one never could make alive again."

She said that, looking right into my face with her innocent eyes. This girl, from her habit of speaking exactly as she thinks, and whether from her solitary country rearing, or her innate simplicity of character, thinking at once more naturally and originally than most women, will, doubtless, often say things like these.

An idea once or twice this morning had flitted across my mind, whether it would not be better for me to break through my hermit ways, and allow myself to pay occasional visits among happy households, or the occasional society of good and cultivated women; now it altogether vanished. It would be a thing impossible.

This young lady must have very quick perceptions, and an accurate memory of trivial things, for scarcely had she uttered the last words when all her face was dyed crimson and red, as if she thought she had hurt or offended me. I judged it best to answer her thoughts out plain.

"I agree with you that to kill wantonly even a flower is an evil deed. But you need not have minded saying that to me, even after our argument at the Cedars. I am not in your sense a soldier—a professed man-slayer; my vocation is rather the other way. Yet even for the former I could find arguments of defence."

"You mean, there are higher things than mere life, and greater crimes than taking it away? So I have been thinking myself, lately. You set me thinking, for the which I am glad to own myself your debtor."

I had not a word of answer to this acknowledgment, at once frank and dignified. She went on—

"If I said foolish or rude things that night, you must remember how apt one is to judge from personal experience, and I have never seen any fair specimen of the Army. Except," and her manner prevented all questioning of what duty elevated into a truth—"except, of course, Captain Treherne."

He caught his name.

"Eh, good people. Saying nothing bad of me, I hope? Anyhow, I leave my character in the hands of my friend Urquhart. He rates me soundly to my face, which is the best proof of his not speaking ill of me behind my back."

"So that is Doctor Urquhart's idea of friendship! bitter outside, and sweet at the core. What does he make of love, pray? All sweet and no bitter?"

"Or all bitter and no sweet?"

These speeches came from the two other sisters, the latter from the eldest; their flippancy needed no reply, and I gave none. The second sister was silent: which, I thought, showed better taste, under the circumstances.

For a few minutes longer we sauntered on, leaving the wood and passing into the sunshine, which felt soft and warm as spring. Then there happened—I have been slow in coming to it—one of those accidents, trivial to all but me, which, whenever occurring, seem to dash the peaceful present out of my grasp, and throw me back years—years, to the time when I had neither present nor future, but dragged on life, I scarcely know how, with every faculty tightly bound up in an inexorable, intolerable past.

She was carrying her prayer-book, or Bible I think it was, though English people oftener carry to church prayer-books than Bibles, and seem to reverence them quite as much, or more. I had noticed it, as being not one of those velvet things with gilt crosses that ladies delight in, but plain-bound, with slightly soiled edges, as if with continual use. Passing through a gate, she dropped it: I stooped to pick it up, and there on the fly-leaf I saw written— "Theodora Johnston."—*Johnston*.

Let me consider what followed, for my memory is not clear.

I believe I walked with her to her own door, that there was a gathering and talking, which ended in Treherne's entering with the ladies, promising to overtake me before I reached the camp. That the gate closed upon them, and I heard their lively voices inside the garden-wall while I walked rapidly down the road and back into the fir-wood. That gaining its shadow and shelter, I sat down on a felled tree, to collect myself.

Johnson her name is not, but *Johnston*. Spelled precisely the same as I remember noticing on his handkerchief—Johnston, without the final *e*.

Yet, granting that identity, it is still a not uncommon name; there are whole families, whole clans of Johnstons along the Scottish border, and plenty of English Johnstons and Johnstones likewise.

Am I fighting with shadows, and torturing myself in vain? God grant it!

Still, after this discovery, it is vitally necessary to learn more. I have sat up till midnight, waiting Treherne's return. He did not overtake me—I never expected he would—or desired it. I came back, when I did come back, another way. His hut, next to mine, is still silent.

So is the whole camp at this hour. Refreshing myself a few minutes since by standing bareheaded at my hut-door, I saw nothing but the stars overhead, and the long lines of lamps below; heard nothing but the sigh of the moorland wind, and the tramp of the sentries relieving guard.

I must wait a little longer; to sleep would be impossible till I have tried to find out as much as I can.

What if it should be *that*—the worst? which might inevitably produce—or leave me no reason longer to defer—the end?

Here it seemed as if with long pondering my faculties became torpid. I fell into a sort of dream; which, being broken by a face looking in at me through the window, a sickness of perfectly childish terror came over me. For an instant only—and then I had put away my writing-materials and unbolted the door.

Treherne came in, laughing violently. "Why, Doctor, did you take me for a ghost?"

"You might have been. You know what happened last week to those poor young fellows coming home from a dinner-party in a dog-cart."

"By George I do!" The thought of this accident, which had greatly shocked the whole camp, sobered him at once. "To be knocked over in action is one thing; but to die with one's head under a carriage-wheel—ugh!—Doctor, did ye really think something of the sort had befallen me? Thank you; I had no idea you cared so much for a harum-scarum fellow like me."

He could not be left believing an untruth; so I said my startled looks were not on his account; the fact was, I had been writing closely for some hours, and was nervous—rather.

The notion of my having "nerves" afforded him considerable amusement. "But that is just what Dora persisted—good sort of creature, isn't she? the one you walked with from church. I told her you were as strong as iron and as hard as a rock, and she said she didn't believe it; that yours was one of the most sensitive faces she had ever seen."

"I am very much obliged to Miss Theodora—I really was not aware of it myself."

"Nor I either, faith! but women are so sharp-sighted. Ah, Doctor, you don't half know their ways."

I concluded he had stayed at Rockmount; had he spent a pleasant day?

"Pleasant? ecstatic. Now, acknowledge—isn't she a glorious girl? Such a mouth—such an eye—such an arm! Altogether a magnificent creature. Don't you think so? Speak out, I shan't be jealous."

I said, with truth, she was an extremely handsome young woman.

"Handsome? Divine. But she's as lofty as a queen—won't allow any nonsense; I didn't get a kiss the whole day. She will have it we are not even engaged till I hear from the governor; and I can't get a letter till Tuesday, at soonest. Doctor, it's maddening. If all is not settled in a week, and that angel mine within six more—as she says she will be, parents consenting—I do believe it will drive me mad."

"Having her, or losing?"

"Either. She puts me nearly out of my senses."

"Sit down then, and put yourself into them again. For a few minutes, at least."

For I perceived the young fellow was warm with something besides love. He had been solacing himself with wine and cigars in the mess-room. Intemperance was not one of his failings, nor was he more than a little excited now; not by any means what men consider "overtaken," or, to use the honester and uglier word, "drunk." Yet, as he stood there, lolling against the door, with hot cheeks and watery eyes, talking and laughing louder than usual, and diffusing an atmosphere both nicotian and alcoholic, I thought it was as well on the whole that his divinity did not see her too human young adorer. I have often pitied women—mothers, wives, sisters. If they could see some of us men as we often see one another!

Treherne talked rapturously of the family at Rockmount—the father and the three young ladies.

I asked if there were no mother.

"No. Died, I believe, when my Lisabel was a baby. Lisabel; isn't it a pretty name? Lisabel Treherne, better still—beats Lisabel Johnston hollow."

This seemed an opportunity for questions, which must be put; safer put them now, than when Treherne was in a soberer and more observant mood.

"Johnston is a Border name. Are they Scotch?"

'Not to my knowledge—I never inquired. Will, if you wish, Doctor. You canny Scots always hang together, ha! ha! But I say, did you ever see three nicer girls? Shouldn't you like one of them for yourself?"

I!

"Thank you—I am not a marrying man; but you will find them a pleasant family, apparently. Are there any more sisters?"

"No!—quite enough, too."

"Nor brothers?"

"Not the ghost of one!"

"Perhaps"—was it I, or some mocking imp speaking through my lips—"perhaps only the ghost of one. None now living, probably?"

"None at all that I ever heard of. So much the better; I shall have her more to myself. Heigho! it's an age till Tuesday."

"You'd better go to your bed, and shorten the time by ten hours."

"So I will. Night, night, old fellow—as they teach little brats to say, on disappearing from dessert. 'Pon my life, I see myself the venerated head of a household, and pillar of the state already. You'll be quite proud of my exceeding respectability."

He put his head in again, two minutes after, with a nod and a wink.

"I say, think better of it. Try for Miss Dora—the second. Charteris one, me the other, and you the third. What a jolly lot of brothers-in-law! Do think better of it."

"Hold your tongue, and go to your bed."

It was not possible to go to mine, till I had arranged my thoughts.

What he stated must be correct. If otherwise, it is next to impossible that, in his position of intimacy, he should not have heard it. Families do not, I suppose, so easily forget one who is lost. There must have been only those *three* daughters.

I may lay me down in peace. Thou who seest not as man sees, wilt Thou make it peace, even for me?

Chapter 6

HER STORY

"Gone to be married? gone to swear a peace?
Shall Lewis have Blanche, and Blanche these provinces?"

Which means, "shall Treherne have Lisa, and Lisa Treherne Court?"

Yes, it is to be: I suppose it must be. Though not literally "gone to be married," they are certainly "going."

For seven days the balance hung doubtful. I do not know exactly what turned the scale; sometimes a strong suspicion strikes me that it was Dr. Urquhart; but I have given up cogitating on the subject. Where one is utterly powerless—a mere iota in a house—when, whatever one might desire, one's opinion has not a straw's weight with anybody, what is the good of vexing one's self in vain!

I shall content myself with giving a straightforward, succinct account of the week; this week which, I cannot deny, has made a vital difference in our family. Though outwardly all went on as usual—our quiet, monotonous life, unbroken by a single "event"—breakfast, dinner, tea, and sleep coming round in ordinary rotation; still the change is made. What a long time it seems since Sunday week!

That day, after the tumult of Saturday, when I fairly shut myself up to escape out of the way of both suitors, the coming and the going one,—sure that neither of my sisters would particularly want me—that Sunday was not a happy one. The only pleasant bit in it was the walk home from church; when, Penelope mounting guard over the lovers, I thought it no more than right to be civil to Dr. Urquhart. In so doing, I resolutely smothered down my annoyance at their joining us, and at the young gentleman's taking so much upon himself already, forsooth: lest Captain Treherne's friend should discover that I was not in the most amiable mood possible with regard to this marriage. And in so valorously "putting myself into my pocket,"—the bad self which had been uppermost all day—somehow it slipped away, as my pin-cushions and pencil-cases are wont to do—slid down to the earth and vanished.

A Life for a Life

I enjoyed the walk. I like talking to Dr. Urquhart, for he seems honest. He makes one feel as if there were some solid good somewhere in the world, if only one could find it; instead of wandering among mere shams of it, pretences of heroism, simulations of virtue, selfish abortions of benevolence. It seems to me, at times, as if this present world were not unlike that place in Hades—is it Dante's or Virgil's making?—where trees, beasts, ghosts, and all, are equally shadowy and unsubstantial. That Sunday morning, which happened to be a specially lovely one, was one of the few days lately when things about me have seemed tangible and real. Including myself who not seldom appear to myself as the biggest sham of all.

Dr. Urquhart left us at the gate: would not come in, though Penelope invited him. Indeed, he went away rather abruptly; I should say, rudely—but that he is not the sort of man to be easily suspected of discourtesy. Captain Treherne declared his secession was not surprising, as he has a perfect horror of ladies' society. In which case, why did he not avoid mine? I am sure he need not have had it unless he chose: nor did he behave as if in a state of great martyrdom. Also, a lover of flowers is not likely to be a woman-hater, or a bad mars either: and those must be bad men who have an unqualified "horror" of women. I shall take the liberty, until further evidence, of doubting Captain Treherne—no novelty! The difficulty is to find any man in whom you can believe.

We spent Sunday afternoon chiefly in the garden, Lisabel and her lover strolling about together, as Penelope and Francis used to do.

Penelope sat with me some time, on the terrace before the drawing-room windows; then bidding me stay where I was, and keep a look-out after those two, lest they should get too sentimental, she went indoors, and I saw her afterwards, through the parlour-window, writing—probably one of those long letters which Francis gets every Monday morning. What on earth can she find to say?

The lecture against sentimentalism was needless. Nothing of that in Lisabel. Her courtship will be of the most matter-of-fact kind. Every time they passed me, she was talking or laughing. Not a soft or serious look has there been on her face since Friday night; or, rather, Saturday morning, when my sobbing made her shed a few tears. She did not afterwards—not even when she told what has occurred to papa and Penelope.

A Life for a Life

Penelope bore it well—if there was anything to bear, and perhaps there was—to her. It might be trying to have her youngest sister married first, and to a young man but for whom Francis would himself long ago have been in a position to marry. He told us, on Saturday, the whole story: how, as a boy, he was meant for his uncle's heir, but late in life Sir William married. There was a coldness afterwards, till Mrs. Charteris died, when her brother got Francis this Government situation, from which we hoped so much, but which still continues, he says, "a mere pittance." It is certainly rather hard for Francis. He had a long talk with papa, before he left, ending, as usual, in nothing.

After he went away, Penelope did not appear till tea-time, and was "as cross as two sticks," to use a childish expression, all evening. If these are lover's visits, I heartily wish Francis would keep away.

She was not in much better humour on Sunday, especially when, coming hastily into the parlour with a message from Lisabel, I gave her a start—for she was sitting, not writing, but leaning over her desk, with her fingers pressed upon her eyes. It startled me, too, to see her; we have grown so used 'to this affair, and Penelope is so sharp-tempered, that we never seem to suspect her of feeling anything. I was foolish enough to apologise for interrupting, and to attempt to kiss her, which irritated her so that we had almost a quarrel. I left the room, put on my bonnet, and went off to evening church—God forgive me! for no better purpose than to get rid of home.

I wonder, do sisters ever love one another? Not after our fashion, out of mere habit and long familiarity, also a certain pride, which, however we differ among ourselves, would make us, I believe, defend one another warmly against strangers— but out of voluntary sympathy and affection. Do families ever live in open-hearted union, feeling that blood is blood, closer than acquaintance, friendship, or any tie in the world, except marriage? That is, it ought to be. Perhaps it may so happen, once in a century, as true love does, or there would not be so much romancing about both.

Thus I meditated, as, rather sick and sorry at heart, I returned from church, tramping through the dark lanes after papa, who marched ahead, crunching the sand and dead leaves in his usual solid, solitary way, now and then calling out to me—

"Keep close behind me. What a pity you came to church to-night!"

It was foolish, but I think I could have cried.

At home, we found my sisters waiting tea. Captain Treherne was gone. They never mentioned to papa that he had been at Rockmount to-day.

On Monday he did not make his appearance. I asked Lisabel if she had expected him.

"What for? I don't wish the young man to be always tied to my apron-strings."

"But he might naturally want to see you."

"Let him want then. My dear little simpleton, it will do him good. The less he has of me, the more he will value me."

I observed that that was an odd doctrine with which to begin married life, but she laughed at me, and said the cases were altogether different.

Nevertheless, when Tuesday also passed, and no word from her adorer, Lisabel looked a little less easy. Not unhappy—our Lis was never seen unhappy since she was born—but, just a little what we women call "fidgety"; a state of mind, the result of which generally affects other people rather than ourselves. In short, the mood for which, as children, we are whipped and sent to bed as "naughty"; as young women, petted, and pitied for "low spirits"; as elderly people, humoured on account of "nerves."

On Wednesday morning, when the post came and brought no letter, Lisabel declared she would stay indoors no longer, but would go out for a drive.

"To the camp, as usual?" said Penelope.

Lisa laughed, and protested she should drive wherever she liked.

"Girls, will you come or not?"

Penelope declined, shortly. I said I would go anywhere except to the camp, which I thought decidedly objectionable under the circumstances.

"Dora, don't be silly. But do just as you like. I can call at the Cedars for Miss Emery."

"And Colin too, who will be exceedingly happy to go with you," suggested Penelope.

But the sneer was wasted. Lisabel laughed again, smoothed her collar at the glass, and left the parlour, looking as contented as ever.

Ere she went Out, radiant in her new hat and feathers, her blue cloth jacket, and her dainty little driving-gloves (won in a bet with Captain Treherne), she put her head in at my door, where I was working at German, and trying to forget all these follies and annoyances.

"You'll not go, then?"

I shook my head, and asked when she intended to be back.

"Probably at lunch; or I may stay dinner at the Cedars. Just as it happens. Good-bye."

"Lisabel," I cried, catching her by the shoulders, "what are you going to do?"

"I told you. Oh, take care of my feather! I shall drive over to the Cedars."

"Any further? To the camp?"

"It depends entirely upon circumstances."

"Suppose you should meet him?"

"Captain Treherne? I shall bow politely, and drive on."

"And what if he comes here in your absence?"

"My compliments and regrets that unavoidable engagements deprived me of the pleasure of seeing him."

"Lisabel, I don't believe you have a bit of heart in you."

"Oh yes, I have; quite as much as is convenient."

Mine was full, and she saw it. She patted me on the shoulder good-naturedly.

"If there ever was a dear little dolt, its name is Theodora Johnston. Why, child, at the worst, what harm am I doing? Merely showing a young fellow, who, I must say, is behaving rather badly, that I am not breaking my heart about him, nor mean to do it."

"But I thought you liked him?"

"So I do; but not in your sentimental sort of way. I am a practical person. I told him, exactly as papa told him, that if he came with his father's consent, I would be engaged to him at once, and marry him as soon as he liked. Otherwise, let him go! That's all. Don't fret, child; I am quite able to take care of myself."

Truly, she was! But I thought, if I were a man, I certainly should not trouble myself to go crazy after a woman—if men ever do such a thing.

Scarcely was my sister gone, than I had the opportunity of considering that latter possibility. I was called downstairs to Captain Treherne. Never did I see an unfortunate youth in such a state of mind.

What passed between us I cannot set down clearly; it was on his side so incoherent, on mine so awkward and uncomfortable. I gathered that he had just had a letter from his father, refusing consent, or at least insisting on the delay of the marriage, which his friend Dr. Urquhart also advised. Exceedingly obliged to that gentleman for his polite interference in our family affairs, thought I.

The poor lover seemed so much in earnest that I pitied him. Missing Lisabel, he had asked to see me, in order to know where she was gone.

A Life for a Life

I told him, to the Cedars. He turned as white as a sheet.

"Serves me right, serves me right, for my confounded folly and cowardice. I never will take anybody's advice again. What did she think of my keeping away so long? Did she despise—hate me?"

I said my sister had not confided to me any such opinion of him.

"She shan't meet Granton, that fool—that knave—that——Could I overtake her before she reaches the Cedars?"

I informed him of a short cut across the moor, and he was out of the house in two minutes, before Penelope came into the drawing-room.

Penelope said I had done exceedingly wrong—that to send him after our Lisa, and allow her to be seen driving with him about the country, was the height of indecorum—that I had no sense of family dignity, or prudence, or propriety—was not a woman at all, but a mere sentimental bookworm.

I answered, I was glad of it, if to be a woman was to resemble the women I knew best.

A bitter, wicked speech, bitterly repented of when uttered. Penelope has a sharp tongue, though she does not know it; but when she rouses mine, I do know it, therefore am the more guilty. Many an unkind or sarcastic word that women drop, as carelessly as a minute seed, often fructifies into a whole garden-full of noisome weeds, sprung up—they have forgotten how—but the weeds are there. Yet still I cannot always command my tongue. Even sometimes when I do, the effort makes me think all the more angrily of Penelope.

It was not now in an angry, but a humbled spirit, that, when Penelope was gone to her district visiting—she does far more in the parish than either Lis or I—I went out alone, as usual, upon the moor.

My moorlands looked dreary; the heather is fading from purple to brown; the autumn days are coming on fast. That afternoon they had that leaden uniformity which always weighs me down; I felt weary, hopeless—longed for some change in my dull life; wished I were a boy, a man—anything, so that I might be something—do something.

A Life for a Life

Thus thinking, so deeply that I noticed little, a person overtook, and passed me. It is so rare to meet any one above the rank of a labourer hereabouts, that I looked round; and then saw it was Dr. Urquhart. He recognised me, apparently—mechanically I bowed, so did he, and went on.

This broke the chain of my thoughts—they wandered to my sister, Captain Treherne, and this Dr. Urquhart, with whom, now I came to think of it—I had not done so in the instant of his passing—I felt justly displeased. What right had he to meddle with my sister's affairs—to give his sage advice to his obedient young friend, who was foolish enough to ask it? Would I marry a man who went consulting his near, dear, and particular friends as to whether they were pleased to consider me a suitable wife for him? Never! Let him out of his own will love me, choose me, and win me, or leave me alone.

So, perhaps, the blame lay more at Mr. Treherne's door than his friend's—whom I could not call either a bad man or a designing man—his countenance forbade it. Surely I had been unjust to him.

He might have known this, and wished to give me a chance of penitence, for I shortly saw his figure reappearing over the slope of the road, returning towards me. Should I go back? But that would seem too pointed, and we should only exchange another formal bow.

I was mistaken. He stopped, bade me "Good morning," made some remarks about the weather, and then abruptly told me that he had taken the liberty of turning back because he wanted to speak to me.

I thought, whatever will Penelope say! This escapade will be more "improper" than Lisabel's, though my friend is patriarchal in his age and preternatural in his gravity. But the mischievous spirit, together with a little uncomfortable surprise, went out of me when I looked at Dr. Urquhart. In spite of himself, his whole manner was so exceedingly nervous that I became quite myself; if only out of compassion.

"May I presume on our acquaintance enough to ask you a question—simple enough, but of great moment to me. Is Captain Treherne at your house?"

"No."

"Has he been there to-day?"

"Yes."

"I see, you think me extremely impertinent."

"Not impertinent, but more inquisitive, than I consider justifiable in a stranger. I really cannot engage to answer any more questions concerning my family or acquaintance."

"Certainly not. I beg your pardon. I will wish you good morning."

"Good morning." But he lingered.

"You are too candid yourself not to permit candour in me—may I, in excuse, state my reasons for thus interrupting you?" I assented.

"You are aware that I know, and have known all along, the present relations of my friend Treherne with your family?"

"I had rather not discuss that subject, Doctor Urquhart."

"No, but it will account for my asking questions about Captain Treherne. He left me this morning in a state of the greatest excitement. And at his age, with his temperament, there is no knowing to what a young man may not be driven."

"At present, I believe, to nothing worse than the Cedars, with my sister as his charioteer."

"You are satirical."

"I am exceedingly obliged to you."

Dr. Urquhart regarded me with a sort of benignant smile, as if I were a naughty child, whose naughtiness partly grieved, and partly amused him.

"If, in warrant of my age and my profession, you will allow me a few words of serious conversation with you, I, in my turn, shall be exceedingly obliged."

"You are welcome."

"Even if I speak about your sister and Captain Treherne?"

There he roused me.

"Doctor Urquhart, I do not see that you have the slightest right to interfere about my sister and Captain Treherne. He may choose to make you his confidant—I shall not; and I think very meanly of any man who brings a third person, either as umpire or go-between, betwixt himself and the woman he professes to love."

Dr. Urquhart looked at me again fixedly, with that curious, half-melancholy smile, before he spoke.

"At least, let me beg of you to believe one thing—I am not that go-between."

He was so very gentle with me in my wrath, that, perforce, I could not be angry. I turned homeward, and he turned with me; but I was determined not to give him another syllable. Nevertheless, he spoke.

"Since we have said thus much, may I be allowed one word more? This matter has begun to give me extreme uneasiness. It is doing Treherne much harm. He is an only son, the son of his father's old age: on him much hope rests. He is very young—I never knew him to be serious in anything before. He is serious in his attachment—I mean in his ardent desire to marry your sister."

"You think so? We are deeply indebted to him."

"My dear young lady, when we are talking on a matter so important, and which concerns you so nearly, it is a pity to reply in that tone."

To be reproved in this way by a man and a stranger! I was so astonished that it made me dumb. He continued— "You are aware that, for the present, Sir William's consent has been refused?"

"I am aware of it."

"And indignant, probably. Yet there are two sides to the subject. It is rather trying to an old man, when his son writes suddenly, and insists upon bringing home a daughter-in-law, however charming, in six weeks; natural, too, that the father should urge,—'Take time to consider, my dear boy.'"

"Very natural."

"Nay, should he go further, and wish some information respecting the lady who is to become one of his family—desire to know her family, in order to judge more of one on whom are to depend his son's happiness and his house and honour, you would not think him unjust or tyrannical?"

"Of course not. We," I said, with some pride, alas! more pride than truth, "we should exact the same."

"I know, Sir William well and he trusts me. You will, perhaps, understand how this trust and the—the flexible character of his son, make me feel painfully responsible. Also, I know what youth is when thwarted. If that young fellow should go wrong, it would be to me—you cannot conceive how painful it would be to me."

His hands nervously working one over the other, the sorrowful expression of his eyes, indicated sufficient emotion to make me extremely grieved for this good-hearted man. I am sure he is good-hearted.

I said I could not, of course, feel the same interest that he did in Captain Treherne, but that I wished the young man well.

"Can you tell me one thing: is your sister really attached to him?"

This sudden question, which I had so many times asked of myself—ought I to reply to it? Could I? Only by a prevarication.

"Mr. Treherne is the best person from whom to obtain that information."

And I began to walk quicker, as a hint that this very odd conversation had lasted quite long enough.

"I shall not detain you two minutes," my companion said, hastily. "It is a strange confidence to put in you, and yet I feel I may. Sir William wrote to me privately to-day. On my answer to his inquiries his consent will mainly depend."

"What does he want to know? If we are respectable; if we have any money; if we have been decently educated, so that our connection shall not disgrace his family?"

"You are almost justified in being angry; but I said nothing of the kind. His questions only referred to the personal worth of the lady, and her personal attachment to his son."

"My poor Lisa! That she should have her character asked for like a housemaid! That she should be admitted into a grand family, condescendingly, on sufferance!"

"You quite mistake," said Dr. Urquhart, earnestly. "You are so angry that you will not listen to what I say. Sir William is wealthy enough to be indifferent to money. Birth and position he might desire, and his son has already satisfied him upon yours; that your father is a clergyman, and that you come of an old English family."

"We do not; we come of nothing and nobody. My grandfather was a farmer; he wrote his name Johnson, plain, plebeian Johnson. We are, by right, no Johnstons at all."

The awful announcement had not the effect I anticipated. True, Dr. Urquhart started a little, and walked on silently for some minutes, but when he turned his face round it was quite beaming.

"If I did tell this to Sir William, he is too honourable a man not to value honour and honesty in any family, whether plebeian, as you call it, or not. Pardon me this long intrusion, with all my other offences. Will you shake hands?"

We did so—quite friendly, and parted.

A Life for a Life

I found Lisabel at home. By some chance, she had missed the Grantons, and Captain Treherne had missed her. I know not of which accident I was the most glad.

Frankly and plainly, as seemed to me best, I told her of my meeting Dr. Urquhart, and of all that had passed between us; saving only the fact of Sir William's letter to him, which, as he said it was "in confidence," I felt I was not justified in communicating even to my sister.

She took everything very easily—laughed at Mr. Treherne's woes, called him "poor fellow," was sure all would come right in time, and went upstairs to dress for dinner.

On Thursday she got a letter from him which she gave me to read—very passionate, and full of nonsense. I wonder any man can write such rubbish, or any woman care to read it— still more to show it. It gave no information on facts—only implored her to see him; which, in a neat little note, also given for my perusal, Lisabel declined.

On Friday evening, just after the lamp was lit and we were all sitting round the tea-table, who should send in his card with a message begging a few minutes' conversation with Mr. Johnston, but Dr. Urquhart? "Max T. Urquhart, M.D."—as his card said. How odd he should be called "Max."

Papa, roused from his nap, desired the visitor to be shown in, and with some difficulty I made him understand that this was the gentleman Mrs. Granton had spoken of—also—as Penelope added ill-naturedly, "the particular friend of Captain Treherne."

This—for though he has said nothing, I am sure he has understood what has been going on—made papa stand up rather frigidly when Dr. Urquhart entered the parlour. He did so, hesitatingly, as if coming out of the dark night, the blaze of our lamp confused him. I noticed he put up his hand to shade his eyes.

"Doctor Urquhart, I believe? Mrs. Granton's friend, and Captain Treherne's?"

"The same."

A Life for a Life

"Will you be seated?"

He took a chair opposite; and he and papa scanned one another closely. I caught, in Dr. Urquhart's face, that peculiar uneasy expression about the mouth. What a comfort a beard must be to a nervous person!

A few commonplace remarks passed, and then our visitor asked if he might speak with papa alone. He was the bearer of a message—a letter in short—from Sir William Treherne, of Treherne Court.

Papa said, stiffly—he had not the honour of that gentleman's acquaintance.

"Sir William hopes, nevertheless, to have the honour of making yours."

Lisabel pinched me under the table; Penelope gazed steadily into the teapot; papa rose and walked solemnly into his study—Dr. Urquhart following.

It was—as Lisa cleverly expressed it—"all right." All parties concerned had given full consent to the marriage.

Captain Treherne came the day following to Rockmount, in a state of exuberant felicity, the overplus of which he vented in kissing Penelope and me, and requesting us to call him "Augustus." I am afraid I could willingly have dispensed with either ceremony.

Dr. Urquhart we have not seen again—he was not at church yesterday. Papa intends to invite him to dinner shortly. He says he likes him very much.

Chapter 7

HIS STORY

Hospital-work, rather heavy this week, with other things of lesser moment, have stopped this my correspondence with an "airy nothing": however, the blank will not be missed—nought concerning Max Urquhart would be missed by anybody.

Pardon, fond and faithful Nobody, for whose benefit I write, and for whose good opinion I am naturally anxious. I believe two or three people would miss me, my advice and conversation, in the hospital.

By-the-bye, Thomas Hardman, to my extreme satisfaction, seems really reforming. His wife told me he has not taken a drop too much since he came out of hospital. She says "this illness was the saving of him, since, if he had been flogged, or discharged for drunkenness, he would have been a drunkard all his days." So far, so good.

I was writing about being missed, literally, by Nobody And, truly, this seems fair enough; for is there anybody I should miss? Have I missed, or been relieved by the lost company of my young friend who has so long haunted my hut, but who, now, at an amazing expense in carriage-hire, horseflesh, and shoe-leather, manages to spend every available minute at a much more lively abode, as Rockmount probably is, for he seems to find a charm in the very walls which enclose his jewel.

For my part, I prefer the casket to the gem. Rockmount must be a pleasant house to live in; I thought so the first night, when, by Sir William's earnest desire, I took upon myself the part of "father" to that wilful lad, and paid the preliminary visit to the lady's father, Mr. Johnston.

Johnson it is, properly, as I learned from that impetuous young daughter of his, when, meeting her on the moor, the idea suddenly struck me to gain from her some knowledge that might guide my conduct in the very anxious position wherein I was placed. Johnson, only Johnson. Poor child! had she known the load she lifted off me by those few impetuous words, which accident only won; for Treherne's matter had for once driven out of my mind all other thoughts, or doubts, or fears, which may now henceforward be completely set aside.

I must, of course, take no notice of her frank communication, but continue to call them "Johnston." Families which "come from nothing and nobody"—the foolish lassie! as if we did not all come alike from Father Adam—are very tenacious on these points; which may have their value—to families. Unto isolated individuals they seem ridiculous. To me, for instance, of what benefit is it to bear an ancient name, bequeathed by ancestors whom I owe nothing besides, and which I shall leave to no descendants? I, who have no abiding-place on the whole earth, and to whom, as I read in a review extract yesterday, "My home is any room where I can draw a bolt across the door."

Speaking of home, I revert to my first glimpse of the interior of Rockmount, that rainy night, when, weary with my day and night journey, and struck more than ever with the empty dreariness of Treherne Court, and the restlessness of its poor gouty old master, able to enjoy so little out of all his splendours, I suddenly entered this snug little "home." The fire, the tea-table, the neatly-dressed daughters, looking quite different from decked-out beauties, or hospital slatterns, which are the two phases in which I most often see the sex. Certainly, to one who has been much abroad, there is a great charm in the sweet looks of a thorough English woman by her own fireside.

This picture fixed itself on my mind, distinct as a photograph; for truly it was printed in light. The warm, bright parlour, with a delicate-tinted paper, a flowered carpet, and amber curtains, which I noticed because one of the daughters was in the act of drawing them, to screen the draught from her father's arm-chair. The old man—he must be seventy, nearly—standing on the hearth-rug, met me coldly enough, which was not surprising, prior to our conversation. The three ladies I have before named.

Of these, the future Mrs. Treherne is by far the handsomest; but I still prefer the countenance of my earliest acquaintance, Miss Theodora—a pretty name. Neither she nor her sisters gave me more than a formal bow; shaking hands is evidently not their custom with strangers. I should have thought of that, two days before.

Mr. Johnston took me into his study. It is an antique room, with dogs for the fireplace, and a settle on either side the hearth; many books or papers about, and a large, neatly arranged library on shelves.

I noticed these things, because, as I say, my long absence from England caused them to attract me more than they might have done a person accustomed to English domestic life. That old man, gliding peacefully downhill in the arms of his three daughters, was a sight pleasant enough. There must be many compensations in old age—in such an old age as this.

Mr. Johnston—I am learning to write the name without hesitation—is not a man of many words. His character appears to me of that type which I have generally found associated with those specially delicate and regular features; shrinking from anything painful or distasteful, putting it aside, forgetting it, if possible, but anyhow trying to get rid of it. Thus, when I had delivered Sir William Treherne's most cordial and gentlemanly letter, and explained his thorough consent to the marriage, the lady's father took it much more indifferently than I had expected.

He said, "that he had never interfered with his daughters' choice in such matters, nor should he now; he had no objection to see them settled; they would have no protector when he was gone." And here he paused.

I answered, it was a very natural parental desire, and I trusted Captain Treherne would prove a good brother to the Misses Johnston, as well as a good son to himself.

"Yes—yes," he said hastily, and then asked me a few questions as to Treherne's prospects, temper, and moral character, which I was glad to be able to answer as I did. "Harum-scarum" as I call him—few young men of fortune can boast a more stainless life, and so I told Mr. Johnston. He seemed satisfied, and ended our interview by saying, "that he should be happy to see the young gentleman to-morrow."

So I departed, declining his invitation to re-enter the drawing-room, for it seemed that, at the present crisis in their family history, there was an indelicacy in any strangers breaking in upon that happy circle. Otherwise, I would have liked well another peep at the pretty

A Life for a Life

home-picture, which, in walking to the camp through a pelting rain, flitted before my eyes again and again.

Treherne was waiting in my hut. He looked up, fevered with anxiety.

"Where the devil have you been gone to, Doctor? Nobody has known anything about you for the last two days. And I wanted you to write to the governor, and—"

"I have seen the 'governor,' as you will persist in calling the best of fathers—"

"Seen him!"

"And the Rockmount father too. Go in and win, my boy; the coast's all clear. Mind you ask me to the wedding."

Truly there is a certain satisfaction in having had a hand in making young folks happy. The sight does not happen often enough to afford my smiling even at the demonstrations of that poor lad on this memorable evening.

Since then, I have left him to his own devices, and followed mine, which have little to do with happy people. Once or twice, I have had business with Mr. Granton, who does not seem to suffer acutely at Miss Lisabel's marriage. He need not cause a care, even to that tender-hearted damsel, who besought me so pitifully to take him in hand. And so, I trust the whole Rockmount family are happy, and fulfilling their destiny—in the which, little as I thought it, when I stood watching the solitary girl in the sofa corner, Max Urquhart has been made more an instrument than he ever dreamed of, or than they are likely ever to be aware.

The matter was beginning to fade out of my memory, as one of the many episodes which are always occurring to create passing interests in a doctor's life, when I received an invitation to dine at Rockmount.

I dislike accepting casual invitations. Primarily, on principle—the bread-and-salt doctrine of the East, which considers hospitality neither as a business nor an amusement, but as a sacred rite, entailing permanent responsibility to both host and guest. When I sit by a man's fireside, or (Treherne *loquitur*) "put my feet under his mahogany," I feel bound not merely to give him back the same quantity and quality of meat and drink, but to regard myself as henceforth his friend and guest, under obligations closer and more binding than one would submit to from the world in general. It is, therefore, incumbent on me to be very choice in those with whom I put myself under such bonds and obligations.

My secondary reasons are so purely personal, that they will not bear enlarging upon. Most people of solitary life, and conscious of many peculiarities, take small pleasure in general society, otherwise to go out into the world, to rub up one's intellect, enlarge one's social sympathies, enjoy the commingling of wit, learning, beauty, and even folly, would be a pleasant thing—like sitting to watch a pyrotechnic display, knowing all the while, that when it was ended one could come back to see one's heart in the perennial warmth of one's own fireside. If not,—better stay away:—for one is inclined to turn cynical, and perceive nothing but the smell of the gunpowder, the wrecks of the catherine-wheels, and the empty shells of the Roman-candles.

The Rockmount invitation was rather friendly than formal, and it came from an old man. The feeble hand-writing, the all but illegible signature, weighed with me, in spite of myself. I had no definite reason to refuse his politeness, which is not likely to extend beyond an occasional dinner-party, of the sort given hereabouts periodically, to middle-aged respectable neighbours—in which category may be supposed to come Max Urquhart, M.D. I accepted the courtesy and invitation.

Yet let me confess to thee, compassionate unknown, the ridiculous hesitation with which I walked up to this friendly door, from which I should certainly have walked away again, but for my dislike to break any engagement, however trivial, or even a promise made only to myself. Let me own the morbid dread with which I contemplated four mortal hours to be spent in the society of a dozen friendly people, made doubly sociable by the influence of a good dinner, and the best of wines.

But the alarm was needless, as a little common-sense, had I exercised it, would soon have proved.

A Life for a Life

In the drawing-room, lit with the warm duskiness of firelight, sat the three ladies. The eldest received me politely: the youngest apologetically.

"We are only ourselves, you see; we understand you dislike dinner-parties, so we invited nobody."

"We never do give dinner-parties more than once or twice a year."

It was the second daughter who made that last remark. I thought whether it was for my sake or her own, that one young lady had taken the trouble to give me a false impression, and the other to remove it. And how very indifferent I was to both attempts! Surely, women hold trifles of more moment than we men can afford to do.

Curious enough to me was the thoroughly feminine atmosphere of the dainty little drawing-room, set out, not with costly splendours, like Treherne Court, but pretty home-made ornaments, and, above all, with plenty of flowers. My olfactories are acute; certain rooms always possess to me certain associated scents through which, at whatever distance of time I revisit them, the pristine impression survives; sometimes pleasant, sometimes horribly painful. That pretty parlour will, I fancy, always carry to me the scent of orange-flowers. It came through the door of a little greenhouse, from a tree there, the finest specimen I had yet seen in England, and I rose to examine it. There followed me the second daughter, Miss Theodora.

In the minute picture which I have been making of my evening at Rockmount, I ought not to omit this young girl, or young woman, for she appears both by turns; indeed, she has the most variable exterior of any person I ever met. I recall her successively: the first time of meeting, quite childlike in her looks and ways; the second, sedate and womanly, save in her little obstinacy about the bluebells; the third, dignified, indignant, pertinaciously reserved; but this night I saw her in an entirely new character, neither childish nor woman-like, but altogether gentle and girlish—a thorough English girl.

Her dress, of some soft, dark colour, which, fell in folds, and did not rustle or spread; her hair, which was twisted at the back, without any bows or laces, such as I see ladies wear, and brought down, smooth and soft over the forehead, formed a sufficient contrast to her sisters to make me notice her; besides, it was a style more according to my own taste. I hate to see a woman all flounces and filligigs, or with her hair torn up by the roots like a Chinese Mandarin. Hair, curved over the brow like a Saxon arch, under the doorway of which two modest intelligent eyes stand sentinel, vouching for the worth of what is within—grant these, and the rest of the features may he anything you choose, if not absolutely ugly.

The only peculiarity about hers was, a squareness of chin, and closeness of mouth, indicating more strength than sweetness of disposition, until the young lady smiled.

Writing this, I am smiling myself, to reflect how little people would give me credit for so much observation; but a liking to study character is, perhaps, of all others, the hobby most useful to a medical man.

I have left my object of remark all this while, standing by her orange-tree, and contemplating a large caterpillar slowly crawling over one of its leaves. I recommended her to get Treherne to smoke in her conservatory, which would remove the insects from her flowers.

"They are not mine, I rarely pay them the least attention."

I thought she was fond of flowers.

"Yes, but wild flowers, not tame, like these of Penelope's. I only patronise those she throws away as being not 'good.' Can you imagine mother Nature making a 'bad' flower?"

I said, I concluded Miss Johnston was a scientific horticulturist.

"Indeed she is. I never knew a girl so learned about flowers, well-educated, genteel, greenhouse flowers, as our Penelope."

"Our" Penelope. There must be a pleasure in these family possessive pronouns.

I had the honour of taking into dinner this lady, who is very sprightly, with nothing at all Odyssean about her. During a lack of conversation—for Treherne, of course, devoted himself to his ladye-love; and Mr. Johnston is the most silent of hosts—I ventured to remark that this was the first time I had ever met a lady with that old Greek name.

"Penelope!" cried Treherne. "'Pon my life, I forget who was Penelope. Do tell us, Dora. That young lady knows everything, Doctor; a regular blue-stocking; at first she quite frightened me, I declare."

Captain Treherne seems to be making himself uncommonly familiar with his future sisters-in-law. This one did not exactly relish it, to judge by her look. She has a will of her own, and a temper too, "that young lady." It is as well Treherne did not happen to set his affections upon her.

Poor youth! he never knows when to stop.

"Ha! I have it now, Miss Dora. Penelope was in the *Odyssey*—that book of engravings you were showing my cousin Charteris and me that Friday night. And how I laughed at what Charteris said—that he thought the good lady was very much over-rated, and Ulysses in the right of it to ride away again, when, coming back after ten years, he found her a prudish, psalm-singing, spinning old woman. Hollo!—have I put my foot into it, Lisabel?"

It seemed so, by the constrained silence of the whole party. Miss Johnston turned scarlet, and then white, but immediately said to me, laughing—

"Mr. Charteris is an excellent classic; he was papa's pupil for some years. Have you ever met him?"

I had not, but I had often heard of him in certain circles of our camp society, as well as from Sir William Treherne. And I now suddenly recollected that, in talking over his son's marriage, the latter had expressed some surprise at the news Treherne had given, that this gay bachelor about town, whose society he had been always chary of cultivating for fear of harm to "the boy," had been engaged for some time to a member of the Johnston family. This was, of course, Miss Johnston—Penelope.

I would have let the subject drop, but Miss Lisabel revived it.

"So you have heard a deal about Francis? No wonder!—is he not a charming person?—and very much thought of in London society? Do tell us all you heard about him?"

Treherne gave me a look.

"Oh! you'll never get anything out of the Doctor. He knows everybody, and everybody tells him everything, but there it ends. He is a perfect tomb—a sarcophagus of silence, as a fellow once called him."

Miss Lisabel held up her hands, and vowed she was really afraid of me. Miss Johnston said sharply, "She liked candid people: a sarcophagus of silence implied a 'body' inside." At which all laughed, except the second sister, who said, with some warmth, "She thought there were few qualities more rare and valuable than the power of keeping a secret."

"Of course, Dora thinks so. Doctor, my sister, there, is the most secretive little mouse that ever was born. Red-hot pincers could not force from her what she did not choose to tell, about herself or other people."

I well believe that. One sometimes finds that combination of natural frankness and exceeding reticence, when reticence is necessary.

The "mouse" had justified her name by being silent nearly all dinner-time, though it was not the silence of either sullenness or abstraction. But when she was afterwards accused of delighting in a secret, "running away with it, and hiding it in her hole, like a bit of cheese," she looked up, and said emphatically—

"That is a mistake, Lisabel."

"A fib, you mean. Augustus, do you know my sisters call me a dreadful story-teller," smiling at him, as if she thought it the best joke in the world.

"I said, a mistake, and meant nothing more."

"Do tell us, child, what you really meant, if it is possible to get it out of you," observed the eldest sister; and the poor "mouse," thus driven into a corner, looked round the table with those bright eyes of hers.

"Lisabel mistakes; I do not delight in secrets. I think people ought not to have any, but to be of one mind in a house." (She studies her Bible, then, for the phrase came out as naturally as one quotes habitual phrases, scarcely conscious whence one has learned them). "Those who really care for one another, are much happier when they tell one another everything; there is nothing so dangerous as a secret. Better never have one, but, having it, if one ought to keep it at all, one ought to keep it to the death."

She looked—quite accidentally, I do believe—but still she looked at me. Why is it, that this girl should be the instrument of giving me continual stabs of pain? yet there is a charm in them. They take away a little of the feeling of isolation—the contrast between the inside and outside of the sarcophagus. Many true words are spoken in jest! They dart, like a thread of light, even to "the body" within. Corruption has its laws. I marvel in what length of time might a sunbeam, penetrating there, find nothing worse than harmless dust?

But I will pass into ordinary life again. Common-sense teaches a man in my circumstances that this is the best thing for him. What business has he to set himself up as a Simon Stylites on a solitary column of woe? as if misery constituted saintship? There is no arrogance like the hypocrisy of humility.

When Treherne had joined the ladies, Mr. Johnston and myself started some very interesting conversation, *à propos* of Mrs. Granton and her doings in the parish, when I found that he has the feeling, very rare among country gentlemen of his age and generation—an exceeding aversion for strong drinks. He discountenances Father Mathew and the pledge as popish, a crotchet not surprising in an old Tory, whose opinions, never wide, all run in one groove, as it were; but he advocates temperance, even to teetotalism.

I tried to draw the line of moderation, and argued that, because some men, determined on making beasts of themselves, required to be treated like beasts, by compulsion only; that was no reason why the remainder should not have freewill, man's glorious privilege, to prove their manhood by the choice of good or evil.

"Like Adam—and Adam fell."

"Like a Greater than Adam; trusting in whom, we need never fall."

The old man did not reply, but he looked much excited. The subject seemed to rouse in him something beyond the mere disgust of an educated gentleman, at what offended his refined tastes. Had not certain other reasons made that solution improbable, I could have imagined it the shudder of one too familiar with the vice he now abhorred: that he spoke about drunkenness with the terrified fierceness of one who had himself been a drunkard.

As we sat talking across the table, philosophically, abstractedly, yet with a perceptible undertone of reserve,—I heard it in his voice; I felt it in my own,—or listening silently to the equinoctial gale, which rattled the window, made the candles flicker, almost caused the wine to shake in the untouched decanters—as I have heard table-rapping tales, of wine beginning to shake when there was "a spirit present,"—the thought struck me more than once—if either of us two men could lift the curtain from one another's past, what would be found there?

He proceeded to close our conversation, by saying— "You will understand now, Doctor Urquhart, and I wish to name it as a sort of apology for former close questioning, my extreme horror of drunkenness, and my satisfaction at finding that Mr. Treherne has no propensity in this direction."

I answered—

"Certainly not; that, with all the temptations of a mess-table, to take much wine was, with him, a thing exceedingly rare."

"Rare! I thought you said he never drank at all?"

"I said he was no drunkard, nor at all in the habit of drinking."

"Habits grow, we know not how," cried the old man, irritably. "Does he take it every day?"

"I suppose so. Most military men do."

A Life for a Life

Mr. Johnston turned sharp upon me.

"I must have no modifications, Doctor Urquhart. Can you declare positively that you never saw Captain Treherne the worse for liquor?"

To answer this question directly was impossible. I tried to remove the impression I had unfortunately given, and which the old man had taken up so unexpectedly and fiercely, by enlarging on the brave manner in which Treherne had withstood many a lure to evil ways.

"You cannot deceive me, sir. I must have the truth."

I was on the point of telling him to seek it from Treherne himself, when, remembering the irritation of the old man, and the hot-headed imprudence of the young one, I thought it would be safer to bear the brunt myself. I informed Mr. Johnston of the two only instances when I had seen Treherne not himself. Once after twenty-four hours in the trenches, when unlimited brandy could hardly keep life in our poor fellows, and again when Miss Lisabel herself must be his excuse.

"Lisabel? Do not name her. Sir, I would rather see a daughter of mine in her grave, than the wife of a drunkard."

"Which, allow me to assert, Captain Treherne is not, and is never likely to be."

Mr. Johnston shook his head incredulously. I became more and more convinced about the justness of my conjecture about his past life, which delicacy forbade me to inquire into, or to use as any argument against his harshness now. I began to feel seriously uneasy.

"Mr. Johnston," I said, "would you for this accidental error—"

I paused, seeing at the door a young lady's face, Miss Theodora's.

"Papa, tea is waiting."

"Let it wait then: shut the door. Well, sir?"

A Life for a Life

I repeated, would he, for one accidental error, condemn the young man entirely?

"He has condemned himself; he has taken the first step, and his downward course will be swift and sudden. There is no stopping it, sir," and he struck his hand on the table. "If I had a son, and he liked wine, as a child does, perhaps; a pretty little boy, sitting at table and drinking healths at birthdays, or a schoolboy, proud to do what he sees his father doing,—I would take his glass from him, and fill it with poison, deadly poison—that he might kill himself at once, rather than grow up to be his friends' and his own damnation—a *drunkard*."

I urged, after a minute's pause, that Treherne was neither a child nor a boy; that he had passed through the early perils of youth, and succumbed to none; that there was little fear he would ever become a drunkard.

"He may."

"Please God, he never shall! Even if he had yielded to temptation; it even in your sense, and mine, Mr. Johnston, the young man had once been 'drunk,' should he for that be branded as a hopeless drunkard? I think not—I trust not."

And, strongly excited myself, I pleaded for the lad as if I had been pleading for my own life,—but in vain.

It was getting late, and I was in momentary dread of another summons to the drawing-room.

In cases like these there comes a time when, be our opponents younger or older, inferior or superior to ourselves, we feel we must assert what we believe to be right, "taking the upper hand," as it is called; that is, using the power which the few have in guiding the many. Call it influence, decision, will,—one who possesses that quality rarely gets through half a lifetime without discovering the fact, and what a weighty and solemn gift it is.

I said to Mr. Johnston, very respectfully, yet resolutely, that, in so serious a matter, of which I myself was the unhappy cause, I must request him, as a personal favour, to postpone his decision for to-night.

"And," I continued, "forgive my urging that, both as a father and a clergyman, you are bound to be careful how you decide. By one fatal word you may destroy your daughter's happiness for life."

I saw him start; I struck bolder.

"Also, as Captain Treherne's friend, let me remind you that he has a future, too. It is a dangerous thing for a young man's future when he is thwarted in his first love. What if he should go all wrong, and you had to answer to Sir William Treherne for the ruin of his only son?"

I was not prepared for the effect of my words.

"His only son—God forgive me! is he his only son?"

Mr. Johnston turned from me; his hands shook violently, his whole countenance changed. In it there was as much remorse and anguish as if he, in his youth, had been some old man's only and perhaps erring son.

I could pity him—if he were one of those who suffer to their life's end for the evil deeds of their youth. I abstained from any further remarks, and he made none. At last, as he expressed some wish to be left alone, I rose.

"Doctor," he said, in a tremulous voice, "I will thank you not to name this conversation to my family. For the subject of it—we'll pass it over—this once."

I thanked him, and earnestly begged forgiveness for any warmth I had shown in the argument.

"Oh yes, oh yes! Did I not say we would pass it over?"

He sank wearily back in his arm-chair, but I felt the point was gained.

A Life for a Life

In course of the evening, when Treherne and Miss Lisabel, in happy ignorance of all the peril their bliss had gone through, were making believe to play chess in the corner, and Miss Johnston was reading the newspaper to her father, I slipped away to the green-house, where I stood examining some orchids, and thinking how curious it was that I, a perfect stranger, should be so mixed up with the private affairs of this family.

"Doctor Urquhart."

Soft as the whisper was, it made me start. I apologised for not having seen Miss Theodora enter, and began admiring the orchidaceous plants.

"Yes, very pretty. But I wanted to ask you, what were you and papa talking about?"

"Your father wished me not to mention it."

"But I heard part of it, I could not help hearing,—and I guessed the rest. Tell me only one thing. Is Captain Treherne still to marry our Lisa?"

"I believe so. There was a difficulty, but Mr. Johnston said he would 'pass it over.'"

"Poor papa," was all she replied. "Poor papa."

I expressed my exceeding regret at what had happened.

"No, never mind, you could not help it; I understand exactly how it was. But the storm will blow over; papa is rather peculiar. Don't tell Captain Treherne."

She stood meditative a good while, and then said—

"I think you are right about Mr. Treherne, I begin to like him myself a little. That is—No, I will not make pretences. I did not like him at all until lately."

I told her I knew that.

A Life for a Life

"How? Did I show it? Do I show what I feel?"

"Tolerably," said I, smiling. "But you do like him now?'

"Yes."

Another pause of consideration and then a second decisive "yes."

"I like him," she went on, "because he is good-natured and sincere. Besides, he suits Lisabel, and people are so different, that it would be ridiculous to expect to choose one's sister's husband after the pattern of one's own. The two would probably not agree in any single particular."

"Indeed," said I, amused at her frankness. "For instance?"

"Well, for instance, Lisa likes talking, and I silence, or being talked to, and even that in moderation. Hark!"

We listened a minute to Treherne's hearty laugh and incessant chitter-chatter.

"Now, my sister enjoys that, she says it amuses her; I am sure it would drive me crazy in a week."

I could sympathise a little in this sentiment.

"But," with sudden seriousness, "I beg you to understand, Doctor Urquhart, that I am not speaking against Captain Treherne. As I told you, I like him; I am quite satisfied with him, as a brother-in-law. Only, he is not exactly the sort of person one would choose to spend a week with in the Eddystone Lighthouse."

I asked if that was her test for all her friends? since so few could stand it.

She laughed.

"Possibly not. When one comes to reflect, there are very few whose company one can tolerate so well as one's own."

A Life for a Life

"Which is itself not always agreeable."

"No, but the less evil of the two. I don't believe there is a creature living whose society I could endure, without intermission, for a month, a week, or even two days. No. Emphatically no."

She must then, though a member of a family, live a good deal alone—a fact I had already begun to suspect.

"Therefore, as I try to make Lisa feel—being the elder, I have a right to preach, you know—what an awful thing marriage must be, even viewed as mere companionship. Putting aside love, honour, obedience, and all that sort of thing, to undertake the burthen of any one person's constant presence and conversation for the term of one's natural life! the idea is frightful!"

"Very, if you do put aside love, honour, 'and all that sort of thing.'"

She looked up, as if she thought I was laughing at her.

"Am I talking very foolishly? I am afraid I do so sometimes."

"Not at all," I said, "it was pleasant to hear her talk."

Which unlucky remark of mine had the effect of wholly silencing her.

But, silent, it was something to watch her moving about the drawing-room, or sitting still over her work. I like to see a woman sewing; it gives her an air of peaceful homelikeness, the nearest approach to which, in us men, who are either always sullenly busy or lazily idle, is the ungainly lounge with our feet on the fender. Mr. Johnston must be happy in his daughters, particularly in this one. He can scarcely have regretted that he has had no sons.

It seems natural, seeing how much too well acquainted we are with our sex, its weaknesses and wickednesses, that most men long for, and make much of daughters. Certainly, to have in one's old age a bright girlish face to look at, a lively original girlish tongue to freshen one's mind with new ideas, must be a pleasant thing. Whatever may have been the sorrows of his past life, Mr. Johnston is a fortunate man now.

A Life for a Life

With regard to Treherne, I had the satisfaction of perceiving that, as Miss Theodora had prophesied, the old man's anger had blown over. His manner indicated not merely forgiveness, but a degree of kindly interest in that light-hearted youth, who was brimming over with fun and contentment.

I had an opportunity of satisfying myself on this point, in another quarter, while waiting in the hall for Treherne's protracted adieu in the drawing-room; when Miss Theodora, passing me, stopped, to interchange a word with me.

"Shall you tell your friend what occurred to-night?—with papa, I mean."

I replied, I was not sure—but perhaps I should. It might act as a warning.

"Do you think he needs a warning?"

"I do not. I believe Treherne is as likely to turn out a good man, especially with a good wife to help him, as any young fellow of my acquaintance; and I sincerely hope that you, as well as your father, will think no worse of him, for anything that is past. An old man has had time to forget, and a girl is never likely to understand, the exceeding temptations which every young man has to fight through,—more especially a young man of fortune, and in the army."

"Ah, yes!" she sighed, "that is too true. Papa must have felt it. Papa wished this to he kept secret between himself and you?"

"I understood him so."

"Then keep it. Do not tell Mr. Treherne. And have no fear that I shall be too hard upon him. It would be sad indeed, for all of us, who do wrong every day, if every error of youth were to be regarded as unpardonable."

God bless her good heart, and the kindly hand she held out to me; which for the second time I dared to take in mine. Ay, even in *mine*.

Chapter 8

HER STORY

I do not feel inclined for sleep, and there is a large round moon looking in at my window. My foolish old moon, what a time it is since you and I had a quiet serious look at one another. What things you used to say to me, and what confidences I used to make in you—at this very window, leaning my elbow in this very spot. That was when I was a child, and fond of Colin—"Colin, my dear." How ridiculous it seems now, and what a laugh it would raise against me if anybody had known it. Yet what an innocent, simple, devoted child-love it was! I hardly think any after-love, supposing I should ever feel one, will be, in its way, more tender, or more true.

Moon, have you forgotten me? Am I becoming a middle-aged person; and is a new and younger generation growing up to have confidences with you as I used to have? Or is it I who have forsaken you? Most likely. You have done me a deal of harm—and good, too—in my time. Yet you seem friendly and mild to-night. I will forgive you, my poor old moon.

It has been a pleasant day. My head aches a little, with the unusual excitement—query, of pleasure?—Is pleasantness so very rare, then ?—No: I am weary with the exertion of having to make myself agreeable: for Penelope is full of housekeeping cares, and a few sad thoughts, too, may be, concerning the wedding; so that she takes little trouble to entertain visitors. And Lisabel is "in love," you know, moon.

You would not think it, though, except from the licence she takes to be lazy when Augustus is here, and up to the eyes in business when he is away. I never thought a wedding was such a "piece of work," as the old women say; such a time of incessant bustle, worry, and confusion. I only saw the "love" side of it, Lisabel avers, and laughs at me when I wonder at her for wearing herself out from morning till night in consultation over her trousseau, and how we shall possibly manage to accommodate the eight-and-forty particular friends who must be asked to the breakfast.

A Life for a Life

Happily, they are only the bride's friends. Sir William and Lady Augusta Treherne cannot come, and Augustus does not care a straw for asking anybody. He says he only wants his Lisa. His Lisa unfortunately requires a few trifles more to constitute her bridal happiness; a wreath, a veil, a breakfast, and six bridesmaids in Indian muslin. Rather cold, for autumn, but which she says she cannot give up on any account, since a wedding-day comes but once, and she has been looking forward to hers ever since she was born.

A wedding-day! Probably there are few of us who have not speculated on it a little, as the day which, of all others, is the most decisive in a woman's life. I am not ashamed to confess having occasionally thought of mine. A foolish dream that comes and goes with one's teens; imagined paradise of utterly impossible joy, to be shared with some paragon of equally impossible perfection—I could sit and laugh at it now, if the laughter were not bitterer than tears.

There, after writing this, I went and pulled down my hair, and tied it under my chin to prevent cold—oh! most prudent five-and-twenty—leaned my elbow on the window-sill, in the old attitude of fifteen, staring up at the moon and out across the fir-woods for a long time. Returning, I have relit my candle, and taken once more to my desk, and I say again, O inquisitive moon, that this has been a pleasant day.

It was one of our quiet Rockmount Sundays, which Dr. Urquhart says he enjoys so much. Poor Lisabel's last Sunday but one. She will be married to-morrow week. We had our indispensable lover to dinner, and Dr. Urquhart also. Papa told me to ask him as we were coming out of the church. In spite of the distance, he often attends our church now—at which papa seems gratified.

I delivered the message, which was not received with as much warmth as I thought it ought to have been, considering that it came from an elderly gentleman, who does not often pay a younger man than himself the compliment of liking his society. I was turning away, saying I concluded he had some better engagement, when Dr. Urquhart replied quickly—

"No, indeed. That were impossible."

"Will you come then? Pray don't, if you dislike it."

A Life for a Life

For I was vexed at a certain hesitation and uneasiness in his manner, which implied this, when I had been so glad to bring him the invitation and had taken the trouble to cross half the churchyard after him, in order to deliver it, which I certainly would not have done for a person whom everybody liked.

N.B.—This may be one of the involuntary reasons for my liking Dr. Urquhart—that papa and I myself are the only two persons of our family who unite in that opinion. Lisabel makes fun of him; Penelope is scarcely civil to him; but that is because Francis, coming down last week for a day, took a violent aversion to him.

I heard the girls laughing within a stone's throw of where we stood.

"Pray please yourself; Doctor Urquhart; come, or not come; but I can't wait."

He looked at me with an amused air;—yes, I certainly have the honour of amusing him, as a child or a kitten would—then said,—

"He would be happy to join us."

I was ashamed of myself for being thus pettish with a person so much older and wiser than I, and who ought to be excused so heartily for any peculiarities he has; yet he vexed me. He does vex me very much, sometimes. I cannot understand why; it is quite a new feeling to be so irritated with anybody. Either it is his manner, which is rather variable, sometimes cheerful and friendly, and then again restless and cold; or an uncomfortable sensation of being under control, which I never yet had, even towards my own father. Once, when I was contesting something with him, Augustus noticed it, and said, laughing—

"Oh, the Doctor makes everybody do what he likes: you'd better give in at once. I always do."

But I cannot, and I will not.

To feel vexed with a person, to know they have the power of vexing you—that a chance word or look can touch you to the quick, make you feel all over in a state of irritation, as if all the world went wrong, and you were ready to do anything cross, or sullen, or childishly naughty—until another chance word or look happens to set you right again—this is an extremely uncomfortable state of things.

I must guard against it. I must not allow my temper to get way. Sensitive it is, I am aware, quick to feel sore, and to take offence; but I am not a thoroughly ill-tempered woman. Dr. Urquhart does not think so: he told me he did not. One day, when I had been very cross with him, he said, "I had done him no harm; that I often did him good."

Me—to do good to Dr. Urquhart! What an extraordinary thing!

I like to do people good—to do it my own self, too—a mean pleasure, perhaps, yet it is a pleasure, and I was pleased by this saying of Dr. Urquhart's. If I could but believe it! I do believe it sometimes. I know that I can make him smile, let him be ever so grave; that something in me and my ways interests and amuses him in an inglorious, kittenish fashion, as I said; yet, still, I draw him out of himself, I make him merry, I bring light into his face till one could hardly believe it was the same face that I first saw at the Cedars; and it is pleasant to me to think that, by some odd sympathy or other, I am pleasant to him, as I am to few—alas! to very few.

I know when people dislike me: know it keenly, painfully; I know, too, with a sort of stolid patience, when they are simply indifferent to me. Doubtless, in both cases, they have every reason; I blame nobody, not even myself; I only state a fact. But with such people I can no more be my natural self; than I can run about, bare-footed and bare-headed, in our north winds or moorland snows. But if a little sunshine comes, my heart warms to it, basks in it, dances under it, like the silliest young lamb that ever frisked in a cowslip-meadow, rejoicing in the May.

I am not, and never pretend to be, a humble person. I feel there is that in me which is worth something, but a return for which I have never yet received. Give me its fair equivalent, its full and honest price, and oh, if I could expend it every mite, how boundlessly rich I should grow!

A Life for a Life

This last sentence means nothing; nor do I quite understand it myself. Writing a journal is a safety-valve for much folly; yet I am by no means sure that I ought to have written the last page.

However, no more of this; let me tell the story of my day.

Walking from church, Dr. Urquhart told me that Augustus had asked him to be best-man at the wedding.

I said I knew it, and wished he would consent.

"Why?"

Though the abrupt question surprised me, I answered, of course, the truth. "That if the best-man were not himself; it would be one of the camp officers, and I hated—"

"Soldiers?"

I told him, it was not kind to be always throwing in my teeth that unfortunate speech; that he ought not to tease me so.

"Do I tease you? I was not aware of it."

"Very likely not; and I am a great simpleton for allowing myself to be teased with such trifles. But Doctor Urquhart cannot expect me to be as wise as himself; he is a great deal older than I."

"Tell me, then," he continued, in that kind tone, which always makes me feel something like a little pet donkey I once had, which, if I called it across the field, would come and lay its head on my hand,—not that, donkey as I am, I incline to trouble Dr. Urquhart in that way.—"Tell me what it is you do hate?"

"I hate to have to entertain strangers."

"Then you do not consider me a stranger?"

"No; a friend."

A Life for a Life

I may say that; for short as our acquaintance dates, I have seen more of Dr. Urquhart, and seem to know him better than any man in the whole course of my life. He did not refuse the title I gave him, and I think he was gratified, though he said only—

"You are very kind, and I thank you."

Presently I recurred to the subject of discussion, and wished him to promise what Augustus, and Lisabel, and we all desired. He paused a moment, then said, decisively—

"I will come."

"That is right. I know we can always depend upon Doctor Urquhart's promises."

Was my gladness over-bold? Would he misconstrue it? No—he is too clear-sighted, too humble-minded, too wise. With him, I have always the feeling that I need take no trouble over what I do or say, except that it should be true and sincere. Whatever it is, he will judge it fairly. And if he did not, why should I care?

Yes, I should care. I like him—I like him very much. It would be a comfort to me to have him for a friend—one of my very own. In some degree, he treats me as such; to-day, for instance, he told me more about himself than he ever did to any one of us. It came out accidentally. I cannot endure a man who, at first acquaintance, indulges you with his autobiography in full. Such an one must be either a puppy or an idiot.

—Ah, there I am again, at my harsh judgments, which Dr. Urquhart has so often tacitly reproved. This good man, who has seen more of the world and its wickedness than I am ever likely to see, is yet the most charitable man I ever knew. To return.

Before we reached Rockmount, the sky had clouded over, and in an hour it was a thoroughly wet afternoon. Penelope went upstairs to write her Sunday letter, and Augustus and Lisabel gave broad hints that they wished the drawing-room all to themselves. Perforce, Dr. Urquhart and I had to entertain ourselves.

I took him into the green-house, where he lectured to me on the orchidacea and vegetation of the tropics generally,—to his own content, doubtless, and partially to mine. I like to hear his talking, so wise, yet so simple; a freshness almost boyish seems to linger in his nature still, and he has the thoroughly boyish peculiarity of taking pleasure in little things. He spent half-an-hour in reviving a big brown bee which had grown torpid with cold, and there was in his eyes a kindness, as over a human creature, when he gave into my charge his "little patient," whom I promised to befriend. (There he is, poor old fellow, fast asleep on a flower-pot, till the first bright morning I can turn him out.)

"I am afraid, though, he will soon get into trouble again, and not find so kind a friend," said I to Dr. Urquhart. "He will intoxicate himself in the nearest flower-cup, and seek repentance and restoration too late."

"I hope not," said the Doctor, sadly and gravely.

I said I was sorry for having made a jest upon his favourite doctrine of repentance and restoration of sinners, which he seemed always both to preach and to practise.

"Do I? Perhaps. Do you not think it's very much needed in this world?"

I said I had not lived long enough in the world to find out.

"I forgot how young you were."

He had once, in his direct way, asked my age, and I had told him, much disposed likewise to return the question, but was afraid. Sometimes I feel quite at home with him, as if I could say anything to him, and then again he makes me, not actually afraid—thank goodness, I never was afraid of any man yet, and hope I never shall be—but shy and quiet. I suppose it is because he is so very good; because in his presence my little follies and wickednesses hide their heads. I cease perplexing myself about them, or about myself at all, and only think—not of him so much as of something higher and better than either him or me. Surely this cannot be wrong.

The bee question settled, we sat down, silent, listening to the rain pattering on the glass roof of the green-house. It was rather a dreary day. I began thinking of Lisabel's leaving more than was good for me; and with that penetrative kindness which I have often noticed in him, Dr. Urquhart turned my sad thoughts away, by various information about Treherne Court, and the new relations of our Lisa—not many. I said, "happily, she would have neither brother nor sister-in-law."

"Happily! You cannot be in earnest?"

I half wished I had not been, and yet I could not but speak my mind—that brothers and sisters, in law or in blood, were often anything but a blessing.

"I must emphatically differ from you there. I think it is, with few exceptional cases, the greatest misfortune to be an only child. Few are so naturally good, or reared under such favourable circumstances, that such a position does not do them harm. A lonely childhood and youth may make a great man, a good man, but it rarely makes a happy man. Better all the tussles and troubles of family life, where the angles of character are rubbed off and its inclinations to morbidness, sensitiveness, and egotism knocked down. I think it is a great wonder to see Treherne such a good fellow as he is, considering he has been an only child."

"You speak as if you knew what that was yourself."

"No, we were orphans, but I had one brother."

This was the first time Dr. Urquhart had reverted to any of his relatives, or to his early life. My curiosity was strong. I risked a question: was this brother older or younger than he?

"Older."

"And his name?"

"Dallas."

"Dallas Urquhart—what a nice name."

"It is common in the family. There was a Dallas Urquhart, younger brother to a Sir John Urquhart, who, in the religious troubles, seceded to Episcopacy. He was in love with a minister's sister—a Presbyterian. She died broken-hearted, and in despair at her reproaches, Dallas threw himself down a precipice, where his whitened bones were not found till many years after. Is not that a romantic history?"

I said romantic and painful histories were common enough; there had been some, even in our matter-of-fact family. But he was not so inquisitive as I; nor should I have told him further; we never speak on this subject if we can help it. Even the Grantons—our intimate friends ever since we came to live at Rockmount—have never been made acquainted with it. And Penelope said there was no need to tell Augustus, as it could not affect him, or any person now living, and, for the sake of the family, the sad story was better forgotten. I think so, too.

With a sigh, I could not help observing to Dr. Urquhart, that it must be a very happy thing to have a brother—a good brother.

"Yes. Mine was the best that any one ever had. He was a minister of the Kirk—that is, he would have been, but he died."

"In Scotland?"

"No—at Pau, in the Pyrenees."

"Were you with him?"

"I was not."

This seemed a remembrance so acutely painful, that shortly afterwards I tried to change the subject, by asking a question or two about himself,—and especially what I had long wanted to find out—how he came by that eccentric Christian-name.

"Is it eccentric?—I really never knew or thought after whom I was called."

I suggested, Max Piccolomini.

"Who was he, pray? My unprofessional reading has been small. I am ashamed to say I never heard of Max Piccolomini."

Amused by this naïve confession of ignorance, I offered jestingly to give him a course of polite literature, and begin with that grandest of German dramas, Schiller's *Wallenstein*.

"Not in German, if you please; I don't know a dozen words of the language."

"Why, Doctor Urquhart, I must be a great deal cleverer than you."

I had said this out of utter incredulity at the ludicrous idea; but, to my surprise, he took it seriously.

"You are right. I know I am a coarse, uneducated person; the life of an army-surgeon allows few opportunities of refinement, and, like many another boy, I threw away my chances when I had them."

"At school?"

"College, rather."

"Where did you go to college?"

"At St. Andrews."

The interrogative mood being on me, I thought I would venture a question which had been often on my mind to ask—namely, what made him choose to be a doctor, which always seemed to me the most painful and arduous of professions.

He was so slow in answering, that I began to fear it was one of my too blunt queries, and apologised.

"I will tell you, if you desire it. My motive was not unlike one you once suggested—to save life instead of destroying it; also, because I wished to have my own life always in my hand. I cannot justly consider it mine. It is *owed*."

To heaven, I conclude he meant, by the solemnity of his manner. Yet, are not all lives owed? And, if so, my early dream of perfect bliss — namely, for two people to spend their lives together in a sort of domestic Pitcairn's Island, cradled in a spiritual Pacific Ocean, with nothing to do but to love one another — must be a delusion, or worse. I am beginning to be glad I never found it. We are not the birds and butterflies, but the labourers of the earthly vineyard. To discover one's right work and do it, must be the grand secret of life. — With or without love, I wonder? With it — I should imagine. But Dr. Urquhart in his plan of existence, never seems to think of such an insignificant necessity.

Yet let me not speak lightly. I like him — I honour him. Had I been his dead brother, or a sister whom he never had, I would have helped, rather than have hindered him in his self-sacrificing career. I would have scorned to put in my poor claim over him or his existence. It would have seemed like taking for daily uses the gold of the sanctuary.

And here pondering over all I have heard of him and seen in him: the self-denial, the heroism, the religious purity of his daily life — which has roused in even the light heart of Augustus Treherne an attachment approaching to positive devotion, that all the jesting of Lisabel is powerless to shake, I call to mind one incident of this day, which startled, shocked me: concerning which even now I can scarcely credit the evidence of my own ears.

We had all gathered round the fire waiting papa's return from the second service, Penelope, Lisabel, Augustus, Dr. Urquhart, I. The rain had cleared off and there was only a soft drip, drip, on the glass of the green-house outside. We were very peaceful and comfortable: it felt almost like a family circle — which indeed it was, with one exception. The new member of our family seemed to make himself considerably at his ease — sat beside his Lisa, and held her hand under cover of her apron — at which I thought I saw Dr. Urquhart smile. Why should he? The caress was quite natural.

Penelope was less restless than usual, owing may be to her long letter and the prospect of seeing Francis in a week: he comes to the marriage, of course. Poor fellow, what a pity we cannot have two weddings instead of one! — it is rather hard for him to be only a wedding-guest and Penelope only a bridesmaid. But I am ceasing to laugh at even Francis and Penelope.

A Life for a Life

I myself; in my own little low chair in its right angle on the hearthrug, felt perfectly happy. Is it the contrast between it and the life of solitude of which I have only lately had any knowledge that makes my own home-life so much sweeter than it used to be?

The gentlemen began talking together about the difference between this quiet scene and that of November last year: when, Sebastopol taken, the army was making up its mind to winter in idleness, as merrily as it could. And then Dr. Urquhart reverted to the former winter, the terrible time— until its miseries reached and touched the English heart at home. And yet, as Dr. Urquhart said, such misery seems often to evoke the noblest half of man's nature. Many an anecdote, proving this, he told about "his poor fellows," as he called them; tales of heroism, patient endurance, unselfishness, and generosity,—such as, in the mysterious agency of Providence, are always developed by that great purifier as well as avenger, war.

Listening, my cheek burned to think I had ever said I hated soldiers. It is a solemn question, too momentous for human wisdom to decide upon, and, probably, never meant to be decided in this world—the justice of carnage, the necessity of war. But thus far I am convinced— and intend, the first opportunity, to express my thanks to Dr. Urquhart for having taught me the lesson—that to set one's self in fierce aversion against any class as a class, is both foolish and wicked. We should "hate" nobody. The Christian warfare is never against sinners, but against sin.

Speaking of the statistics of mortality in the army, Dr. Urquhart surprised us by stating how small a percentage—bless me, I am beginning to talk like a blue-book—results from death in battle and from wounds. And, strange as it may appear, the mortality in a campaign, with all its fatal chances, is less than in barracks at home. He has long suspected this, from the accounts of the men, and having lately, from clear data, ascertained its accuracy, intends urging it at the Horse Guards, or failing there, in the public press,— that the causes may be inquired into and remedied. It will be at some personal risk: Government never likes being meddled with; but he seems the sort of man who, having once got an idea into his head, would pursue it to the death—and very right to. If I had been a man, I would have done exactly the same.

All this while, I have never told—that thing. It came out, as well as I can remember, thus:—

A Life for a Life

Dr. Urquhart was saying that the average mortality of soldiers in barracks was higher than that of any corresponding class of working-men. He attributes this to want of space, cleanliness, fresh air, and good food.

"Also, to another cause, which you always find flourishing under such circumstances—drink. It is in a barracks just as in the courts and alleys of a large city—wherever you find people huddled together in foul air, ill smells, and general wretchedness—they drink. They cannot help it, it seems a natural necessity."

"There, we have the Doctor on his hobby. Gee-up, Doctor!" cried Augustus. I wonder his friend stands his nonsense so good-humouredly.

"You know it is true, though, Treherne," and he went on speaking to me. "In the Crimea, the great curse of our army was drink. Drink killed more of us than the Russians did. You should have seen what I have seen—the officer maddening himself with champagne at the mess-table—the private stealing out to a rum-store to booze secretly over his grog. The thing was obliged to be winked at, it was so common."

"In hospital, too," observed Captain Treherne, gradually listening. "Don't you remember telling me there was not a week passed that you had not cases of death solely from drinking?"

"And, even then, I could not stop it, nor keep the liquor outside the wards. I have come in and found drunken orderlies carousing with drunken patients; nay, more than once I have taken the brandy-bottle from under a dead man's pillow."

"Ay, I remember," said Augustus, looking grave.

Lisabel, who never likes his attention diverted from her charming self; cried saucily—

"All very fine talking, Doctor, but you shall not make me a teetotaller, nor Augustus either, I hope."

"I have not the slightest intention of the kind, I assure you: nor does there seem any necessity. Though, for those who have not the power to resist intoxication, it is much safer never to touch stimulants."

"Do you never touch them?"

"I have not done so for many years."

"Because you are afraid? Well, I daresay you were no better once than your neighbours"

"Lisabel!" I whispered, for I saw Dr. Urquhart wince under her rude words: but there is no stopping that girl's tongue.

"Now confess, Doctor, just for fun. Papa is not here, and we'll tell no tales out of school—were you ever in your life, to use your own ugly word, *drunk*?"

"Once."

Writing this, I can hardly believe he said it, and yet he did, in a quiet, low voice, as if the confession were forced from him as a sort of voluntary expiation.

Dr. Urquhart *drunk*! What a frightful idea! Under what circumstances could it possibly have happened? One thing I would stake my life upon,—it never happened but that once.

I have been thinking, how horrible it must be to see anybody one cared for drunk: the honest eyes dull and meaningless; the wise lips jabbering foolishness; the whole face and figure, instead of being what one likes to look at, takes pleasure to see in the same room, even,—growing ugly, irrational, disgusting—more like a beast than a man.

Yet some women have to bear it, have to speak kindly to their husbands, hide their brutishness, and keep them from making worse fools of themselves than they can help. I have seen it done, not merely by working-men's wives, but lady-wives in drawing-rooms. I think, if I were married, and I saw my husband the least overcome by wine, not "drunk" may be, but just excited, silly, otherwise than his natural self; it would nearly drive me wild. Less on my own account than his. To see him sink—not for a great crime, but a contemptible, cowardly bit of sensualism—from the height where my love had placed him; to have to take care of him, to pity him—ay, and I might pity him, but I think the full glory and passion of my love would die out, then and there, for ever.

Let me not think of this, but go on relating what occurred to-day.

Dr. Urquhart's abrupt confession, which seemed to surprise Augustus as much as anybody, threw an awkwardness over us all; we slipped out of the subject, and plunged into the never-ending theme—the wedding and its arrangements. Here I found out that Dr. Urquhart had, at first, refused, point-blank, his friend's request that he would be best-man, but, on my entreating him this morning, had changed his mind. I was glad, and expressed my gladness warmly. I would not like Dr. Urquhart to suppose we thought the worse of him for what he had confessed, or rather been forced into confessing. It was very wrong of Lisabel. But she really seemed sorry, and paid him special attention in consultations about what she thinks the important affairs of Monday week. I was almost cross at the exemplary patience with which he examined the orange-tree, and pronounced that the buds would open in time, he thought; that if not, he would try, as in duty bound, to procure some. He also heroically consented to his other duty, of returning thanks for "the bridesmaids," for we are to have healths drunk, speeches made, and all the rest of it. Mercy on us! how will papa ever stand it?

These family events have always their painful side. I am sure papa will feel it. I only trust that no chance observations will strike home, and hurt him. This fear haunted me so much, that I took an opportunity of suggesting to Dr. Urquhart that all the speeches had better be as short as possible.

"Mine shall be, I promise. Were you afraid of it?" asked he, smiling; it was just before the horses were brought up, and we were all standing out in the moonlight—for shame, moon, leading us to catch cold just before our wedding, and very thoughtless of the Doctor to allow it, too. I could see by his smile that he was now quite himself again,—which was a relief.

"Oh, nonsense; I shall expect you to make the grandest speech that ever was heard. But, seriously, these sort of speeches are always trying, and will be so, especially to papa."

"I understand. We must take care: you are a thoughtful little lady."—He sometimes has called me "Little lady," instead of "Miss Theodora."—"Yes, your father will feel acutely this first break in the family."

I said I did not mean that exactly, as it was not the case. And, for the first time, it struck me as sad, that one whom I never knew, whom I scarcely ever think of, should be lost from among us, so lost as not to be even named.

Dr. Urquhart asked me why I looked so grave. At first I said I had rather not tell him, and then I felt as if at that moment, standing quietly talking in the lovely night, after such a happy day, it were a comfort, almost a necessity, to tell him anything, everything.

"I was thinking of some one belonging to me whom nobody knows of, whom we never speak about. Hush, don't let them hear."

"Who was it? But I beg your pardon, do not tell me unless you like."

From his tone,—he thought, I know he thought—Oh, what a ridiculous, impossible thing! Then I was determined to tell.

"It was one—who was Papa's favourite among us all."

"A sister?"

"No, a brother."

I had not time to say any more, for they were just starting, nor am I satisfied that I was right in saying so much. But the confidence is safe with him, and he will never refer to it; he will feel, as we do, that a subject so painful is best avoided, even among ourselves—on the whole I am glad he knows.

Coming indoors, the girls made me very angry by their jests, but the anger has somehow evaporated now. What does it matter? As I told

A Life for a Life

Lisabel, friends do not grow on every hedge, though lovers may, and when one finds a good man one ought to value him, nor be ashamed of it either.

No, no, my sweet moon, setting so quickly behind that belt of firs, I *will* like him if I choose, as I like everything true and noble wherever I find it in this world.

Moon, it is a good world, a happy world, and grows happier the longer one lives in it. So I will just watch your silver ladyship—a nice "little lady" you are too, slipping away from it with that satisfied farewell smile, and then—I shall go to bed.

Chapter 9

HIS STORY

It is a fortnight since I wrote a line here.

Last Sunday week I made a discovery—in truth, two discoveries—after which I lost myself, as it were, for many days.

It will be advisable not to see any more of that family. Not that I have any proof that they are *the* family—the name itself, Johnson, and their acknowledged plebeian origin, is sufficient evidence to the contrary. But, if they had been!

The mere supposition, coming, instinctively, that Sunday night, before reason argued it down—was enough to cause me twelve such hours as would be purchased dearly with twelve years of life—even a life full of such happiness as, I then learned, is possible for a man. But not for me.—Never for me!

This phase of the subject is, however, so exclusively my own, that even here I will pass it over. It will be conquered by-and-by—being discovered in time.

I went to the marriage — having promised. She said, Dr. Urquhart never breaks his promises. No. There is one promise— nay, vow — kept unflinchingly for twenty years, could it be broken now? It never could. Before it is too late — I will take steps to teach myself that it never shall.

I only joined the marriage-party during the ceremony. They excused me the breakfast, speeches, etc.—Treherne knew I was not well. Also, she said I looked "over-worked,"—and there was a kind of softness in her eye, the pity that all women have, and so readily show.

She looked the very picture of a white fairy, or a wood-nymph—or an angel, sliding down on a sunshiny cloud to a man asleep.—He wakes and it is all gone.

A Life for a Life

While the register was being signed—and they wished me to be one of the attesting witnesses—an idea came into my mind.

The family must have settled at Rockmount for many years. Probably, the grandfather, the farmer who wrote himself, plebeianly, "Johnson," was buried there. Or—if he were dead, but whether it was so or not, I had no clue—here, probably, would be registered the interment of that brother to whom allusion had been made as "papa's favourite," but in such a manner, and with such evident distress, that to make further inquiry about him was impossible. Besides, I must have no more private talk with her—with the one of the Misses Johnston whom I know best.

This brother—I have calculated his possible age, compared with theirs. Even were he the eldest of them, he could not now be much above thirty—if alive. *That person* would now be at least fifty.

Still, at once and for ever to root up any such morbid, unutterable fancies, I thought it would be as well to turn over the register-books, as, without suspicion, it was this day easy to do. On my way home I stopped at the church—and, helped by the half-stupid sexton and bell-ringer, went over the village records of, he declared, the last twenty years, and more. In none of them was once named the family of Johnston.

No proof, therefore, of my cause of dread—not an atom, not a straw. All evidence hitherto going directly counter to a supposition—the horror of which would surpass all horrible coincidences that fate could work out for a man's punishment. Let me put it aside.

The other thing—God help me! I believe I shall also be able to put aside—being entirely my own affair—and I myself being the only sufferer.

Now Treherne is married and away, there will be no necessity to visit at Rockmount any more.

Chapter 10

HER STORY

What a change a marriage makes—what a blank it leaves in a house! Ours has been very dull since poor Lisa went away.

I know not why I call her "poor Lisa." She seems the gayest of the gay, and the happiest of the happy, two characters which, by the way, are not always identical. Her letters from Paris are full of enjoyment. Augustus takes her everywhere, and introduces her to everybody. She was the "belle mariée" of a ball at the British Embassy, and has been presented to my old aversion, though he is really turning out a creditable individual in some things; "never too late to mend," even for a Louis Napoleon. Of course, Lisabel now thinks him "the most charming man in the world," except Augustus.

Strange that she should take delight in such dissipations. She, not three weeks married. How very little she must have of her husband's society. Now, I should think the pleasantest way of spending a honeymoon would be to get out of everybody's way, and have a little peace and quiet, rambling about at liberty, and looking at pretty places together. But tastes differ; that is not Lisabel's fancy, nor was hers the sort of marriage likely to make such a honeymoon desirable. She used to say she should get tired of the angel Gabriel if she had him all to herself for four mortal weeks. Possibly; I remember once making a similar remark.

But surely that dread and weariness of two people, in being left to one another's sole society, must apply chiefly to cases of association for mere amusement or convenience; not to those who voluntarily bind their lives together, "for better for worse, for richer for poorer, in sickness and in health, to love and to cherish, till death us do part"; how solemn the words are! They thrilled me all through, on the morning of Lisabel's marriage.

I have never set down here anything about that day. I suppose it resembled most other wedding-days—came and went like a dream, and not a very happy dream either. There seemed a cloud over us all.

One of the reasons was, Francis did not come: at the last minute, he sent an apology; which was not behaving well, I thought. Nor did the excuse seem a valid one. But it might have been a painful day to him, and Francis is one of those sort of people—very pleasant, and not ill-meaning people either—who like to escape pain, if possible. Still, he might have considered that it was not likely to be the happiest of days to Penelope herself, nor made more so by his absence;—which she bore in perfect silence; and nobody, except Augustus, who observed, laughingly, that it was "just like cousin Charteris," ventured any comment on the subject.

I do not join Mrs. Granton and our Lisa in their tirades against long engagements. I do not see why, when people are really fond of one another, and cannot possibly be married, they should not live contentedly betrothed for an indefinite time: it is certainly better than living wholly apart, forlorn and hopeless, neither having towards the other any open right, or claim, or duty. But then every betrothal should resemble marriage itself, in its perfect confidence, patience, and un-exacting tenderness. Also, it ought never to be made so public, or allowed to be so cruelly talked over, as this engagement of Penelope's.

Well, Francis did not appear, and everybody left earlier than we had expected. On the marriage evening, we were quite alone; and the day after, Rockmount was its dull self again, except the want of poor Lisa.

I still call her so—I cannot help it. We never discover the value of things till we have lost them. Out of every corner I miss our Lisa— her light laugh that used to seem heartless, yet was the merriest sound in the house; her tall, handsome figure sailing in and about the rooms; her imperturbable good-temper, which I often tried—her careless, untidy ways, that used for ever to aggravate Penelope— down to her very follies and flirtations, carried on to the last in spite of Augustus.

My poor Lisa! The putting away of her music from the piano, her books from the shelf, and her clothes from the drawers, cost me as sharp an agony as I ever had in my life. I was not half good enough to her when I had her,—if I had her again, how different it should be. Ah, that is what we always say, as the great shadow Time keeps advancing and advancing, yet we always let it slip by, and we cannot make it go back for a single hour.

A Life for a Life

Mrs. Granton and Colin came to tea to-night. Their company was a relief; our evenings are often very dull. We sit all three together, but no one has much sympathy with what the other is doing or thinking. As not seldom happens in families, we each live in a distinct world of our own, never intruded on, save when we collectively entertain visitors. Papa asked Dr. Urquhart to dinner twice, but received an apology both times, which rather offended him, and he says he shall not invite him again until he has called. He ought to call, for an old man likes attention, and is justified in exacting it.

To-night, while Mrs. Granton gossiped with papa and Penelope, Colin talked to me. He bears Lisabel's marriage far better than I expected, probably because he has got something to do. He told me along story about a row of labourers' cottages, which Dr. Urquhart advised him to build at the corner of the moor, each with its bit of land, convertible into a potato-field or a garden. There Colin busies himself from morning till night, superintending, planning, building, draining, "working like a horse," he protests, "and never enjoyed anything more in his life." He says he has seen a great deal of Dr. Urquhart lately, and had great assistance from him in the matter of these cottages.

Then can he be so exceedingly occupied as not to have an hour or two for a visit? Shame on me for the suspicion! The idea that Dr. Urquhart would, even in a polite excuse, state a thing which was not true!

Colin is much improved. He is beginning to suspect that Colin Granton, Esq., owner of a free estate, and twenty-seven years old, has got something to do besides lounge about, shoot rabbits, and play billiards. He opened up to my sympathy a long series of schemes about these cottages: how he meant to instigate industry, cleanliness, and, indeed, all the cardinal virtues, by means of cottagers' prizes for tidy houses, well-kept gardens, and the best brought-up and largest families. He will never be clever, poor Colin! but he may be a most useful character in the county, and he has the kindest heart in the world. By the way, he told me in his ultra-simple fashion, that somebody had informed him one of the Rockmount young ladies said so! I felt myself grow hot to the ears, which exceedingly astonished Colin.

A Life for a Life

Altogether, a not unpleasant evening. But oh, moon!—whom I saw making cross-panes on the carpet, when I came in—it was not like the evenings a month ago, when Lisabel was at home.

I think women, as well as men, require something to do. I wish I had it; it would do me as much good as it has done Cohn. I am beginning to fear I lead a wretchedly idle life: all young ladies at home do, it seems, except perhaps the eldest sister, if she chances to be such a woman as our Penelope. Why cannot I help Penelope? Mrs. Granton took it for granted that I do; that I shall be the greatest comfort and assistance to Miss Johnston, now Miss Lisabel is gone.

I am not, the least in the world! which I would fain have explained, only mere friends can never understand the ins and outs of a family. If I offered to assist her in the house, how Penelope would stare! Or even in her schools and parish—but that I cannot do. Teaching is to me perfectly intolerable. The moment I have to face two dozen pairs of round eyes, every particle of sense takes flight, and I become the veriest of cowards, ready to sink through the floor. The same, too, in district visiting. What business have I, because I happen to be the clergyman's daughter, to go lifting the latch, and poking about poor people's houses, obliging them to drop me curtseys, and receive civilly my tracts and advice—which they neither read nor follow, and might be none the better for it if they did?

Yet this may be only my sophistries for not doing what I so heartily dislike. Others do it—and successfully: take by storm the poor folks' hearts, and, what is better, their confidence; never enter without a welcome, and depart without a blessing; as, for instance, Dr. Urquhart. Mrs. Granton was telling about his doings among the poor families down with fever and ague, near the camp, at Mooredge.

Why cannot I do the same good? not so much, of course, but just a little? Why cannot somebody show me how to do it?

No, I am not worthy. My quarter century of life has been of no more use to myself or any human creature than that fly's which my fire has stirred up to a little foolish buzzing in the window-curtain, before it drops and dies. I might drop down and die in the same manner, leaving no better memorial.

A Life for a Life

There—I hear Penelope in her room fidgeting about her drawers, and scolding the housemaid—she is always taking juvenile incompetent housemaids out of her village school, teaching and lecturing them for a twelvemonth, and then grumbling because they leave her. Yet, this is doing good. Sometimes they cone back and thank her for having made capital servants of them; and very seldom, indeed, does such a case happen, as pretty, silly Lydia Cartwright's, who went up to London and never came back any more.

My dear sister Penelope, who, except in company, hardly has a civil word for anybody—Francis excepted:—Penelope, who has managed the establishment ever since she was a girl of sixteen; has kept the house comfortable, and maintained the credit of the family to the world without,—truly, with all your little tempers, sneers, and crabbednesses, you are worth a dozen of your sister Theodora.

I wonder if Dr. Urquhart thinks so. He looked at her closely, more than once, when we were speaking about Francis. He and she would have many meeting points of interest, if they only knew it, and talked much together. She is not very sweet to him, but that would not matter; he only values people for what they are, and not for the manner in which they behave to himself. Perhaps, if they were better acquainted, Penelope might prove a better friend for him than the "little lady."

"Little lady!" that is just such a name as one would give to an idle, useless butterfly-creature, of no value but as an amusement, a plaything of leisure-hours; in time of business or care to be altogether set aside and forgotten.

Does he think me *that*? If he does—why, let him.

A fine proof of how dull Rockmount is, and how little I have to write about when I go on scribbling such trivialities as these. If no better subjects can be found, I shall give up my journal. Meantime I intend next week to begin a serious course of study, in history, Latin and German; for the latter, instead of desultory reading, I shall try written translations, probably from my favourite, *Wallenstein*.—To think that anybody should have been ignorant even of the name of Max Piccolomini! He always was my ideal of a hero,—faithful, trustful, brave, and infinitely loving; yet able to renounce love itself for the sake of conscience.—And then, once a week I shall have a long letter to write to Lisabel—I who never had a regular correspondence in my life. It will be almost as good as Penelope's with Francis Charteris.

At last, I hear Penelope dismiss her maiden, bolt the door, and settle for the night. When, for a wonder, she finds herself alone and quiet, with nothing to do, and nobody to lecture,—I wonder what Penelope thinks about? Is it Francis? Do people in their position always think about one another the last thing? Probably. When all the day's cares and pleasures are ended, and the rest of the world shut out, the heart would naturally turn to the only one in whom, next to Heaven, is its real rest, its best comfort, closer than either friend, or brother, or sister—less another person than half itself.

No sentiment! Go to bed, Theodora.

Chapter 11

HIS STORY

I had almost given up writing here. Is it wise to begin again? Yet, to-day, in the silent hut, with the east wind howling outside almost as fiercely as it used to howl last winter over the steppes of the Caucasus, one must do something, if only to kill time.

Usually, I have little need for that resource; this barrack business engrosses every leisure hour.

The Commander-in-Chief has at length promised a commission of inquiry, if sufficient data can be supplied to him to warrant it. I have, therefore, been collecting evidence from every barrack in the United Kingdom,—and visiting personally all within a day or two days' leave from the camp. The most important were those of the metropolis.

It is needless here to recur to details of which my head has been full all the week, till a seventh day's rest and change of ideas becomes almost priceless. Unprofessional men cannot understand this; young Granton could not, when, coming down from town with me last night, he was lamenting that he should not get at his cottage-building, which he keeps up in defiance of winter weather, till Monday morning.

Mr. Granton indulged me with much conversation about some friends of his, which inclines me to believe that "the kindest heart in the world" has not suffered an incurable blow, and is already proceeding to seek consolation elsewhere. It may be so. The young are pleasant to the young: the happy delight in the happy.

To return to my poor fellows—my country bumpkins and starving mechanics, caught by the thirteenpence a day, *and* after all the expensive drilling that is to make them proper food for powder, herded together like beasts in a stall, till, except under strong coercion, the beast nature is apt to get uppermost—and no wonder. I must not think of rest till I have left no stone unturned for the furtherance of this scheme concerning my poor fellows.

A Life for a Life

And yet, the older one grows, the more keenly one feels how little power one individual man has for good—whatever he may have for evil. At least, this is the suggestion of a morbid spirit, after aiming at everything and doing almost nothing—which seemed the brief catalogue of my week's labour, last night.

People are so slow to join in any reformatory schemes. They will talk enough of the need for it,—but they will not act—it is too much trouble. Most men are engrossed in their own private concerns, business, amusements, or ambitions. It is incredible, the difficulty I had in hunting up some, who were the most active agents of good in the Crimea—and of these, how few could be convinced that there was anything needed to be done at home.

At the Horse Guards, where my face must be as familiar as that of the clock on the quadrangle to those gentlemanly young clerks—no attention was wanting, but that of furthering my business. However, the time was not altogether wasted, as in various talks with former companions, whom I there by chance waylaid, ideas were thrown out that may be brought to bear in different quarters. And, as always happens, from some of the very last quarters where anything was to be expected, the warmest interest and assistance came.

Likewise—and this forms the bright spot in a season not particularly pleasant—during my brief stay in London, the first for many years, more than one familiar face has come across me out of far-back times, with a welcome and remembrance, the warmth and heartiness of which both surprised and cheered me.

Among those I met on Thursday, was an old colonel, under whom I went out on my first voyage as assistant-surgeon, twelve years ago. He stopped me in the Mall, addressing me by name; I had almost forgotten his, till his cordial greeting brought it to mind. Then we fell to upon many mutual questions and reminiscences.

He said that he should have known me anywhere, though I was altered a good deal in some respects.

"All for the better, though, my boy—beg pardon, Doctor—but you were such a slip of a lad, then. Thought we should have had to throw you overboard before the voyage was half over, but you cheated us all, you see,—and 'pon my life, hard as you must have been at it since then, you look as if you had many years more of work in you yet."

I told him I hoped so,—which I do, for some things, and then, in answer to his friendly questions, I entered into the business which had brought me to London.

The good Colonel was brimful of interest. He has a warm heart, plenty of money, thinks that money can do everything. I had the greatest difficulty in persuading him that his cheque-book would not avail me with the Commander-in-Chief, or the honourable British officers whom I hoped to stir up to some little sympathy with the men they commanded.

"But can't I help you at all?—can't my son, either?—you remember Tommy, who used to dance the sailor's hornpipe on the deck. Such a dandy young fellow;—got him a place under Government—capital berth, easy hours, eleven till four, and regular work—the whole *Times* to read through daily. Ha! ha! you understand, eh?"

I laughed too, for it was a pretty accurate description of what I had this week seen in Government offices; indeed, in public offices of all kinds, where the labour is so largely subdivided as to be in the responsible hands of very few, and the work and the pay generally follow in an opposite ratio of progression. In the present instance, from what I remember of him, no doubt such a situation would exactly suit Master Tommy Turton.

His father and I strolled up and down the shiny half-dried pavement till the street-lamps were lighted, and the club-windows began to brighten and glow.

"You'll dine with me, of course—not at the United Service—it's my day with Tom at his club, the New Universal, capital club too. No apologies; we'll quarter ourselves upon Tommy; he will be delighted. He's extremely proud of his club; the young rogue costs me—it's impossible to say what Tom costs me per annum, over and above his pay. Yet he is a good lad, too—as lads go—holds up his head among all the young fellows of the club, and keeps the very best of company."

So went on the worthy old father—with more, which I forget. I had been on my feet all day, and was what women call "tired,"—when they delight to wheel out arm-chairs and push warmed slippers under wet feet—at least, so I have seen done.

London club-life was new to me; nor was I aware that in this England, this "home,"—words, which abroad we learn to think synonymous and invest with an inexpressible charm,—so large a proportion of the middle classes assume by choice the sort of life which, on foreign service, we put up with of necessity; the easy selfish life into which a male community is prone to fall. The time-honoured United Service, I was acquainted with; but the New Universal was quite a dazzle of brilliant plate, a palace of upholstery. Tom had not come in, but his father showed me over his domains with considerable pride.

"Yes; this is how we live—he at his club and I at mine. We have two tidy bedrooms, somewhere or other, hard by,—and that's all. A very jolly life, I assure you, if one hasn't the gout or the blues; we have kept to it ever since the poor mother died, and Henrietta married. I sometimes tell Tom he ought to settle; but he says it would be slow, and he can't afford it. Hollo! here's the boy."

Tom—a "boy" six feet high, good-looking and well dressed, after the exact pattern of a few dozen more, whom we had met strolling arm-in-arm down Pall Mall—greeted me with great civility, and said he remembered me perfectly—though my unfortunately quick ears detected him asking his father, aside, "where on earth he had picked up that old fogie?"

We dined well—and a good dinner is not a bad thing. As a man gets old, he may be allowed some cheer—in fact, he needs it. Whether, at twenty-four, he needs five courses and half-a-dozen kinds of wine is another question. But Master Tom was my host, so silence! Perhaps I am becoming "an old fogie."

After dinner, the Colonel opened out warmly upon my business, which his son evidently considered a bore.

"He really did not understand the matter; it was not in his department of public business; the governor always thought they must know everything that was going on, when, in truth, they knew nothing at all. He should be most happy, but had not the least notion what it was in his power to do for Doctor Urquhart."

Dr. Urquhart laboured to make the young gentleman understand that he really did not want him to do anything, to which Tom listened with that philosophical *laissez-faire*, kept just within the bounds of politeness, that we of an elder generation are prone to find fault with. At last, an idea struck him.

"Why, father, there's Charteris,—knows everything and everybody—would be just the man for you. There he is."

And he pointed eagerly to a gentleman, who, six tables off, lounged over his wine and newspaper.

That morning, as I stood talking in an ante-room, at the Horse Guards, this gentleman had caught my notice, leaning over one of the clerks, and enlivening their dulness by making a caricature. Now my phiz was quite at their service, but it seemed scarcely fair for any but that king of caricature, *Punch*, to make free with the honest, weather-beaten features of the noble old veteran who was talking with me. So I just intervened—not involuntarily—between the caricaturist and my—shall I honour myself by calling him my friend? the good old warrior, might not deny it. For Mr. Charteris, he apparently did not wish to own my acquaintance, nor had I any desire to resume his. We passed without recognition, as I would willingly have done now, had not Colonel Turton seized upon the name.

"Tom's right. Charteris is the very man. Has enormous influence, and capital connections—though, between you and me, Doctor, calls himself as poor as a church-mouse."

"Five hundred a year," said Tom grimly. "Wish I'd as much! Still, he's a nice fellow, and jolly good company. Here, waiter, take my compliments to Mr. Charteris, and will he do us the honour of joining us?"

Mr. Charteris came.

He appeared surprised at sight of me, but we both went through the ceremony of introduction without mentioning that it was not for the first time. And during the whole conversation, which lasted until the dinner-sounds ceased, and the long, bright, splendid dining room was all but deserted, we neither of us once adverted to the little parlour where, for a brief five minutes, Mr. Charteris and myself had met some weeks before.

I had scarcely noticed him then; now I did. He bore out Tom's encomium and the Colonel's. He is a highly intelligent, agreeable person, apparently educated to the utmost point of classical refinement. The sort of man who would please most women, and who, being intimate in a family of sisters, would with them involuntarily become their standard of all that is admirable in our sex.

In Mr. Charteris was much really to be admired: a grace bordering on what in one sex we call sweetness, in the other effeminacy. Talent, too, not original or remarkable, but indicating an evenly-cultivated, elegant mind. Rather narrow, might be—all about him was small, neat, regular; nothing in the slightest degree eccentric, or diverging from the ordinary, being apparently possible to him; a pleasure-loving temperament, disinclined for active energy in any direction—this completed my impression of Mr. Francis Charteris.

Though he gave me no information,—indeed, he seemed like my young friend Tom to make a point of knowing as little and taking as slight interest as possible in the state machinery of which he formed a part—he contributed very considerably to the enjoyment of the evening. It was he who suggested our adjournment to the theatre.

"Unless Doctor Urquhart objects. But I daresay we can find a house where the performance trenches on none of the Ten Commandments, about which, I am aware, he is rather particular."

"Oh," cried Tom, "'Thou shalt not steal,' from the French; and 'Thou shalt do no murder' on the Queen's English, are the only commandments indispensable on the stage. Come away, father."

"You're a sad dog," said the father, shaking his fist at him, with a delighted grin, which reminded me of hornpipe days.

But the sad dog knew where to find the best bones to pick, and by no means dry, either. Now, though I am not a bookman, I love my

Shakespeare well enough not to like him acted—his grand old flesh and blood digged up and served out to this modern taste as a painted, powdered, dressed-up skeleton. But this night I saw him "in his habit as he lived," presented "in very form and fashion of the time." There was a good deal of show, certainly, it being a pageant play; but you felt show was natural; that just in such a way the bells must have rung, and the people shouted, for the living Bolingbroke. The acting, too, was natural; and to me, a plain man, accustomed to hold women sacred, and to believe that a woman's arms should be kept solely for the man who loves her, I own it was a satisfaction when the stage Queen clung to the stage King Richard, in that pitiful parting, where,—

> "Bad men, ye violate
> A twofold marriage—'twixt my crown and me,
> And then between me and my married wife,"

it was a satisfaction, I say, to know that it was her own husband the actress was kissing.

This play, which Tom and the Colonel voted "slow," gave me two hours of the keenest, most utterly oblivious enjoyment; a desideratum not easily attainable.

Mr. Charteris considered it fine in its way; but, after all, there was nothing like the opera.

"Oh, Charteris is opera-mad," said Tom. "Every subscription-night, there he is, wedged in the crowd at the horrid little passage leading out of the Haymarket—among a knot of his cronies, who don't mind making martyrs of themselves for a bit of tootle-te-tooing, a kick-up, and a twirl. Well, I'm not fond of music."

"I am," said Mr. Charteris dryly.

"And of looking at pretty women, too, eh, my dear fellow?"

"Certainly."

And here he diverged to a passing criticism on the pretty women in the boxes round us: who were not few. I observed them, also—for I notice women's faces more than I was wont—but none were satisfactory, even to the eye. They all seemed over-conscious of themselves and their looks, except one small creature, in curls, and a red mantle—about the age of the poor wounded Russ, who might have been my own little adopted girl by this time, if she had not died.

I wish, sometimes, she had not died. My life would have been less lonely, could I have adopted that child.

There may be more beauty—I have heard there is, in the upper class of Englishwomen than in any race of women on the globe. But a step lower in rank, less smoothly cosmopolitan, more provincially and honestly Saxon; reserved, yet frank; simple, yet gay, would be the Englishwoman of one's heart. The man who dare open his eyes, fearlessly, to the beauties of such a one—seek her in a virtuous middle-class home, ask her of her proud father and mother; then win her and take her, joyfully, to sit by his happy hearth, wife—matron—*mother*—

I forget how that sentence was to have ended; however, it is of little consequence. It was caused partly by some reflection on this club-life, and another darker side of it, of which I caught some glimpses when I was in London.

We finished the evening at the theatre pleasantly. In the sort of atmosphere we were in, harmless enough, but glaring, unquiet, and unhome-like, I was scarcely surprised that Mr. Charteris did not once name the friends at whose house I first met him; indeed, he seemed to avoid the slightest approach to the subject. Only once, as we were pushing together, side by side, into the cool night air, he asked me, in a low, hurried tone, if I had been to Rockmount lately. He had heard I was present at the marriage.

I believe I made some remark about his absence being much regretted that day.

"Yes—yes. Shall you be there soon?"

The question was put with an anxiety which my answer in the negative evidently relieved.

A Life for a Life

"Oh, then—I need send no message. I thought you were very intimate. A charming family—a very charming family."

His eyes were wandering to some ladies of fashion who had recognised him—whom he put into their carriage with that polite assiduity which seems an instinct with him, and in the crowd we lost sight of Mr. Charteris.

Twice afterwards I saw him; once, driving in the park with two ladies in a coroneted carriage: and again walking in the dusk of the afternoon down Kensington Road. This time he started, gave me the slightest recognition possible, and walked on faster than ever. He need not have feared:—I had no wish or intention of resuming our acquaintance. The more I hear of him, the more increases my surprise—nay, even not unmixed with anxiety—at his position in the family at Rockmount.

Here I was suddenly called out to a bad accident case, some miles across the country; whence I have only returned in time for bed.

It was impossible to do anything for the poor fellow, one of Granton's labourers, who knew me by sight. I could only wait till all was over, and the widow a little composed.

At her urgent request, I sent a note to Rockmount, hard by, begging Miss Johnston would let her know if there had been heard anything of Lydia—a daughter, once in service with the Johnstons, afterwards in London—now—as the poor old mother mournfully expressed it—"gone wrong."

To my surprise, Miss Johnston answered the message in person, and a most painful conversation ensued. She is a good woman—no doubt of that: but she is, as Treherne once said of her father, "as sharp as a needle and as hard as a rock."

It being already dark, of course I saw her safe back to her own gate. She informed me that the family were all quite well, which was the sole conversation that passed between us, except concerning the poor dead labourer, James Cartwright, and his family, of whom, save Lydia, she spoke compassionately, saying they had gone through much trouble.

A Life for a Life

Walking along by her side, and trying to find a cause for the exceeding bitterness and harshness of spirit she had evidenced, it struck me that this lady was herself not ignorant of trouble.

I left her at the gate under the bush of ivy. Through the bars I could see, right across the wet garden, the light streaming from the hall-door.

Now to bed, and to sleep, if this heart will allow: it has been rather unmanageable lately, necessitating careful watching, as will be the case till there is nothing here but an empty skull.

If only I could bring this barrack matter to a satisfactory start, from which good results might reasonably be expected, I would at once go abroad. Anywhere—it is all the same. A rumour is afloat that we may soon get the route for the East, or China; which I could be well content with, as my next move.

Far away—far away; with thousands of miles of tossing sea between me and this old England; far away out of all sight or remembrance. So best.

Next time I call on Widow Cartwright shall be after dark, when, without the slightest chance of meeting any one, it will be easy to take a few steps farther up the village. There is a cranny in one place in the wall, whence I know one can get a very good view of the parlour-window, where they never close the shutters till quite bed-time.

And, before our regiment leaves, it will be right I should call—to omit this would hardly be civil, after all the hospitality I have received. So I will call some wet day, when they are not likely to be out,—when, probably, the younger sister will be sitting at her books upstairs in the attic, which, she told me, she makes her study, and gets out of the way of visitors. Perhaps she will not take the trouble to come down. Not even for a shake of the hand and a good-bye—good-bye for *ever*.

O mother—unknown mother—who must have surely loved my father; well enough, too, to leave all friends and follow him, a poor lieutenant of a marching regiment, up and down the world—if I had but died with you when you brought me into this same troublesome world, how much it would have saved!

A Life for a Life

Chapter 12

HER STORY

Just finished my long letter to Lisabel, and lingered over the direction, "Mrs. Treherne, Treherne Court."

How strange to think of our Lisa as mistress there. Which she is in fact, for Lady Treherne, a mild elderly lady, is wholly engrossed in tending Sir William, who is very infirm. The old people's rule seems merely nominal—it is Lisabel and Augustus who reign. Their domain is a perfect palace—and what a queen Miss Lis must look therein! How well she will maintain her position, and enjoy it too! In her case are no poetical sufferings from haughty parents, delighted to crush a poor daughter-in-law

> "With the burthen of an honour
> Unto which she was not born."

Already, they both like her and are proud of her—which is not surprising. I thought I had never seen a more beautiful creature than my sister Lisa, when, on her way to Treherne Court, she came home for a day.

Home? I forget, it is not her home now. How strange this must have been to her—if she thought about it. Possibly she did not; being never given to sentiment. And, though with us she was not the least altered, it was amusing to see how, to everybody else, she appeared quite the married lady; even with Mrs. Granton, who, happening to call that day, was delighted to see her, and seems not to cherish the smallest resentment in the matter of "my Colin." Very generous—for it is not the good old lady's first disappointment—she has been going a-wooing for her son ever since he was one-and-twenty, and has not found a daughter-in-law yet.

Colin, too, conducted himself with the utmost *sangfroid;* and when Augustus, who is beaming with benevolence to the whole human race, invited him to escort his mother, Penelope and me, on our first visit to Treherne Court, he accepted the invitation as if it were the pleasantest in the world. Truly, if women's hearts are as impressionable as wax, men's are as tough as gutta-percha. Talk of breaking them—faugh!

I hope it indicates no barbarity on my part, if I confess that it would have raised my opinion of him, and his sex in general, to have seen Colin for a month or so, at least, wholesomely miserable.

Lisabel behaved uncommonly well with regard to him, and, indeed, in every way. She was as bright as a May morning, and full of the good qualities of her Augustus—whom she really likes very much after her fashion. She will doubtless be among the many wives who become extremely attached to their husbands, after marriage. To my benighted mind, it has always seemed advisable to have a slight preference before that ceremony.

She told me, with a shudder that was altogether natural and undisguised, how glad she was that they had been married at once, and that Augustus had sold out—for there is a chance of the regiment's being soon ordered on foreign service. I had not heard of this before. It was some surprise.

Lisabel was very affectionate to me the whole day, and, in going away, said she hoped I did not miss her much, and that I should get a good husband of my own soon; I did not know what a comfort it was.

"Somebody to belong to you—to care for you—to pet you—your own personal property in short—who can't get rid of you, even when you're old and ugly. Yes, I'm glad I married poor dear Augustus. And, child, I hope to see you married also. A good little thing like you would make a capital wife to somebody. Why, simpleton, I declare she's crying!"

It must have been the over-excitement of this day; but I felt as if, had I not cried, my temples and throat would have burst with a choking pain, that lasted long after Lisabel was gone.

They did not altogether stay more than four hours. Augustus talked of riding over to the camp, to see his friend, Dr. Urquhart, whom he has heard nothing of since the wedding-day; but Lisabel persuaded him against it. Men's friendship with one another is worth little, apparently.

A Life for a Life

Penelope here said she could answer for Dr. Urquhart's being in the land of the living, as she had met him a week before at Cartwright's cottage, the day the poor old man was killed. Why did she not tell me of this? But then she has taken such a prejudice against him, and exults so over what she calls his "rude behaviour to the family."

It always seemed to me very foolish to be for ever defending those whose character is itself a sufficient defence. If a false word is spoken of a friend, one must of course deny it, disprove it. But to be incessantly battling with personal prejudice or animosity, I would scorn it! Ay, as utterly as I would scorn defending myself under similar attacks. I think, in every lesser affection that is worth the name—the same truth holds good—which I remember being struck with in a play, the only play I ever saw acted. The heroine is told by her sister—

"Katherine,
You love this man—defend him."

She answers—

> "You have said,
> I love him. That's my defence. I'll not
> Assert, in words, the truth on which I've cast
> The stake of life. I love him, and am silent."

At least, I think the passage ran thus—for I cut it out of a newspaper afterwards, and long remembered it. What an age it seems since—that one play, to which Francis took us. And what a strange, dim dream, has become the impression it left; something like that I always have in reading of Thekla and Max; of love so true and strong—so perfect in its holy strength, that neither parting, grief, nor death have any power over it. Love, which makes you feel that once to have possessed it, must be bliss unutterable, unalienable—better than any happiness or prosperity that this world could give—better than anything in the world or out of it, except the love of God.

I sometimes think of this Katherine in this play, when she refuses to let her lover barter conscience for life, but when the test comes, says to him, herself, "No, *die!*" Also, of that scene in *Wallenstein*, when Thekla bids her lover be faithful to his honour and his country, not to her—when, just for one minute, he holds her tight, tight in his arms—Max, I mean. Death, afterwards, could not have been so very hard.

I am beginning to give up—strange, perhaps, that it should have lasted so long—my belief in the possible happiness of life. Apparently, people were never meant to be happy. Small flashes of pleasantness come and go; or, it may be that in some few lives, are ecstatic moments, such as this I have been thinking of, and then it is all over. But many people go plodding along to old age, in a dull, straight road, with little sorrow and no joy. Is my life to be such as this? Probably. Then the question arises, what am I to do with it?

It sometimes crosses my mind what Dr. Urquhart said, about his life being "owed." All our lives are, in one sense: to ourselves, to our fellow-creatures, or to God; or, is there some point of union which includes all three? If I only could find it out!

Perhaps, according to Colin Granton's lately learned doctrine—I know whence learned—it is the having something to do. Something to be, your fine preachers of self-culture would suggest; but self-culture is often no better than idealised egotism; people sick of themselves want something to do.

Yesterday, driving with papa along the edges of the camp, where we never go now, I caught sight of the slope where the hospital is, and could even distinguish the poor fellows sitting in the sun, or lounging about in their blue hospital clothes. It made me think of Smyrna and Scutari.

No; while there is so much misery and sin in the world, a man has no right to lull himself to sleep in a paradise of self-improvement and self-enjoyment; in which there is but one supreme Adam, one perfect specimen of humanity, namely himself. He ought to go out and work—fight, if it must be, wherever duty calls him. Nay, even a woman has hardly any right, in these days, to sit still and dream. The life of action is nobler than the life of thought.

So I keep reasoning with myself. If I could only find a good and adequate reason for some things which perplex me sorely, about myself and—other people, it would be a great comfort.

To-day, among a heap of notes which papa gave me to make candle-lighters of, I found this note, which I kept, the handwriting being peculiar,—and I have a few crotchets about handwriting.

"Dear Sir,—Press of business, and other unforeseen circumstances, with which I am fettered, make it impossible for me to accept any invitations at present. I hope you will believe that I can never forget the hospitalities of Rockmount, and that I am ever most gratefully

"Your faithful servant,

"Max Urquhart."

Can he, then, mean our acquaintance to cease? Should we be a hindrance in his busy, useful life—such a frivolous family as ours? It may be so. Yet I fear papa will be hurt.

This afternoon, though it was Sunday, I could not stay in the house or the garden, but went out, far out upon the moor, and walked till I was weary. Then I sat me down upon a heather-bush, all in a heap, my arms clasped round my knees, trying to think out this hard question—what is to become of me; what am I to do with my life? It lies before me, apparently as bleak, barren, and monotonous as these miles of moorland—stretching on and on in dull undulations, or dead flats, till a range of low hills ends all! Yet, sometimes, this wild region has looked quite different. I remember describing it once— how beautiful it was, how breezy and open, with the ever-changing tints of the moor, the ever-shifting and yet always steadfast arch of the sky. To-day I found it all colourless, blank, and cold; its monotony almost frightened me. I could do nothing but crouch on my heather-bush and cry.

Tears do one good occasionally. When I dried mine, the hot weight on the top of my head seemed lighter. If there had been anybody to lay a cool hand there, and say, "Poor child, never mind!" it might have gone away. But there was no one: Lisa was the only one who ever "petted" me.

I thought I would go home and write a long letter to Lisa.

Just as I was rising from my heather-bush, my favourite haunt, being as round as a mushroom, as soft as a velvet cushion, and hidden by two great furze-bushes, from the road—I heard footsteps approaching, Having no mind to be discovered in that gipsy plight, I crouched down again.

People's footsteps are so different, it is often easy to recognise them. This, I think, I should have known anywhere—quick, regular, determined; rather hasty, as if no time could be lost; as if, according to the proverb, it would never "let the grass grow under it." Crouching lower, I listened; I heard him stop and speak to an old woman, who had been coming up the road towards the village. No words were distinguishable, but the voice—I could not have mistaken it—it was not like our English voices.

What a strange feeling it is, listening to people's steps or voices, when they do not know you are near them. Something like being a ghost, and able to watch them—perhaps watch over them—without its being unnatural or wrong.

He stood talking—I should say, Dr. Urquhart stood talking—for several minutes. The other voice, by its querulousness, I guessed to be poor Mrs. Cartwright's; but it softened by degrees, and then I heard distinctly her earnest "thank'ee, Doctor—God bless'ee, sir," as he walked away, and vanished over the slope of the hill. She looked after him a minute, and then, turning, toddled on her way.

When I overtook her, which was not for some time, she told me the whole story of her troubles, and how good Dr. Urquhart had been. Also, the whole story about her poor daughter—at least as much as is known about it. Mrs. Cartwright thinks she is still somewhere in London, and Dr. Urquhart has promised to find her out, if he can. I don't understand much about these sort of dreadful things—Penelope never thought it right to tell us: but I can see that what Dr. Urquhart has said has given great comfort to the mother of unfortunate Lydia.

"Miss," said the old woman, with the tears running down, "the Doctor's been an angel of goodness to me, and there's many a one in these parts as can say the same—though he be only a stranger, here to-day and gone to-morrow, as one may say. Eh, dear, it'll be an ill day for many a poor body when he goes."

A Life for a Life

I am glad I saw him—glad I heard all this. Somehow, hearing of things like this makes one feel quieter.

It does not much matter after all—it does not, indeed! I never wanted anybody to think about me, to care for me—half as much as somebody to look up to—to be satisfied in—to honour and reverence. I can do that—still!

Like a fool, I have been crying again, till I ought, properly, to tear this leaf out, and begin again afresh. No, I will not. Nobody will ever see it, and it does no harm to any human being.

"God bless him," the old woman said. I might say something of the like sort, too. For he did me a deal of good: he was very kind to me.

A Life for a Life

Chapter 13

HER STORY

Papa and Penelope are out to dinner—I myself was out yesterday, and did not return till they were gone; so I sit up for them; and, meantime, shall amuse myself with writing here.

The last date was Sunday, and now it is only Tuesday, but much seems to have happened between. And yet nothing really has happened but two quiet days at the Cedars, and one gay evening—or people would call it gay.

It has been the talk of the neighbourhood for weeks—this amateur concert at the camp. We got our invitation, of course. The such-and-such Regiments (I forget which, all but one) presenting their compliments to the Reverend William Henry and the Misses Johnston, and requesting their company; but papa shook his head, and Penelope was indifferent. Then I gave up all idea of going, if I ever had any.

The surprise was almost pleasant when Mrs. Granton, coming in, declared she would take me herself, as it was quite necessary I should have a little gaiety to keep me from moping after Lisabel. Papa consented, and I went.

Driving along over the moors was pleasant, too—even though it snowed a little. I found myself laughing back at Colin, who sat on the box, occasionally turning to shake the white flakes off him like a great Polar bear. His kindly, hearty face was quite refreshing to behold.

I have a habit of growing attached to places, independently of the persons connected with them. Thus, I cannot imagine any time when it would not be an enjoyment to drive up to the hall-door of the Cedars, sweeping round in the wide curve that Colin is so proud of making his carriage-wheels describe: to look back up the familiar hill-side, where the winter sun is shining on that slope of trees,—then run into the house, through the billiard-room, and out again by the dining-room windows, on to the broad terrace. There, if there is any sunshine, you will be sure to get it,—any wind, it will blow in your face; any bit of colour or landscape beauty, you will catch it on this green lawn; the grand old cedars—the distant fir-woods, lying in a still mass of dark blue shadow, or standing up, one by one, cut out sharply against the brilliant west. Whether it is any meteorological peculiarity I know not; but it seems to me as if, whatever the day has been, there is always a fair sunset at the Cedars.

I love the place. If I went away for years—if I never saw it again—I should always love it and remember it. Mrs. Granton too, for she seems an integral part of the picture. Her small, elderly figure, trotting in and out of the rooms; her clear loud voice—she is a little deaf—along the upstairs passages; her perpetual activity—I think she is never quiet but when she is asleep. Above all, her unvarying goodness and cheerfulness—truly the Cedars would not be the Cedars without my dear old lady!

I don't think she ever knew how fond I was of her, even as a little girl. Nobody could help it; never anybody had to do with Mrs. Granton without becoming fond of her. She is almost the only person living of whom I never heard any one speak an unkind word; because she herself never speaks an ill word of any human being. Every one she knows is "the kindest creature," "the nicest creature," "the cleverest creature"—I do believe if you presented to her Diabolus himself, she would only call him "poor creature"; would suggest that his temper must have been aggravated by the unpleasant place he had to live in, and set about some plan for improving his complexion, and concealing his horns and tail.

At dinner, I took my favourite seat, where, seen through this greatest of the three windows,—a cedar with its "broad, green layers of shade," is intersected by a beech—still faintly yellow—as I have seen it, autumn after autumn, from the same spot. It seemed just like old times. I felt happy, as if something pleasant were about to happen, and said as much.

Mrs. Granton looked delighted.

"I am sure, my dear, I hope so. And I trust we shall see you here very often indeed. Only think, you have never been since the night of the ball. What a deal has happened between then and now."

I had already been thinking the same.

A Life for a Life

It must be curious to any one who, like our Lisa, had married a stranger and not an old acquaintance, to analyse afterwards the first impressions of a first meeting—most likely brought about by the merest chance. Curious to try and recall the face you then viewed critically, carelessly, or with the most absolute indifference—how it gradually altered and altered, till only by a special effort can memory reproduce the pristine image, and trace the process by which it has become what it is now—a face by itself, its peculiarities pleasant, its plainness sacred, and its beauties beautiful above all faces in the world.

In the course of the afternoon, Colin was turned out, that is corporeally, for his mother talked about him the whole time of his absence, a natural weakness rather honourable than pardonable. She has been very long a widow, and never had any child but Colin.

During our gossip, she asked me if we had seen Dr. Urquhart lately, and I said no.

"Ah, that is just like him. Such an odd creature. He will keep away for days and weeks, and then turn up as unexpectedly as he did here yesterday. By-the-bye, he inquired after you—if you were better. Colin had told him you were ill."

I testified my extreme surprise and denial of this.

"Oh, but you looked ill. You were just like a ghost the day Mrs. Treherne was at Rockmount—my son noticed it. Nay, you need not flush up so angrily—it was only my Colin's anxiety about you—he was always fond of his old play-fellow.

I smiled, and said his old play-fellow was very much obliged to him.

So, this business is not so engrossing, but that Dr. Urquhart can find time to pay visits somewhere. And he had been inquiring for me. Still he might have made the inquiry at our own door. Ought people, even if they do head a busy life, to forget ordinary courtesy—accepting hospitality, and neglecting it—cultivating acquaintance and then dropping it? I think not; all the respect in the world cannot make one put aside one's common-sense judgment of another's actions. Perhaps the very respect makes one more tenacious that no single action should be even questionable. I did think, then, and even to-day I have thought sometimes, that Dr. Urquhart has been somewhat in the wrong towards us at Rockmount. But as to acknowledging it to any of them at home—never!

Mrs. Granton discussed him a little, and spoke gratefully of Colin's obligations to him, and what a loss it would be for Colin when the regiment left the camp.

"How fortunate that your brother-in-law sold out when he did. He could not well have done so now, when there is a report of their being ordered on active service shortly. Colin says we are likely to have war again, but I do hope not."

"Yes," I said.

And just then Colin came to fetch me to the green-houses to choose a camellia for my hair.

Likely to have war again! When Mrs. Granton left me to dress, I sat over my bedroom fire, thinking—I hardly know what. All sorts of visions went flitting through my mind— of scenes I have heard talked about, in hospital, in battle, on the battlefield afterwards. Especially one, which Augustus has often described, when he woke up, stiff and cold, on the moonlight plain, from under his dead horse, and saw Dr. Urquhart standing over him.

Colin whistling through the corridor,—Mrs. Granton's lively "Are you ready, my dear?" made me conscious that this would not do.

I stood up, and dressed myself in the silver-grey silk I wore at the ball; tried to stick the red camellia in my hair, but the buds all broke off under my fingers, and I had to go down without it. It was all the same. I did not much care. However, Colin insisted on going with a lantern to hunt for another flower, and his mother took a world of pains to fasten it in, and make me look "pretty."

They were so kind—it was wicked not to try and enjoy one's self.

Driving along in the sharp, clear twilight, till we caught sight of the long lines of lamps which make the camp so picturesque at night-time, I found that compelling one's self to be gay sometimes makes one so.

A Life for a Life

We committed all sorts of blunders in the dark—came across a sentry who challenged us, and, nobody thinking of giving the password, had actually levelled his gun, and was proceeding in the gravest manner to do his duty and fire upon us—when our coachman shrieked, and Colin jumped out; which he had to do a dozen times, tramping the snow with his thin boots, to his mother's great uneasiness—and laughing all the time— before we discovered the goal of our hopes—the concert-room. Almost any one else would have grown cross, but this good mother and son have the gayest spirits and the best tempers imaginable. The present—the present is, after all, the only thing certain. I began to feel as cheery as they.

Giving up our ticket to the most gentlemanly of sergeants, we entered the concert-room. Such a blaze of scarlet—such a stirring of pretty heads, between—such a murmur of merry chat. For the first minute, coming out of the dark—it dazzled me. I grew sick and could see nothing; but when we were quietly seated, I looked round.

There were many of our neighbours and acquaintances whom I knew by sight or to bow to—and that was all. I could see every corner of the room—still that was all.

The audience seemed in a state of exuberant enjoyment, especially if they had a bit of scarlet beside them, which nearly everybody had, except ourselves.

"You'll be quite ashamed of poor Colin in his plain black, Dora, my dear?"

Not very likely—as I told her, with my heart warmly grateful to Colin, who had been so attentive, thoughtful, and kind.

Altogether a gay and pretty scene. Grave persons might possibly eschew it or condemn it—but no, a large liberal spirit judges all things liberally, and would never see evil in anything but sin.

I sat—enjoying all I could. But more than once ghastly imaginations intruded—picturing these young officers other-where than here, with their merry moustached faces pressed upon the reddened grass, their goodly limbs lopped and mangled, or worse, themselves, their kindly, lightsome selves, changed into what soldiers are—must be— in battle, fiends rather than men, bound to execute that slaughter

A Life for a Life

which is the absolute necessity of war. To be the slain or the slayer—which is most horrible? To think of a familiar hand—brother's or husband's—dropping down powerless, nothing but clay; or of clasping, kissing it, returned with red blood upon it—the blood of some one else's husband or brother!

To have gone on pondering thus would have been dangerous. Happily, I stopped myself before all self-control was gone.

The first singer was a slim youth, who, facing the footlights with an air of fierce determination, and probably more inward cowardice than he would have felt towards a regiment of Russians, gave us, in a rather uncertain tenor, his resolution to "love no more,"—which was vehemently applauded—and vanished. Next came "The Chough and Crow," executed very independently, none of the vocalists being agreed as to their "opening day." Afterwards, the first soprano, a professional, informed us with shrill expression, that—"Oh yes, she must have something to love,"—which I am sure I hope she had, poor body! There was a duet, of some sort, and then the *primo tenore* came on for an Italian song.

Poor youth!—a fourth-rate opera-singer might have done it better; but 'tis mean to criticise: he did his best; and when, after a grand roulade, he popped down, with all his heart and lungs, upon the last note, there arose a cordial English cheer, to which he responded with an awkward duck of the head, and a delighted smile; very unprofessional, but altogether pleasant and natural.

The evening was now half over. Mrs. Granton thought I was looking tired, and Colin wrapped my feet up in his fur coat, for it was very cold. They were afraid I was not enjoying myself, so I bent my whole appreciative faculties to the comical-faced young officer who skipped forward, hugging his violin, which he played with such total self-oblivious enjoyment that he was the least nervous and the most successful of all the amateurs; the timid young officer with the splendid bass voice, who was always losing his place and putting his companions out; and the solemn young officer who marched up to the pianoforte as if it were a Redan, and pounded away at a heavy sonata as if feeling that England expected him to do his duty; which he did, and was deliberately retreating, when, in that free-and-easy way with which audience and stage intermingled, some one called him—

"Ansdell, you're wanted!"

"Who wants me?"

"Urquhart." At least I was almost sure that was the name.

There was a good deal more of singing and playing; then "God save the Queen," with a full chorus and military band. That grand old tune is always exciting; it was so, especially, here to-night.

Likely to have war. If so, a year hence, where might be all these gay young fellows, whispering and flirting with pretty girls, walked about the room by proud mothers and sisters! I never thought of it, never understood it, till now—I who used to ridicule and despise soldiers! These mothers—these sisters!—they might not have felt it for themselves, but my heart felt bursting. I could hardly stand.

We were some time in getting out to the door through the long line of epaulets and swords, the owners of which—I beg their pardon, but cannot help saying it—were not too civil; until a voice behind cried—

"Do make way there—how do you expect those ladies to push past you?"

And a courteous helping hand was held out to Mrs. Granton, as any gentleman ought to any lady—especially an old lady.

"Doctor, is that you? What a scramble this is! Now, will you assist my young friend here?"

Then—and not till then, I am positive—he recognised me.

Something has happened to him—something has altered him very much. I felt certain of that on the very first glimpse I caught of his face. It shocked me so that I never said "how d'ye do?" I never even put out my hand. Oh that I had!

He scarcely spoke, and we lost him in the crowd almost immediately.

A Life for a Life

There was a great confusion of carriages. Colin ran hither and thither, but could not find ours. Some minutes after, we were still out in the bitter night; Mrs. Granton talking to somebody, I standing by myself. I felt very desolate and cold.

"How long have you had that cough?"

I knew who it was, and turned round. We shook hands.

"You had no business out here on such a night. Why did you come?"

Somehow, the sharpness did not offend me, though it was rare in Dr. Urquhart, who is usually extremely gentle in his way of speech.

I told him my cough was nothing—it was indeed as much nervousness as cold, though of course I did not confess that—and then another fit came on, leaving me all shaking and trembling.

"You ought not to have come: is there nobody to take better care of you, child?—No—don't speak. You must submit, if you please."

He took off a plaid he had about him, and wrapped me up in it, close and warm. I resisted a little, and then yielded.—

"You must!"

What could one do but yield? Protesting again, I was bidden to "hold my tongue."

"Never mind me!—I am used to all weathers;—I'm not a little delicate creature like you."

I said, laughing, I was a great deal stronger than he had any notion of—but as he had begun our acquaintance by taking professional care of me, he might just as well continue it; and it certainly was a little colder here than it was that night at the Cedars.

"Yes."

Here Colin came up, to say "we had better walk on to meet the carriage, rather than wait for it." He and Dr. Urquhart exchanged a few words, then he took his mother on one arm—good Colin, he never neglects his old mother—and offered me the other.

"Let me take care of Miss Theodora," said Dr. Urquhart, rather decidedly. "Will you come?"

I am sure he meant me to come. I hope it was not rude to Colin, but I could not help coming, I could not help taking his arm. It was such a long time since we had met.

But I held my tongue, as I had been bidden: indeed, nothing came into my head to say. Dr. Urquhart made one only observation, and that not particularly striking—

"What sort of shoes have you got on?"

"Thick ones."

"That is right. You ought not to trifle with your health."

Why should one be afraid of speaking the truth right out, when a word would often save so much of misunderstanding, doubt, and pain? Why should one shrink from being the first to say that word, when there is no wrong in it, when in all one's heart there is not a feeling that one need be ashamed of before any good man or woman, or—I humbly hope—before God?

I determined to speak out.

"Doctor Urquhart, why have you never been to see us since the wedding? It has grieved papa."

My candour must have surprised him; I felt him start. When he replied, it was in that peculiar nervous tone I know so well—which always seems to take away my nervousness, and makes me feel that for the moment I am the stronger of the two.

"I am very sorry. I would not on any account grieve your papa."

"Will you come, then, some day this week?"

A Life for a Life

"Thank you, but I cannot promise."

A possibility struck me.

"Papa is rather peculiar. He vexes people, sometimes, when they are not thoroughly acquainted with him. Has he vexed you in any way?"

"I assure you, no."

After a little hesitation, determined to get at the truth, I asked—

"Have I vexed you?"

"You! What an idea!"

It did seem, at this moment, preposterous, almost absurd. I could have laughed at it. I believe I did laugh. Oh, when one has been angry or grieved with a friend, and all of a sudden the cloud clears off—one hardly knows how or why, but it certainly is gone, perhaps never existed—save in imagination— what an infinite relief it is! How cheerful one feels, and yet humbled; ashamed, yet inexpressibly content. So glad, so satisfied to have only one's self to blame.

I asked Dr. Urquhart what he had been doing all this while? that I understood he had been a good deal engaged; was it about the barrack business, and his memorial?

"Partly," he said, expressing some surprise at my remembering it.

Perhaps I ought not to have referred to it. And yet that is not a fair code of friendship. When a friend tells you his affairs, he makes them yours, and you have a right to ask about them afterwards. I longed to ask,—longed to know all and everything. For by every carriage-lamp we passed I saw that his face was not as it used to be, that there was on it a settled shadow of pain, anxiety—almost anguish.

I have only known Dr. Urquhart three months, yet in those three months I have seen him every week, often twice and thrice a week, and, owing to the pre-occupation of the rest of the family, almost all his society has devolved on me. He and I have often and often sat talking, or in "playing decorum" to Augustus and Lisabel, walked up and down the garden together for hours at a time. Also, from my brother-in-law, always most open and enthusiastic on the subject, I have heard about Dr. Urquhart nearly everything that could be told.

All this will account for my feeling towards him, after so short an intimacy, as people usually feel, I suppose, after a friendship of years.

As I have said, something must have happened to make such a change in him. It touched me to the quick. Why not, at least, ask the question, which I should have asked in a minute of anybody else,—so simple and natural was it?—

"Have you been quite well since we saw you?"

"Yes.—No, not exactly. Why do you ask?"

"Because I thought you looked as if you had been ill."

"Thank you, no. But I have had a great deal of anxious business on hand."

More than that he did not say, nor had I a right to ask. No right! What was I, to be wanting rights—to feel that in some sense I deserved them—that if I had them I should know how to use them? For it is next to impossible to be so sorry about one's friends without having also some little power to do them good, if they would only give you leave.

All this while Colin and his mother were running hither and thither in search of the carriage, which had disappeared again. As we stood, a blast of moorland wind almost took my breath away. Dr. Urquhart turned, and wrapped me up closer.

"What must be done? You will get your death of cold, and I cannot shelter you. Oh, if I could!"

Then I took courage. There was only a minute more. Perhaps, and the news of threatened war darted through my mind like an arrow—

perhaps the last minute we might ever be together in all our lives. My life—I did not recollect it just then, but his, busy indeed, yet so wandering, solitary, and homeless—he once told me that ours was the only family-hearth he had been familiar at for twenty years. No, I am sure it was not wrong, either to think what I thought, or to say it.

"Doctor Urquhart, I wish you would come to Rockmount. It would do you good, and papa good, and all of us; for we are rather dull now Lisabel is gone. Do come."

I waited for an answer, but none was given. No excuse, or apology, or even polite acknowledgment. Politeness!—that would have been the sharpest unkindness of all.

Then they overtook us, and the chance was over.

Colin advanced, but Dr. Urquhart put me into the carriage himself, and as Colin was restoring the plaid, said rather irritably—

"No, no, let her wrap herself in it, going home."

Not another word passed between us, except that, as I remembered afterwards, just before they came up, he had said, "Good-bye," hastily adding to it, "God bless you."

Some people's words—people who usually express very little—rest in one's mind strangely. Why should he say "God bless you?" Why did he call me "child"?

I sent back his plaid by Colin next morning, with a message of thanks, and that "it had kept me very warm." I wonder if I shall ever see Dr. Urquhart again.

And yet it is not the seeing one's friends, the having them within reach, the hearing of and from them, which makes them ours—many a one has all that, and yet has nothing. It is the believing in them, the depending on them; assured that they are true and good to the core, and therefore could not but be good and true towards everybody else—ourselves included. Ay, whether we deserve it or not. It is not our deserts which are in question, but their goodness, which, once settled, the rest follows as a matter of course. They would be untrue to themselves if they were insincere or untrue to us. I have half-a-dozen friends, living within half-a-dozen miles, whom I feel farther off from than I should from Dr. Urquhart if he lived at the Antipodes.

He never uses words lightly. He never would have said "God bless you!" if he had not specially wished God to bless me—poor me! a foolish, ignorant, thoughtless child.

Only a child—not a bit better nor wiser than a child: full of all kinds of childish naughtinesses, angers, petulances, doubts—oh, if I knew he was at this minute sitting in our parlour, and I could run down and sit beside him, tell him all the hard things I have been thinking of him of late, and beg his pardon; asking him to be a faithful friend to me, and help me to grow into a better woman than I am ever likely to become—what an unutterable comfort it would be!

A word or two more about my pleasant morning at the Cedars, and then I must close my desk and see that the study-fire is all right—papa likes a good fire when he comes home.

There they are! what a loud ring! it made me jump from my chair. This must be finished to-morrow, when—

Chapter 14

HIS STORY

I ended the last page with "I shall write no more here." It used to be my pride never to have broken a promise nor changed a resolution. Pride! What have I to do with pride?

And resolutions, forsooth! What,—are we omnipotent and omniscient, that against all changes of circumstances, feelings, or events, we should set up our paltry resolutions, urge them and hold to them, in spite of reason and conviction, with a tenacity that we suppose heroic, god-like, yet which may be merely the blind obstinacy of a brute?

I will never make a resolution again. I will never again say to myself, "You, Max Urquhart, in order to keep up that character for virtue, honour, and steadfastness, which heaven only knows whether or no you deserve, ought to do so and so; and, come what will, you must do it." Out upon me and my doings! Was I singled out to be the scapegoat of the world?

It is my intention here, regularly to set down, for certain reasons, which I may, or may not, afterwards allude to, certain events, which have happened without any act of mine, almost without my volition, if a man can be so led on by force of circumstances, that there seems only one course of conduct open to him to pursue. Whither these circumstances may lead, I am at this moment as utterly ignorant as on the day I was born, and almost as powerless. I make no determinations, attempt no previsions, follow no set line of conduct; doing only from day to day, what is expected of me, and heaving all the rest to—is it? it must be—to God.

The sole thing in which I may be said to exercise any absolute volition, is in writing down what I mean to write here, the only record that will exist of the veritable me—Max Urquhart,—as he might have been known, not to people in general, but to—any one who looked into his deepest heart, and was his friend, his beloved, his very own.

A Life for a Life

The form of Imaginary Correspondent I henceforward throw aside, I am perfectly aware to whom and for whom I write: yet who, in all human probability, will never read a single line.

Once, an officer in the Crimea, believing himself dying, gave me a packet of letters to burn. He had written them, year by year, under every change of fortune, to a friend he had,, to whom he occasionally wrote other letters, *not* like these; which were never sent nor meant to be sent, during his lifetime— though sometimes I fancy he dreamed of *giving* them, and of their being read, smiling, by two together. He was mistaken. Circumstances which happen not rarely to dreamers like him, made it unnecessary, nay, impossible, for them to be delivered at all. He bade me burn them—at once—in case he died. In so doing there started out of the embers, clear and plain, *the name*. But the fire and I told no tales; I took the poker and buried it. Poor fellow! He did not die, and I meet him still; but we have never referred to those burnt letters.

These letters of mine I also may one day burn. In the meantime, there shall be no name or superscription on them—no beginning or ending, nor, if I can avoid it, anything which could particularise the person to whom they are written. For all others, they will take the form of a mere statement—nothing more.

To begin. I was sitting about eleven at night, over the fire, in my hut. I had been busy all day, and had had little rest the night before.

It was not my intention to attend our camp concert; but I was in a manner compelled to do so. Ill news from home reached poor young Ansdell of ours—and his colonel sent me to break it to him. I then had to wait about, in order to see the good colonel as he came out from the concert-room. It was, therefore, purely by accident that I met those friends whom I afterwards did not leave for several minutes.

The reason of this delay in their company may be told. It was a sudden agony about the uncertainty of life—young life; fresh and hopeful as pretty Laura Ansdell's—whom I had chanced to see riding through the North Camp, not two weeks ago—and now she was dead. Accustomed as I am to almost every form of mortality, I had never faced the grim fear exactly in this shape before. It put me out of myself for a little time.

A Life for a Life

I did not go near Granton the following day, but received from him a message and my plaid. She—the lady to whom I had lent it—was "quite well." No more: how could I possibly expect any more?

I was, as I say, sitting over my hut fire, with the strangest medley in my mind—rosy Laura Ansdell—now galloping across the moor—now lying still and colourless in her coffin; and another face, about the same age, though I suppose it would not be considered nearly as pretty, with the scarlet hood drawn over it; pallid with cold, yet with such a soft light in the eyes, such a trembling sweetness about the mouth! She must be a very happy-minded creature. I hardly ever saw her, or was with her any length of time, that she did not look the picture of content and repose. She always puts me in mind of Dallas's pet song, when we were boys—"Jessie, the Flower o' Dunblane."

> "She's modest as ony, and blithe as she's bonnie,
> And guileless simplicity marks her its ain,
> And far be the villain, divested o' feelin',
> Wha'd blight in its bud the sweet Flower O' Dunblane."

I say amen to that.

It was—to return, for the third time, to simple narrative—somewhere about eleven o'clock, when a man on horseback stopped at my hut door. I thought it might be a summons to the Ansdells, but it was not. It was the groom from Rockmount, bringing me a letter.

Her letter—her little letter! I ought to burn it—but, as yet, I cannot—and where it is kept, it will be quite safe. For reasons, I shall copy it here.

"Dear Sir,—My father has met with a severe accident. Dr. Black is from home, and there is no other doctor in the neighbourhood upon whom we can depend. Will you pardon the liberty I am taking, and come to us at once?

"Yours truly,

"Theodora Johnston."

There it lies, brief and plain; a firm heart guided the shaking hand. Few things show character in a woman more than her handwriting: this, when steady, must be remarkably neat, delicate, and clear. I did well to put it by—I may never get another line.

In speaking to Jack, I learned that his master and one of the young ladies had been out to dinner—that master had insisted on driving home himself, probably from Jack's incompetence, but he was sober enough now, poor lad!—that, coming through the fir-wood, one of the wheels got fixed in a deep rut, and the phaeton was overturned.

I asked, was any one hurt—besides Mr. Johnston?

"Miss Johnston was, a little."

"Which Miss Johnston?"

"Miss Penlope, sir."

"No one else?"

"No, sir."

I had evidence enough of all this before, but just then, at that instant, it went out of my mind in a sudden oppression of fear. The facts of the case gained, I called Jack in to the fire, and went into my bedroom to settle with myself what was best to be done.

Indecision, as to the matter of going or not going, was of course impossible; but it was a sudden and startling position to be placed in. True, I could avoid it by pleading hospital business, and sending the assistant-surgeon of our regiment, who is an exceedingly clever young man—but not ~ young man whom women would like in a sick house, in the midst of great distress or danger. And in that distress and danger, she had called upon *me*, trusted *me*.

I determined to go. The cost, whatever it might be, would be purely personal, and in that brief minute I counted it all. I state this, because I wish to make clear that no secondary motive, dream, or desire, prompted me to act as I have done.

A Life for a Life

On questioning Jack more closely, I found that Mr. Johnston had fallen, they believed, on a stone; that he had been picked up senseless, and had never spoken since. This indicated at once on what a thread of chance the case hung. *The case*—simply that and no more; as to treat it at all, I must so consider it. I have saved lives, by God's blessing—this, then, must be regarded merely as one other life to be saved, if, through His mercy, it were granted me to do it.

I unlocked my desk, and put her letter in the secret drawer; wrote a line to our assistant-surgeon, with hospital orders, in case I should be absent part of the next day; took out any instruments I might want; then, with a glance round my room, and an involuntary wondering as to how and when I might return to it, I mounted Jack's horse and rode off to Rockmount. The whole had not occupied fifteen minutes, for I remember looking at my watch, which stood at a quarter-past eleven.

Hard-riding makes thinking impossible; and, indeed, my whole mind was bent upon not missing my road in the darkness. A *detour* of a mile or two, one lost half-hour, might, humanly speaking, have cost the old man's life; for, in similar cases, it is generally a question of time.

It is said, our profession is that, which, of all others, most inclines a man to materialism. I never found it so. The first time I ever was brought close to death—but that train of thought must be stopped. Since, death and I have walked so long together, that the mere vital principle, common to all breathing creatures, "the life of a beast which goeth downwards," as the Bible has it, I never think of confounding with "the soul of a man which goeth upwards." Quite distinct from the life, dwelling in blood or breath, or at that "vital point" which has been lately discovered, showing that in a spot the size of a pin's head, resides the principle of mortality—quite distinct, I say, from this something which perishes or vanishes so mysteriously from the dead friends we bury, the corpses we anatomise, seems to me the spirit, the ghost; which being able to conceive of and aspire to, must necessarily return to, the one Holy Ghost, the one Eternal Spirit, Himself once manifest in flesh, this very flesh of ours.

And it seemed on that strange, wild night, just such another winter's night as I remember, years and years ago,—as if this distinction between the life and the soul, grew clearer to me than ever before; as if pardoning all that had happened to its mortal part, a ghost, which, were such visitations allowed, though I do not believe they are, might be supposed often to visit me—followed my ghost, harmlessly,—nay, pitifully, I

"Being a thing immortal as itself,"

the whole way between the camp and Rockmount.

I dismounted under the ivy-bush which overhangs the garden gate, which gate had been left open, so I was able to go, at once, up to the hall-door, where the fanlight flickered on the white stone-floor; the old man's stick was in the corner, and the young ladies' hats hung up on the branching stag's horns.

For the moment, I half believed myself dreaming; and that I should wake as I have often done, after half-an-hour's rest, with the salt morning breeze blowing on me, in the outside gallery of Scutari Hospital,—start up, take my lamp, and go round my wards.

But minutes were precious. I rang the bell; and, almost immediately, a figure slid down the staircase, and opened the door. I might not have thought it flesh and blood, but for the touch of its little cold hand.

"Ah! it is you, at last; I was sure you would come."

"Certainly."

Perhaps she thought me cold, "professional," as if she had looked for a friend, and found only the doctor. Perhaps,— nay, it must be so, she never thought of me at all, except as "the doctor."

"Where is your father?"

"Upstairs; we carried him at once to his room. Will you come?"

So I followed—I seemed to have nothing to do but to follow that light figure, with the voice so low, the manner so quiet,—quieter than I ever expected to see hers, or any woman's, under such an emergency. I? what did I ever know of women? What did I deserve to know, except that a woman bore me? It is an old fancy, but I have never thought so much about my mother as within the last few months. And sometimes, turning over the sole relics I have of hers, a ribbon or two, and a curl of hair, and calling to mind the few things Dallas remembered about her, I have imagined my mother, in her youth, must have been something like this young girl.

She entered the bedroom first.

"You may come in now. You will not startle him; I think he knows nobody."

I sat down beside my patient. He lay, just as he had been brought in from the road, with a blanket and counterpane thrown over him, breathing heavily, but quite unconscious.

"The light, please. Can you hold it for me? Is your hand steady?" And I held it a moment to judge. That weakness cost me too much; I took care not to risk it again.

When I finished my examination, and looked up, Miss Theodora was still standing by me. Her eyes only asked the question—which, thank God, I could answer as I did.

"Yes—it is a more hopeful case than I expected."

At this shadow of hope—for it was only a shadow—the deadly quiet in which she had kept herself was stirred. She began to tremble exceedingly. I took the candle from her, and gave her a chair.

"Never mind me. It is only for a minute," she said. One or two deep, hard sighs came, and then she recovered herself.

"Now, what is to be done?"

I told her I would do all that was necessary, if she would bring me various things I mentioned.

"Can I help you? There is no one else. Penelope has hurt her foot, and cannot move, and the servants are mere girls. Shall I stay? If there is to be an operation, I am not afraid."

For I had, unguardedly, taken out of my pocket the case of instruments which, after all, would not be needed. I told her so, adding that I had rather she left me alone with my patient.

"Very well. You will take care of him? You will not hurt him—poor papa!"

Not very likely. If he and I could have changed places,—he assuming my strength and life, I lying on that bed, with death before me, under such a look as his child left him with,—I think I should at that moment have done it.

When I had laid the old man comfortably in his bed, I sat with his wrist under my fingers, counting, beat by beat, the slow pulse, which was one of my slender hopes for his recovery. As the hand dropped over my knee, powerless, almost, as a dead hand, it recalled, I know not how or why, the helpless drop of *that*, the first dead hand I ever saw. Happily the fancy lasted only a moment; in seasons like this, when I am deeply occupied in the practice of my profession, all such phantasms are laid. And the present case was urgent enough to concentrate all my thoughts and faculties.

I had just made up my mind concerning it, when a gentle knock came to the door, and on my answering, she walked in; glided rather, for she had taken off her silk gown, and put on something soft and dark, which did not rustle. In her face, white as it was, there was a quiet preparedness, more touching than any wildness of grief—a quality which few women possess, but which Heaven never seems to give except to women, compelling us men, as it were, to our knees, in recognition of something diviner than anything we have, or are, or were ever meant to be. I mention this, lest it might be thought of me, as is often thought of doctors, that I did not feel.

She asked me no questions, but stood silently beside me, with her eyes fixed on her father. His just opened, as they had done several times before, wandered vacantly over the bed-curtains, and closed again, with a moan.

She looked at me, frightened—the poor child.

I explained to her that this moaning was no additional cause of alarm, rather the contrary; that her father might be in his present state for hours—days.

"And can you do nothing for him?"

If I could—at any cost which mortal man could pay!

Motioning her to the farthest corner of the room, I there, as is my habit, when the friends of the patient seem capable of listening and comprehending, gave her my opinion about the course of treatment I intended to adopt, and my reasons for the same. In this case, of all others, I wished not to leave the relatives in the dark, lest they might afterwards blame me for doing nothing; when, in truth, to do nothing was the only chance. I told her my belief that it would be safest to maintain perfect silence and repose, and leave benignant Nature to work in her own mysterious way—Nature, whom the longer one lives, the more one trusts in as the only true physician.

"Therefore," I said, "will you understand that however little I do, I am acting as I believe to be best? Will you trust me?"

She looked up searchingly, and then said, "Yes." After a few moments she asked me how long I could stay? if I were obliged to return to the camp immediately?

I told her "No; I did not intend to return till morning."

"Ah, that is well! Shall I order a room to be prepared for you?"

"Thank you, but I prefer sitting up."

"You are very kind. You will be a great comfort"

I, "a great comfort!" I—"kind."

My thoughts must needs return into their right channel. I believe the next thing she said was something about my going to see "Penelope": at least I found myself with my hand on the door, all but touching hers, as she was showing me how to open it.

"There: the second room to the left. Shall I go with you? No! I will stay here then, till you return."

So, after she had closed the door, I remained alone in the dim passage for a few moments. It was well. No man can be his own master at all times.

Miss Johnston was a good deal more hurt than she had confessed. As she lay on the bed, still in her gay dress, with artificial flowers in her hair—her face, pallid and drawn with pain, looked almost like that of an old woman. She seemed annoyed at my coming—she dislikes me, I know: but anxiety about her father, and her own suffering, kept her aversion within bounds. She listened to my medical report from the next room, and submitted to my orders concerning herself, until she learned that at least a week's confinement, to rest her foot, would be necessary. Then she rebelled.

"That is impossible. I must be up and about. There is nobody to do anything but me."

"Your sister?"

"Lisabel is married. Oh, you meant Dora?—We never expect any useful thing from Dora."

This speech did not surprise me. It merely confirmed a good deal which I had already noticed in this family. Also, it might in degree be true. I think, so far from being blind to them, I see clearer than most people every fault she has.

Neither contradicting nor arguing, I repeated to Miss Johnston the imperative necessity for her attending to my orders: adding that I had known more than one case of a person being made a cripple for life by neglecting such an injury as hers.

"A cripple for life!" She started—her colour came and went—her eye wandered to the chair beside her, on which was her little writing-case; I conclude that in the intervals of her pain she had been trying to send these ill news, or to apply for help to some one.

"You will be lame for life," I repeated, "unless you take care."

"Shall I now?"

"No—with reasonable caution I trust you will do well."

"That is enough. Do not trouble yourself any more about me. Pray go back to my father."

She turned from me and closed her eyes. There was nothing more to be done with Miss Penelope. Calling a servant who stood by, I gave my last orders concerning her, and departed. A strange person, this elder sister. What differences of character exist in families!

There was no change in my other patient. As I stood looking at him, his daughter glided round to my side. We exchanged a glance only—she seemed quite to understand that talking was inadmissible. Then she stood by me, silently gazing.

"You are sure there is no change?"

"None."

"Lisa—ought she not to know? I never sent a telegraph message; will you tell me how to do it?"

Her quiet assumption of duty—her thoughtful methodical arrangements; surely the sister was wrong,—that is, as I knew well, any great necessity would soon prove her to be wrong— about Miss Theodora.

I said there was no need to telegraph until morning, when, as I rode back to the camp, I would do it myself.

"Thank you."

No objection or apology; only that soft "thank you"—taking all things calmly and naturally, as a man would like to see a woman take the gift of his life, if necessary. No, not life; that is owed—but any or all of its few pleasures would be cheerfully laid down for such another "thank you."

A Life for a Life

While I was considering what should be done for the night, there came a rustling and chattering outside in the passage. Miss Johnston had sent a servant to sit up with her father. She came—knocking at the door-handle, rattling the candlestick, and tramping across the floor like a regiment of soldiers—so that my patient moaned, and put up his hand to his head.

I said—sharply enough, no doubt—that I must have quiet. A loud voice, a door slammed to, even a heavy step across the floor, and I would not answer for the consequences. If Mr. Johnston were meant to recover, there must be no one in his room but the doctor and the nurse.

"I understand—Susan, come away."

There was a brief conference outside; then Miss Theodora re-entered alone, bolted the door, and was again at my side.

"Will that do?"

"Yes."

The clock struck two while we were standing there. I stole a glance at her white, composed face.

"Can you sit up?—do you think?"

"Certainly."

Without more ado—for I was just then too much occupied with a passing change in my patient—the matter was decided. When I next looked for her, she had slipped round the foot of the bed, and taken her place behind the curtain on the other side. There we both sat, hour after hour, in total silence.

I tell everything, you see, just as minutely as I remember it—and shall remember—long after every circumstance, trivial or great, has faded out of every memory except mine. If these letters are ever read by other than myself, words and incidents long forgotten may revive: that when I die, as in the course of nature I shall do long before younger persons, it may be seen that it is not youth alone which can receive impressions vividly and retain them strongly.

A Life for a Life

I could not see her—I could only see the face on the pillow, where a dim light fell; just enough to show me the slightest change, did any come. But, closely as I watched, none did come. Not even a twitch or quiver broke that blank expression of repose which was neither life nor death.

I thought several times that it would settle into death before morning. And then?

Where was all my boasted skill, my belief in my own powers of saving life? Why, sitting here, trusted and looked up to, depended upon as the sole human stay—my countenance examined, as I felt it was, even as if it were the index and arbiter of fate—I—watching as I never watched before by any sick bed, this breath which trembled in the balance, felt myself as ignorant and useless as a child. Nay, I was "as a dead man before Thee," O Thou humbler of pride!

Crying to myself thus—Job's cry—I thought of another Hebrew, who sought "not unto the Lord, but unto the physicians"; and died. It came into my mind, May there not be, even in these days, such a thing as "seeking the Lord"?

I believe there is: I *know* there is.

The candle went out. I had sat with my eyes shut, and had not noticed it, till I heard her steal across the room, trying to get a light. Afraid to trust my own heavy step—hers seemed as soft as snow—I contrived to pull the window-blind aside, so that a pale white streak fell across the hearth where she was kneeling—the cheerless hearth, for I had not dared to risk the noise of keeping up a fire.

She looked up, and shivered.

"Is that light morning?"

"Yes. Are you cold?"

"A little."

"It is always cold at daybreak. Go and get a shawl."

She took no notice, but put the candle in its place and came over to me.

"How do you think he is?"

"No worse."

A sigh, patient, but hopeless. I took an opportunity of examining her closely, to judge how long her self-control was likely to last; or whether, after this great shock and weary night-watch, her physical strength would fail. So looking, I noticed a few blood-drops trickling over her forehead, oozing from under her hair:—

"What is this?"

"Oh, nothing. I struck myself as we were lifting papa from the carriage. I thought it had ceased bleeding."

"Let me look at it a moment. There—I shall not hurt you."

"Oh no. I am not afraid."

I cut the hair from round the place, and plastered it up. It hardly took a minute; was the smallest of surgical operations; yet she trembled. I saw her strength was beginning to yield; and she might need it all.

"Now, you must go and lie down for an hour."

She shook her head.

"You must."

There might have been something harsh in the words—I did not quite know what I was saying—for she looked surprised.

"I mean you ought; which is enough argument with a girl like you. If you do not rest, you will never be able to keep up for another twelve hours, during which your father may need you. He does not need you now."

"And you?"

"I had much rather be alone." Which was most true.

So she left me; but, ten minutes after, I heard again the light step at the door.

"I have brought you this" (some biscuits and a glass of milk). "I know you never take wine."

Wine! O Heaven, no! Would that, years ago, the first drop had burned my lips—been as gall to my tongue—proved to me not drink, but poison—as the poor old man now lying there once wished it might have happened to any son of his. Well might my father, my young, happy father, who married my mother, and, loving and loved, spent with her the brief years of their youth—well, indeed, might my father have wished it for me!

So there I sat, after the food she brought me had been swallowed down somehow—for it would have hurt her to come back and find it untouched. Thus watching, hope lessened by degrees, sank into mere conjectures as to the manner in which the watch would end. Possibly, in this state of half-consciousness, the breath would quietly pass away, without struggle or pain; which would be easiest for them all.

I laid my plans, in that case, either to be of any use to the family if I could, by remaining until the Trehernes arrived, or to leave immediately all was over. Circumstances, and their apparent wish, must be my only guide. Afterwards there would be no difficulty; the less they saw of any one who had been associated with such a painful time, the better. Better for all of them.

The clock below struck—what hour I did not count, but it felt like morning. It was,—must be—I must make it morning.

I went to the window to refresh my eyes with the soft white dawn, which, as I opened the blind, stole into the room, making the candle burn yellow and dim. The night was over and gone. Across the moorland, and up on the far hills, it was already morning.

A Life for a Life

A thought struck me, suggesting one more chance. Extinguishing the candle, I drew aside all the curtains, so as to throw the daylight in a full stream across the foot of the bed; and by the side of it—with the patient's hand between mine, and my eyes fixed steadily on his face—I sat down.

His eyes opened, not in the old blank way, but with an expression in them that I never expected to see again. They turned instinctively to the light; then, with a slow, a wandering, but perfectly rational, look towards me, feebly, the old man smiled.

That minute was worth dying for; or rather, having lived for, all these twenty years.

The rest which I have to tell must be told another time.

Chapter 15

HIS STORY

I have not been able to continue this. Every day has been full of business, and every night I have spent at Rockmount for the last three weeks.

Such was, I solemnly aver—from no fixed intention: I meant only to go as an ordinary doctor—in order, if possible, to serve the life that was valuable in itself, and most precious to some few; afterwards, whichever way the case terminated, to take my leave, like any other medical attendant: receiving thanks, or fee. Yes—if they offered it, I determined to take a fee; in order to show, both to them and myself that I was only the doctor—the paid physician. But this last wound has been spared me—and I only name it now in proof that nothing has happened as I expected or intended.

I remember Dallas, in reading to me the sermons he used to write for practice, preparing for the sacred duties which, to him, never came—had one upon the text "Thy will be done,"—where, in words more beautiful than I dare try to repeat in mine, he explained how good it was for us that things so seldom fell out according to our shortsighted plannings; how many a man had lived to bless God that his own petty will had not been done; that nothing had happened to him according as he expected or intended.

Do you know, you to whom I write, how much it means, my thus naming to you of Dallas—whose name, since he died, has never but once passed my lips?

I think you would have liked my brother Dallas. He was not at all like me—I took after my father, people said, and he after our mother. He had soft, English features, and smooth, fine, dark hair. He was smaller than I, though so much the elder. The very last Christmas we had at St. Andrews, I mind lifting him up and carrying him several yards in play, laughing at him for being as thin and light as a lady. We were merry-hearted fellows, and had many a joke, the two of us, when we were together. Strange to think, that I am a man nigh upon forty, and that he has been dead twenty years.

A Life for a Life

It is you—little as you guess it, who have made me think upon these my dead, my father, mother, and Dallas, whom I have never dared to think of until now. Let me continue.

Mr. Johnston's has been a difficult case—more so in its secondary stages than at first. I explained this to his daughter—the second daughter; the only one whom I found of much assistance, Miss Johnston being extremely nervous and irritable, and Mrs. Treherne, whom I trusted would have taken her share in the nursing, proving more of a hindrance than a help. She could not be made to comprehend why, when her father was out of danger, she should not rush in and out of the sick-room continually, with her chattering voice, and her noisy silk dresses. And she was offended because, when Mr. Charteris, having come for a day from London, was admitted, quiet, scared, and shocked, to spend a few minutes by the old man's bed-side—her Augustus, full of lively rattle and rude animal spirits, was carefully kept out of the room.

"You plan it all between you," she said, one day, half sulkily, to her sister and myself. "You play into one another's hands as if you had lived together all your lives. Confess, Doctor,—confess, Miss Nurse, you would keep me too out of papa's room, if you could."

I certainly would. Though an excellent person, kind-hearted and good-tempered to a degree, Mrs. Treherne contrived to try my temper more than I should like to say, for two intolerable days.

The third, I resolved on a little conversation with Miss Theodora; who, having sat up till my watch began at two, now came in to me while I was taking breakfast, to receive my orders for the day. These were simple enough; quiet, silence; and, except old Mrs. Cartwright, whom I had sent for, only one person to be allowed in my patient's room.

"Ah, yes, I'm glad of that. Just hearken!"

Doors slamming—footsteps on the stairs—Mrs. Treherne calling out to her husband not to smoke in the hall.—"That is how it is all day, when you are away. What can I do? Help me, please, help me!"

An entreaty, almost childish in its earnestness; now and then, through all this time, she has seemed in her behaviour towards me, less like a woman than a trusting, dependent child.

I sent for Treherne and his wife, and told them that the present was a matter of life and death, in which there could be no standing upon ceremony; that in this house, where no legitimate rule existed, and all were young and inexperienced, I, as the physician, must have authority, which authority must be obeyed. If they wished, I would resign the case altogether—but I soon saw that was not desired. They promised obedience; and I repeated the medical orders, adding, that during my absence, only one person, the person I chose, should be left in charge of my patient.

"Very well, Doctor," said Mrs. Treherne, "and that is—"

"Miss Theodora."

"Theodora—oh, nonsense! She never nursed anybody. She never was fit for anything."

"She is fit for all I require, and her father wishes for her also; therefore, if you please, will you at once go up to him, Miss Theodora?"

She had stood patient and impassive till I spoke, then the colour rushed into her face and the tears into her eyes. She left the room immediately.

But, as I went, she was lying in wait for me at the door. "Thank you—thank you so much! But do you really think I shall make a good careful nurse for dear papa?"

I told her "Certainly—better than any one else here—better indeed than any one I knew."

It was good to see her look of happy surprise.

"Do you really think that? Nobody ever thought so well of me before. I will try—ah! won't I try, to deserve your good opinion."

A Life for a Life

Ignorant, simple heart.

Most people have some other person, real or imaginary, who is more "comfortable" to them than any one else—to whom in trouble the thoughts always first fly, who in sickness would be chosen to smooth the weary pillow, and holding whose hand they would like to die. Now, it would be quite easy, quite happy to die in a certain chamber I know, shadowy and still, with a carpet of a green leafy pattern, and bunches of fuchsias papering the walls. And about the room, a little figure moving; slender, noiseless, busy, and sweet—in a brown dress, soft to touch, and making no sound, with a white collar fastened by a little coloured bow above it; the delicate throat and small head like a deer's; and the eyes something like a deer's eyes also, which turn round large and quiet, to look you right in the face—as they did then.

I wonder if any accident or illness were to happen to me here, while staying in the camp—something that would make it certain I had only a few days, or hours, to live, and I happened to have sufficient consciousness and will to say what I wished done, whom I desired to see, in those few last hours, when the longing of a dying man could injure nobody—Enough—this is the merest folly. To live, not to die, is likely to be my portion. I accept it—blame me not.

Day after day has gone on in the same round—my ride to Rockmount after dusk, tea there, and my evening sleep in "the Doctor's room." There, at midnight, Treherne wakes me—I dress and return to that quiet chamber where the little figure rises from beside the bed with a smile and a whisper—"Not at all tired, thank you." A few words more, and I give it my candle, bid it good night, and take its place, sitting down in the same arm-chair, and leaning my head back against the same cushion, which still keeps the indentation, soft and warm; and so I watch by the old man till morning.

This is how it has regularly been.

Until lately, night was the patient's most trying time. He used to lie moaning, or watching the shadows of the fire-light on the curtains, sometimes, when I gave him food or medicine, turning upon me with a wild stare, as if he hardly knew me, or thought I was some one else. Or he would question me vaguely as to where was Dora?— and would I take care that she had a good long sleep—poor Dora!

Dora—Theodora—"the gift of God,"—it is good to have names with meanings to them, though people so seldom resemble their names. Her father seems beginning to feel that she is not unlike hers.

"She is a good girl, Doctor," he said one evening, when, after having safely borne moving from bed to his arm-chair, I pronounced my patient convalescent, and his daughter was sent to take tea and spend the evening downstairs, "she is a very good girl. Perhaps I have never thought of my daughters."

I answered vaguely, daughters were a great blessing—often more so than sons.

"You are right, sir," he said suddenly, after a few minutes' pause. "You were never married, I believe?"

"No."

"If you do marry—never long for a son. Never build your hopes on him—trusting he will keep up your name, and be the stay of your old age. I had one boy, sir; he was more to me than all my daughters."

A desperate question was I prompted to ask—I could not withhold it—though the old man's agitated countenance showed that it must be one passing question only.

"Is your son living?"

"No. He died young."

This, then, must be the secret—simple and plain enough. He was "a boy"—he died "young," perhaps about eighteen or nineteen—the age when boys are most prone to run wild. This lad must have done so; putting all the circumstances together, the conclusion was obvious, that in some way or other he had, before his death, or in his death, caused his father great grief and shame.

I could well imagine it; fancy drew the whole picture, filling it up pertinaciously, line by line. A man of Mr. Johnston's character, marrying late in life—as he must have done, to be seventy when his youngest child was not much over twenty— would be a dangerous father for any impetuous headstrong boy. A motherless boy too; Mrs. Johnston died early. It was easy to understand how strife would rise between him and the father, no longer young, with all his habits and peculiarities formed, sensitive, over-exacting; rigidly good, yet of somewhat narrow-minded virtue: scrupulously kind, yet not tender; alive to the lightest fault, yet seldom warming into sympathy or praise. The sort of man who compels respect, and whom, being oneself blameless, one might even love; but, having committed any error, one's first impulse would be to fly from him to the very end of the earth.

Such, no doubt, had been the case with that poor boy, who "died young." Out of England, no doubt, or surely they would have brought him home and buried him under the shadow of his father's church, and his memory would have left some trace in the family, the village, or the neighbourhood. As it was, it seemed blotted out — as if he had never existed. No one knew about him — no one spoke about him, not even the sisters, his playmates. So she — the second sister — had said. It was a tacit hint for me also to keep silence; otherwise I would have liked to ask her more about him — this poor fallen boy. I know how suddenly, how involuntarily, as it seems, a wretched boy can fall — into some perdition never afterwards retrieved.

Thinking thus — sitting by the bedroom fire, with Mr. Johnston asleep opposite — poor old man, it must have been his boy's case and not his own which has made him so sensitive about only sons — I suddenly called to mind how, in the absorbing anxiety of the last three weeks — *that day* — the anniversary — had slipped by, and I had not even recollected it. It could be forgotten then? — was this a warning that I might let it pass, if it would, into oblivion — and yield like any other man, to pleasant duties, and social ties, the warmth of which stole into me, body and soul, like this blessed household fire? It could not last — but while it did last, why not share it; why persist in sitting outside in the cold?

You will not understand this. There are some things I cannot explain, till the last letter, if ever I should come to write it. Then you will know.

Tea over, Miss Theodora came to see after "our patient," as she called him, asking if he had behaved well, and done nothing he ought not to have done?

I told her that was an amount of perfection scarcely to be exacted from any mortal creature; at which she laughed, and replied, she was sure I said this with an air of deprecation, as if afraid such perfection might be required of me.

Often her little hand carries an invisible sword. I try to hide the wounds, but the last hour's meditation made them sharper than ordinary. For once, she saw it. She came and knelt by the fire, not far from me, thoughtfully. Then, suddenly turning round, said—

"If ever I say a rude thing to you, forgive it. I wish I were only half as good as you."

The tone, so earnest, yet so utterly simple,—a child might have said the same, looking into one's face with the same frank eyes. God forgive me! God pity me!

I rose and went to the bedside to speak to her father, who just then woke, and called for "Dora."

If in nothing else, this illness has been a blessing; drawing closer together the father and daughter. She must have been thinking so, when to-day she said to me—

"It is strange how many mouthfuls of absolute happiness one sometimes tastes in the midst of trouble;" adding—I can see her attitude as she talked, standing with eyes cast down, mouth sweet and smiling, and fingers playing with her apron-tassels—a trick she has—"that she now felt as if she should never be afraid of trouble any more."

That also is comprehensible. Anything which calls out the dormant energies of the character must do a woman good. With some women, to be good and to be happy is one and the same thing.

She is changed too, I can see. Pale as she looks, there is a softness in her manner and a sweet composure in her face, different from the restlessness I once noticed there—the fitful irritability, or morbid pain, perceptible at times, though she tried hard to disguise both. And succeeded doubtless, in all eyes but mine.

She is more cheerful too than she ever used to be, not restlessly lively, like her eldest sister, but seeming to carry about in her heart a well-spring of content, which bubbles out refreshingly upon everything and everybody about her. It is especially welcome in the sick-room, where, she knows, our chief aim is to keep the mind at ease, and the feeble brain in absolute rest. I could smile, remembering the hours we have spent—patient, doctor, and nurse, in the most puerile amusements, and altogether delicious nonsense, since Mr. Johnston became convalescent.

All this is over now. I knew it was. I sat by the fire, watching her play off her loving jests upon her father, and prattle with him, childish-like, about all that was going on downstairs.

"You little quiz!" he cried at last. "Doctor, this girl is growing—I can't say witty—but absolutely mischievous."

I said talents long dormant sometimes appeared. We might yet discover in Miss Theodora Johnston the most brilliant wit of her day.

"Doctor Urquhart, it's a shame! How can you laugh at me so? But I don't care. You are all the better for having somebody to laugh at. You know you are."

I did know it—only too well, and my eyes might have betrayed it, for hers sank. She coloured a little, sat down to her work, and sewed on silently, thoughtfully, for a good while.

What was in her mind? Was it pity? Did she fancy she had hurt me—touched unwittingly one of my many sores? She knows I have had a hard life, with few pleasures in it; she would gladly give me some; she is sorry for me.

Most people's compassion is worse than their indifference; but hers—given out of the fulness of the pure, tender, unsuspicious heart—I can bear it. I can be grateful for it.

On this first evening that broke the uniformity of the sick-room, we thought it better, she and I, considering the peculiarities of the rest of the family, which she seems to take for granted I am aware of, and can make allowance for—that none of them should be admitted this night. A prohibition not likely to afflict them much.

"And pray, Miss Dora, how do you mean to entertain the Doctor and me?"

"I mean to give you a large dose of my brilliant conversation, and, lest it becomes too exciting, to season it with a little reading, out of something that neither of you take the smallest interest in, and will be able to go to sleep over properly. Poetry—most likely."

"Some of yours?"

She coloured deeply. "Hush, papa, I thought you had forgotten—you said it was 'nonsense,' you know."

"Very likely it was. But I mean to give it another reading some day. Never mind—nobody heard."

So she writes poetry. I always knew she was very clever, besides being well educated. Talented women—modern Corinnes—my impression of them was rather repulsive. But she—that soft, shy girl, with her gay simplicity, her meek, household ways—I said, if Miss Theodora were going to read, perhaps she might remember she had once promised to improve my mind with a course of German literature. There was a book about a gentleman of my own name—Max—Max something or other—

"Piccolomini. You have not forgotten him! What a memory you have for little things."

She thought so! I said, if she considered a poor doctor, accustomed to deal more with bodies than souls, could comprehend the sort of books she seemed so fond of, I would like to hear about Max Piccolomini.

"Certainly. Only—"

"You think I could not understand it."

"I never thought any such thing," she cried out in her old abrupt way, and went out of the room immediately.

A Life for a Life

The book she fetched was a little dainty one. Perhaps it had been a gift. I asked to look at it.

"Can you read German?"

"Not a line." For my few words of conversational foreign tongues have been learned orally, the better to communicate with stray patients in hospitals. I told her so. "I am very ignorant, as you must have long since found out, Miss Theodora."

She said nothing, but began to read. At first translating line by line; then saying a written translation would be less trouble, she fetched one. It was in her handwriting—probably her own doing.

No doubt every one, except such an unlearned ass as myself, is familiar with the story—historical, I believe she said—how a young soldier, Max Piccolomini, fell in love with the daughter of his General, Wallenstein, who, heading an insurrection, wished the youth to join in promising him the girl's hand. There is one scene where the father tempts, and brings the daughter to tempt him by hope of this bliss, to turn rebel; but the young man is firm—the girl, too, when he appeals to her, bids him keep to his duty, and renounce his love. It is a case such as may have happened—might happen in these days— were modern men and women capable of such attachments. Something of the sort of lose upon which Dallas used to theorise when we were boys, always winding up with his favourite verse—how strange that it should come back to my mind now!—

>"I could not love thee, dear, so much,
>Loved I not honour more."

Max—odd enough the name sounded, and she hesitated over it at first, with a half-laughing apology, then forgetting all but her book, it came out naturally and sweetly—oh, so sweetly sometimes—Max *died.* How, I do not clearly remember, but I know he died, and never married the girl he loved; that the time when he held her in his arms, and kissed her before her father and them all, was the last time they ever saw one another.

She read, sometimes hurriedly and almost inaudibly, and then just like the people who were speaking, as if quite forgetting herself in them. I do not think she even recognised that there was a listener in the room. Perhaps she thought, because I sat so still, that I did not hear or feel, that I, Max Urquhart, have altogether forgotten what it is to be young and to love.

When she ceased, Mr. Johnston was sound asleep; we both sat silent. I stretched out my hand for the written pages, to go over some of the sentences again; she went on reading the German volume to herself. Her face was turned away, but I could see the curve of her cheek, and the smooth, spiral twist of her hair behind—I suppose, if untwisted, it would reach down to her knees. This German girl, Thekla, might have had just such hair; this boy—this Max—might have been allowed sometimes to touch it—reverently to kiss it.

I was interrupted here. A case at the hospital; James McDermot—fever-ward—cut his throat in a fit of delirium. There must have been great neglect in the nurse or orderly—perhaps in more than they. These night absences were bad—this pre-occupation—though I have tried earnestly to fulfil all my duties. Yet, as I walked back, the ghastly figure of the dead man was ever before me.

Have I not a morbid conscience, which revels in self-accusation? Suppose there were one who knew me as I knew myself—could show myself unto myself, and say, "Poor soul, 'tis nothing. Forget thyself, think of another—thy other self—of me."

Why recount this, one of the countless painful incidents that are always recurring to our profession? Because, having begun, I must tell you all that happens to me, as a man would, coming home after his day's labour to his—let me write down the word steadily—his wife; nearer to him than any mortal thing—bone of his bone and flesh of his flesh; his rest, comfort, and delight—whom, more than almost any man, a doctor requires, seeing that on the dark side of human life his path must continually lie.

Sometimes, though, bright bits come across us—such as when the heavy heart is relieved, or the shadow of death lifted off from a dwelling moments when the doctor, much to his own conscious humiliation, is apt to be regarded as an angel of deliverance—seasons when he is glad to linger a little amidst the glow of happiness he has been instrumental in bringing, before he turns out again into the shadows of his appointed way.

A Life for a Life

And such will always be this, which I may consider the last of my nights at Rockmount. They would not hear of my leaving, though it was needless to sit up. And when I had seen Mr. Johnston safe and snug for the night, they insisted on my joining the merry supper-table, where, relieved now from all care, the family assembled. The family included, of course, Mr. Charteris. I was the only stranger.

They did not treat me as a stranger—you know that. Sometimes falling, as the little party naturally did, into two, and two, and two, it seemed as if the whole world were conspiring to wrap me in the maddest of delusions; as if I always had sat, and were meant to sit, familiarly, brotherly, at that family table; as if my old solitude were quite over and gone, never to return more. And, over all, was the atmosphere of that German love-tale, which came up curiously to the surface, and caused a conversation, which, in some parts of it, seems the strangest thing of all that strange evening.

It was Mrs. Treherne who originated it. She asked her sister what had we been doing that, we were so exceedingly quiet upstairs?

"Reading—papa wished it." And being further questioned, Miss Theodora told what had been read.

Mrs. Treherne burst out laughing immoderately.

It would hardly be expected of such well-bred and amiable ladies, but I have often seen the eldest and youngest sisters annoy her—the second one—in some feminine way—men would never think of doing it, or guess how it is done— sufficient to call the angry blood to her cheeks, and cause her whole manner to change from gentleness into defiance. It was so now.

"I do not see anything so very ridiculous in my reading to papa out of any book I choose."

I explained that I myself had begged for this one.

"Oh! and I'm sure she was delighted to oblige you."

"I was," she said boldly; "and I consider that anything, small or great, which either I, or you, or Penelope can do to oblige Doctor

Urquhart, we ought to be happy and thankful to do for the remainder of our lives."

Mrs. Treherne was silenced. And here, Mr. Charteris—breaking the uncomfortable pause—good-naturedly began a disquisition on the play in question. He bore, for some time, the chief part in a literary and critical conversation, of which I did not hear or follow much. Then the ladies took up the story in its moral and personal phase, and talked it over pretty well.

The youngest sister was voluble against it. She hated doleful books: she liked a pleasant ending, where the people were all married, cheerfully and comfortably.

It was suggested, from my side of the table, that this play had not an uncomfortable ending, though the lovers both died.

"What an odd notion of comfort Dora has," said Mr. Charteris.

"Yes, indeed," added Mrs. Treherne. "For if they hadn't died, were they not supposed never to meet again? My dear child, how do you intend to make your lover happy? By bidding him an eternal farewell, allowing him to get killed, and then dying on his tomb?"

Everybody laughed. Treherne said he was thankful his Lisa was not of her sister's mind.

"Ay, Gus dear, well you may! Suppose I had come and said to you, like Dora's heroine, 'My dear boy, we are very fond of one another, but we can't ever be married. It's of no consequence. Never mind. Give me a kiss, and good-bye,'— what would you have done, eh, Augustus?"

"Hanged myself," replied Augustus forcibly.

"If you did not think better of it while searching for a cord," dryly observed Mr. Charteris. (I have for various reasons noticed this gentleman rather closely of late.) "Dora's theories about love are pretty enough, but too much on the gossamer style. Poor human nature requires a little warmer clothing than these 'sky robes of iris woof,' which are *not* 'warranted to wear.'"

As he spoke, I saw Miss Johnston's black eyes dart over to his face in keen observation, but he did not see them. Immediately afterwards she said—"Francis is quite right. Dora's heroics do her no good—nor anybody; because such characters do not exist, and never did. Max and Thekla, for instance, are a pair of lovers utterly impossible in this world."

"True," said Mr. Charteris, "even as Romeo and Juliet are impossible, Shakespeare himself owns

'These violent delights have violent ends.'

Had Juliet lived, she would probably not by force, but in the most legal, genteel, and satisfactory way, have been 'married to the County'; or, supposing she had got off safe to Mantua, obtained parental forgiveness, and returned to set up housekeeping as Mrs. R. Montague; depend upon it, she and Romeo would have wearied of one another in a year, quarrelled, parted, and she might, after all, have consoled herself with Paris, who seems such a sweet-spoken, pretty-behaved young gentleman throughout. Do you not think so, Doctor Urquhart? that is, if you are a reader of Shakespeare."

Which he apparently thought I was not. I answered, what has often struck me about this play, "that Shakespeare only meant it as a tale of boy and girl passion. Whether it would have lasted, or grown out of passion into love, one need not speculate, any more than the poet does. Enough, that while it lasts, it is a true and beautiful picture of youthful love—that is, youth's ideal of love. Though the love of maturer life is often a far deeper, higher, and better thing."

Here Mrs. Treherne, bursting into one of her hearty laughs, accused her sister of having "turned Doctor Urquhart poetical."

It is painful to appear like a fool, even when a lively young woman is trying to make you do so. I sat, cruelly conscious how little I have to say—how like an awkward, dull clod I often feel—in the society of young and clever people, when I heard her speaking from the other end of the table—I mean, Miss Theodora.

"Lisabel, you are talking of what you do not understand. You never did, and never will understand my Max and Thekla, any more than

Francis there, though he once thought it so fine, when he was teaching Penelope German, a few years ago."

"Dora, your excitement is unlady-like."

"I do not care," she answered, turning upon her elder sister with flashing eyes. "To sit by quietly and hear such doctrines is worse than unlady-like—unwoman-like! You two girls may think as you please on the matter; but I know what I have always thought—and think still"

"Pray, will you indulge us with your creed?" cried Mr. Charteris.

She hesitated—her cheeks burned like fire—but still she spoke out bravely.

"I believe, spite of all you say, that there is, not only in books, but in the world, such a thing as love, unselfish, faithful, and true, like that of my Thekla and my Max. I believe that such a love—a *right* love—teaches people to think of the *right* first, and themselves afterwards; and, therefore, if necessary, they could bear to part for any number of years—or even for ever."

"Bless us all; I wouldn't give two farthings for a man who would not do anything—do wrong even—for my sake."

"And I, Lisabel, should esteem a man a selfish coward, whom I might pity, but I don't think I could ever love him again, if in any way he did wrong for mine."

From my corner, whither I had gone and sat down a little out of the circle, I saw this young face—flashing, full of a new expression. Dallas, when he talked sometimes, used to have just such a light in his eyes—just such a glory streaming from all his features; but then he was a boy, and this was a woman. Ay, one felt her womanhood, the passion and power of it, with all its capabilities for either blessing or maddening, in the very core of one's being.

The others chattered a little more, and then I heard her speaking again.

"Yes, Lisabel, you are quite right; I do *not* think it of so very much importance, whether people who are very deeply attached, ever live to be married or not. In one sense they are married already, and nothing can come between them, so long as they love one another."

This seemed an excellent joke to the Trehernes, and drew a remark or two from Mr. Charteris, to which she refused to reply.

"No; you put me in a passion, and forced me to speak; but I have done now. I shall not argue the point any more."

Her voice trembled, and her little hands nervously clutched and plaited the table-cloth; but she sat in her place, without moving features or eyes. Gradually the burning in her cheeks faded, and she grew excessively pale; but no one seemed to notice her. They were too full of themselves.

I had time to learn the picture by heart, every line; this little figure sitting by the table, bent head, drooping shoulders, and loose white sleeves shading the two hands, which were crushed so tightly together, that when she stirred I saw the finger-marks of one imprinted on the other. What could she have been thinking of?

"Miss Dora, please."

It was only a servant, saying her father wished to speak to her before he went to sleep.

"Say I am coming." She rose quickly, but turned before she reached the door. "I may not see you again before you go. Good night, Doctor Urquhart."

We have said good night, and shaken hands every night for three weeks. I know I have done my duty; no lingering, tender clasping what I had no right to clasp; a mere "good night," and shake of the hand. But, to-night?

I did not say a word—-I did not look at her. Yet the touch of that little cold, passive hand has never left mine since. If I lay my hand down here, on this table, it seems to creep into it and nestle there; if I let it go, it comes back again; if I crush my fingers down upon it, though there is nothing, I feel it still—feel it through every nerve and pulse, in heart, soul, body, and brain.

This is the merest hallucination, like some of the spectral illusions I have been subject to at times;—the same which made Coleridge once say "he had seen too many ghosts to believe in them."

Let me gather up my faculties.

I am sitting in my hut. There is no fire—no one ever thinks of lighting a fire for me, of course, unless I specially order it. The room is chill, warning me that winter is nigh at hand: disorderly—no one ever touches my goods and chattels, and I have been too much from home lately to institute any arrangement myself. All solitary, too; even my cat, who used to be the one living thing lingering about me, marching daintily over my books, or stealing up purring to lay her head upon my knee, even my cat, weary of my long absence, has disappeared to my next-door neighbour. I am quite alone.

Well, such is the natural position of a man without near kindred, who has reached my years, and has not married. He has no right to expect aught else to the end of his days.

I rode home from Rockmount two hours ago, leaving a still lively group sitting round the fire in the parlour—Miss Johnston on her sofa, with Mr. Charteris beside her; Treherne sitting opposite, with his arm round his wife's waist.

And upstairs, I know how things will look—the shadowy bed-chamber, the little white china lamp on the table, and one curtain half-looped back, so that the old man may just catch a glimpse of the bending figure, reading to him the Evening Psalms; or else she will, by this time, have said "Good night, papa," and kissed him, and gone away to the upper part of the house, of which I know nothing, and have never seen. Therefore, I can only fancy her as I one night happened to see, going upstairs, candle in hand, softly, step by step, as saintly souls slip away into paradise, and we below, though we would cling to the hem of their garments, crush our lips in the very print of their feet, can neither bold them, nor dare beseech them to stay.

Oh, if I were only dead, that you might have this letter, — might know, feel, comprehend all these things!

I have been "doing wrong." I owe it to myself — to more than myself, not to yield to weak lamentation or unmanly bursts of frenzy against inevitable fate.

Is it inevitable?

Before beginning to write to-night, for two hours I sat arguing with myself this question; viewing the circumstances of both parties, for such a question necessarily includes both, with a calmness which I believe even I can attain, when the matter involves not myself alone. I have come to the conclusion that it *is* inevitable.

When you reach these my years, when you have experienced all those changes which you now dream over, and theorise upon in your innocent, unconscious heart, you also will see that my judgment was right.

To seek and sue a woman's yet unwon love, implies the telling her, when won, the whole previous history of her lover, concealing nothing, fair or foul, which does not compromise any other than himself. This confidence she has a right to expect, and the man who withholds it is either a coward in himself, or doubts the woman of his choice, as, should he so doubt his wife, — woe to him and to her! To carry into the sanctuary of a true wife's breast some accursed thing which must be for ever hidden in his own, has always seemed to me one of the blackest treasons against both honour and love of which a man could be capable.

Could I tell my wife, or the woman whom I would fain teach to love me, my whole history? And if I did, would it not close the door of her heart eternally against me? or, supposing it was too late for that, and she already loved me, would it not make her, for my sake, miserable for life? I believe it would.

On this account merely, things are inevitable.

There is another reason; whether it comes second or first in my arguments with myself, I do not know. When a man has vowed a vow, dare he break it?

A Life for a Life

There is a certain vow of mine, which, did I marry, *must* be broken. No man in his senses, or possessing the commonest feelings of justice and tenderness, would give his name to a beloved woman, with the possibility of children to inherit it, and then bring upon each and all of them *the end*, which I have all my life resolutely contemplated as a thing necessary to be done—either immediately before my death, or after it.

Therefore, also, it is inevitable.

That word—inevitable—always calms me. It is the will of God. If He had meant otherwise, He would have found out a way—perhaps by sending me some good woman to love me, as men are loved sometimes, but not such men as I. There is no fear—or hope—which shall I say?—of any one ever loving me.

Sleep, child! You are fast asleep by this hour, I am sure: you once said, you always fall asleep the instant your head touches the pillow. Blessed pillow! precious, tender, lovely head!

"Good night." Sleep well, happy ignorant child.

Chapter 16

HER STORY

"Finished to-morrow." What a lifetime seems to have elapsed since I wrote that line!

A month and four days ago I sat here, waiting for papa and Penelope to come home from their dinner-party. Trying to be cheerful—wondering why I was not so: yet with my heart as heavy as lead all the time.

I think it will never be quite so heavy any more. Never weighed down by imaginary wrongs and ideal woes. It has known real anguish and been taught wisdom.

We have been very near losing our beloved father. Humanly speaking, we should have lost him but for Dr. Urquhart, to whose great skill and unremitting care, Dr. Black himself confessed yesterday, papa has, under God, owed his life.

It is impossible for me to write down here the particulars of dear papa's accident, and the illness which followed, every day of which seems at once so vivid and so unreal. I shall never forget it while I live, and yet, even now, am afraid to recall it. Though at the time I seemed afraid of nothing—strong enough for everything. I felt—or it now appears as though I must have done so—as I did on one sunshiny afternoon, at a picnic, about a dozen years ago—when I, following Colin Granton, walked round the top of a circular rock, on a ledge two feet wide, a sloping ledge of short slippery grass, where, if we had slipped, it was about ninety perpendicular feet to fall.

I shudder to think of that feat, even now; and telling it to Dr. Urquhart in illustration of what I am here mentioning, namely, the quiet unconsciousness with which one sometimes passes through exceeding great danger, he too shuddered, turned deadly white. I never saw a strong man lose colour so suddenly and completely as he does, at times.

Can he be really strong? Those nights of watching must have told upon his health; which is so valuable. Doubly valuable to one in his profession. We must try to make him take care of himself, and allow us—Rockmount generally—to take care of him. Though, since his night-watchings ceased, he has not given us much opportunity, having only paid his due medical visit once a day, and scarcely stayed ten minutes afterwards,—until to-day, when, by papa's express desire, Augustus drove over and fetched him to dinner.

It is pleasant to be able to write down here, how very much better I like my brother-in-law. His thorough goodness of nature, his kindly cheering ways, and his unaffected, if rather obstreperous love for his wife, which is reflected, as it should be, upon every creature belonging to her, make it impossible not to like him. I am heartily glad he has sold out, so that even if war breaks out again, there will be no chance of his being ordered off on foreign service. Though in that case, he declares he should feel himself in honour bound to volunteer. But Lisabel only laughs; she knows better.

Still, I trust there may be no occasion. War, viewed in the abstract, is sufficiently terrible; but when it comes home, when one's self, and one's own, are bound up in the chances of it, the case is altogether changed. Some misfortunes contemplated as personal possibilities, seem more than human nature could bear. How the mothers, sisters, wives, have borne them all through this war is—

My head turned dizzy here, and I was obliged to leave off writing and lie down. I have not felt very strong lately—that is, not bodily strong. In my heart I have—thoroughly calm, happy, and thankful—as God knows we have all need to be, since. He has spared our dear father, never loved so dearly as now. But physically, I am rather tired and weak, as if I would fain rest my head somewhere and be taken care of. If there were anybody to do it, which there is not. Since I can remember, nobody ever took care of me.

While writing this last line, old Mrs. Cartwright came up to bring me some arrowroot with wine in it, for my supper, entreating me to go to bed "like a good child." She said "the Doctor" told her to look after me; but she should have done it herself; anyhow. She is a good old body—I wish we could find out anything about her poor lost daughter.

A Life for a Life

What was I writing about? Oh, the history of to-day: where I take up the thread of my journal, leaving the whole interval between, a blank. I could not write about it if I would.

I did not go to church with them this morning, feeling sure I could not walk so far, and some one ought to stay with papa. So the girls went, and Dr. Urquhart also, at which papa seemed just a little disappointed, he having counted on a long morning's chat.

I never knew papa attach himself to any man before, or take such exceeding delight in any one's company. He said the other day, when Augustus annoyed him about some trifle or other, that "he wished he might have chosen his own son-in-law—Lisabel had far better have married Doctor Urquhart."

Our Lisabel and Dr. Urquhart! I could not help laughing. Day and night—fire and water, would have best described their union.

Penelope now, though she has abused him so much—but that was Francis's fault,—would have suited him a deal better. They are more friendly than they used to be—indeed, he is on good terms with all Rockmount. We feel, every one of us, I trust, that our obligations to him are of a kind of which we never can acquit ourselves while we live.

This great grief has been in many ways, like most afflictions, "a blessing in disguise." It has drawn us all together, as nothing but trouble ever does, as I did not think anything ever would, so queer a family are we. But we are improving. We do not now shut ourselves up in our rooms, hiding each in her hole like a selfish bear until feeding time—we assemble in the parlour—we sit and talk round papa's study-chair. There, this morning after church, we held a convocation and confabulation before papa came down.

And, strange to say—almost the first time such a thing ever happened in ours, though a clergyman's family—we talked about church and the sermon.

It was preached by the young man whom papa has been obliged to take as curate, and who, Penelope said, she feared would never suit, if he took such eccentric texts, and preached such out-of-the-way sermons as the one this morning. I asked what it was about, and was answered, "The cities of refuge."

I fear I do not know my Bible—the historic portion of it—so well as I might; for I scandalised Penelope exceedingly by inquiring what were "the cities of refuge." She declared any child in her school would have been better acquainted with the Old Testament, and I had it at my tongue's end to say that a good many of her children seemed far too glibly and irreverently acquainted with the Old Testament, for I once overheard a knot of them doing the little drama of Elijah, the mocking children, and the bears in the wood, to the confusion of our poor bald-headed organist, and their own uproarious delight, especially the two boys who enacted the bears. But 'tis wicked to tease our good Penelope—at least I think it wicked now.

So I said nothing; but after the sermon had been well talked over as "extraordinary," "unheard of in our church," "such a mixing of politics and religion, and bringing up everyday subjects into the pulpit,"—for it seems he had alluded to some question of capital punishment, which now fills the newspapers—I took an opportunity of asking Dr. Urquhart what the sermon really had been about. I can often speak to him of things which I never should dream of discussing with my sisters, or even papa. For, whatever the subject is, he will always listen, answer, explain; either laughing away my follies, or talking to me seriously and kindly.

This time, though, he was not so patient; asked me abruptly, "Why I wanted to know?"

"About the sermon? From harmless curiosity. Or rather,"—for I would not wish him to think that in any religious matter I was guided by no higher motive than curiosity, "because I doubt Penelope's judgment of the curate. She is rather harsh sometimes."

"Is she?"

"Will you find for me,"—and I took out of my pocket my little Bible, which I had been reading in the garden,—"about the cities of refuge? That is, unless you dislike to talk on the subject."

"Who—I—what made you suppose so?"

A Life for a Life

I replied candidly, his own manner, while they were arguing it.

"You must not mind my manner—it is not kind—it is not friendly." And then he begged my pardon, saying he knew he often spoke more rudely to me than to any one else.

If he does, it harms me not. He must have so many causes of anxiety and irritation, which escape by expression. I wish he would express them a little more, indeed. One could bear to be really scolded, if it did him any good. But, of course, I should have let the theological question slip by, had he not, some minutes after, referred to it himself. We were standing outside the window; there was no one within hearing; indeed, he rarely talks very seriously unless he and I happen to be alone.

"Did you think as they do—your sisters, I mean—that the Mosaic law is still our law—an eye for an eye—a tooth for a tooth—a life for a life—and so on?"

I said I did not quite understand him.

"It was the subject of the sermon. Whether he who takes life forfeits his own. The law of Moses enacted this. Even the chance murderer, the man guilty of manslaughter, as we should term it now, was not safe out of the bounds of the three cities of refuge. The avenger of blood finding him, might slay him."

I asked what he thought was meant by "the avenger of blood." Was it divine or human retribution?

"I cannot tell. How should I know? Why do you question me?"

I might have said, because I liked to talk to him, and hear him talk; because, in many a perplexed subject over which I had been wearying myself; his opinion had guided me and set me right. I did hint something of the kind, but he seemed not to hear or heed it, and continued—

"Do you think, with the minister of this morning, that, except in very rare cases, we—we Christians, have no right to exact a life for a life? Or do you believe, on religious as well as rational grounds, that every man-slayer should inevitably be hanged?"

A Life for a Life

I have often puzzled over that question, which Dr. Urquhart evidently felt as much as I did. Truly, many a time have I turned sick at the hangings which I have had to read to papa in the newspapers—have wakened at seven in the morning, and counted, minute by minute, some wretched convict's last hour—till the whole scene grew so vivid that the execution seemed more of a murder than the original crime of which it was the expiation. But still, to say that there ought to be no capital punishments? I could not tell. I only repeated softly words that came into my mind at that instant.

"For we know that no murderer hath eternal life in him."

"But if he were *not* a wilful murderer?—if life were taken—let us suppose such a case—in violent passion, or under circumstances which made the man not himself?—if his crime were repented of and atoned for in every possible way—the lost life re-purchased by his own—not by dying, but by the long torment of living?"

"Yes," I said, "I could well imagine a convict's existence, or that of one convicted in his own conscience—a duellist, for instance—far more terrible than death upon the scaffold."

"You are right; I have seen such cases."

No doubt he has, since, as an officer once told me, the army still holds duelling to be the necessary defence of a gentleman's "honour." The recollections aroused were apparently very sore; so much so that I suggested our changing the subject, which seemed both painful and unprofitable.

"Not quite. Besides, would you quit a truth because it happened to be painful? That is not like you."

"I hope not."

After a few minutes' silence, he continued—

"This is a question I have thought over deeply. I have my own opinion concerning it, and I know that of most men; but I should like to hear a woman's—a Christian woman's. Tell me, do you believe the avenger of blood walks through the Christian world, as through the land of Israel, requiring retribution; that for blood-shedding as for all other crimes, there is, in this world, whatever there may be in another, expiation, but no pardon? Think well, answer slowly, for it is a momentous question."

"I know that—the one question of our times." Dr. Urquhart bent his head without replying. He hardly could speak; I never saw him so terribly in earnest. His agitation roused me from the natural shyness I have in lifting up my own voice and setting forth my own girlish opinion on topics of which every one has a right to think, but very few to speak.

"I believe that in the Almighty's gradual teaching of His creatures, a Diviner than Moses brought to us a higher law— in which the sole expiation required is penitence, with obedience: *'Repent ye.' 'Go and sin no more.'* It appears to me, so far as I can judge and read here"— my Bible was still in my hand—"that throughout the New, and in many parts of the Old Testament, runs one clear doctrine, namely, that any sin, however great, being repented of and forsaken, is by God, and ought to be by man, altogether pardoned, blotted out and done away."

"God bless you!"

For the second time he said to me those words—said them twice over, and left me. Rather abruptly; but he is sometimes abrupt when thinking deeply of anything.

Thus ended our little talk: yet it left a pleasant impression. True, the subject was strange enough; my sisters might have been shocked at it; and at my freedom in asking and giving opinions. But oh! the blessing it is to have a friend to whom one can speak fearlessly on any subject; with whom one's deepest as well as one's most foolish thoughts come out simply and safely. Oh, the comfort—the inexpressible comfort of feeling *safe* with a person—having neither to weigh thoughts nor measure words, but pouring them all right out, just as they are, chaff and grain together; certain that a faithful hand will take and sift them, keep what is worth keeping, and then with the breath of kindness blow the rest away.

Somebody must have done a good deal of the winnowing business this afternoon; for in the course of it I gave him as much nonsense as any reasonable man could stand—even such an ultra-reasonable man as Dr. Urquhart. Papa said once, that she was "taking too great liberty of speech with our good friend, the Doctor—that foolish little Dora"; but foolish little Dora knows well enough what she is about—when to be silly and when to be wise. She believes in her heart that there are some people to whom it does great good to be dragged down from their heights of wisdom, and forced to talk and smile, until the clouds wear off, and the smile becomes permanent—grows into a sunshine that warms every one else all through.

Oh, if he had had a happy life—if Dallas had lived—this Dallas, whom I often think about, and seem to know quite well—what a cheerful, blithe nature his would have been!

Just before tea; when papa was taking his sleep, Dr. Urquhart proposed that we should all go for a walk. Penelope excused herself; besides, she thinks it wrong to walk out on a Sunday; but Lisabel and Augustus were very glad to go. So was I, having never been beyond the garden since papa's illness.

If I try to remember all the trivial incidents of to-day at full length, it is because it has been such an exceedingly happy day: to preserve which from the chances of this mortal life, "the sundry and manifold changes of this world," as the prayer says, I here write them down.

How vague, how incompatible with the humdrum tenor of our quiet days at Rockmount that collect used to sound!

"That amidst the sundry and manifold changes of this world our hearts may surely there be fixed, where true joys are to be found, through Jesus Christ our Lord, Amen." Now, as if newly understanding it, I also repeat, "Amen."

We started, Lisabel, Augustus, Dr. Urquhart, and I. We went through the village, down the moorland-road, to the ponds, which Augustus wanted to examine, with a view to wild-duck shooting, next, or, rather, I might say, this winter, for Christmas is coming close upon us, though the weather is still so mild.

Lisa and her husband walked on first, and quickly left us far behind; for, not having been out for so long, except the daily stroll round the garden, which Dr. Urquhart had insisted upon, the fresh air seemed to turn me dizzy. I managed to stumble on through the village, keeping up talk, too, for Dr. Urquhart hardly said anything, until we came out upon the open moor, bright, breezy, sunshiny. Then I felt a choking—a longing to cry out or sob—my head swam round and round.

"Are you wearied?—you look as if you were." "Will you like to take my arm?" "Sit down—sit down on this stone— my child!"

I heard these sentences distinctly, one after the other, but could not answer. I felt my bonnet-strings untied, and the wind blowing on my face—then all grew light again, and I looked round.

"Do not be frightened; you will be well in a minute or two. I only wonder that you have kept up so bravely, and are so strong."

This I heard too—in a cheerful, kind voice—and soon after I became quite myself; but ready to cry with vexation, or something, I don't know what.

"You will not tell anybody?" I entreated.

"No, not anybody," said he, smiling, "if turning faint was such a crime. Now, you can walk? Only not alone, just at present, if you please."

I do not marvel at the almost unlimited power which, Augustus says, Dr. Urquhart has over his patients. A true physician—not only of bodies, but souls.

We walked on, I holding his arm. For a moment I was half afraid of Lisabel's laugh, and the silly etiquette of our neighbourhood; which holds that if a lady and gentleman walk arm-in-arm they must be going to be married., Then I forgot both, and only thought what a comfort it was in one's weakness to have an arm to lean on, and one that you knew, you felt, was not unwilling to have you resting there.

I have never said, but I will say it here, that I know Dr. Urquhart likes me—better than any other of my family; better, perhaps, than any friend he has, for he has not many. He is a man of great kindliness of nature, but few personal attachments. I have heard him say "that though he liked a great many people, only one or two were absolutely necessary to him." Dallas might have been, had he lived.

He told me, one day, there was a certain look in me which occasionally reminded him of Dallas. It is by these little things that I guess he likes me—at least, enough to make me feel, when with him, that rest and content that I never feel with those who do not care for me.

I made him laugh, and he made me laugh, several times, about trifles that, now I call them to mind, were not funny at all. Yet "it takes a wise man to make a fool, and none but a fool is always wise."

With which sapient saying we consoled ourselves, standing at the edge of the larger pool, watching the other couple strolling along, doubtless very busy over the wild-duck affair.

"Your sister and Treherne seem to suit one another remarkably well. I doubted once if they would."

"So did I. It ought to be a warning to us against hasty judgments. Especially here."

Mischief prompted the latter suggestion, for Dr. Urquhart must have recollected, as well as I did, the last and only time he and I walked across this moorland road, when we had such a serious quarrel, and I was more passionate and rude to him than I ever was to anybody— out of my own family. I hope he has forgiven me. Yet he was a little wrong too.

"Yes, especially here," he repeated, smiling—so I have no doubt he did remember.

Just then, Lisabel's laugh, and her husband's with it, rang distantly across the pool.

"They seem very happy, those two."

I said I felt sure they were, and that it was a blessed thing to find, the older one grew, how very much of happiness there is in life.

"Do you think so?"

"Do *you* not think so?"

"I do; but not in your sense exactly. Remember, Miss Theodora, people see life in a different aspect at twenty-five and at—"

"Forty. I know that."

"That I am forty? Which I am not quite, by-the-bye. No doubt it seems to you a most awful age."

I said it was perhaps for a woman, but for a man no more than the prime of life, with many years before him in which both to work and enjoy.

"Yes, for work is enjoyment, the only enjoyment that ever satisfies."

He stood gazing across the moorland, *my* moorland, which put on its best smile for us to-day. Ay, though the heather was brown, and the furze-bushes had lost their gold. But so long as there is free air, sunshine, and sky, the beauty never can vanish from my beloved moor. I wondered how any one could look at it and not enjoy it; could stand here as we stood and not be satisfied Perhaps in some slight way I hinted this, at least, so far as concerned myself; to whom everything seemed so delicious, after this month of sorrow.

"Ah, yes, I understand," said Dr. Urquhart, "and so it should be with me also. So it is, I trust. This is a lovely day, lovely to its very close, you see."

For the sun was sinking westward, and the clouds robing themselves for one of those infinitely varied late autumn sunsets, of the glory of which no human eye can ever tire.

"You never saw a tropical sunset? I have, many. I wonder if I shall ever see another."

After a little hesitation, I asked if he thought it likely? Did he wish to go abroad again?

"For some reasons, yes!" Then speaking forcibly—"Do not think me morbid; of all things, morbid, cowardly sentimentality is my abhorrence—but I am not naturally a cheerful-minded man. That is, I believe I was, but circumstances have been stronger than nature; and it now costs me an effort to attain what I think every man ought to have, if he is not absolutely a wicked man."

"You mean an even, happy temper, that tries to make the best of all things, which I am sure you do."

"An idle life," he went on, unheeding, "is of all things the very worst for me. Unless I have as much work as ever I can do, I am never happy."

This was comprehensible in degree. Though one thing surprised and pained me, that even Dr. Urquhart was not "happy." Is anybody happy?

"Do not misunderstand me." (I had not spoken, but he often guesses my thoughts in a way that makes me thankful I have nothing to hide.) "There are as many degrees of happiness as of goodness, and the perfection of either is impossible. But I have my share. Yes, truly, I have my share."

"Of both?"

"Don't—don't!"

Nor ought I to have jested when he was in such heavy earnest.

And then for some time we were so still, that I remember hearing a large bee, deluded by the mild weather, come swinging and singing over the moor, and stop at the last, the very last, bluebell—I dared not call it a harebell with Dr. Urquhart by—of the year, for his honey-supper. While he was eating it, I picked one of the flower-stalks, and stroked it softly over his great brown back and wings.

"What a child you are still!"

(But for once Dr. Urquhart was mistaken.)

"How quiet everything is here!" he added.

"Yes, that wavy purple line always reminded me of the hills in the 'Happy Valley' of Prince Rasselas. Beyond them lies the world."

A Life for a Life

"If you knew what 'the world' is, as you must one day. But I hope you will only see the best half of it. I hope you will have a happy life."

I was silent.

"This picture; the moorland, hills, and lake,—your pond is as wide and bright as a lake—will always put me in mind of Rasselas, but one cannot live for ever in our 'Happy Valley,' nor in our lazy camp either. I often wish I had more work to do."

"How—and where?"

As soon as I had put it I blushed at the intrusiveness of this question. In all he tells me of his affairs I listen, but never dare to inquire, aware that I have no right to ask of him more than he chooses to reveal.

Right or not, he was not offended; he replied to me fully and long; talking more as if I had been a man and his confidential friend, than only a simple girl, who has in this at least some sense, that she feels she can understand him.

It appears, that in peace-time, the duties of a regimental surgeon are almost nothing, except in circumstances where they become as hopeless as they are heavy; such as the cases of unhealthy barracks, and other avoidable causes of mortality, which Dr. Urquhart and Augustus discussed, and which he has since occasionally referred to, when talking to papa and me. He told me with what anxiety he had tried to set on foot reforms in these matters; how all his plans had been frustrated by the tardiness of Government; and how he was hopeless of ever attaining his end. Indeed he showed me an official letter, received that morning, finally dismissing the question.

"You see, Miss Theodora,

'To mend the world's a vast design,'

too vast for my poor powers."

"Are you discouraged?"

"No. But I suspect I began at the wrong end; that I attempted too much, and gave myself credit for more influence than I possessed. It does not do to depend upon other people; much safer is that amount of work which a man can do with his own two hands and head. I should be far freer, and therefore more useful, if I left the army altogether, and set up practice on my own account."

"That is, if you settled somewhere as a consulting physician, like Doctor Black?"

"No," he smiled—"not exactly like Doctor Black. Mine would be a much humbler position. You know, I have no income except my pay."

I confessed that I had never given a thought to his income, and again smiling, he answered—"No, he was sure of that."

He then went on to explain that he believed moral and physical evil to be so bound up together, that it was idle to attack one without trying to cure the other. He thought, better than all building of gaols and reformatories, or even of churches—since the Word can be spread abroad without need of bricks and mortar—would be the establishing of sanitary improvements in our great towns, and trying to teach the poor, not how to be taken care of in workhouses, prisons, and hospitals, but how to take care of themselves, in their own homes. And then, in answer to my questions, he told me many things about the life, say rather existence, of the working-classes in most large towns, which made me turn sick at heart; marvelling how, with all this going on around me, I could ever sit dreamily gazing over my moorland, and play childish tricks with bees!

Yes, something ought to be done. I was glad, I was proud, that it had come into his mind to do it. Better far to labour thus in his own country than to follow an idle regiment into foreign parts, or even a fighting regiment into the terrible campaign. I said so.

"Ah—you 'hate soldiers' still."

I did not answer, but met his eyes. I know mine were full—I know my lips were quivering. Horribly painful it was to be jested with just then.

A Life for a Life

Dr. Urquhart said gravely: "I was not in earnest; I beg your pardon."

We then returned to the discussion of his plans and intentions. I asked him how he meant to begin his labours?

"From a very simple starting-point. 'The doctor' has, of all persons, the greatest influence among the poor—if only he cares to use it. As a commencement, and also because I must earn salt to my porridge, you know, my best course would be to obtain the situation of surgeon to some dispensary, workhouse, hospital, or even gaol. Thence, I could widen my field of work at pleasure, so far as time and money were forthcoming."

"If some one could only give you a fortune now!"

"I do not believe in fortunes. A man's best wealth consists of his personal labours, personal life. 'Silver and gold have I none'—but wherever I am, I can give myself; my labours, and my life."

I said something about that being a great gift—many men would call it a great sacrifice.

"Less to me than to most men—since, as you know, I have no relatives; nor is it likely I shall ever marry."

I believed so. Not constantly; but at intervals. Something in his manner and mode of thought fixed the conviction in my mind, from our earliest acquaintance.

Of course, I merely made some silent assent to this confidence. What was there to say? Perhaps he expected something—for as we turned to walk home, the sun having set, he remained a long time silent. But I could not speak. In truth, nothing came into my head to say.

At last I lifted my eyes from the ground, and saw the mist beginning to rise over my moorland—my grey, soft, dreamy moorland. Ay, dreamy it was, and belonging only to dreams. But the world beyond—the struggling, suffering, sinning world of which be had told me—that was a reality.

I said to my friend who walked beside me, feeling keenly that he was my friend, and that I had a right to look up into his good noble face, wherein all his life was written as clearly as on a book—thinking too what a comfort and privilege it was to have more than any one else had the reading of that book—I said to Dr. Urquhart—my old hesitation having somehow altogether vanished—that I wished to know all he could possibly tell me of his plans and projects; that I liked to listen to them, and would fain do more than listen—help.

He thanked me. "Listening is helping. I hope you will not refuse sometimes to help me in that way—it is a great comfort to me. But the labour I hope for is exclusively a man's—if any woman could give aid you could, for you are the bravest woman I ever knew."

"And do you think I never can help you?"

"No."

So our walk ended.

I say "ended," because, though there was a great deal of laughing with Augustus and Lisabel—who had pushed one another ankle-deep into the pond, and behaved exactly like a couple of school-children out on a holiday, and though, they, hurrying home, Dr. Urquhart and I afterwards followed leisurely, walking together slowly, along the moorland road—we did not renew our conversation. We scarcely exchanged more than a few words;—but walking thus arm-in-arm we did not feel—that is, I did not feel, either apart, or unfriendly, or sad.

There is more in life than mere happiness—even as there are more things in the world than mere marrying and giving in marriage. If, from circumstances, he has taken that resolution, he is perfectly justified in having done so, and in keeping to it. I would do exactly the same. The character of a man who marries himself to a cause, or a duty—has always been an ideal of mine—like my Max—Max and Thekla.—But they were lovers, betrothed lovers; free to *say* "I love you" with eyes and lips—just once, for a day or two—a little hour or two.—Would this have made parting less bitter or more?" I cannot tell; I do not know. I shall never know aught about these things. So I will not think of them.

When we came home—Dr. Urquhart and myself—I left him at the door, and went up into my own room.

A Life for a Life

In the parlour I found Colin Granton come to tea—he had missed me at church, he said, and was afraid I had made myself ill; so walked over to Rockmount to see. It was very kind—though, while acknowledging it, he seemed half ashamed of the kindness.

He and Augustus, now on the best of terms, kept us alive all the evening with their talking and laughing. They planned all sorts of excursions—hunting, shooting, and what not—to take place during the grand Christmas gathering which is to be at Treherne Court. Dr. Urquhart—one of the invited guests, listened to all, with a look of amused content.

Yes—he is content. More than once, as I caught his eye following me about the room, we exchanged a smile—friendly, even affectionate.—Ay, he does like me. If I were a little younger—if I were a little girl in curls, I should say he is "fond" of me.—"Fond of"—what an idle phrase!—such as one would use towards a dog, or cat, or bird. What a difference between that and the holy words, "I love"—not as silly young folks say, I am "in love"—but *"I love"*; with all my reason, will, and strength; with all the tenderness of my heart, all the reverence of my soul.

Be quiet, heart—be silent, soul! I have, as I said before—nought to do with these things.

The evening passed pleasantly and calmly enough, all parties seeming to enjoy themselves: even poor Colin coming out his brilliantest and best, and making himself quite at home with us. Though he got into a little disgrace before going away, by saying something which irritated papa; and which made me glad that the little conversation this morning between Dr. Urquhart and myself had been not in family conclave, but private.

Colin was speaking of the sermon, and how "shocked" his mother had been at its pleading against capital punishment.

"Against capital punishment, did you say?"—cried papa.

"Did my curate bring this disgraceful subject into my pulpit in order to speak against the law of the land—the law of God?—Girls, why did you not tell me? Dora, remind me I must see the young man to-morrow."

A Life for a Life

I was mortally afraid this would end in the poor young man's summary dismissal; for papa never allows any "new fangled notions" in his curates; they must think and preach as he does—or quit. I pleaded a little for this one, who has a brother and sister dependent on him, lodging in the village, and, as far as I dared and could, I pleaded for his sermon. Colin tried to aid me, honest fellow, backing my words, every one, with the most eager asseverations—well-meant, though they did not exactly help the argument.

"Dora," cried papa, in utmost astonishment, "what do you mean?"

"Miss Dora's quite right: she always is," said Colin stoutly. "I don't think anybody ever ought to be hanged; least of all a poor fellow who, like—" he mentioned the name, but I forget it—it was the case that has been so much in the newspapers—"killed another fellow out of jealousy—or in a passion—or being drunk—which was it? I say, Urquhart—Treherne—won't you bear me out?"

"In what?" asked Augustus, laughing.

"That many a man has sometimes felt inclined to commit murder?—I have myself—ha! ha!—and many a poor devil is kicked out of the world dancing upon nothing, who isn't a bit worse, may be better, than a great many young scoundrels who die unhung. That's truth, Mr. Johnston, though I say it."

"Sir," said papa, turning white with anger, "you are at perfect liberty to say exactly what you please—provided it is not in my presence. No one, before me, shall so insult my cloth, and blaspheme my Maker, as to deny His law set down here" (dropping his hand over our great Family Bible, which he allows no one but himself to touch, because, as we know, there is the fly-leaf pasted down, not to be read by any one, nor written on again during poor papa's lifetime). "God's law is blood for blood. '*Whoso sheddeth man's blood, by man shall his blood be shed.*' That law, sir, my Church believes never has been—never will be—annulled. And though your maudlin, loose charity may sympathise with hanged murderers, uphold duellists, and exalt into heroes cowardly man-slayers, I say that I will no more have in my house the defenders of such, than I would, under any pretext, grasp in mine the hand of a man who had taken the life of another."

A Life for a Life

To see papa so excited, alarmed us all. Colin, greatly distressed, begged his pardon and retracted everything—but the mischief was done. Though we anticipate no serious results, indeed he has been now for some hours calmly asleep in his bed, still he was made much worse by this unfortunate dispute.

Dr. Urquhart stayed, at our earnest wish, till midnight, though he did not go into papa's room. When I asked him what was to be done in case of papa's head suffering for this excitement—if we should send to the camp for him—he said, "No, he would rather we sent for Doctor Black."

Yet he was anxious, I know; for after Colin left, he sat by himself in the study, saying he had a letter to write and post, but would come upstairs to papa if we sent for him. And when, satisfied that the danger was past and papa asleep, he prepared to leave—I never, in all the time of our acquaintance, saw him looking so exceedingly pale and weary.

I wanted him to take something—wine or food; or at least to have one of our ponies saddled that he might ride instead of walking home. But he would not.

We were standing at the hall—only he and I—the others having gone to bed. He took both my hands, and looked long and steadily in my face as he said good-bye.

"Keep up heart. I do not think any harm will come to your father."

"I hope not. Dear, dear papa—it would indeed be terrible."

"It would. Nothing must be allowed to grieve him in any way—as long as he lives."

"No."

Dr. Urquhart was not more explicit than this; but I am sure he wished me to understand that in any of those points discussed to-day, wherein he and I agreed, and both differed from my father—it was our duty henceforth, as much as possible, to preserve a respectful silence. And I thanked him in my heart—and with my eyes too, I know—for this, and for his forbearance in not having contradicted papa, even when most violent and unjust.

"When shall you be coming again, Doctor Urquhart?"

"Some day—some day."

"Do not let it be very long first. Good-bye."

"Good-bye."

And here befell a thing so strange—so unexpected, that if I think of it, it seems as if I must have been dreaming; as if, while all the rest of the events of to-day, which I have so quietly written down, were perfectly natural, real, and probable—this alone were something unreal, and impossible to tell—hardly right to tell.

And yet—oh me! it is not wrong—though it makes my cheek burn and my hand tremble—this poor little hand. I thought he had gone—and was standing on the door-step, preparing to lock up—when Dr. Urquhart came back again along the walk. It was he—though in manner and voice so unlike himself—that even now I can hardly believe the whole is not a delusion.

"For God's sake—for pity's sake—do not utterly forget me, Theodora."

And then—then—

He said once, that every man ought to hold every woman sacred; that, if not of her own kindred, he had no right, except as the merest salutation, even to press her hand. Unless—unless he loved her.

Then, why—

No: I ought not to write it, and I will not. It is—if it is anything—something sacred between him and me—something in which no one else has any part—which may not be told to any one—except in my prayers.

My heart is so full. I will close this and say my prayers.

Chapter 17

HER STORY

Treherne Court.

Where, after another month's pause, I resume my journal.

Papa and I have been here a week. At the last moment Penelope declined going, saying that some one ought to keep house at Rockmount. I wished to do so; but she would not allow me.

This is a fine place, and papa enjoys it extremely. The enforced change, the complete upsetting of his former solitary ways, first by Lisabel's marriage, and then by his own illness, seem to have made him quite young again. Before we left, Dr. Black pronounced him entirely recovered; that he might reasonably look forward to a healthy, green old age. God grant it! For, altered as he is, in so many ways, by some imperceptible influence; having wider interests—is it wrong to write affections?—than he has had for the last twenty years, he will enjoy life far more than ever before. Ah me; how can anybody really enjoy life without having others to make happy, and to draw happiness from?

Dr. Black wished, as a matter of professional etiquette, that papa should once again consult Dr. Urquhart about his taking this long northern journey; but on sending to the camp we found he was "absent on leave," and had been for some time. Papa was disappointed and a little annoyed. It was strange, rather; but might have been sudden and important business, connected with the plans of which he told me, and which I did not quite feel justified in communicating further, till he informs papa himself.

I had a week of that restless laziness, which I suppose most people unaccustomed to leave home experience for the first few days of a visit: not unpleasant laziness, neither, for there was the Christmas week to anticipate and plan for, and every nook in this beautiful place to investigate, as its own possessors scarcely care to do; but which I, and other visitors, shall so intensely enjoy. I am trying to feel settled now.

A Life for a Life

In this octagon room, which Lisabel—such a thoughtful, kindly hostess, as Lisa makes I has specially appropriated mine, I take up my rest. It is the wee-est room attainable in this great, wide, wandering mansion, where I still at times feel as strange as a bird in a crystal palace; such birds as in the Aladdin Palace of 1851 we used to see flying about the tops of these gigantic, motionless trees, caught under the glass, and cheated by those green, windless, unstirred leaves into planning a natural wild-wood nest. Poor little things! To have once dreamed of a nest, and then never to be able to find or build it, must be a sore thing.

This grand "show" house has no pretensions to the character of "nest," or "home." To use the word in it seems half-ridiculous, or pathetic; though Lisa does not find it so. Stately and easy, our girl moves through these magnificent rooms, and enjoys her position as if she were born to it. She shows good taste and good feeling too—treats meek, prosy, washed-out Lady Augusta Treherne, and little, fussy, infirm Sir William, whose brown scratch-wig and gold spectacles rarely appear out of his own room, with unfailing respect and consideration. They are mightily proud of her, as they need to be. Truly the best thing this their patrician blood could do, was to ally itself with our plebeian line.

But, thank goodness that Lisa, not I, was the victim of that union! To me, this great house, so carefully swept and garnished, sometimes feels like a beautiful body without a soul: I should dread a demon's entering and possessing it, compelling me to all sorts of wild and wicked deeds, in order to break the suave harmony of things. For instance, the three drawing-rooms, *en suite,* where Lis and I spend our mornings, amidst a labyrinth of costly lumber—sofas, tables, and chairs, with our choice of five fires to warm at, glowing in steel and gilded grates, and glittering with pointed china tiles; having eleven mirrors, large and small, wherein to catch, at all points, views of our sweet selves—in this splendid wilderness, I should, did trouble seize me, roam, rage, or ramp about like any wild animal. The oppression of it would be intolerable. Better, a thousand times, my little room at Rockmount, with its little window, in at which the branches wave; I can see them as I lie in bed. My own dear little bed, beside which I flung myself down the night before I left it, and prayed that my coming back might be as happy as my going.

This is the first time since then, that I have suffered myself to cry. When people feel happy causelessly, it is said to be a sign that the joy cannot last, that there is sorrow coming. So, on the other hand, it may be a good omen to feel one's heart aching, without cause. Yet, a tear or two seems to relieve it and do it good. Enough now.

I was about to describe Treherne Court. Had any of us seen it before the wedding, ill-natured people might have said that Miss Lisabel Johnston married the Court and not the master—so magnificent is it. Estate, extending goodness knows where; park, with deer; avenue, two miles long; plantations, sloping down to the river—one of the "principal rivers of England," as we used to learn in *Pinnock's Geography*—the broad, quiet, and yet fast-running Dee. How lovely it must look in summer, with those great trees dipping greenly into it, and those meadows dotted with lazy cows.

There are gardens, too, and an iron bridge, and statues, and a lawn with a sun-dial, though not half so pretty as that one at the Cedars, and a quadrangular stable, almost as grand as the house; and which Augustus thinks of quite as much importance. He has made Lisa a first-rate horsewoman, and they used to go careering half over the country, until lately. Certainly, those two have the most thorough enjoyment of life, fresh, young, animal life and spirits, that it is possible to conceive. Their whole existence, present and future, seems to be one blaze of sunshine.

I broke off here to write to Penelope. I wish Penelope were with us. She will find her Christmas very dull without us all; and, consequently, without Francis; though he could not have come to Rockmount under any circumstances, he said. "Important business."—This "business," alack, is often hard to brook. Well!

"Men must work, and women must weep."

No, they ought not to weep; they are cowards if they do. They ought to cheer and encourage the men, never to bemoan and blame them. Yet, I wish—I wish Penelope could get a sight of Francis this Christmas-time. It is such a holy time, when hearts seem "knit together in love"—when one would like to have all one's best-beloved about one. And she loves Francis—has loved him for so long.

Dr. Urquhart said to me once, the only time he ever referred to the matter—for he is too delicate to gossip about family love-affairs;

"that he wished sincerely my sister and Mr. Charteris had been married—it would have been the best thing which could have happened to him—and to her, if she loved him." I smiled; little doubt about that "if." In truth, though I once thought differently, it is one of the chief foundations of the esteem and sympathy which I take shame to myself for not having hitherto given to my elder sister. I shall do better, please God, in time to come; better in every way.

And to begin:—In order to shake off a certain half-fretful dreaminess that creeps over me, it may be partly in consequence of the breaking-up of home-habits, and the sudden plunge into a life so totally new, I mean to write regularly at my journal; to put down everything that happens from this time; so that it may be a complete history of this visit at Treherne Court; if at a future time, I, or any one, should ever read it. Will any one ever do so? Will any one ever have the right? No; rights enforced are ugly things; will any one ever come and say to me, "Dora," or "Theodora,"—I think I like my full name best—"I *should like* to read your journal"?

Let me see: to-night is Sunday; I seem always to choose Sunday for these entries, because we usually retire early, and it is such a peaceful family day at Rockmount; which indeed is the case here. We only went to church once, and dined as usual at seven, so that I had a long afternoon's wander about the grounds; first with papa, and then by myself. I hope it was a truly Sunday walk; that I was content and thankful, as I ought to be.

So endeth Sunday. Let us see what Monday will bring.

Monday.—It brought an instalment of visitors; the first for our Christmas week.

At church-time a fly drove up to the door, and who should leap out of it, with the brightest faces in the world, but Colin Granton and his mother. I was so surprised—startled indeed, for I happened to be standing at the hall-door when the fly appeared; that I hardly could find two words to say to either. Only my eyes might have shown—I trust they did—that, after the first minute, I was very glad to see them.

I tucked the dear old lady under my arm, and marched her through all the servants into the dining-room, leaving Colin to take care of himself, a duty of which the young man is well capable. Then I had a grand hunt after Papa and Lisa; finally waylaying the shy Lady Augusta, and begging to introduce to her my dear old friend. Every friend's face is so welcome when one is away from home.

After lunch, the gentlemen adjourned to the stables; while Mrs. Treherne escorted her guest in hospitable state through the long corridors to her room, and I was glad to see the very best bedroom of all was assigned to the old lady. Lisa—bless the girl!—looked just a little bit proud of her beautiful house, and not unnatural either. A wife has a right to be proud of all the good things her husband's love endows her with; only they might be better things than houses and lands, clothes and furniture. When Lisa has said sometimes, "My dear, I am the happiest girl in the world. Don't you envy me?" my heart has never found the least difficulty in replying.

Yet she is happy. There is a look of contented matronhood growing in her face day by day, far sweeter than anything her girlhood could boast. She is very fond of her husband too. It was charming to see the bright blush with which she started up from Mrs. Granton's fireside, the instant Augustus was heard calling outside, "Lis! Lis! Mrs. Treherne! Where's Mrs. Treherne?"

"Run away to your husband, my dear. I see he can't do without you. How well she looks, and how happy she seems!" added the old lady, who has apparently forgotten the slight to "my Colin."

By the way, I do not suppose Colin ever actually proposed to our Lisa; only it was a sort of received notion in our family that he would. If he had, his mother never would have brought him here, to be a daily witness of Mrs. Treherne's beauty and contentment; which he bears with a stoicism most remarkable in a young man who has ever been in love with her. Do men so easily forget?—Some, perhaps; not all. It is oftentimes honourable and generous to conquer an unfortunate love; but there is something discreditable in totally ignoring and forgetting it. I doubt, I should rather despise a man who despised his first love, even for me.

Let me see: where did I leave myself? Oh, sitting by Mrs. Granton's fire; or helping her to take off her things—a sinecure office, for her "things"—no other word befits them—are popped off and on with the ease and untidiness of fifteen, instead of the preciseness of sixty-five: order and regularity being omitted by Providence in the manufacture of this dear old lady. Also listening—which is no sinecure; for she always has plenty to say about everything and everybody, except herself.

I may never have said it in so many words, but I love Mrs. Granton. Every line in her nice old withered face is pleasant to me; every creak of her quick footstep; every angular fold in her everlasting black silk gown—a very shabby gown often, for she does not care how she dresses. She is by no means one of your picturesque, ancient gentlewomen, looking as if they had just stepped out of a gilt frame—she is only a little, active, bright old lady. As a girl, she might have been pretty—I am not sure, though she has still a delicate expressive mouth, and soft grey eyes; but I am very sure that she often looks beautiful now.

And why?—for, guessing what all the grand people at the dinner to-night will think of her and myself, I cannot help smiling at this application of the word—because she has one of the most beautiful natures that can adorn an old woman—or a young one, either: all loving-kindness, energy, cheerfulness. Because age has failed to sour her; affliction to harden her heart. Of all people I know, she is the quickest to praise, the slowest to judge, the gentlest to condemn. A living homily on the text, which, specifying the trinity of Christian virtues, names—"these three—but *the greatest of these is charity.*"

Long familiarity made me unmindful of these qualities in her, till, taught by the observations of others, and by my own comparison of the people I meet out in the world, which may be supposed to mean Treherne Court, with my good old friend.

"Have you much company, then?" asked she, while I was trying to persuade her to let me twist into a little more form the shapeless "bob" of her dear old grey hair, and put her cap not quite so much on one side. "And do you enjoy it, my dear? Have you seen anybody you liked very much?"

"None that I liked better than myself, be sure. How should I?"

A true saying, though she did not understand its under-meaning. I have set more value on myself of late, and taken pains to be pleasant to every one. It would not do to have people saying, "What a disagreeable girl is that Theodora Johnston! I wonder how anybody can like her?" Has Mrs. Granton an idea that anybody—nay, let it come out—that anybody does like me?

Her eyes were very sharp, and her questions keen, as I entertained her with our doings at Treherne Court, and the acquaintances we had made—a large number—from county nobility to clerical dignitaries, and gay young officers from Whitchester, which seems made up entirely of barracks and cathedral. But she gave me no news in return, except that Colin found the Cedars so dull that he had never rested till he had got his mother away here; which fact did not extremely interest me. He was always a restless youth, but I trusted his late occupations had inclined him to home-quietness. Can his interest in them have ended?—or is there no friend at hand to keep him steadily at work?

We sat so long gossiping, that Lisabel, ready for dinner, with Treherne diamonds blazing on her white neck and arms, called us to order, and sent me away to dress. As I left, I heard her say, Augustus had sent her to ask if Mrs. Granton had seen Dr. Urquhart lately?

"Oh yes! Colin saw him a few days since. He is quite well, and very busy."

"And where is he? Will he be here this week; Augustus wants to know?'

"I have not the slightest idea. He did not say a word about it."

Lisabel inquired no further, but began exhibiting her velvet dress, and her beautiful point-lace ruffles, Lady Treherne's present—to her a far more interesting subject. Verily gratitude is not the most lasting of human emotions in young women who have homes, and husbands, and everything they can desire.

Quite well and very busy; though not too busy to write to Colin Granton I am glad. I have sometimes thought he might be ill.

The dinner-party was the largest since we have been here. Two long rows of faces; not one in whom I took the slightest interest, save Mrs. Granton and Colin. I tried to sit next the former, and the latter to sit next to me; but both designs failed, and we fell among strangers, which is sometimes as bad as falling among thieves. I did not enjoy my evening as much as I expected; but I hope I behaved well; that, as Mrs. Treherne's sister, I tried to be attentive and courteous to the people, that no one need have been ashamed of poor Theodora.

And it was some comfort when, by the merest chance, I overheard Mrs. Granton say to Lisabel, "that she never saw a girl so much improved as Miss Dora."

Improved! Yes, I ought to be. There was room for it. Oh that I may go on improving—growing better and better every day! Too good I cannot be.

"Quite well and very busy." Again runs in my head that sweet, sad ditty—

> "Men must work and women must weep,
> For there's little to earn and many to keep."

Oh! to think of any one's ever working *for me!*

Tuesday.—Nothing at all happened. No letters, no news. Colin drove out his mother and me towards the Welsh hills, which I had expressed a wish to see, and after lunch, asked if I would go with him to the river-side in search of a boat, for he thought we may still have a row, though it is December, the weather being so mild. He remembered how I used to like his pulling Lisabel and me up and down the ponds in the moorland—we won't say how many years ago. I think Colin also is "improved." He is so exceedingly attentive and kind.

Wednesday.—A real event happened to-day—quite a surprise. Let me make the most of it; for this journal seems very uninteresting.

I was standing "flattening my nose," as children say, against the great iron gates of the avenue; peering through them at the two lines of bare trees, planted three deep, and the broad gravel-drive, straight as an arrow, narrowing in perspective almost to a point—the lodge plainly visible at the end of the two miles, which seems no distance at all; but when you have to walk it, it's "awfu' lang," as says the old Scotch gardener, who is my very particular friend, and my informant on all subjects, animal, vegetable, and historical, pertaining to

Treherne Court. And, looking at it from these gates, the road does seem "awfu' lang," like life. I was thinking so, when some one touched me, and said, "Dora."

Francis startled me so: I am sure I must have blushed as much as if I had been Penelope; that is, as Penelope used to blush in former days. The next minute I thought of her, and felt alarmed.

"Oh, Francis, nothing is the matter—nothing has happened to Penelope?"

"You silly girl, what should happen? I do not know anything about Rockmount, was not aware but that you were all at home, till I saw you here, and knew by the sentimental attitude it could be nobody but Dora. Tell me, when did you come?"

"When did *you* come? I understood it was impossible for you to leave London."

"I had business with my uncle, Sir William. Besides, if Penelope is here—"

"You must know quite well, Francis, that Penelope is not here."

I never scruple to speak my mind to Francis Charteris. We do not much like one another, and are both aware of it. His soft, silken politeness often strikes me as insincere, and my "want of refinement," as he terms it, may be quite as distasteful to him. We do not suit, and were we ever so fond of one another, this incompatibility would be apparent. People may like and respect one another extremely, yet not suit, even as two good tunes are not always capable of being harmonised. I once heard an ingenious performer try to play at once, "The Last Rose of Summer" and "Garry Owen." The result resembled many a conversation between Francis and me.

This promised to be one of them; so, as a preventive measure, I suggested luncheon-time.

"Oh, thank you, I am not hungry; I lunched at Birmingham.' Still, it might have struck Francis that other people had not. We crossed the gardens towards the river, under the great Portugal laurels, which he stood to admire.

"I have watched their growth ever since I was a boy. You know, Dora, once this place was to have been mine."

"It would have given you a vast deal of trouble, and you don't like trouble. You will enjoy it much more as a visitor."

Francis made no reply, and when I asked the reason of his sudden change of plans, and if Penelope were acquainted with it, he seemed vexed.

"Of course Penelope knows; I wrote to-day, and told her my purpose in coming here was to see Sir William. Cannot a man pay his respects to his uncle without being questioned and suspected?"

"I never suspected you, Francis,—until now, when you look as if you were afraid I should. What is the matter? Do tell me."

For, truly, I felt alarmed. He was so extremely nervous and irritable, and his sensitive features, which he cannot keep from telling tales, betrayed so much inward discomfiture, that I dreaded some ill, threatening him or Penelope. If one, of course both.

"Do tell me, Francis. Forgive my rudeness. We are almost brother and sister."

"Which tie is supposed to excuse any rudeness. But really I have nothing to tell—except that your ladyship is growing blunter than ever, under the instruction, no doubt, of your friend, Doctor Urquhart. Pray, is he here?"

"Is he expected?"

"You had better ask Captain Treherne."

"Pshaw! What do men care for one another? I thought a young lady was the likeliest person to take an interest in the proceedings of a young—I beg his pardon—a middle-aged gentleman."

If Francis thought either to irritate or confuse me, he was disappointed. A month ago it might have been. Not now. But probably,—and I have since felt sure of it—he was merely pursuing his own ends without heeding me.

"Now, Dora, seriously, I want to know something of Doctor Urquhart's proceedings, and where a letter might reach him. Do find out for me, there's a good girl."

And he put his arm round me, in the elder-brotherly caressing manner which he sometimes adopted with Lisa and me, and which I never used to mind. Now, I felt as if I could not endure it, and slipped away.

"I don't see, Francis, why you should not ask such a simple question yourself. It is no business of mine."

"Then you really know nothing of Doctor Urquhart's whereabouts lately? He has not been to Rockmount?"

"No."

"Nor written?"

"I believe not. Why do you want to know? Have you been quarrelling with him?"

For, aware that they two were not over fond of one another—a sudden idea, so ridiculously romantic that I laughed at it the next minute—made me, for one second, turn quite sick and cold.

"Quarrelling, my dear child—young lady, I mean—am I ever so silly, so ungentlemanly, as to quarrel with anybody? I assure you not. There is the Dee! What a beautiful view this is!"

He began to expatiate on its beauties, with that delicate appreciative taste which he has in such perfection, and in the expression of which he never fails. tinder such circumstances, when he really seems pleased—not languidly, but actively, and tries to please others, I grant all Francis's claims to be a charming companion—for an hour's walk. For life—ah! that is a different matter! When with him, I often think of *Beatrice's* answer when *Don Pedro* asks if she will have him as a husband?—"*No, my lord, unless I might have another for working-days. Your Grace is too costly to wear every day.*"

Love—fit for constant wear and tear, able to sink safely down

> "to the level of every day's
> Most quiet need; by sun and candle-light,"

must be a rare thing, and precious as rare.

"I think I never saw such a Christmas-eve. Look, Dora, the sky is blue as June. How sharp and clear the reflection of those branches in the river. Heigho! this is a lovely place. What a difference it would have made to me if Sir William had never married, and I had been heir to Treherne Court."

"No difference to you in yourself," said I stoutly. "Penelope would not have loved you one whit the more, only you would have been married a little sooner, which might have been the better for both parties."

"Heaven knows—yes," muttered he, in such anguish of regret, that I felt sorry for him. Then, suddenly: "Do you think your sister is tired of waiting? Would she wish the—our engagement broken?"

"Not at all. Indeed, I meant not to vex you. Penelope wishes no such thing."

"If she did," and he looked more vexed still, "it would be quite natural."

"No, indeed," I cried, in some indignation, "it would not be natural. Do you suppose we women are in such a frightful hurry to be married, that love promised and sure, such as Penelope has—or ought to have—is not sufficient to make us happy for any number of years? If you doubt it, you ought to be ashamed of yourself. You don't know women; least of all such women as my sister Penelope."

"Ay, she has been a good, faithful girl," said he, again sighing.

"Poor Penelope."

A Life for a Life

And then he recurred to the beautiful scenery which I, feeling that extreme want of topics of conversation which always appals me in *tête-à-têtes* with Francis Charteris—gladly accepted. It lasted till we re-entered the house, and, not unwillingly, parted company.

After luncheon—being unable to find anybody in this great, wide house—I sat in my own room awhile; till, finding it was not good to be lazy and dreaming, I went to Mrs. Granton's and listened to her pleasant gossip about people with whom she had been mixed up during her long life. Who have every one this remarkable characteristic, that they are all the very best people that ever lived. The burthen of her talk is, of course, "my Colin," who she makes out to have been the most angelic babe, the sweetest school-boy, the noblest youth, and the most perfect man upon this poor earth. One cannot smile at the fond old mother. Besides, I am fond of Colin myself. Was he not my first love?

Hush! let me not, even in jest, profane that holy word.

I sat with Mrs. Granton a long time—sometimes hearing, sometimes not; probably saying, "yes," and "no," and "certainly," to many things which now I have not the least idea of. My thoughts wandered—lulled by the wind, which began to rise into a regular Christmas blast.

Yes, to-night was Christmas-eve, and all the Christmas guests were now gathering in country-houses. Ours, too; there were rings at the resonant door-bell, and feet passing up and down the corridor. I like to recall—just for a moment's delusion— the sensations of that hour, between the lights, resting by Mrs. Granton's fire, lazy, warm, content. The only drawback to my content was the thought of Penelope—poor girl—all alone at Rockmount, and expecting nobody.

At the dressing-bell, I slipped through the long, half-dark staircases—to my room. As it was to be a large party at dinner I thought I would put on my new dress—Augustus's present; black velvet; "horridly old-womanish" Lisa had protested. Yet it looked well—I stood before the glass and admired myself in it—just a little. I was so glad to look well.

Foolish vanity—only lasting a minute. Yet that minute was pleasant. Lisabel, who came into my room with her husband following her to the very door, must have real pleasure in her splendours. I told her so.

"Oh, nonsense, child. Why, I am as vexed and cross as possible. So many disappointments to-night. People with colds, and rheumatism, and dead relatives."

"Oh, Lisa!"

"Well, but is it not annoying? Everybody wanted, does not come; those not wanted, do. For instance: Doctor Urquhart—who always keeps both papa and Sir William in the best of humours, is not here. And Francis, who fidgets them both to death, and whom I was so thankful was not coming—he is just come. You stupid girl, you seem not the least bit sorry. You are thinking of something else the whole time."

I said I was sorry, and was not thinking of anything else.

"Augustus wanted to see him particularly; but I forgot, you don't know—however, you will soon, child. Still, isn't it a downright shame of Doctor Urquhart neither to come nor send?"

I suggested something might have happened.

"A railway accident. Dear me, I never thought of that."

"Nor I. Heaven knows, no!"

I had a time-table, and searched through it for the last train stopping at Whitchester, then counted how long it would take to drive to Treherne Court, and looked at my watch. No, he could not be here to-night.

"And if there had been any accident, there was time for us to have heard of it," said Lisa carelessly, as she took up her fan and gloves to go downstairs. "So, child, we must make the best we can of your friend's behaviour. Are you ready for dinner?"

A Life for a Life

"In two minutes."

I shut the door after my sister, and stood still before the glass, fastening a brooch, or something.

Mine, my friend. He was that. Whenever they were vexed with him, all the family usually called him so.

It was very strange his not coming—having promised Augustus, for some reason which I did not know of. Also, there was another reason—which they did not know of—he had promised *me*. He once said to me, positively, that this, the first Christmas he has kept in England for many years, should be kept with us—with me.

Now, a promise is a promise. I, myself, would keep one at all costs, that involved no wrong to any other person. He is of the same mind. Then something must have happened.

For a moment I had been angry, though scarcely with him; for wherever he was he would be doing his duty. Yet, why should he be always doing his duty to every one, *except* me? Had I no right? I, to whom even Lisa, who knew nothing, called him my friend?

Yes, *mine*. Of a sudden I seemed to feel all that the word meant, and to take all the burthen of it. It quieted me.

I went downstairs. There were the usual two lines of dinner-table faces—the usual murmur of dinner-table talk; but all was dim and uncertain, hike a picture, or the sound of people chattering very far off. Colin beside me, kept talking about how well I looked in my new gown—how he would like to see me dressed as fine as a queen—and how he hoped we should spend many a Christmas as merry as this—till something seemed tempting me to bid him hold his tongue—myself to start up and scream.

At dessert, the butler brought a large letter to Sir William. It was a telegraph message—I recognised the look of the thing, we had several during papa's illness. Easy to sit still now. I seemed to know quite well what was coming, but the only clear thought was "mine—mine."

Sir William read, folded up the message, and passed it on to Augustus, then rose.

"Friends, fill your glasses. I have just had good news; not unexpected, but still good news. Ladies and gentlemen, I have the honour to give you the health of my nephew, Francis Charteris, Esquire, Governor-elect of—."

In the cheering, confusion, and congratulation that followed, Lisa passed the telegram to me, and I saw it was from "Max Urquhart, London."

As soon as we got into a corner by ourselves, my sister burst out with the whole mystery.

"Thank goodness, it's over; I never kept a secret before, and Augustus was so frightened lest I should tell—and then what would Doctor Urquhart have said? It's Doctor Urquhart's planning, and he was to have brought the good news to-day; and I'm very sorry I abused him, for he has been working like a horse for Francis's interest, and—did you ever see a young fellow take a piece of good fortune so coolly—a lovely West Indian Island, with Government house, and salary large enough to make Penelope a most magnificent Governor's wife—yet he is not a bit thankful for it—I declare I am ashamed of Francis Charteris."

She went on a good deal more in this fashion, but I had nothing to say—I felt so strange and confused; till at last I leaned my head on her shoulder, and cried softly. Which brought me into great opprobrium, and subjected me to the accusation of always weeping when there was the least prospect of a marriage in the family.

Marriage! just at that moment, there might not have been such a thing as marriage in the world. I never thought of it. I only thought of life, a life still kept safe, labouring busily to make everybody happy, true to itself and to its promises, forgetting nothing and no one, kind to the thankful and unthankful alike. Compared to it, my own insignificant life, with its small hopes and petty pains, all crumbled down into nothingness.

"Well, are you glad, Dora?"

Ay, I was; very glad—very content.

Papa came in soon, and he and I walked up and down, arm-in-arm, talking the matter over; till, seeing Francis sitting alone in a recess, we went up to him, and papa again wished him all happiness. He merely said, "Thank you," and muttered something about "wishing to explain by-and-by."

"Which means, I suppose, that I am shortly to be left with only one girl to take care of me—eh! Francis," said papa, smiling.

"Sir—I did not mean—I," he actually stammered. "I hope, Mr. Johnston, you understand that this appointment is not yet accepted—indeed I am uncertain if I shall accept it."

Papa looked exceedingly surprised; and remembering some of Francis's sayings to me this morning, I was rather more than surprised—indignant. But no remark was made, and just then Augustus called the whole party to go down into the great kitchen and see the Christmas mummers or guisers, as they are called in that county.

We looked at them for a long half-hour, and then everybody, great and small, got into the full whirl of Christmas merriment. Colin, in particular, grew so lively, that he wanted to lead me under the mistletoe; but when I declined, first gaily and then seriously, he desisted, saying he would not offend me for the world. Nevertheless, he and one or two more kissed Lisabel. How could she endure it? when I,—I now sometimes feel jealous over even a strange touch of this my hand.

The revels ended early, and, as I sit writing, the house is quite still. I have just drawn up my blind and looked out. The wind has sunk; snow is falling. I like snow on a Christmas morning.

Already it is Christmas morning. Unto whom have I silently to wish those good wishes which always lie nearest to one's heart? My own family, of course; papa and Lisa, and Penelope, far away. Poor dear Penelope! may she find herself a happy woman this time next year. Are these all? They were, last Christmas. But I am richer now. Richer, it often seems to me, than anybody in the whole world.

Good night! a merry—no—for "often in mirth the heart is sad"—a happy Christmas, and a good new year!

Chapter 18

HIS STORY

Dec. 31st, 1855.

The merry-making of my neighbours in the flat above—probably Scotch or Irish, both of which greatly abound in this town—is a sad counteraction of work for to-night. But why grumble, when I am one of the few people who pretend to work at all on this holiday—a night which used to be such a treat to us boys? The sounds overhead put me in mind of that old festival of Hogmanay, which, for a good many things, would be "more honoured in the breach than the observance."

This Liverpool is an awful town for drinking. Other towns may be as bad; statistics prove it; but I know no place where intoxication is so open and shameless. Not only in by-streets and foul courts, where one expects to see it, but everywhere. I never take a short railway journey in the after part of the day but I am liable to meet at least one drunken "gentleman" snoozing in his first-class carriage; or, in the second class, two or three drunken "men," singing, swearing, or pushed stupidly about by pale-faced wives. The sadness of 'the thing is, that the wives do not seem to mind it, that everybody takes it quite as a matter of course. The "gentleman," often grey-haired, is but "merry," as he is accustomed to be every night of his life; the poor man has only "had a drop or two," as all his comrades are in the habit of taking, whenever they get the chance: they see no disgrace in it; so they laugh at him a bit, and humour him, and are quite ready to stand up for him against all in-corners who may object to such a fellow-passenger. *They* don't; nor do the women belonging to them, who are well used to tolerate drunken sweethearts, and lead about and pacify drunken husbands. It makes me sick at heart sometimes to see a decent, pretty girl sit tittering at a foul-mouthed beast opposite; or a tidy young mother, with two or three bonnie children, trying to coax home, without harm to himself or them, some brutish husband, who does not know his right hand from his left, so utterly stupid is he with drink. To-night, but for my chance hand at a railway-station, such a family party as this might have reached home fatherless, and no great misfortune, one might suppose. Yet the wife had not even looked sad—had only scolded and laughed at him.

A Life for a Life

In this, as in most cases of reform, it is the woman who must make the first step. There are two great sins of men: drunkenness in the lower classes; a still worse form of vice in the higher, which I believe women might help to stop, if they tried. Would to God I could cry to every young working woman, "Never encourage a drunken sweetheart!" and to every young lady thinking of marriage, "Beware! better die than live to give children to a loose-principled, unchaste father."

These are strong words—dare I leave them for eyes that may, years hence, read this page?—Ay, for by then they will—they must, in the natural course of things—have gained at least a tithe of my own bitter knowledge of the world. God preserve them from all knowledge beyond what is actually necessary I when I think of any suffering coming to them, any sight of sin or avoidable sorrow troubling those dear eyes, it almost drives me mad. If, for instance, you were to marry a man, like some men I have known, and who indeed form the majority of our sex, and he were unkind to you, or wronged you in the smallest degree, I think I could murd—

Hush!—not that word!

You see how my mind keeps wandering purposelessly, having nothing to communicate. I had indeed, for some time, avoided writing here at all. And I have been, and am, necessarily occupied, laying the groundwork of that new plan of life which I explained to you.

Its whole bearing you did not see, nor did I intend you should; though your own words originated it; lit it with a ray of hope so exquisite that I could follow on cheerfully for indefinite years.

It only lasted an hour or two; and then your father's words—though, heaven be praised, they were not yours—plunged me into darkness again; a darkness out of which I had never crept, had I been still the morbid coward I was a year ago.

As it was, you little guessed all the thoughts you shut in with me behind the study door, till your light foot came back to it—that night. Nor that in the interval I had had strength to weigh all circumstances, and form a definite, deliberate plan, firm as I believe my heart to be—since I have known you.

A Life for a Life

I have resolved, in consequence of some words of yours, to change my whole scheme of life. That is, I will at some future day, whether near or far circumstances must decide, submit to you every event of my history, and then ask you dispassionately as a friend, to decide if I shall still live on according to my purpose, in prospect of *the end,* or, shaking off the burthen of it, shall trust in God's mercy, consider all things past and gone, and myself at liberty like any other, to love, and woo, and marry.

Afterwards, according to your decision, may or may not follow that other question—the very hope and suspense of which is like passing into a new life, through the gate of death.

Your father said distinctly—but I will not repeat it. It is enough to make me dread to win my best blessing, lest I might also win her father's curse. To evoke that curse, knowingly to sow dissension between a man and his own daughter, is an awful thing. I dare not do it. During his lifetime I must wait.

So, for the present, farewell, innocent child! for no child can be more innocent and happy than you.

But you will not always be a child. If you do not marry—and you seem of an opposite mind to your sisters in that particular—you will, years hence, be a woman no longer young, perhaps little sought after, for you are not beautiful to most eyes, nor from your peculiar temperament do you please many people. By then, you may have known care and sorrow—will be an orphan and alone. I should despise myself for reckoning up these possibilities, did I not know that, in so far as any human hand can shield you from trouble, you shall be shielded, that while one poor life lasts, you never shall be left desolate.

I have given up entirely my intention of quitting England. Even if I am not able to get sight of you from year's end to year's end, if I have to stretch out and diminish to the slenderest link which will remain unbroken my acquaintance with your family, I must keep within reach of you. Nothing must happen to you or any one belonging to you, without my informing myself of it. And though you may forget—I say not you will, but you may—I am none the less resolved that you shall never lose me, while a man can protect a woman, a friend sustain and comfort a friend.

You will probably set down to mere friendship one insane outburst of mine. Wrong, I confess; but to see you standing in the lamplight, looking after me into the dark, with a face so tender, mild, and sweet, and to know I should not look at that face again for so long, it nearly maddened me. But you were calm—you would not understand.

It will never do for me to see you often, or to live in your neighbourhood, and therefore it was best to take immediate steps for the change I contemplate, and of which I told you. Accordingly, the very next day, I applied for leave of absence. The colonel was just riding over to call at Rockmount, so I sent a message to your father. I shrank from writing to him: to you, it was of course impossible. In this, as in many a future instance, I can only trust to that good heart which knows me—not wholly—alas, will it ever know me wholly? but better than any other human being does, or ever will. I believe it will judge me charitably, patiently, faithfully; for is it not itself the truest, simplest, faithfullest heart?

Let me here say one word. I believe there is no love in it; nothing that need make a man hesitate lest his own happiness should not be the only sacrifice. Sympathy, affection, you have for me; but I do not think you ever knew what love was. Any one worthy of you may yet have free opportunity of winning you—of making you happy. And if I saw you happy, thoroughly and righteously happy, I could endure it.

I will tell you my plans.

I am trying for the appointment of surgeon to a gaol near this town. I hope to obtain it: for it will open a wide field of work—to me the salt of life: and it is only fifty miles from Treherne Court, where you will visit, and where, from time to time, I may be able to meet you.

You see—this my hope, dim as it is in the future, and vague enough as to present comfort—does not make me weaker but stronger for the ordinary concerns of life; therefore I believe it to be a holy hope, and one that I dare carry along with me in all my worldly doings and plannings. Believe one fact, for my nature has sufficient unity of purpose never to do things by halves—that no single plan, act, or thought is without reference to you.

A Life for a Life

Shall I tell you my ways and means, as calculated to-night, the last night of the year?

Selling out of the army will supply me with a good sum. Which I mean to put by, letting the interest accumulate, as a provision for accidental illness, or old age, if I live to be old: or for—do you guess?

My salary will be about £300 a year. Now, half of that ought to suffice a man of my moderate habits. Many a poor clerk, educated, and obliged to appear as a gentleman, has no larger income, and contrives to marry upon it, too, if love seizes hold of him while still in the venturesome stage of existence.

We men are strange animals: at twenty, ready to rush into matrimony on any prospects whatever, or none at all; at thirty, having thought better of it, rejoice in our escape; but after forty, when the shadows begin to fall, when the outer world darkens, and the fireside feels comfortless and lone, then, we sit and ponder—I mean, most men. Mine is an individual and special case, not germane to the subject.

With all deference to young Tom Turton, his friend Mr. Charteris, and others of the set which I have lately been among in London, the sum of one hundred and fifty pounds a year seems to me amply sufficient to maintain in as much comfort as is good for him, and in all the necessary outward decencies of middle-class life, a man without any expensive habits or relations dependent on him, and who has neither wife nor child.

Neither wife nor child! As I write them, the words smite hard.

To have no wife, no child! Never to seek what the idlest, most drunken loon of a mechanic may get for the asking; never to experience the joy which I saw on a poor fellow's face only yesterday; when, in the same room with one dead lad, and another sickening, the wife brought into the world a third, a living child, and the ragged, starved father cried out, "Lord be thankit!" that it *was* a living child.

O Lord, Thy ways are equal: it is ours only which are unequal. Forbid it Thou that I should have given Thee of that which cost me nothing!

A Life for a Life

Yet, on this night—this last night of a year so momentous—let me break silence, and cry—Thou alone wilt hear.

I want her—I crave her; my very heart and soul are hungry for her! Not as a brief possession, like gathering a flower and wearying of it, or throwing it away. I want her for always—to have her morning, noon, and night; day after day and year after year; happy or sorrowful, good or faulty, young or old; only mine, mine! I feel sometimes as if, found thus late, all eternity could not give me enough of her. It is not the body she inhabits,—though, from head to foot, my love is all fair, fair as daylight and pure as snow—it is herself I want, ever close at hand to be the better self of this me, who have tried vainly all these years to stand alone, to live and endure alone! Folly I—proud folly! such is not a natural state of things; God Himself said, "It is not good for man to be alone."

I think I never shall be so solitary as I have been. That good heart, pure and unselfish as I never saw woman's before, will always incline kindly to as much of mine as I dare show; those sweet, honest eyes will never be less trustful than now—unless I gave them cause to doubt me. Her friendship, like her character, is steadfast as a rock.

But oh! if she *loved* me! If I were one of those poor clerks at a hundred a year; if we had only meat, raiment, and a roof to cover us, and she loved me! If I were, as I might have been, a young doctor, toiling day and night, with barely time for food and sleep; but with a home to come to, and her to love me! If we sat in this room, poor and mean as it is, with this scanty supper between us, asking a blessing upon it, while, her hand in mine and her lips on my forehead, told me, "Max, I love you!"

God forgive me if I murmur! I am not young; my life is slipping away—my life, which is *owed*. Oh! that I might live long enough to teach her to say, "Max, I love you!"

Enough. The last minutes of this year—this blessed year! shall not be wasted in moans.

Already the streets are growing quiet. People do not seem to keep this festival here as we do, north of the Tweed; they think more of Christmas. Most likely she will have forgotten all about the day, and be peacefully sleeping the old year out and the new year in—this little English girl. Well, I am awake, and that will do for both.

My letter to Treherne—could you have seen it? I suppose you did. It made no excuses for not coming at Christmas, because I intended to come and see you as to-morrow. I mean to wish you a happy New Year, on this, the first since I knew you, since I was aware of there being such a little creature existing in the world.

Also, I mean to come and see you every New Year, if possible. The word possible, implying so far as my own will can control circumstances. I desire to see you; it is life to me to see you, and see you I will. Not often, for I dare not, but as often as I dare. And—for I have faith in anniversaries, always on the anniversary of the day I first saw you, and on New Year's Day.

One—two—three; I waited for the clock to cease striking, and now all the bells are ringing from every church tower. Is this an English custom? I must ask you to-morrow—that is, to-day, for it is morning—it is the New Year.

My day-dawn, my gift of God, my little English girl, a happy New Year!

Max Urquhart.

Chapter 19

HER STORY

New year's morning. So, this long-anticipated festival-week is ended, and the old year gone. Poor old year!

> "He gave me a friend and true, true love,
> And the New Year will take them away."

Ah, no, no, no!

Things are strange. The utmost I can say of them is, that they seem very strange. One would suppose, if one liked a friend, and there existed no reasonable cause for not showing it, why one would show it, just a little? That, with only forty miles between—a half-hour's railway ride not to run over and shake hands—to write a letter and not to mention one's name therein, was, at least, strange. Such a small thing, even under any pressure of business—just a line written, an hour spared. Talk of want of time! Why, if I were a man I would make time, I would—Simpleton! what would you do, indeed, when your plainest duty you do not do,—just to wait and trust.

Yet I do trust. Once believing in people, I believe in them always, against all evidence except their own—ay, and should to the very last—"until death us do part."

Those words have set me right again, showing me that I am not afraid, either for myself or any other, even of that change. As I have read somewhere, all pure love of every kind partakes in this of the nature of the love divine, "neither life nor death, nor things present nor things to come, nor height nor depth, nor any other creature," are able to separate or annihilate it. One feels that—or if one does not feel it, it is not true love, is worth nothing, and had better be let go.

I write idly,—perhaps from having been somewhat tired this week. Let me tell my troubles, it is only to this paper. Troubles indeed, they would scarcely deserve to be called, had they not happened in this festive week, when every one expected to be so uncommonly happy.

First, there was Francis's matter, which ought to have been a great joy, and yet has seemed to weigh us down like a great care; perhaps because the individual most concerned took it as such, never once looking pleased, nor giving a hearty "thank you," to a single congratulation. Also, instead of coming to talk over his happy prospects with papa and me, he has avoided us pertinaciously. Whenever we lighted upon him, it was sure to be by accident, and he slipped away as soon as he could, to do the polite to Treherne cousins, or to play interminably at billiards, which he considered "the most fascinating game in the world."

I hate it. What can be the charm of prowling for hours round and round a green-baize table, trying to knock so many red and white balls into so many holes? I never could discover, and told him so. He laughed, and said it was only my ignorance; but Colin, who stood by, blushed up to the eyes, and almost immediately left off playing. Who would have supposed the lad so sensitive?

I am beginning to understand the interest taken by a friend of theirs and mine in these two young men. Augustus Treherne and Colin Granton. Though neither particularly clever, they have both two qualities sufficiently rare in all men to make one thankful to find them in any—uprightness of character and unselfishness of disposition. By-the-bye, I never knew but one thoroughly unselfish man in all my life, and that was—

Well, and it was *not* Francis Charteris, of whom I am now speaking. The aforesaid little interchange of civility passed between him and me on the Saturday after Christmas Day, when I had been searching for him with a letter from Penelope. (There was in the post-bag another letter, addressed to Sir William, which made me feel sure we should have no more guests to-day, nor, consequently, till Monday. Indeed, the letter, which, after some difficulty, I obtained in the shape of cigar-lighters, made no mention of any such possibility at all; but then it had been a *promise*.)

Francis put my sister's note into his pocket, and went on with the game so earnestly that when Augustus came behind and caught hold of him, he started as if he had been collared by a policeman.

"My dear fellow, beg pardon, but the governor wants to know if you have written that letter."

Lisa had told me what it was—the letter of acceptance of the appointment offered him, which ought to have been sent immediately.

Francis looked annoyed. "Plenty of time.—My compliments to Sir William, and I'll—think about it."

"Cool!" muttered Augustus. "'Tis your look-out, Charteris, not mine—only, one way or other, your answer must go to-day, for my father has heard from—"

Here he reined up, as he himself would say; but having seen the handwriting in the post-bag, I guessed who was meant.

"Heard from whom, did you say? Some of the officious persons who are always so obliging as to keep my uncle informed of my affairs?"

"Nonsense—that is one of your crotchets. You have no warmer friend than my father, if only you wouldn't rub him up the wrong way. Come along, and have done with it. Otherwise—you know him of old—the old gentleman will get uncommon savage."

"Though I have the honour of knowing Sir William Treherne of old, I really cannot be accountable for his becoming 'uncommon savage,'" said Francis haughtily. "Mr. Granton, will you be marker this game?"

"Upon my word, he is the coolest customer! By George, Charteris, if you wanted Penelope as much as I did my wife—"

"Excuse me," returned Francis, "I have never mentioned Miss Johnston's name."

Certainly Augustus goes awkwardly to work with his cousin, who has good points if you know how to take hold of them. To use my brother-in-law's own phrase, Francis too gets "rubbed up the wrong way," especially when something has annoyed him. I saw him afterwards stand by a window of the library, reading Penelope's letter, with an expression of such perplexity and pain that I should have been alarmed, had not hers to me been so cheerful. They cannot have been quarrelling, for then she is never cheerful. No wonder. Silences, or slight clouds of doubt between friends are hard enough to bear: a real quarrel, and between lovers, must be heartbreaking. With all Francis's peculiarities, I trust it will never come to that.

Yet something must have been amiss, for there he stood, looking out vacantly on the Italian garden, with the dreary statues half clad in snow—on Antinous, almost seeming to shiver under anything but an Egyptian sky; and a white-limbed Egeria pouring out of her urn a stream of icicles. Of my presence he was scarcely conscious, I do believe, until I ventured to speak.

"Francis, do you see how near it is to post-time?"

Again a start, which with difficulty he concealed. "Et tu Brute? You also among my tormentors?—I quit the field."

—And the room: whence he was just escaping, had not his uncle's wheeled-chair filled up the door-way?

"Just in search of you"—cried the querulous voice, which Francis declares goes through his nervous system like a galvanic shock. "Have you written that letter?"

"My dear Sir William—"

"Have you written that letter?"

"No, sir, but—"

"Can't wait for 'buts'—I know your ways. There's pen and ink—and—I mean to wait here till the letter is done."

I thought Francis would have been indignant. And with reason; Sir William, despite his good blood, is certainly a degree short of a gentleman:—but old habit may have force with his nephew, who, without more remonstrance, quietly sat down to write.

A long half-hour, only broken by the rustle of Sir William's *Times*, and Lady Augusta's short cough—she was more nervous than usual, and whispered me that she hoped Mr. Charteris would not offend his uncle, for the gout was threatening. An involuntary feeling of suspense oppressed even me; until, slipping across the room, I saw that a few stray scribblings were the only writing on Francis's sheet of paper.

That intolerable procrastination of his! he would let everything slip—his credit, his happiness—nor his alone. And, the more people irritated him, the worse he was. I thought, in despair, I would try my hand at this incorrigible young man, who makes me often feel as if, clever and pleasing as he is, he were not half good enough for our Penelope.

"Francis"—I held out my watch with a warning whisper. He caught at it with great relief and closed the letter-case.

"Too late for to-day; I'll do it to-morrow."

"To-morrow will indeed be too late: Augustus said so distinctly. The appointment will be given to some one else—and then—"

"And then, you acute, logical, and business-like young lady?"

There was no time for ultra-delicacy. "And then you may not be able to marry Penelope for ten more years."

"Penelope will be exceedingly obliged to you for suggesting the possibility, and taking me to task for it in this way—such a child as you?"

Am I a child? but it mattered not to him how old I seem to have grown. Nor did his satirical tone vex me as it once might have done.

"Forgive me," I said; "I did not mean to take you to task. But it is not your own happiness alone which is at stake, and Penelope is my sister."

Strange to say, he was not offended. Perhaps, if Penelope had sometimes spoken her mind to him, instead of everlastingly adoring him, he might have been the better for it.

Francis sighed, and made another scribble on his paper—"Do you think, you who seem to be well acquainted with your sister's mind, that Penelope would be exceedingly unhappy if—if I were to decline this appointment?"

"Decline—oh!—you're jesting."

"Not at all. The governorship looks far finer than it is. A hot climate—and I detest warm weather: no society—and I should lose all my London enjoyments—give up all my friends and acquaintance."

"So would Penelope."

"So would Penelope, as you say. But—"

"But women count that as nothing—they are used to it. Easy for them to renounce home and country, kindred and friends, and follow a man to the ends of the earth. Quite natural, and they ought to be exceedingly obliged to him for taking them."

He looked at me; then begged me not to fly into a passion, as somebody might hear.

I said he might trust me for that; I would rather not, for his sake—for all our sakes, that anybody did hear—and then the thought of Penelope's gay letter suddenly choked me.

"Don't cry, Dora—I never could bear to see a girl cry. I am very sorry. Heaven help me! was there ever such an unfortunate fellow born? but it is all circumstances: I have been the sport of circumstances during my whole life. No, you need not contradict. What the devil do you torment me for?"

I have thought since, how great must have been the dormant irritation and excitement which could have forced that ugly word out of the elegant lips of Francis Charteris. And, the smile being off it, I saw a face, haggard and sallow with anxiety.

I told him, as gently as I could, that the only thing wanted of him was to make up his mind, either way.—If he saw good reasons for declining—why, decline; Penelope would be content.

"Do as you think best—only do it—and let my sister know. There are two things which you men, the best of you, count for nought; but which are the two things which almost break a woman's heart—one is, when you keep secrets from her; the other when you hesitate and hesitate, and never know your own minds. Pray, Francis, don't do so with Penelope. She is very fond of you."

"I know that. Poor Penelope!" He dropped his head, with something very like a groan.

Much shocked, to see that what ought to have been his comfort seemed to be his worst pain, I forgot all about the letter in my anxiety lest anything should be seriously amiss between them: and my great concern roused him.

"Nonsense, child. Nothing is amiss. Very likely I shall be Governor of—after all, and your sister Governor's lady, if she chooses. Hush!—not a word; Sir William is calling.—Yes, sir, nearly ready. There, Dora, you can swear the letter is begun." And he hastily wrote the date—Treherne Court.

Even then, though, I doubt if he would have finished it, save for the merest accident, which shows what trifles apparently cause important results, especially with characters so impressible and variable as Francis.

Sir William, opening his letters, called me to look at one with a name written on the corner.

"Is that meant for my nephew? His correspondent writes an atrocious hand, and cannot spell. 'Mr. F. Chatters!'—the commonest tradesman might have had the decency to put 'Francis Charteris, Esquire.' Perhaps it is not for him, but for one of the servants."

It was not: for Francis, looking rather confused, claimed it as from his tailor—and then, under his uncle's keen eyes, turned scarlet. These two must have had some sharp encounters in former days, since, even now, their power of provoking one another is grievous to see. Heartily vexed for Francis, I took up the ugly letter to give to him, but Sir William interfered.

A Life for a Life

"No, thank you, young lady. Tradesmen's bills can always wait. Mr. Francis shall have this letter when he has written his own."

Rude as this behaviour was, Francis bore with it. I was called out of the library, but half-an-hour afterwards I learned that the letter was written—a letter of acceptance.

So I conclude his hesitation was all talk—or else his better self sees that a good and loving wife, in any nook of the world, outweighs a host of grand London acquaintance, miscalled "friends."

Dear old Mrs. Granton beamed with delight at the hope of another marriage at Rockmount.

"Only," said she—"what will become of your poor papa, when he has lost all his daughters?"

I reminded her that Francis did not intend marrying more than one of us, and the other was likely to be a fixture for many years.

"Not so sure of that, my dear; but it is very pretty of you to say so. We'll see—something will be thought of for your good papa when the time comes."

What could she mean!—But I was afterwards convinced that only my imagination suspected her of meaning anything beyond her usual old-ladyish eagerness in getting young people "settled."

Sunday was another long day—they seem so long and still in spite of all the gaiety with which these country cousins fill Treherne Court, which is often so oppressive to me, and affects me with such a strange sensation of nervous irritation, that when Colin and his mother, who take a special charge of me, have hunted me out of stray corners, their affectionate kindness has made me feel like to cry.

—Now, I did not mean to write about myself—I have been trying desperately to fill my mind with other people's affairs— but it will out. I am not myself I know. All Sunday, a formal and dreary day at Treherne Court, I do think a dozen gentle words would have made me cry like a baby. I did cry once, but it was when nobody saw me, in the firelight, by Mrs. Granton's arm-chair.

"What is ailing you, my dear?" she had been saying. "You are not near so lively as you were a week ago. Has anybody been vexing my Dora?"

Which, of course, Dora at once denied, and tried to be as blithe as a lark, all the evening.

No, not vexed, that would be impossible—but just a little hurt. If I could only talk about some things that puzzle me—talk in a cursory way, or mention names carelessly, like other names, or ask a question or two, that might throw a light on circumstances not clear, then they would be easier to bear. But I dare not trust my tongue, or my cheeks, so all goes inwards—I keep pondering and wondering till my brain is bewildered, and my whole heart sore. People should not—cannot—that is good people cannot—say things they do not mean; it would not be kind or generous; it would not be *right*, in short; and as good people usually act rightly, or what they believe to be right, that doubt falls to the ground.

Has there risen up somebody better than I? with fewer faults and nobler virtues? God knows I have small need to be proud. Yet I am myself—this Theodora Johnston—as I was from the first, no better and no worse; honest and true if nothing else, and he knew it. Nobody ever knew me so thoroughly—faults and all.

We women must be constituted differently from men. A word said, a line written and we are happy; omitted, our hearts ache—ache as if for a great misfortune. Men cannot feel it, or guess at it—if they did, the most careless of them would be slow to wound us so.

There's Penelope, now, waiting alone at Rockmount. Augustus wanted to go post haste and fetch her here, but Francis objected. He had to return to London immediately, he said, and yet, here he is still. How can men make themselves so content abroad, while the women are wearing their hearts out at home?

I am bitter—naughty—I know I am. I was even cross to Colin to-day, when he wanted me to take a walk with him, and then persisted in staying beside me indoors. Colin likes me—Colin is kind to me—Colin would walk twenty miles for an hour of his old playmate's company—he told me so. And yet I was cross with him.

Oh, I am wicked, wicked! But my heart is so sore. One look into eyes I knew—one clasp of a steadfast kindly hand, and I would be all right again. Merry, happy, brave—afraid of nothing and nobody—not even of myself; it cannot be so bad a self if it is worth being cared for. I can't see to write. There new, there now—as one would say to a child in a passion—cry your heart out, it will do you good, Theodora.

After that, I should have courage to tell the last thing, which, this evening, put a climax to my ill-humours, and in some sense cleared them off, thunderstorm fashion. An incident so unexpected, a story so ridiculous, so cowardly, that had Francis been less to me than my expected brother-in-law, I declare I would have cut his acquaintance for ever and ever, and never spoken to him again.

I was sitting in a corner of the billiard-room, which, when the players are busy, is as quiet, unobserved a nook as any in the house. I had a book—but read little, being stopped by the eternal click-clack of the billiard-balls. There were only three in the room—Francis, Augustus, and Colin Granton, who came up and asked my leave to play just one game. My leave? How comical! I told him he might play on till midsummer, for all I cared.

They were soon absorbed in their game, and their talk between whiles went in and out of my head as vaguely as the book itself had done, till something caught my attention.

"I say, Charteris, you know Tom Turton? He was the cleverest fellow at a cannon. It was refreshing only to watch him hold the cue, so long as his hand was steady, and even after he got a little 'screwed.' He was a wild one, rather. What has become of him?"

"I cannot say. Doctor Urquhart might, in whose company I last met him."

Augustus stared.

"Well, that is a good joke. Doctor Urquhart with Tom Turton. I was nothing to boast of myself before I married; but Tom Turton!"

"They seemed intimate enough; dined, and went to the theatre together and finished the evening—I really forget where. Your friend the doctor made himself uncommonly agreeable."

"Urquhart and Tom Turton," Augustus kept repeating, quite unable to get over his surprise at such a juxtaposition; from which I conclude that Mr. Turton, whose name I never heard before, was one of the not too creditable associates of my brother-in-law in his bachelor days. When, some one calling, he went out, Colin took up the theme; being also familiar with this notorious person, it appeared.

"Very odd, Doctor Urquhart's hunting in couples with Tom Turton. However, I hope he may do him good—there was room for it."

"In Tom, of course; your doctor being one of those china patterns of humanity, in which it is vain to find a flaw, and whose mission it is to go about as patent cementers of all cracked and unworthy vessels."

"Eh?" said Colin, opening his good, stupid eyes.

"Query—whether your humdrum Scotch doctor is one whit better than his neighbours. (Score that as twenty, Granton.) I once heard he has a wife and six children living in the shade, near some cathedral town, Canterbury, or Salisbury."

"What!" and Colin's eyes almost started out of his head with astonishment.

I laugh now—I could have laughed then, the minute after, to recollect what a "stound" it gave us both, Colin and me, this utterly improbable and ridiculous tale, which Francis so coolly promulgated.

"I don't believe it," said Colin doggedly, bless his honest heart! "Beg your pardon, Charteris, but there must be some mistake. I don't believe it."

"As you will—it is a matter of very little consequence. Your game, now."

A Life for a Life

"I won't believe it," persisted Colin, who, once getting a thing into his head, keeps it there. "Doctor Urquhart isn't the sort of man to do it. If he had married ever so low a woman, he would have made the best of her. He'd never take a wife and keep her in the background. Six young ones, too—and he so fond of children." Francis laughed.

And all this while I sat quiet in my chair.

"Children are sometimes inconvenient—even to a gentleman of your friend's parental propensities. Perhaps—we know such things do occur, and can't be helped, sometimes—perhaps the tale is all true, except that he omitted the marriage ceremony."

"Charteris, that girl's sitting there."

It was this hurried whisper of Colin's, and a certain tone of Francis's, which made me guess at the meaning, which, when I clearly caught it—for I was not a child exactly, and Lydia Cartwright's story has lately made me sorrowfully wise,—sent me burning hot all over, and then so cold.

"That girl." Yes, she was but a girl. Perhaps she ought to have crept blushing away, or pretended not to have heard a syllable of these men's talk. But, girl as she was, she scorned to be such a hypocrite—such a coward. What! sit still to hear a friend sneered at, and his character impeached. While one—the only one at hand to do it—durst not so much as say "The tale is false—prove it." And why? Because she happened to be a woman! Out upon it! I should despise the womanhood that skulked behind such rags of miscalled modesty as these.

"Mr. Granton," I said, as steadily and coolly as I could, "your caution comes too late. If you gentlemen wished to talk about anything I should not hear, you ought to have gone into another room. I have heard every word you uttered."

"I'm sorry for it," said Colin bluntly.

Francis proposed carelessly "to drop the subject." What! take away a man's good name, behind his back, and then merely "drop the subject." Suppose the listener had been other than I, and had believed: or Colin had been a less honest fellow than he is, and he had believed, and we had both gone and promulgated the story, with a few elegant improvements of our own, where would it have ended? These are the things that destroy character—foul tales, that grow up in darkness, and before a man can seize hold of them, root them up, and drag them to light, homes are poisoned, reputation gone.

Such thoughts came in a crowd upon me. I hardly knew till then how much I cared for him—I mean his honour, his stainless name, all that helps to make his life valuable and noble. And he absent, too, unable to defend himself. I was right to do as I did; I take shame to myself even for this long preamble, lest it might look like an apology.

"Francis," I said, holding fast by the billiard-table, and trying to smother down the heat of my face, and the beat at my heart, which nearly choked me, "if you please, you have no right to say such things, and then drop the subject. You are quite mistaken. Doctor Urquhart was never married, he told papa so. Who informed you that he had a wife and six children living at Salisbury?"

"My dear girl, I do not vouch for any such fact; I merely 'tell the tale, as it was told to me.'"

"By whom? Remember the name, if you can. Any one who repeated it ought to be able to give full confirmation."

"Faith, I almost forgot what the story was."

"You said he had a wife and six children living near Salisbury. Or," and I looked Francis direct in the face, "a woman who was not his wife, but who ought to have been."

He must have been ashamed of himself, I think; for he turned away and began striking irritably at the balls.

"I must say, Dora, these are extraordinary questions to put. Young ladies ought to know nothing about such things; what possible concern is this of yours?"

I did not shrink; or I am sure he could not have seen me do so. "It is my concern, as much as it is Colin's, there; or that of any honest stander-by. Francis, I think that to take away a man's character behind his back, as you have been doing, is as bad as murdering him."

"She's right," cried Colin; "upon my soul she is!—Dora—Miss Dora, if Charteris will only give me the scoundrel's name that told him this, I'll hunt him down and unearth him, wherever he is. Come, my dear fellow, try and remember. Who was it?"

"I think," observed Francis, after a pause, "his name was Augustus Treherne."

Colin started—but I only said, "Very well, I shall go and ask him."

And just then it chanced that papa and Augustus were seen passing the window. I was well-nigh doing great mischief by forgetting, for the moment, how that the name of the place was Salisbury. It would never have done to hurt papa even by the mention of Salisbury, so I let him go by. I then called in my brother-in-law, and at once, without an instant's delay, put the question.

He utterly and instantly denied having said any such thing. But afterwards, just in time to prevent a serious fracas between him and Francis, he suddenly burst out laughing violently.

"I have it, and if it isn't one of the best jokes going! Once, when I was chaffing Urquhart about marrying, I told him he 'looked as savage as if he had a wife and six children hidden somewhere on Salisbury Plain.' And I dare say afterwards, I told some fellow at the camp, who told somebody else, and so it got round."

"And that was all?"

"Upon my word of honour, Granton, that was all."

Mr. Charteris said he was exceedingly happy to hear it. They all seemed to consider it a capital joke, and in the midst of their mirth I slipped out.

But, the thing ended, my courage gave way. O the wickedness of this world and of the men in it! Oh ! if there were any human being to speak to, to trust, to lean upon! I laid my head in my hands and cried. If he could know how bitterly I have cried.

New Year's night.

Feeling wakeful, I will just put down the remaining occurrences of this New Year's day.

When I was writing the last line, Lisa knocked at the door.

"Dora, Doctor Urquhart is in the library; make haste, if you care to see him; he says he can only stop half-an-hour."

So, after a minute, I shut and locked my desk. Only half-an-hour!

I have the credit of "flying into a passion," as Francis says, about things that vex and annoy me. Things that wound, that stab to the heart, affect me quite differently. Then, I merely say "yes," or "no," or "of course," and go about quietly, as if nothing were amiss. Probably, did there come any mortal blow, I should be like one of those poor soldiers one hears of, who, being shot, will stand up as if unhurt, or even fight on for a minute or so, then suddenly drop down—dead.

I fastened my neck-ribbon, smoothed my hair, and descended. I knew I should have entered the library all proper, and put out my hand. Ah! he should not—he ought not, that night—this very same right hand.

I mean to say, I should have met Dr. Urquhart exactly as usual, had I not, just in the corridor, entering from the garden, come upon him and Colin Granton in close talk.

"How do you do?" and "It is a very cold morning." Then they passed on. I have since thought that their haste was Colin's doing. He looked confused, as if it were a confidential conversation I had interrupted, which very probably it was. I hope, not the incident of the morning, for it would vex Dr. Urquhart so; and blunt as Colin is, his kind heart teaches him tact, oftentimes.

Dr. Urquhart stayed out his half-hour punctually, and over the luncheon-table there was plenty of general conversation. He also

A Life for a Life

took an opportunity to put to me, in my character of nurse, various questions about papa's health, and desired me, still in the same general half-medical tone,' to be careful of my own, as Treherne Court was a much colder place than Rock-mount, and we were likely to have a severe winter. I said it would not much signify, as we did not purpose remaining more than a week longer; to which he merely answered, "Oh, indeed!"

We had no more conversation, except that on taking leave, having resisted all the Trehernes' entreaties to remain, he wished me "a happy New Year."

"I may not see you again for some time to come; if not, good-bye; good-bye!"

Twice over, good-bye; and that was all.

A happy New Year. So now, the Christmas time is over and gone; and to-morrow, January 2nd, 1857, will be like all other days in all other years. If I ever thought or expected otherwise, I was mistaken.

One thing made me feel deeply and solemnly glad of Dr. Urquhart's visit to-day. It was, that if ever Francis, or any one else, was inclined to give a moment's credence to that atrocious lie, his whole appearance and demeanour were its instantaneous contradiction. Whether Colin had told him anything, I could not discover; he looked grave, and somewhat anxious, but his manner was composed and at ease—the air of a man whose life, if not above sorrow, was wholly above suspicion; whose heart was steadfast and whose conscience free.

"A thoroughly good man, if ever there was one," said papa emphatically, when he had gone away.

"Yes," Augustus answered, looking at Francis and then at me. "As honest and upright a man as God ever made."

Therefore, no matter—even if I was mistaken.

Chapter 20

HIS STORY

I continue these letters, having hitherto been made aware of no reason why they should cease. If that reason comes, they shall cease at once, and for ever; and these now existing be burned immediately, by my own hand, as I did those of my sick friend in the Crimea. Be satisfied of that.

You will learn to-morrow morning, what, had an opportunity offered, I meant to have told you on New Year's Day—my appointment as surgeon to the gaol, where I shall shortly enter upon my duties. The other portion of them, my private practice in the neighbourhood, I mean to commence as soon as ever I can, afterwards.

Thus, you see my "Ishmaelitish wanderings," as you once called them, are ended. I have a fixed position in one place. I begin to look on this broad river with an eye of interest, and am teaching myself to grow familiar with its miles of docks, forests of shipping, and its two busy, ever-growing towns along either shore, even as one accustoms one's self to the natural features of the place, wherever it be, that we call "home."

If not home, this is at least my probable sphere of labour for many years to come: I shall try to take root here, and make the best of everything.

The information that will reach you to-morrow, comes necessarily through Treherne. He will get it at the breakfast-table, pass it on to his wife, who will make her lively comments on it, and then it will be almost sure to go on to you. You will, in degree, understand, what they will not, why I should give up my position as regimental surgeon to establish myself here. For all else, it is of little moment what my friends think, as I am settled in my own mind—strengthened by certain good works of yours, that soft, still, autumn day, with the haze over the moorland and the sun setting in the ripples of the pool.

A Life for a Life

You will have discovered by this time a fact of which, so far as I could judge, you were a week since entirely ignorant—that you have a suitor for your hand. He himself informed me of his intentions with regard to you—asking my advice and good wishes. What could I say?

I will tell you, being unwilling that in the smallest degree a nature so candid and true as yours could suppose me guilty of double-dealing. I said, "that I believed you would make the best of wives to any man you loved, and that I hoped when you did marry, it would be under those circumstances. Whether he himself were that man, it rested with your suitor alone to discover and decide." He confessed honestly that on this point he was as ignorant as myself, but declared that he should "do his best." Which implies that while I have been occupied in this gaol business, he has had daily, hourly access to your sweet company, with every opportunity in his favour—money, youth, consent of friends,—he said you have been his mother's choice for years. With, best of all, an honest heart, which vows that, except a passing "smite" or two, it has been yours since you were children together. That such an honest heart should not have its fair chance with you, God forbid.

Though I will tell you the truth, I did not believe he had any chance. Nothing in you has ever given me the slightest indication of it. Your sudden blush when you met him surprised me, also your exclamation—I was not aware you were in the habit of calling him by his Christian name. But that you love this young man, I do not believe.

Some women can be persuaded into love, but you are not of that sort, so far as I can judge. Time will show. You are entirely and absolutely free.

Pardon me, but after the first surprise of this communication I rejoiced that you were thus free. Even were I other than I am—young, handsome, with a large income and everything favourable, you should still, at this crisis, be left exactly as you are, free to elect your own fate, as every woman ought to do. I may be proud, but were I seeking a wife, the only love that ever would satisfy me would be that which was given spontaneously and unsought:—dependent on nothing I gave, but on what I was. If you choose this suitor, my faith in you will convince me that your feelings were such for him, and I shall be able to say, "Be happy, and God bless you."

A Life for a Life

Thus far, I trust, I have written with the steadiness of one who, in either case, has no right to be even surprised—who has nothing whatever to claim, and who accordingly claims nothing.

Treherne will of course answer—and I shall find his letter at the camp when I return, which will be the day after to-morrow. It may bring me—as, indeed, I have expected day by day, being so much the friend of both parties—definite tidings.

Let me stop writing here. My ghosts of old have been haunting me, every day this week; is it because my good angel is vanishing—vanishing—far away? Let me recall your words, which nothing ever can obliterate from my memory—and which in any case I shall bless you for as long as I live.

"I believe that every sin, however great, being repented of and forsaken, is by God and ought to be by men, altogether forgiven, blotted out and done away."

A truth, which I hope never to forget, but to set forth continually—I shall have plenty of opportunity, as a gaol-surgeon. Ay, I shall probably live and die as a poor gaol-surgeon.

And you?

"The children of Alice call Bartrum father."

This line of Elia's has been running in my head all day. A very quiet, patient, pathetically sentimental line. But Charles Lamb was only a gentle dreamer—or he wrote it when he was old.

Understand, I do *not* believe you love this young man. If you do—marry him! But if, not loving him, you marry him—I had rather you died. Oh, child, child, with your eyes so like my mother and Dallas—I had rather, ten thousand times, that you died.

Chapter 21

HER STORY

Penelope has brought me my desk to pass away the long day during her absence in London—whither she has gone up with Mrs. Granton to buy the first instalment of her wedding-clothes. She looked very sorry that I could not accompany her. She is exceedingly kind—more so than ever in her life before, though I have given her a deal of trouble, and seem to be giving more every day.

I have had "fever-and-agur," as the poor folk hereabouts call it—caught, probably, in those long walks over the moor-lands, which I indulged in after our return from the north—supposing they would do me good. But the illness has done me more; so it comes to the same thing in the end.

I could be quite happy now, I believe, were those about me happy too; and, above all, were Penelope less anxious on my account, so as to have no cloud on her own prospects. She is to be married in April, and they will sail in May; I must contrive to get well long before then, if possible. Francis has been very little down here, being fully occupied in official arrangements; but Penelope only laughs, and says he is better out of the way during this busy time. She is so happy, she can afford to jest. Mrs. Granton takes my place in assisting her, which is good for the dear old lady too.

Poor Mrs. Granton! it cut me to the heart at first to see how puzzled she was at the strange freak which took Colin off to the Mediterranean—only puzzled, never cross—how could she be cross at anything "my Colin" does? he is always right, of course. He was really right this time, though it made her unhappy for awhile; but she would have been more so, had she known all. Now, she only wonders a little; regards me with a sort of half-pitying curiosity; is specially kind to me, brings me every letter of her son's to read—thank Heaven, they are already very cheerful letters—and treats me altogether as if she thought I were breaking my heart for her Colin, and that Colin had not yet discovered what was good for himself concerning me, but would in time. It is of little consequence—so as she is content and discovers nothing.

A Life for a Life

Poor Colin! I can only reward him by loving his old mother for his sake.

After a long pause, writing being somewhat fatiguing, I have thought it best to take this opportunity of setting down a circumstance which befell me since I last wrote in my journal. It was at first not my intention to mention it here at all, but on second thoughts I do so, lest, should anything happen to prevent my destroying this journal during my lifetime, there might be no opportunity, through the omission of it, for any misconstructions as to Colin's conduct or mine. I am weak enough to feel that, not even after I was dead would I like it to be supposed I had given any encouragement to Colin Granton, or cared for him in any other way than as I shall always care for him, and as he well deserves.

It is a most painful thing to confess, and one for which I still take some blame to myself for not having seen and prevented it, but the day before we left Treherne Court, Colin Granton made me an offer of marriage.

When I state that this was unforeseen, I do not mean up to the actual moment of its befalling me. They say women instinctively find out when a man is in love with them, so long as they themselves are indifferent to him; but I did not, probably because my mind was so full of other things. Until the last week of our visit, such a possibility never entered my mind. I mention this, to explain my not having prevented—what every girl ought to prevent if she can—the final declaration, which it must be such a cruel mortification to any man to make, and be denied.

This was how it happened. After the new year came in, our gaieties and late hours, following the cares of papa's illness, were too much for me, or else this fever was coming on. I felt—not ill exactly—but not myself, and Mrs. Granton saw it. She petted me like a mother, and was always telling me to regard her as such, which I innocently promised; when she would hook at me earnestly, and say, often with tears in her eyes, that "she was sure I would never be unkind to the old lady," and that "she should get the best of daughters."

Yet still I had not the least suspicion. No, nor when Colin was continually about me, watching me, waiting upon me, sometimes almost irritating me, and then again touching me inexpressibly with his unfailing kindness, did I suspect anything for long. At last, I did.

There is no need to relate what trifles first opened my eyes, nor the wretchedness of the two intermediate days between my dreading and being sure of it.

I suppose it must always be a very terrible thing to any woman, the discovery that some one whom she likes heartily, and only likes, loves her. Of course, in every possible way that it could be done, without wounding him, or betraying him to other people, I avoided Colin; but it was dreadful, notwithstanding. The sight of his honest, happy face, was sadder to me than the saddest face in the world, yet when it clouded over, my heart ached. And then his mother, with her caresses and praises, made me feel the most conscience-stricken wretch that ever breathed.

Thus things went on. I shall set down no incidents, though bitterly I remember them all. At last it came to an end. I shall relate this, that there may be no doubt left as to what passed between us—Colin and me.

We were standing in the corridor, his mother having just quitted us, to settle with papa about to-morrow's journey, desiring us to wait for her till she returned. Colin suggested waiting in the library, but I preferred the corridor, where continually there were persons coming and going. I thought if I never gave him any opportunity of saying anything, he might understand what I so earnestly wished to save him from being plainly told. So we stood looking out of the hall-windows. I can see the view this minute, the large, level circle of snow, with the sundial in the centre, and beyond, the great avenue-gates, with the avenue itself, two black lines and a white one between, lessening and fading away in the mist of a January afternoon.

"How soon the day is closing in—our last day here!"

I said this without thinking. The next minute I would have given anything to recall it. For Colin answered something—I hardly remember what—but the manner, the tone, there was no mistaking. I suppose the saying is true;—no woman with a heart in her bosom can mistake for long together when a man really loves her. I felt it was coming; perhaps better let it come, and then it would be over, and there would be an end of it.

So I just stood still, with my eyes on the snow, and my hands locked tight together, for Colin had tried to take one of them. He was trembling much, and so I am sure was I. He had said only half-a-dozen words, when I begged him to stop, "unless he wished to break my heart." And seeing him turn pale as death, and lean against the wall, I did indeed feel as if my heart were breaking.

For a moment the thought came—let me confess it—how cruel things were, as they were; how happy had they been otherwise, and I could have made him happy—this good honest soul that loved me, his dear old mother, and every one belonging to us; also, whether anyhow I ought not to try.—No: that was not possible. I can understand women's renouncing hove, or dying of it, or learning to live without it: but marrying without it, either for "spite," or for money, necessity, pity, or persuasion, is to me utterly incomprehensible. Nay, the self-devoted heroines of the *Emilia Wyndham* school seem creatures so weak that if not compassionating, one would simply despise them. Out of duty or gratitude, it might be possible to work, live, or even die for a person, but *never* to marry him.

So, when Colin, recovering, tried to take my hand again, I shrunk into myself, and became my right self at once. For which, lest tried overmuch, and liking him as I do, some chance emotion might have led him momentarily astray, I most earnestly thank God.

And then I had to look him in the eyes and tell him the plain truth.

"Colin, I do not love you; I never shall be able to love you, and so it would be wicked even to think of this. You must give it all up, and let us go back to our old ways."

"Dora?"

"Yes, indeed, it is true. You *must* believe it."

For a long time the only words he said were—

"I knew it—knew I was not half good enough for you."

A Life for a Life

It being nearly dark, no one came by until we heard his mother's step, and her cheerful "Where's my Colin?"—loud enough as if she meant—poor dear!—in fond precaution, to give us notice of her coming. Instinctively we hid from her in the library. She looked in at the door, but did not, or would not, see us, and went trotting away down the corridor. Oh, what a wretch I felt!

When she had departed, I was stealing away, but Colin caught my dress.

"One word—just one. Did you never care for me—never the least bit in all the world?"

"Yes," I answered sorrowfully, feeling no more ashamed of telling this, or anything, than one would be in a dying confession. "Yes, Colin, I was once very fond of you, when I was about eleven years old."

"And never afterwards"

"No—as my saying this proves. Never afterwards, and never should, by any possible chance—in the sort of way you wish."

"That is enough—I understand," he said, with a sort of mournful dignity quite new in Colin Granton. "I was only good enough for you when you were a child, and we are not children now. We never shall be children any more."

"No—ah, no." And the thought of that old time came upon me like a flood—the winter games at the Cedars—the blackberrying and bilberrying upon the sunshiny summer moors—the grief when he went to school, and the joy when he came home again—the love that was so innocent, so painless. And he had loved me ever since—me, not Lisabel; though for a time he tried flirting with her, he owned, just to find out whether or not I cared for him. I hid my face and sobbed.

And then, I had need to recover self-control; it is such an awful thing to see a man weep.

I stood by Colin till we were both calmer, trusting all was safe over, and that without the one question I most dreaded. But it came.

"Dora, *why* do you not care for me? Is there—tell me or not, as you like—is there any one else?"

Conscience! let me be as just to myself as I would be to another in my place.

Once, I wrote that I had been "mistaken," as I have been in some things, but not in all. Could I have honestly said so, taking all blame on myself and freeing all others from everything save mere kindness to a poor girl who was foolish enough, but very honest and true, and wholly ignorant of where things were tending, till too late; if I could have done this, I believe I should then and there have confessed the whole truth to Colin Granton. But as things are, it was impossible.

Therefore I said, and started to notice how literally my words imitated other words, the secondary meaning of which had struck me differently from their first, "that it was not likely I should ever be married."

Colin asked no more.

The dressing-bell rang, and I again tried to get away; but he whispered "Stop one minute—my mother—what am I to tell my mother?"

"How much does she know?"

"Nothing. But she guesses, poor dear—and I was always going to tell her outright; but somehow I couldn't. But now, as you will tell your father and sisters, and—"

"No, Colin; I shall not tell any human being."

And I was thankful that if I could not return his love I could at least save his pride, and his mother's tender heart.

"Tell her nothing; go home and be brave for her sake. Let her see that her boy is not unhappy. Let her feel that not a girl in the land is more precious to him than his old mother."

"That's true!" he said, with a hard breath. "I won't break her dear old heart. I'll hold my tongue and bear it. I will, Dora."

"I know you will," and I held out my hand. Surely, that clasp wronged no one; for it was hardly like a lover's—only my old playmate—Colin, my dear.

We then agreed, that if his mother asked any questions, he should simply tell her that he had changed his mind concerning me, and that otherwise the matter should be buried with him and me, now and always. "Except only"—and he seemed about to tell me something, but stopped, saying it was of no matter—it was all as one now. I asked no further, only desiring to get away.

Then, with another long, sorrowful, silent clasp of the hand, Colin and I parted.

A long parting it has proved; for he kept aloof from me at dinner, and instead of travelling home with us, went round another way. A week or two afterwards, he called at Rockmount, to tell us he had bought a yacht, and was going a cruise to the Mediterranean. I, being out on the moor, did not see him. He left next day, telling his mother to "wish good-bye for him to his playmate Dora."

Poor Colin! God bless him and keep him safe, so that I may feel I only wounded his heart, but did his soul no harm. I meant it not! And when he comes back to his old mother, perhaps bringing her home a fair daughter-in-law, as no doubt he will one day, I shall be happy enough to smile at all the misery of that time at Treherne Court and afterwards, and at all the tender compassion which has been wasted upon me by good Mrs. Granton, because "my Colin" changed his mind, and went away without marrying his playmate Dora. Only "Dora." I am glad he never called me my full name. There is but one person who ever called me "Theodora."

I read in a book, the other day, this extract:—

"People do not sufficiently remember that in every relation of life as in the closest one of all, they ought to take one another 'for better, for worse.' That, granting the tie of friendship, gratitude, or esteem be strong enough to have existed at all, it ought, either actively or passively, to exist for ever. And seeing we can, at best, know our

A Life for a Life

neighbour, companion, or friend, as little as, alas! we often find he knoweth of us, it behoveth us to treat him with the most patient fidelity, the tenderest forbearance; granting, unto all his words and actions that we do not understand, the utmost limit of faith that common-sense and Christian justice will allow. Nay, these failing, is there not still left Christian charity? which, being past 'believing' and 'hoping,' still 'endureth all things'?"

I hear the carriage-wheels.

They will not let me go downstairs at all to-day.

I have been lying looking at the fire alone, for Francis returned with Mrs. Granton and Penelope yesterday. They have gone a long walk across the moors. I watched them, strolling arm-in-arm—Darby and Joan fashion—till their two small black figures vanished over the hilly road, which always used to remind me of the Sleeping Beauty and her prince.

> "And on her lover's arm she leant,
> And round her waist she felt it fold,
> And far across the hills they went,
> To that new world which is the old."

They must be very happy—Francis and Penelope.

I wonder how soon I shall be well? This fever and ague lasts sometimes for months; I remember Dr. Urquhart's once saying so.

Here, following my plan of keeping this journal accurate and complete, I ought to put down something which occurred yesterday, and which concerns Dr. Urquhart.

Driving through the camp, my sister Penelope saw him, and papa stopped the carriage and waited for him. He could not pass them by, as Francis declared he seemed intending to do, with a mere salutation, but stayed and spoke. The conversation was not told me, for, on mentioning it, a few sharp words took place between papa and Penelope. She protested against his taking so much trouble in cultivating the society of a man who, she said, was evidently, out of his own profession, "a perfect boor."

A Life for a Life

Papa replied more warmly than I had at all expected.

"You will oblige me, Penelope, by allowing your father to have a will of his own in this as in most other matters, even if you do suppose him capable of choosing for his associate and friend 'a perfect boor.' And were that accusation as true as it is false, I trust I should never forget that a debt of gratitude, such as I owe to Doctor Urquhart, once incurred, is seldom to be repaid, and never to be obliterated."

So the discourse ended. Penelope left my room, and papa took a chair by me. I tried to talk to him, but we soon both fell into silence. Once or twice, when I thought he was reading the newspaper, I found him looking at me, but he made no remark.

Papa and I have had much less of each other's company lately, though we have never lost the pleasant footing on which we learned to be during his illness. I wonder if, now that he is quite well, he has any recollection of the long, long hours, nights and days, with only daylight or candle-light to mark the difference between them, when he lay motionless in his bed, watched and nursed by us two?

I was thinking thus, when he asked a question, the abrupt coincidence of which with my secret thoughts startled me out of any answer than a simple "No, papa."

"My dear, have you ever had any letter from Doctor Urquhart?"

How could he possibly imagine such a thing? Could Mrs. Granton, or Penelope, who is quick-sighted in some things, have led papa to think—to suppose—something, the bare idea of which turned me sick with fear? Me, they might blame as they hiked; it would not harm me; but a word, a suggestion of blame to any other person, would drive me wild, furious. So I summoned up all my strength.

"You know, papa, Doctor Urquhart could have nothing to write to me about. Any message for me he could have put in a letter to you."

"Certainly. I merely inquired, considering him so much a friend of the family, and aware that you had seen more of him, and liked him better than your sisters did. But if he had written to you, you would, of course, have told me?"

A Life for a Life

"Of course, papa."

I did not say another word than this.

Papa went on, smoothing his newspaper, and looking direct at the fire:—

"I have not been altogether satisfied with Doctor Urquhart of late, much as I esteem him. He does not appear sufficiently to value what—I may say it without conceit—from an old man to a younger one, is always of some worth. Yesterday, when I invited him here, he declined again, and a little too—too decidedly."

Seeing an answer waited for, I said, "Yes, papa."

"I am sorry, having such great respect for him, and such pleasure in his society." Papa paused. "When a man desires to win or retain his footing in a family, he usually takes some pains to secure it. If he does not, the natural conclusion is that he does *not* desire it." Another pause. "Whenever Doctor Urquhart chooses to come here, he will always be welcome—most welcome; but I cannot again invite him to Rockmount."

"No, papa."

This was all. He then took up his *Times*, and read it through: I lay quiet; quiet all the evening—quiet until I went to bed.

To-day I find in the same old book before quoted:—

"The true theory of friendship is this: Once a friend, always a friend. But, answerest thou, doth not every day's practice give the lie to that doctrine? Many, if not most friendships, be like a glove, that however well fitting at first, doth by constant use wax loose and ungainly, if it doth not quite wear out. And others, not put off and on, but chose to a man as his own skin and flesh, are yet liable to become diseased: he may have to lose them, and live on without them, as after the lopping off of a limb, or the blinding of an eye. And likewise, there be friendships which a man groweth out of, naturally and blamelessly, even as out of his child-clothes: the which, though no longer suitable for his needs, he keepeth religiously, Un-forgotten and undestroyed, and often visiteth with a kindly tenderness, though he knoweth they can cover and warm him no more. All these instances do clearly prove that a friend is not always a friend."

"'Yea,' quoth Fidelis, 'he is. Not in himself, may be, but unto thee. The future and the present are thine and his; the past is beyond ye both; an unalienable possession, a bond never disannulled. Ye may let it slip, of natural disuse, throw it aside as worn-out and foul; cut it off, cover it up, and bury it; but it hath been, and therefore in one sense for ever must be. Transmutation is the law of all mortal things; but so far as we know, there is not, and will not be, until the great day of the second death—in the whole universe, any such thing as annihilation.'

"And so take heed. Deceive not thyself, saying that, because a thing is not, it never was. Respect thyself—thine old self, as well as thy new. Be faithful to thyself, and to all that ever was thine. Thy friend is always thy friend. Not to have or to hold, to love or rejoice in, but *to remember*.

"And if it befall thee, as befalleth most, that in course of time nothing will remain for thee, except to remember, be not afraid! Hold fast that which was thine—it is thine for ever. Deny it not—despise it not; respect its secrets—be silent over its wrongs. And, so kept, it shall never lie hike a dead thing in thy heart, corrupting and breeding corruption there, as dead things do. Bury it, and go thy way. It may chance that, one day, long hence, thou shalt come suddenly upon the grave of it—and behold! it is dewy-green!"

Chapter 22

HIS STORY

That face,—that poor little white, patient face! How she is changed

I wish to write down how it was I chanced to see you, though chance is hardly the right word. I *would* have seen you, even if I had waited all day and all night, like a thief, outside your garden-wall. If I could have seen you without your seeing me (as actually occurred) all the better; but in any case I would have seen you. So far as relates to you, the will of Heaven only is strong enough to alter this resolute "I will," of mine.

You had no idea I was so near you. You did not seem to be thinking of anybody or anything in particular, but came to your bedroom window, and stood there a minute, looking wistfully across the moorlands; the still, absorbed, hopeless look of a person who has had some heavy loss, or resigned something very dear to the heart— Dallas's look almost, as I remember it when he quietly told me that, instead of preaching his first sermon, he must go away at once abroad, or give up hope of ever living to preach at all. Child, if you should slip away and leave me as Dallas did!

You must have had a severe illness. And yet, if so, surely I should have heard of it, or your father and sister would have mentioned it when I met them. But no mere bodily illness could account for that expression—it is of the mind. You have been suffering mentally also. Can it be out of pity for that young man, who, I hear, has left England? Why, it is not difficult to guess, nor did I ever expect otherwise, knowing him and you. Poor fellow! But he was honest, and rich, and your friends would approve him. Have they been urging you on his behalf? Have you had family feuds to withstand? Is it this which has made you waste away, and turn so still and pale? You would just do that; you would never yield, but only break your heart quietly, and say nothing about it. I know you; nobody knows you half so well. Coward that I was, not to have taken care of you. I might have done it easily, as the friend of the family—the doctor—a grim fellow of forty. There was no fear for anybody save myself. Yes, I have been a coward. My child,—my gentle, tender, childlike child—they have been breaking your heart, and I have held aloof and let them do it.

You had a cough in autumn, and your eyes are apt to get that bright, limpid look, dilated pupils, with a dark shade under the lower eyelid, which is supposed to indicate the consumptive tendency. Myself, I differ; believing it in you, as in many others, merely to indicate that which for want of a clearer term we call the nervous temperament; exquisitely sensitive, and liable to slight derangements, yet healthy and strong at the core. I see no trace of disease in you, no reason why, even fragile as you are, you should not live to be an old woman. That is, if treated as you ought to be, judiciously, tenderly; watched over, cared for, given a peaceful, cheerful life with plenty of love in it. Plenty of anxieties also, maybe; no one could shield you from these—but the love would counterbalance all, and you would feel that—you should feel it—I could make you feel it.

I must find out what has ailed you and who has been attending you. Dr. Black, probably. You disliked him, had almost a terror of him, I know. Yet they would of course have placed you in his hands, my little tender thing, my dove, my flower. It makes me mad.

Forgive! Forgive also that word "my," though in one sense you are even now mine. No one understands you as I do, or loves you. Not selfishly either; most solemnly do I here protest that if I could find myself now your father or your brother, through the natural tie of blood, which for ever prevents any other, I would rejoice in it, rather than part with you, rather than that you should slip away like Dallas, and bless my eyes no more.

You see now what you are to me, that a mere apparition of your little face at a window could move me thus.

I must go to work now. To-morrow I shall have found out all about you.

I wish you to know how the discovery was made; since, be assured, I have ever guarded against the remotest possibility of friends or strangers finding out my secret, or gossiping neighbours coupling my name with yours.

Therefore, instead of going to Mrs. Granton, I paid a visit to Widow Cartwright, whom I had news to give concerning her daughter. And here, lest at any time evil or careless tongues should bring you a garbled statement, let me just name all I have had to do with this matter of Lydia Cartwright, which your sister once spoke of as my "impertinent interference."

Widow Cartwright, in her trouble, begged me to try and learn something about her child, who had disappeared from the family where, by Miss Johnston's recommendation, she went as parlour-maid, and in spite of various inquiries set on foot by Mr. Charteris and others, had, to your sister's great regret, never more been heard of. She was believed not to be dead, for she once or twice sent money to her mother; and lately she was seen in a private box at the theatre by a person named Turton, who recognised her, having often dined at the house where she once was servant. This information was what I had to give to her mother.

I would not have mentioned such a story to you, but that long ere you read these letters, if ever you do read them, you will have learned that such sad and terrible facts do exist, and that even the purest woman dare not ignore them. Also, who knows but, in the infinite chances of life, you may have opportunities of doing in other cases what I would fain have done, and one day entreated your sister to do—to use every effort for the redemption of this girl, who, from all I hear, must have been unusually pretty, affectionate, and simpleminded?

Her poor old mother being a little comforted, I learned tidings of you. Three weeks of fever and ague, or something like it, nobody quite knew what; they, your family, had no notion till lately that there was anything ailing you.

No—they never would. They would let you go on in your silent, patient way, sick or well, happy or sorry, till you suddenly sunk, and then they would turn round astonished:—"Really, why did she not say she was ill? Who would have guessed there was anything the matter with her?"

And I—I who knew every change in your little face, every mood in that strange, quaint, variable spirit—I have let you slip, and been afraid to take care of you. Coward!

A Life for a Life

I proceeded at once to Rockmount, but learned from the gardener that your father and sister were out, and "Miss Dora was ill in her room." So I waited, hung about the road for an hour or more, till at last it struck me to seek for information at the Cedars.

Mrs. Granton was glad to see me. She told me all about her son's departure—gentle heart! you have kept his secret—and, asking if I had seen you lately, poured out in a stream all her anxieties concerning you.

So, something must be done for you—something sudden and determined. They may all think what they like—act as they choose—and so shall I.

I advised Mrs. Granton to fetch you at once to the Cedars, by persuasion if she could; if not, by compulsion—bringing you there as if for a drive and keeping you. She has a will, that good old lady, when she sees fit to use it—and she has considerable influence with your father. She said she thought she could persuade him to let her have you, and nurse you.

"And if the poor child herself is obstinate—she has been rather variable of temper lately—I may say that you ordered me to bring her here? She has a great respect for your opinion. I may tell her I acted by Doctor Urquhart's desire?"

I considered a moment, and then said she might.

We arranged everything as seemed best for your removal—a serious undertaking for an invalid. You an invalid, **my** bright-eyed, light-footed, moorland girl!

I do not think Mrs. Granton had a shadow of suspicion. She thanked me continually, in her warm-hearted fashion, for my "great kindness." Kindness! She also begged me to call immediately—as *her* friend, lest I might have any professional scruples of etiquette about interfering with Dr. Black.

Scruples! I cast them all to the winds. Come what will, I must see you, must assure myself that there is no danger, that all is done for you which gives you a fair chance of recovery.

A Life for a Life

If not—if with the clear vision that I know I can use on occasion, I see you fading from me—I shall snatch at you. I will have you—be it only for a day or an hour, I will have you, I say,—on my heart, in my arms. My love, my darling, my wife that ought to have been—you could not die out of my arms. I will make you live—I will make you love me. I will have you for my wife yet. I will—God's will be done!

Chapter 23

HER STORY

I am at home again. I sit by my bedroom fire in a new easy-chair. Oh, such care am I taken of now! I cast my eyes over the white waves of moorland—

"Moor and pleasaunce looking equal in one snow."

Let me see, how does that verse begin?

> "God be with thee, my beloved, God be with thee,
> As alone thou goest forth
> With thy face unto the North,
> Moor and pleasaunce looking equal in one snow:
> While I follow, vainly follow
> With the farewell and the hollow,
> But cannot reach thee so."

Ah, but I can—I can! Can reach anywhere: to the north or the south, over the land or across the sea, to the world's end. Yea, beyond there if need be; even into the other unknown world.

Since I last wrote here, in this room, things have befallen me, sudden and strange. And yet so natural do they seem that I almost forget I was ever otherwise than I am now. I, Theodora Johnston, the same, yet not the same. I, just as I was, to be thought worthy of being— what I am, and what I hope some one day to be—God willing. My heart is full—how shall I write about these things—which never could be spoken about, which only to think of makes me feel as if I could but lay my head down in a wonder-stricken silence, that all should thus have happened unto me, this unworthy me.

It is not likely I shall keep this journal much longer—but, until closing it finally, it shall go on as usual. Perhaps it may be pleasant to read over some day when I am old—when *we* are old.

One morning, I forget how long after the last date here, Mrs. Granton surprised me and everybody by insisting that the only thing for me was change of air, and that I should go back at once with her to be nursed at the Cedars. There was an invalid-carriage at the gate, with cushions, mats, and furs; there was papa waiting to help me downstairs, and Penelope with my trunk packed—in short, I was taken by storm, and had only to submit. They all said it was the surest way of recovering, and must be tried.

Now, I wished to get well, and fast, too; it was necessary I should, for several reasons.

First, there was Penelope's marriage, with the after responsibility of my being the only daughter now left to keep the house and take care of papa.

Secondly, Lisabel wrote that, before autumn, she should want me for a new duty and new tie; which, though we never spoke of it to one another, we all thought of with softened hearts; even papa, who, Penelope told me she had seen brushing the dust off our old rocking-horse in an absent sort of way, and stopping in his walk to watch Thomas, the gardener, toss his grandson. Poor dear papa!

I had a third reason. Sometimes I feared, by words Penelope dropped, that she and my father had laid their heads together concerning me and my weak health, and imagined—things which were not true. No; I repeat they were not true. I was ill of fever and ague, that was all; I should have recovered in time. If I were not quite happy, I should have recovered from that also, in time. I should not have broken my heart. No one ought who has still another good heart to believe in; no one need, who has neither done wrong nor been wronged. So, it seemed necessary, or I fancied it so, thinking over all things during the long wakeful nights, that, not for my own sake alone, I should rouse myself, and try to get well as fast as possible.

Therefore, I made no objections to what, on some accounts, was to me an excessively painful thing—a visit to the Cedars.

Pain or no pain, it was to be, and it was done. I lay in a dream of exhaustion that felt like peace, in the little sitting-room, which looked on the familiar view—the lawn, the sundial, the boundary of evergreen bushes, and, farther off, the long, narrow valley, belted by fir-topped hills, standing out sharp against the western sky.

Mrs. Granton bustled in and out, and did everything for me as tenderly as if she had been my mother.

When we are sick and weak, to find comfort; when we are sore at heart, to be surrounded by love; when, at five-and-twenty, the world looks blank and dreary, to see it looking bright and sunshiny at sixty—this does one good. If I said I loved Mrs. Granton, it but weakly expressed what I owed and now owe her—more than she is ever likely to know

I had been a day and a night at the Cedars without seeing any one, except the dear old lady, who watched me incessantly, and administered perpetual doses of "kitchen physic," promising me faithfully that if I continued improving, the odious face of Dr. Black should never cross the threshold of the Cedars.

"But for all that, it would be more satisfactory to me if you would consent to see a medical friend of mine, my dear."

Sickness sharpens our senses, making nothing seem sudden or unnatural. I knew as well as if she had told me who it was she wanted me to see—who it was even now at the parlour-door.

Dr. Urquhart came in, and sat down beside my sofa. I do not remember anything that was said or done by any of us, except that I felt him sitting there, and heard him in his familiar voice talking to Mrs. Granton, about the pleasant view from this low window, and the sunshiny morning, and the blackbird that was solemnly hopping about under the sundial.

I will not deny it, why should I? The mere tone of his voice—the mere smile of his eyes, filled my whole soul with peace. I neither knew how he had come, nor why. I did not want to know; I only knew he was there; and in his presence I was like a child who has been very forlorn, and is now taken care of; very hungry and is satisfied.

Some one calling Mrs. Granton out of the room, he suddenly turned and asked me, "how long I had been ill?"

I answered briefly; then said, in reply to further questions, that I believed it was fever and ague, caught in the moorland cottages, but that I was fast recovering—indeed, I was almost well again now.

"Are you? Give me your hand." He felt my pulse, counting it by his watch; it did not beat much like a convalescent's then, I know. "I see Mrs. Granton in the garden—I must have a little talk with her about you."

He went out of the room abruptly, and soon after I saw them walking together, up and down the terrace. Dr. Urquhart only came to me again to bid me good-bye.

But after that, we saw him every day for a week.

He used to appear at uncertain hours, sometimes forenoon, sometimes evening; but faithfully, if ever so late, he came. I had not been aware he was thus intimate at the Cedars, and one day when Mrs. Granton was speaking about him, I happened to say so.

She smiled.

"Yes, certainly; his coming here daily is a new thing; though I was always glad to see him, he was so kind to my Colin. But, in truth, my dear, if I must let out the secret, he now comes to see *you*."

"Me!" I was glad of the dim light we sat in, and horribly ashamed of myself when the old lady continued, matter-of-fact and grave.

"Yes, you, by my special desire. Though he willingly consented to attend you; he takes a most kindly interest in you. He was afraid of your being left to Doctor Black, whom in his heart I believe he considers an old humbug; so he planned your being brought here, to be petted and taken care of. And I am sure he himself has taken care of you in every possible way that could be done without your finding it out. You are not offended, my dear?"

"No."

"I can't think how we shall manage about his fees; still it would have been wrong to have refused his kindness—so well meant and so delicately offered. I am sure he has the gentlest ways, and the tenderest heart of any man I ever knew. Don't you think so?"

"Yes."

But, for all that, after the first week, I did not progress so fast as these two expected—also papa and Penelope, who came over to see me, and seemed equally satisfied with Dr. Urquhart's "kindness." Perhaps this very "kindness," as I, like the rest, now believed it, made things a little more trying for me. Or else the disease—the fever and ague—had taken firmer hold on me than anybody knew. Some days I felt as if health were a long way off—in fact, not visible at all in this mortal life, and the possibility seemed to me sometimes easy to bear, sometimes hard. I had many changes of mood and temper, very sore to struggle against—for all of which I now humbly crave forgiveness of my dear and kind friends, who were so patient with me, and of Him, the most merciful of all.

Dr. Urquhart came daily, as I have said. We had often very long talks together, sometimes with Mrs. Granton, some-times alone. He told me of all his doings and plans, and gradually brought me out of the narrow sick-room world into which I was falling, towards the current of outward life—his own active life, with its large aims, duties, and cares. The interest of it roused me; the power and beauty of it strengthened me. All the dreams of my youth, together with one I had dreamed that evening by the moorland pool, came back again. I sometimes longed for life, that I might live as he did; in any manner, anywhere, at any sacrifice, so that it was a life in some way resembling, and not unworthy of his own. This sort of life—equally solitary, equally painful, devoted more to duty than to joy, was—heaven knows—all I then thought possible. And I still think, with it, and with my thorough reverence and trust in him, together with what I now felt sure of—his sole, special, unfailing affection for me, I could have been content all my days.

My spirit was brave enough, but sometimes my heart was weak. When one has been accustomed to rest on any other—to find each day the tie become more familiar, more necessary, belonging to daily life and daily want; to feel the house empty, as it were, till there comes the ring at the door or the step in the ball, and to be aware that all this cannot last, that it must come to an end, and one must go back to the old, old life—shut up in oneself, with no arm to lean on,

A Life for a Life

no smile to cheer and guide, no voice to say, "You are right, do it," or "There I think you are wrong," then, one grows frightened.

When I thought of his going to Liverpool, my courage broke down. I would hide my head in my pillow of nights, and say to myself, "Theodora, you are a coward; will not the good God make you strong enough by yourself, even for any sort of life He requires of you? Leave all in His hands." So I tried to do: believing that from any feeling that was holy and innocent He would not allow me to suffer more than I could bear, or more than is good for all of us to suffer at times.

(I did not mean to write thus; I meant only to tell my outward story; but such as is written let it be. I am not ashamed of it.)

Thus things went on, and I did not get stronger.

One Saturday afternoon Mrs. Granton went a long drive, to see some family in whom Dr. Urquhart had made her take an interest, if, indeed, there was need to do more than mention any one's being in trouble, in the dear woman's hearing, in order to unseal a whole torrent of benevolence. The people's name was Ansdell; they were strangers, belonging to the camp; there was a daughter dying of consumption.

It was one of my dark days: and I lay, thinking bow much useless sentiment is wasted upon the young who die; how much vain regret at their being so early removed from the enjoyments they share, and the good they are doing, when they often do no good and have little joy to lose. Take, for instance, Mrs. Granton and me: if Death hesitated between us, I know which he had better choose: the one who had least pleasure in living, and who would be easiest spared — who, from either error or fate, or some inherent faults, which, become almost equal to a fate, had lived twenty-five years without being of the smallest use to anybody; and to whom the best that could happen would apparently be to be caught up in the arms of the Great Reaper, and sown afresh in a new world, to begin again.

Let me confess all this—because it explains the mood which I afterwards betrayed; and because it caused me to find out that I was not the only person into whose mind such wild and wicked thoughts have come, to be reasoned down—battled down—prayed down.

A Life for a Life

I was in the large drawing-room, supposed to be lying peacefully on the sofa—but in reality, cowering down all in a heap, within the small circle of the fire-light. Beyond, it was very dark—so dark that the shadows would have frightened me, were there not too many spectres close at hand: sad, or evil spirits,—such as come about us all in our dark days. Still, the silence was so ghostly, that when the door opened, I slightly screamed.

"Do not be afraid. It is only I."

I was shaken hands with; and I apologised for having been so startled. Dr. Urquhart said it was he who ought to apologise, but he had knocked and I did not answer, and he had walked in, being "anxious." Then he spoke about other things, and I soon became myself, and sat listening, with my eyes closed, till, suddenly seeing him, I saw him looking at me.

"You have been worse to-day."

"It was my bad day."

"I wish I could see you really better."

"Thank you."

My eyes closed again—all things seemed dim and far off, as if my life were floating away, and I had no care to seize hold of it—easier to let it go.

"My patient does not do me much credit. When do you intend to honour me by recovering, Miss Theodora?"

"I don't know;—it does not much matter." It wearied me to answer even him.

He rose, walked up and down the room several times, and returned to his place.

"Miss Theodora, I wish to say a few words to you seriously, about your health. I should like to see you better—very much better than now—before I go away."

"Possibly you may."

"In any case, you will have to take great care—to be taken great care of—for months to come. Your health is very delicate. Are you aware of that?"

"I suppose so."

"You must listen—"

The tone roused me.

"If you please, you *must* listen, to what I am saying. It is useless telling any one else, but I tell *you,* that if you do not take care of yourself you will die."

I looked up. No one but he would have said such a thing to me—if he said it, it must be true.

"Do you know that it is wrong to die—to let yourself carelessly slip out of God's world, in which He put you to do good work there?"

"I have no work to do."

"None of us can say that. You ought not—you shall not. I will not allow it."

His words struck me. There was truth in them—the truth, the faith of my first youth, though both had faded in after years—till I knew him. And this was why I clung to this friend of mine, because amidst all the shams and falsenesses around me, and even in myself—in him I ever found, clearly acknowledged, and bravely outspoken—the *truth.* Why should he not help me now?

Humbly I asked him, "if he were angry with me?"

"Not angry, but grieved; you little know how deeply."

Was it for my dying, or my wickedly wishing to die? I knew not; but that he was strongly affected, more even than he liked me to see, I did see, and it lifted the stone from my heart.

"I know I have been very wicked. If any one would thoroughly scold me—if I could only tell anybody—"

"Why cannot you tell me?"

So I told him, as far as I could, all the dark thoughts that had been troubling me this day; I laid upon him all my burthens; I confessed to him all my sins; and when I ended, not without agitation, for I had never spoken so plainly of myself to any creature before, Dr. Urquhart talked to me long and gently upon the things wherein he considered me wrong in myself and in my home; and of other things where he thought I was only "foolish," or "mistaken." Then he spoke of the manifold duties I had in life; of the glory and beauty of living; of the peace attainable, even in this world, by a life which, if ever so sad and difficult, has done the best it could with the materials granted to it—has walked, so far as it could see, in its appointed course, and left the rewarding and the brightening of it solely in the hands of Him who gave it, who never gives anything in vain.

This was his "sermon"—as, smiling, I afterwards called it, though all was said very simply, and as tenderly as if he had been talking with a child. At the end of it, I looked at him by a sudden blaze of the fire; and it seemed as if mortal man as he was, with faults enough doubtless—and some of them I already knew, though there is no necessity to publish them here—I "saw his face as it had been the face of an angel." And I thanked God, who sent him to me—who sent us each to one another.

For what should Dr. Urquhart reply when I asked him how he came to learn all these good things? but—also smiling—

"Some of them I learned from you."

"Me?" I said, in amazement.

"Yes; perhaps I may tell you how it was some day, but not now." He spoke hurriedly; and immediately began talking about other things; informing me,—as he had now got a habit of doing,—exactly how his affairs stood. Now, they were nearly arranged; and it became needful he should leave the camp, and begin his new duties by a certain day.

A Life for a Life

After a little more talk, he fixed—or rather, we fixed, for he asked me to decide—that day; briefly, as if it had been like any other day in the year; and quietly as if it had not involved the total ending for the present, with an indefinite future, of all this—what shall I call it?—between him and me, which, to one, at least, had become as natural and necessary as daily bread.

Thinking now of that two or three minutes of silence which followed—I could be very sorry for myself—far more so than then; for then I hardly felt it at all.

Dr. Urquhart rose, and said he must go—he could not wait longer for Mrs. Granton.

"Thursday week is the day then," he added, "after which I shall not see you again for many months."

"I suppose not."

"I cannot write to you. I wish I could; but such a correspondence would not be possible, would not be right."

I think I answered mechanically, "No."

I was standing by the mantelpiece, steadying myself with one hand, the other hanging down. Dr. Urquhart touched it for a second.

"It is the very thinnest hand I ever saw!—You will remember," he then said, "in case this should be our last chance of talking together—you will remember all we have been saying? You will do all you can to recover perfect health, so as to be happy and useful? You will never think despondingly of your life; there is many a life much harder than yours; you will have patience, and faith, and hope, as a girl ought to have, who is so precious to—many! Will you promise?"

"I will."

"Good-bye, then."

"Good-bye."

Whether he took my hands, or I gave them, I do not know; but I felt them held tight against his breast, and him looking at me as if he could not part with me, or as if, before we parted, he was compelled to tell me something. But when I looked up at him we seemed of a sudden to understand everything, without need of telling. He only said four words,—"Is this my wife?" And I said "Yes."

Then—he kissed me.

Once, I used to like reading and hearing all about love and lovers, what they said and how they looked, and how happy they were in one another. Now, it seems as if these things ought never to be read or told by any mortal tongue or pen.

When Max went away, I sat where I was, almost without stirring, for a whole hour; until Mrs. Granton came in and gave me the history of her drive, and all about Lucy Ansdell, who had died that afternoon. Poor girl—poor girl.

A Life for a Life

Chapter 24

HER STORY

Here, between the locked leaves of my journal, I keep the first letter I ever had from Max.

It came early in the morning, the morning after that evening which will always seem to us two, I think, something like what we read of, that "the evening and the morning were the first day." It was indeed like the first day of a new world.

When the letter arrived, I was still fast asleep, for I had not gone and lain awake all night, which, under the circumstances (as I told Max), it was a young lady's duty to have done: I only laid my head down with a feeling of ineffable rest—rest in Heaven's kindness, which had brought all things to this end—and rest in his love, from which nothing could ever thrust me, and in the thought of which I went to sleep, as safe as a tired child; knowing I should be safe for all my life long, with him—my Max—my husband.

"Lover" was a word that did not seem to suit him—grave as he was, and so much older than I; I never expected from him anything like the behaviour of a lover—indeed, should hardly like to see him in that character; it would not look natural. But from the hour he said, "Is this my wife?" I have ever and only thought of him as "my husband."

My dear Max! Here is his letter—which lay before my eyes in the dim dawn; it did not come by post—he must have left it himself: and the maid brought it in; no doubt thinking it a professional epistle. And I take great credit to myself for the composed, matter-of-fact way in which I said "it was all right, and there was no answer," put down my letter, and made believe to go to sleep again.

Let me laugh—it is not wrong; and I laugh still as much as ever I can; it is good for me and good for Max. He says scarcely anything in the world does him so much good as to see me merry.

It felt very strange at first to open his letter and see my name written in his hand.

A Life for a Life

Saturday night.

"My Dear Theodora,—I do not say 'dearest,' because there is no one to put in comparison with you: you are to me the one woman in the world.

"My dear Theodora;—let me write it over again to assure myself that it may be written at all, which perhaps it ought not to be till you read this letter.

"Last night I left you so soon, or it seemed soon, and we said so little, that I never told you some things which you ought to have been made aware of at once; even before you were allowed to answer that question of mine. Forgive me. In my own defence let me say, that when I visited you yesterday, I meant only to have the sight of you—the comfort of your society—all I hoped or intended to win for years to come. But I was shaken out of all self-control—first by the terror of losing you, and then by a look in your sweet eyes. You know! It was to be, and it was. Theodora—gift of God!—may He bless you for showing, just for that one moment, what there was in your heart towards me.

"My feelings towards you, you can guess—a little: the rest you must believe in. I cannot write about them.

"The object of this letter is to tell you something which you ought to be told before I see you again.

"You may remember my once saying it was not likely I should ever marry. Such, indeed, was long my determination, and the reason was this. When I was a mere boy—just before Dallas died—there happened to me an event so awful, both in itself and its results, that it changed my whole character, darkened my life, turned me from a lively, careless, high-spirited lad, into a morbid and miserable man, whose very existence was a burthen to him for years. And though gradually, thank God! I recovered from this state, so as not to have an altogether useless life; still I never was myself again—never knew happiness, till I knew you. You came to me as unforeseen a blessing as if you had fallen from the clouds: first you interested, then you cheered me, then, in various ways, you brought light into my darkness, hope to my despair. And then I loved you.

"The same cause, which I cannot now fully explain, because I must first take a journey, but you shall know everything within a week or ten days—the same cause which has oppressed my whole life prevented my daring to win you. I always believed that a man circumstanced as I was, had no right ever to think of marriage. Some words of yours led me of late to change this opinion. I resolved, at some future time, to lay my whole history before you—as to a mere friend—to ask you the question whether or not, under the circumstances, I was justified in seeking any woman for my wife, and on your answer to decide either to try and make you love me, or only to love you, as I should have loved and shall for ever.

"What I then meant to tell you is still to be told. I do not dread the revelation as I once did: all things seem different to me.

"I am hardly the same man that I was twelve hours ago. Twelve hours ago I had never told you what you are to me—never had you in my arms—never read the love in your dear eyes—oh, child, do not ever be afraid or ashamed of letting me see you love me, unworthy as I am. If you had not loved me, I should have drifted away into perdition—I mean, I might have lost myself altogether, so far as regards this world.

"That is not likely now. You will save me, and I shall be so happy that I shall be able to make you happy. We will never be two again—only one. Already you feel like a part of me: and it seems as natural to write to you thus as if you had been mine for years. Mine. Some day you will find out all that is sealed up in the heart of a man of my age and of my disposition—when the seal is once broken.

"Since, until I have taken my journey I cannot speak to your father, it seems right that my next visit to you should be only that of a friend. Whether after having read this letter, which at once confesses so much and so little, you think me worthy even of that title, your first look will decide. I shall find out, without need of your saying one word.

"I shall probably come on Monday, and then not again; to meet you only as a friend, used to be sufficiently hard; to meet you with this uncertainty overhanging me, would be all but impossible. Besides, honour to your father compels this absence and silence, until my explanations are made.

A Life for a Life

"Will you forgive me? Will you trust me? I think you will.

"I hope you have minded my 'orders,' rested all evening and retired early? I hope on Monday I may see a rose on your cheeks—a tiny, delicate winter-rose? That poor little thin cheek, it grieves my heart. You *must* get strong.

"If by your manner you show that this letter has changed your opinion of me, that you desire yesterday to be altogether forgotten, I shall understand it, and obey.

"Remember, whatever happens, whether you are ever my own or not, that you are the only woman I ever wished for my wife; the only one I shall ever marry.

"Yours,

"Max Urquhart."

I read his letter many times over.

Then I rose and dressed myself, carefully, as if it had been my marriage morning. He loved me; I was the only woman he had ever wished for his wife. It was in truth my marriage morning.

Coming downstairs, Mrs. Granton met me, all delight at my having risen so soon.

"Such an advance! we must be sure and tell Doctor Urquhart. By-the-bye, did he not leave a note or message early this morning?"

"Yes; he will probably call on Monday."

She looked surprised that I did not produce the note, but made no remark. And I, two days before, I should have been scarlet and tongue-tied; but now things were quite altered. I was his chosen, his wife; there was neither hypocrisy nor deceit in keeping a secret between him and me. We belonged to one another, and the rest of the world had nothing to do with us.

A Life for a Life

Nevertheless, my heart felt running over with tenderness towards the dear old lady;—as it did towards my father and my sisters, and everything belonging to me in this wide world. When Mrs. Granton went to church, I sat for a long time in the west parlour, reading the Bible, all alone; at least as much alone as I ever can be in this world again, after knowing that Max loves me.

It being such an exceedingly mild and warm day—wonderful for the first day of February, an idea came into my head, which was indeed strictly according to "orders"; only I never yet had the courage to obey. Now, I thought I would. It would please him so, and Mrs. Granton too.

So I put on my out-door gear, and actually walked, all by myself, to the hill-top, a hundred yards or more. There I sat down on the familiar bench, and looked round on the well-known view. Ah me! for how many years, and under how many various circumstances, have I come and sat on that bench and looked at that view!

It was very beautiful to-day, though almost death-like in its supernatural sunshiny calm: such as one only sees in these accidental fine days which come in early winter, or sometimes as a kind of spectral antitype of spring. Such utter stillness everywhere. The sole thing that seemed alive or moving in the whole landscape was a wreath of grey smoke, springing from some invisible cottage behind the fir-wood, and curling away upwards till it lost itself in the opal air. Hill, moorland, wood, and sky, lay still as a picture, and fair as the Land of Beulah, the Celestial Country. It would hardly have been strange to see spirits walking there, or to have turned and found sitting on the bench beside me, my mother and my half-brother Harry, who died so long ago, and whose faces in the Celestial Country I shall first recognise.

My mother.—Never till now did I feel the want, of her. It seems only her—only a mother—to whom I could tell, "Max loves me—I am going to be Max's wife."

And Harry—poor Harry, whom also I never knew—whose life was so wretched, and whose death so awful; he might have been a better man, if he had only known my Max. I am forgetting, though, how old he would have been now; and how Max must have been a mere boy when my brother died.

I do not often think of Harry. It would be hardly natural that I should; all happened so long ago that his memory has never been more than a passing shadow across the family lives. But to-day, when every one of my own flesh and blood seemed to grow nearer to me, I thought of him more than once; tried to recall the circumstances of his dreadful end; and then to think of him only as a glorified, purified spirit, walking upon those hills of Beulah. Perhaps now looking down upon me, "baby" that was, whom he was once reported, in one of his desperate visits home, to have snatched out of the cradle and kissed; knowing all that had lately happened to me, and wishing me a happy life with my dear Max.

I took out Max's letter, and read it over again, in the sunshine and open air.

Oh, the happiness of knowing that one can make another happy—entirely happy! Oh, how good I ought to grow!

For the events which have caused him so much pain, and which he has yet to tell papa and me—they did not weigh much on my mind. Probably there is no family in which there is not some such painful revelation to be made; we also have to tell him about poor Harry. But these things are purely accidental and external. His fear that I should "change my opinion of him" made me smile. "Max," I said out loud, addressing myself to the neighbouring heather-bush, which might be considered a delicate compliment to the land where he was born, "Oh, Max, what nonsense you do talk! While you are you, and I am myself, you and I are one."

Descending the hill-top, I pressed all these my happy thoughts deep down into my heart, covered them up, and went back in the world again.

Mrs. Granton and I spent a quiet day; the quieter, that I afterwards paid for my feats on the hill-top by hours of extreme exhaustion. It was my own folly, I told her, and tried to laugh at it, saying, I should be better to-morrow.

But many a time the thought came, what if I should not be better to-morrow, nor any to-morrow? What if, after all, I should have to go away and leave him with no one to make him happy? And then I learned how precious life had grown, and tasted, in degree, what is meant by "the bitterness of death."

But it did not last. And by this I know that our love is holy: that I can now think of either his departure or my own, without either terror or despair. I know that even death itself can never part Max and me.

Monday came. I was really better, and went about the house with Mrs. Granton all the forenoon. She asked me what time Dr. Urquhart had said he should be here; with various other questions about him. All of which I answered without confusion or hesitation; it seemed as if I had now belonged to him for a long time. But when, at last, his ring came to the hall-door, all the blood rushed to my heart, and back again into my face—and Mrs. Granton saw it.

What was I to do? to try and "throw dust" into those keen, kind eyes, to tell or act a falsehood, as if I were ashamed of myself or him? I could not. So I simply sat silent, and let her think what she chose.

Whatever she thought, the good old lady said nothing. She sighed— ah, it went to my conscience that sigh—and yet I had done no wrong either to her or Colin; then, making some excuse, she slipped out of the room, and the four walls only beheld Max and me when we met.

After we had shaken hands, we sat down in silence. Then I asked him what he had been doing with himself all yesterday, and he told me he had spent it with the poor Ansdells.

"They wished this, and I thought it was best to go."

"Yes; I am very glad you went."

Dr. Urquhart (of course I shall go on calling him "Doctor Urquhart," to people in general; nobody but me has any business with his Christian name), Dr. Urquhart looked at me and smiled; then he began telling me about these friends of his; and how broken-hearted the old mother was, having lost both daughters in a few months— did I remember the night of the camp concert, and young Ansdell who sung there?

I remembered some young man being called for, as Dr. Urquhart wanted him.

"Yes—I had to summon him home; his eldest sister had suddenly died. Only a cold and fever—such as you yourself might have caught that night—you thoughtless girl. You little knew how angry you made me."

"Did I? Something was amiss with you—I did not know what—but I saw it in your looks."

"Could you read my looks even then, little lady?"

It was idle to deny it—and why should I, when it made him happy? Radiantly happy his face was now—the sharp lines softened, the wrinkles smoothed out. He looked ten years younger; ah! I am glad I am only a girl still; in time I shall actually make him young.

Here, the hall-bell sounded—and though visitors are never admitted to this special little parlour, still Max turned restless, and said he must go.

"Why?"

He hesitated—then said hastily—

"I will tell you the truth; I am happier out of your sight than in it, just at present."

I made no answer.

"To-night, I mean to start—on that journey I told you of." Which was to him a very painful one, I perceived.

"Go then, and get it over. You will come back to me soon."

"God grant it." He was very much agitated.

The only woman he had ever wished for his wife. This, I was. And I felt like a wife. Talk of Penelope's long courtship—Lisabel's marriage—it was I that was, in heart and soul, the real *wife;* ay, though Max and I were never more to one another than now; though I lived as Theodora Johnston to the end of my days.

So I took courage—and since it was not allowed me to comfort him in any other way, I just stole my hand inside his, which clasped instantly and tightly round it. That was all, and that was enough. Thus we sat side by side, when the door opened—and in walked papa.

How strangely the comic and the serious are mixed up together in life, and even in one's own nature. While writing this, I have gone off into a hearty fit of laughter, at the recollection of papa's face when he saw us sitting there.

Though at the time it was no laughing matter. For a moment he was dumb with astonishment—then he said severely—

"Doctor Urquhart, I suppose I must conclude—indeed, I can only conclude one thing. But you might have spoken to me, before addressing yourself to my daughter."

Max did not answer immediately—when he did, his voice absolutely made me start.

"Sir, I have been very wrong—but I will make amends—you shall know all. Only first—as my excuse," here he spoke out passionately, and told papa all that I was to him, all that we were to one another.

Poor papa! it must have reminded him of his own young days—I have heard he was very fond of his first wife, Harry's mother—for when I hung about his neck, mine were not the only tears. He held out his hand to Max.

"Doctor, I forgive you; and there is not a man alive on whom I would so gladly bestow this little girl as you."

And here Max tried me—as I suppose people not yet quite familiar will be sure to try one another at first. Without saying a word, or even accepting papa's hand, he walked straight out of the room.

It was not right—even if he were ever so much unnerved; why should he be too proud to show it? and it might have seriously offended papa. I softened matters as well as I could, by explaining that he had not wished to ask me of papa till a week hence, when he should be able fully to enter into his circumstances.

A Life for a Life

"My dear," papa interrupted, "go and tell him he may communicate them at whatever time he chooses, When such a man as Doctor Urquhart honestly comes and asks me for my daughter, you may be sure the very last question I should ask him would be about his circumstances."

With my heart brimful at papa's kindness, I went to explain this to Max. I found him alone in the library, standing motionless at the window. I touched him on the arm, with some silly coquettish speech about how he could think of letting me run after him in this fashion. He turned round.

"Oh, Max, what is the matter? Oh, Max!—" I could say no more.

"My child!"—He soothed me by calling me that and several other fond names, but all these things are between him and me alone.—"Now, good-bye. I must bid you good-bye at once."

I tried to make him understand there was no necessity—that papa desired to hear nothing, only wished him to stay with us till evening. That indeed, looking as wretched as he did, I could not and would not let him go. But in vain.

"I cannot stay. I cannot be a hypocrite. Do not ask it. Let me go—oh! my child, let me go."

And he might have gone—being very obstinate, and not in the least able to see what is good for him or for me either—had it not fortunately happened that, overpowered with the excitement of the last ten minutes, my small strength gave way. I felt myself falling—tried to save myself by catching hold of Max's arm, and fell. When I awoke, I was lying on the sofa, with papa and Mrs. Granton beside me.

Also Max—though I did not at first see him. He had taken his rights, or they had been tacitly yielded to him; I do not know how it was, but my head was on my betrothed husband's breast.

So he stayed. Nobody asked any questions, and he himself explained nothing. He only sat by me, all afternoon, taking care of me, watching me with his eyes of love—the love that is to last me my whole life. I know it will.

A Life for a Life

Therefore, in the evening, it was I who was the first to say, "Now, Max, you must go."

"You are quite better?"

"Yes, and it is almost dark—it will be very dark across the moors. You must go."

He rose, and shook hands mechanically with papa and Mrs. Granton. He was going to do the same by me, but I loosed my hands and clasped them round his neck. I did not care for what anybody might say or think; he was mine and I was his—they were all welcome to know it. And I wished him to know and feel that, through everything, and in spite of everything, I—his own—loved him and would love him to the last.

So he went away.

That is more than a week ago, and I have had no letter; but he did not say he would write. He would rather come, I think. Thus, any moment I may hear his ring at the door.

They—papa and Penelope—think I take things quietly. Penelope, indeed, hardly believes I care for him at all! But they do not know; oh, Max, they do not know! *You* know, or you will know, some day.

Chapter 25

HIS STORY

My dear Theodora,—I trust you may never read this letter, which, as a preventive measure, I am about to write; I trust we may burn it together, and that I may tell you its contents at accidental times, after the one principal fact has been communicated.

I mean to communicate it face to face, by word of mouth. It will not seem so awful then: and I shall see the expression of your countenance on first hearing it. That will guide me as to my own conduct—and as to the manner in which it had best be broken to your father. I have hope, at times, that even after such a communication, his regard for me will not altogether fail—and it may be that his present opinions will not be invincible. He may suggest some atonement, some probation, however long or painful I care not, so that it ends in his giving me you.

But first I ought to furnish him with full information about things into which I have never yet dared to inquire. I shall do so to-morrow. Much, therefore, depends upon to-morrow. Such a crisis almost unnerves me; add to that the very sight of this place—and I went by chance to the same inn, the White Hart, Salisbury. When you have read this letter through, you will not wonder that this is a terrible night for me. I never would have revisited this town—but in the hope of learning every particular, so as to tell you and your father the truth and the whole truth.

He will assuredly pity me. The thought of his own boy, your brother, whom you once mentioned, and whom Mr. Johnston informed me "died young" after some great dereliction—this thought may make him deal gently with me. Whether he will ever forgive me, or receive me into his family, remains doubtful. It is with the fear of this, or any other possibility which I cannot now foresee, that I write this letter; in order that whatever happens, my Theodora may be acquainted with my whole history.

My Theodora! Some day, when she comes to read a few pages which I seal up to-night, marking them with her name, and "To be delivered to her after my death," she will understand how I have

A Life for a Life

loved her. Otherwise, it never could have been found out, even by her—for I am not a demonstrative man. Only my wife would have known it.

In case this letter and those other letters do reach you, they will then be your last mementos of me. Read them and burn them; they are solely meant for you.

Should all go well, so that they become needless, we will, as I said, burn them together, read or unread, as you choose. You shall do it with your own hand, sitting by me, at our own fireside. *Our* fireside. The thought of it—the terror of losing it, makes me almost powerless to write on. Will you ever find out how I love you, my love—my love!

I begin by reminding you that I have been long aware your name is not properly Johnston. You told me yourself that the *t* had been inserted of late years. That you are not an aristocratic, but a plebeian family. My thankfulness at learning this, you will understand afterwards.

That cathedral clock—how it has startled me! Striking twelve with the same tongue as it did twenty years ago. Were I superstitious, I might fancy I heard in the coffee-room below, the clink of glasses, the tune of "Glorious Apollo," and the "Bravo" of that uproarious voice.

The town is hardly the least altered. Except that I came in by railway instead of by coach, it might be the very same Salisbury on that very same winter's night—the quaint, quiet English town that I stood looking at from this same window—its streets shining with rain, and its lights glimmering here and there through the general gloom. How I stared, boy-like, till *he* came behind and slapped me on the shoulder. But I have a few things to tell you before I tell you the history of that night. Let me delay it as long as I can.

You know about my father and mother, and how they both died when Dallas and I were children. We had no near kindred: we had to take care of ourselves—or rather he took care of me; he was almost as good as a father to me, from the time he was twelve years old.

A Life for a Life

Let me say a word or two more about my brother Dallas. If ever there was a perfect character on this earth, he was one. Every creature who knew him thought the same. I doubt not the memory of him still lingers in those old cloisters of St. Mary and St. Salvador, where he spent eight years, studying for the ministry. I feel sure there is not a lad who was at college with him—grey-headed lads they would be now, grave professors, or sober ministers of the Kirk, with country manses, wives, and families—not one of them but would say as I say, if you spoke to him of Dallas Urquhart.

Being five years my elder, he had almost ended his curriculum when I began mine; besides, we were at different colleges; but we went through some sessions together, a time on which I look back with peculiar tenderness, as I think all boys do who have studied at St. Andrews. You English do not altogether know us Scotch. I have seen hard-headed, possibly hard-hearted men, grim divines, stern military officers, and selfish Anglo-Indian valetudinarians, melt to the softness of a boy, as they talked of their boyish days at St. Andrews.

You never saw the place, my little lady? You would like it, I know. To me, who have not seen it these twenty years, it still seems like a city in a dream. I could lead you, hand-in-hand, through every one of its quiet old streets, where you so seldom hear the noise of either carriage or cart: could point out the notable historical corners, and tell you which professor lived in this house and which in that; could take you along the Links, to the scene of our celebrated golfing-match, calling over the names of the principal players, including his who won it—a fine fellow he was, too! What became of him, I wonder?

Also, I could show you the exact spot where you get the finest view of the Abbey and St. Regulus' Tower, and then away back to our lodgings—Dallas's and mine—along the Scores, where, of moonlight nights, the elder and more sentimental of the college lads would be caught strolling with their sweethearts—bonnie lassies too they were at St. Andrews—or we beheld them in all the glamour of our teens, and fine havers we talked to them along those Scores, to the sound of the sea below. I can hear it now. What a roar it used to come in with, on stormy nights, against those rocks beyond the Castle, where a lad and his tutor were once both drowned!

A Life for a Life

I am forgetting myself; and all I had to tell you. It is a long time since I have spoken of those old days.

Theodora, I should like you some time to go and see St. Andrews. Go there, in any case, and take a look at the old place. You will likely find, in St. Mary's cloisters, on the third arch to the right hand as you enter, my initials and Dallas's; and if you ask, some old janitor or librarian may still remember "the two Urquharts"—that is, if you like to name us. But, go if you can. Faithful heart! I know you will always care for anything that concerned me.

All the happy days of my life were spent at St. Andrews. They lasted until Dallas fell ill, and had to go abroad at once. I was to follow, and stay with him the winter, missing thereby one session, for he did not like to part with me. Perhaps he foresaw his end, which I, boy-like, never thought of, for I was accustomed to his being always delicate; perhaps he knew what a lad of nineteen might turn out, left to himself.

I was "left to myself," in our Scotch interpretation of the phrase; which, no doubt, originated in the stern Presbyterian belief of what human nature is, abandoned by God. *Left to himself.f* Many a poor wretch's more wretched parents know what that means.

How it came about I do not call to mind, but I found myself in London, my own master, spending money like dross; and spending what was worse, my time, my conscience, my innocence. How low I fell, God knows, for I hardly know myself! Things which happened afterwards made me oblivious even of this time. While it lasted, I never once wrote to Dallas.

A letter from him, giving no special reason for my joining him, but urging me to come, and quickly, made me recoil conscience-stricken from the Gehenna into which I was falling. You will find the letter— the last I had from him, in this packet: read it, and burn it with mine. Of course, no one has ever seen it, or will ever see it, except yourself.

I started from London immediately, in great restlessness and anguish of mind; for though I had been no worse than my neighbours, or so bad as many of them—I knew what Dallas was— and how his pure life, sanctified, though I guessed it not, by the shadow of coming death, would look beside this evil life of mine. I was very miserable; and a lad not used to misery is then in the quicksands of temptation. He is grateful to any one who will save him from himself—give him a narcotic and let his torment sleep.

I mention this only as a fact, not an extenuation. Though, in some degree, Max Urquhart the man has long since learned to pity Max Urquhart the boy.

—Here I paused, to read this over, and see if I have said all I wished therein. The narrative seems clear. You will perceive, I try as much as I can to make it a mere history as if of another person, and thus far I think I have done so. The rest I now proceed to tell you, as circumstantially and calmly as I can.

But first, before you learn any more about me, let me bid you remember how I loved you, how you permitted me to love you—how you have been mine, heart, and eyes, and tender lips; you know you were mine. You cannot alter that. If I were the veriest wretch alive, you once saw in me something worth loving, and you did love me. Not after the fashion of those lads and lassies who went courting along the Scores at St. Andrews—but solemnly—deeply—as those love who expect one day to be husband and wife. Remember, we were to have been married, Theodora.—I found my quickest route to Pau was by Southampton to Havre. But in the dusk of the morning I mistook the coach; my luggage went direct, and I found myself; having travelled some hours, on the road—not to Southampton, but to Salisbury. This was told me after some jocularity, at what he thought a vastly-amusing piece of "greenness" on my part, by the coachman. That is, the gentleman who drove the coach.

He soon took care to let me know he was a gentleman—and that, like many young men of rank and fashion at that time, he was acting Jehu only "for a spree." He talked so large, I should have taken him for a nobleman, or a baronet at least—had he not accidentally told me his name; though he explained that it was not as humble as it seemed, and expatiated much upon the antiquity, wealth, and aristocratic connections of his "family."

His conversation, though loud and coarse, was amusing; and he patronised me extremely.

A Life for a Life

I would rather not say a word more than is necessary concerning this person—he is dead. As before stated, I never knew anything of him excepting his name, which you shall have by-and-by; but I guessed that his life had not been a creditable one. He looked about thirty, or a little older.

When the coach stopped—at the very inn where I am now writing, the "White Hart," Salisbury, he insisted on my stopping too, as it was a bitter cold night and the moon would not rise till two in the morning—he said that, I mind well.

Finally, he let the coach go on without us, and I heard him laying a bet to drive across Salisbury Plain, in a gig, or dogcart, and meet it again on the road to Devizes by daybreak next morning. The landlord laughed, and advised him to give up such a mad, "neck-or-nothing" freak; but he swore, and said he always went at everything "neck-or-nothing."

I can remember to this day nearly every word he uttered, and his manner of saying it. Under any circumstances this might have been the case, for he attracted me, bad as I felt him to be, with his bold, devil-may-care jollity, mixed with a certain English frankness, not unpleasant. He was a small, dark man, hollow-eyed and dissipated looking. His face—no, better not call up his face.

I was persuaded to stay and drink with this man and one or two others—regular topers, as I soon found he was. He appeared poor too; the drinking was to be at my expense. I was very proud to have the honour of entertaining such a clever and agreeable gentleman.

Once, watching him, and listening to his conversation, sudden doubt seized me of what Dallas would think of my new acquaintance, and what he would say, or look—he seldom reproved aloud—were he to walk in, and find me in this present company. And, supper being done, I tried to get away, but this man held me by the shoulders, mocking me, and setting the rest on to mock me as a "milksop." The good angel fled. From that moment, I believe, the devil entered both into him and me.

I got drunk. It was for the first time in my life, though more than once lately I had been "merry," but stopped at that stage. This time I stopped at nothing. My blood was at boiling heat, with just enough of conscience left to make me snatch at any means to deaden it.

Of the details of that orgie, or of those who joined in it, except this one person—I have, as was likely, no distinct recollection. They were habitual drinkers; none of them had any pity for me, and I—I was utterly "left to myself;" as I have said. A raw, shy, Scotch lad, I soon became the butt of the company.

The last thing I remember is their trying to force me to tell my name, which, hitherto, I had not done; first, from natural reserve among strangers, and then from an instinctive feeling that I was not in the most creditable of society, and therefore the less I said about myself the better. All I had told, was that I was on my way to France, to join my brother, who was ill. They could not get any more out of me than that: a few taunts—which some English people are rather too ready to use against us Scotch—made me savage, as well as sullen. I might have deserved it, or not—I cannot tell; but the end was, they turned me out—the obstinate, drunken, infuriated lad—into the street.

I staggered through the dark, silent town, into a lane, and fell asleep on the road-side.

The next thing I call to mind is being awakened by the cut of a whip across my shoulders, and seeing a man standing over me. I flew at his throat like a wild creature; for it was he—the "gentleman" who had made me drunk, and mocked me; and whom I seemed then and there to hate with a fury of hatred that would last to my dying day. Through it all, came the thought of Dallas, sick and solitary, half way towards whom I ought to have travelled by now.

How he—the man—soothed me, I do not know, but I think it was by offering to take me towards Dallas; he had a horse and gig standing by, and said if I would mount, he would drive me to the coast, whence I could take boat to France. At least, that is the vague impression my mind retains of what passed between us. He helped me up beside him, and I dozed off to sleep again.

My next wakening was in the middle of a desolate plain. I rubbed my eyes, but saw nothing except stars and sky, and this black, black plain, which seemed to have no end.

He pulled up, and told me to "tumble out," which I did mechanically. On the other side of the gig was something tall and dark, which I took at first for a half-way inn; but perceived it was only a huge stone—a circle of stones.

"Hollo! what's this?"

"Stonehenge! comfortable lodging for man and beast; so you're all right. Good-bye, young fellow. You're such dull company, that I mean to leave you here till morning."

This was what he said to me, laughing uproariously. At first, I thought he was in jest, and laughed too; then, being sleepy and maudlin, I remonstrated. Lastly, I got half frightened, for when I tried to mount, he pushed me down. I was so helpless, and he so strong; from this solitary place, miles and miles from any human dwelling—how should I get on to Dallas?—Dallas, who, stupefied as I was, still remained my prominent thought.

I begged, as if I had been begging for my life, that he would keep his promise, and take me on my way towards my brother.

"To the devil with your brother!" and he whipped his horse on.

The devil was in me, as I said. I sprang at him, my strength doubled and trebled with rage, and, catching him unawares, dragged him from the gig, and threw him violently on the ground; his head struck against one of the great stones—and—and—Now, you see how it was. I murdered him. He must have died easily—instantaneously; he never moaned nor stirred once; but, for all that, it was murder.

Not with intent, God knows. So little idea had I he was dead, that I shook him as he lay, told him to "get up and fight it out": oh, my God!—my God!

Thus I have told it, the secret, which until now has never been written or spoken to any human being. I was then nineteen—I am now nine-and-thirty; twenty years. Theodora, have pity: only think of carrying such a secret—the blood of a man, on one's conscience for twenty years!

A Life for a Life

If, instead of my telling you all this, as I may do in a few days, you should have to read it here, it will by then have become an old tale. Still, pity me.

To continue, for it is getting far on into the night.

On the first few minutes after I discovered what I had done, you will not expect me to dilate.

I was perfectly sober, now. I had tried every means in my power to revive him, and then to ascertain for certain that he was dead; I forgot to tell you I had already begun my classes in medicine, so I knew a good deal. I sat with his head on my knee, fully aware that I had killed him; that I had taken the life of a man, and that his blood would be upon me for ever and ever.

Nothing, short of the great condemnation of the last judgment-day, could parallel that horror of despair; under it my reason seemed to give way. I was seized with the delusion that, bad and cruel man as he was, he was only shamming to terrify me. I held him up in my arms, so that the light of the gig-lamps fell full on his face.

It was a dead face—not frightful to look at, beautiful rather, as the muscles slowly settled—but dead, quite dead. I laid him down again, still resting his head against my knee, till he gradually stiffened and grew cold.

This was just at moon-rise; he had said the moon would rise at two o'clock, and so she did, and struck her first arrowy ray across the plain upon his face—that still face with its half-open mouth and eyes.

I had not been afraid of him hitherto; now I was. It was no longer a man, but a corpse, and I was the murderer.

The sight of the moon rising is my last recollection of this night. Probably, the fit of insanity which lasted for many months after, at that instant came on, and under its influence, I must have fled, leaving him where he lay, with the gig standing by, and the horse quietly feeding beside the great stones; but I do not recollect anything. Doubtless, I had all the cunning of madness, for I

A Life for a Life

contrived to gain the coast and get over to France; but how, or when, I have not the slightest remembrance to this day.

As I have told you, I never saw Dallas again. When I reached Pau, he was dead and buried. The particulars of his death were explained to me months afterwards by the good curé, who, Catholic as he was, had learned to love Dallas like a son, and who watched over me for his sake, during the long melancholy mania which, as he thought, resulted from the shock of my brother's death.

Some day I should like you, if possible, to see the spot where Dallas is buried—the churchyard of Bilhéres, near Pau; but his grave is not within the churchyard, as he, being a Protestant, the authorities would not allow it. You will find it just outside the hedge—the headstone placed in the hedge—though the little mound is by this time level with the meadow outside. You know, we Presbyterians have not your English feeling about "consecrated" ground; we believe that "the whole earth is the Lord's," and no human consecration can make it holier than it is, both for the worship of the living, and the interment of the dead. Therefore, it does not shock me that the cattle feed, and the grass grows tall, over Dallas's body. But I should like the headstone preserved—as it is; for yearly, in different quarters of the globe, I have received letters from the old curé and his successor, concerning it. You are much younger than I, Theodora; after my death I leave this charge to you. You will fulfil it for my sake, I know.

Must I tell you any more? Yes, for now comes what some might say was a crime as heavy as the first one. I do not attempt to extenuate it. I can only say that it has been expiated—such as it was, by twenty miserable years, and that the last expiation is even yet not come. Your father once said, and his words dashed from me the first hope which ever entered my mind concerning you, that he never would clasp the hand of a man who had taken the life of another. What would he say to a man who had taken a life, and *concealed the fact* for twenty years? I am that man.

How it came about, I will tell you.

For a twelvemonth after that night, I was, you will remember, not myself: in truth, a maniac, though a quiet and harmless one. My insanity was of the sullen and taciturn kind, so that I betrayed nothing; if indeed I had any remembrance of what had happened, which I believe I had not. The first dawn of recollection came through reading in an English newspaper, which the old curé brought to amuse me, an account of a man who was hanged for murder. I read it line by line—the trial—the verdict—the latter days of the criminal—who was a young lad like me—and the last day of all, when he was hanged.

By degrees, first misty as a dream, then ghastly clear, impressed on my mind with a tenacity and minuteness all but miraculous, considering the long blank which followed,— returned the events of that night. I became conscious that I too had killed a man, that if any eye had seen the act, I should have been taken, tried, and hanged, for murder.

Young as I was, and ignorant of English criminal law, I had sufficient common-sense to arrive at the conclusion that, as things stood, there was not a fragment of evidence against me individually, nor, indeed, any clear evidence to show that the man was murdered at all. It was now a year ago—he must have long since been found and buried—probably, with little inquiry; they would conclude he had been killed accidentally through his own careless, drunken driving. But if I once confessed and delivered myself up to justice, I myself only knew, and no evidence could ever prove, that it was not a case of wilful murder. I should be hanged—hanged by the neck till I was dead—and my name—our name, Dallas's and mine, blasted for evermore.

The weeks that elapsed after my first recovery of reason, were such, that when I hear preachers thunder about the literal "worm that dieth not, and fire that is never quenched," I could almost smile. Sufficient are the torments of a spiritual hell.

Sometimes, out of its depths, I felt as if Satan himself had entered my soul, to rouse me into atheistic rebellion. I, a boy not twenty yet, with all my future before me, to lose it through a moment's fury against a man who must have been depraved to the core, a man against whom I had no personal grudge—of whom I knew nothing but his name. Yet I must surrender my life for his—be tried, condemned—publicly disgraced—finally die the death of a dog. I had never been a coward—yet night after night I woke, bathed in a cold sweat of terror, feeling the rope round my neck, and seeing the forty thousand upturned faces—as in the newspaper account of the poor wretch who was hanged.

A Life for a Life

Remember, I plead nothing. I know there are those who would say that the most dishonourable wretch alive, was this same man of honour—this Max Urquhart, who carries such a fair reputation; that the only thing I should have done was to go back to England, surrender myself to justice, and take all the consequences of this one act of drunkenness and ungovernable passion. However, I did it not. But my sin—as every sin must,—be sure has found me out.

Theodora, it is hardly eight hours since your innocent arms were round my neck, and your kisses on my mouth—and now! Well, it will be over soon. However I have lived, I shall not die a hypocrite.

I do not attempt to retrace the course of reasoning by which I persuaded myself to act as I did. I was only a boy; this long sleep of the mind had re-established my bodily health;—life and youth were strong within me—also the hope of honour — the dread of shame. Yet sometimes conscience struggled so fiercely with all these, that I was half tempted to a medium course, the coward's last escape—suicide.

You must remember, religion was wanting in me—and Dallas was dead. Nay, I had for the time already forgotten him.

One day,—when, driven distracted with my doubts, I had almost made up my mind to end them in the one sharp easy way I have spoken of,—while putting my brother's papers in order, I found his Bible.—Underneath his name he had written—and the date was that of the last day of his life—my name. I looked at it, as we look at a handwriting long familiar, till of a sudden we remember that the hand is cold, that no earthly power can ever reproduce of this known writing a single line. Child, did you ever know—no, you never could have known—that total desolation, that helpless craving for the dead who return no more?

After I grew calmer, I did the only thing which seemed to bring me a little nearer to Dallas—I read in his Bible. The chapter I opened at was so remarkable that at first I recoiled as if it had been my brother—he who being now a spirit, might, for all I could tell, have a spirit's knowledge of all things—speaking to me out of the invisible world. The chapter was Ezekiel xvii.; and among other verses were these:—

A Life for a Life

"When the wicked man turneth away from his wickedness that he hath committed, and doeth that which is lawful and right, he shall save his soul alive.

"Because he considereth and turneth away from all his transgressions that he hath committed, he shall surely live; he shall not die.

"For I have no pleasure in the death of him that dieth, saith the Lord God: wherefore turn yourselves and live ye."

I turned and lived. I resolved to give a life—my own—for the life which I had taken; to devote it wholly to the saving of other lives;—and at its close, when I had built up a good name, and shown openly that after *any* crime a man might recover himself, repent and atone, I meant to pay the full price of the sin of my youth, and openly to acknowledge it before the world.—

How far I was right or wrong in this decision, I cannot tell—perhaps no human judgment ever can tell: I simply state what I then resolved, and have never swerved from—till I saw you.

Of necessity, with this ultimate confession ever before me, all the pleasures of life, and all its closest ties, friendship, love, marriage—were not to be thought of. I set them aside as impossible. To me, life could never be enjoyment, but simply atonement.

My subsequent history you are acquainted with—how, after the needful term of medical study in Britain (I chose Dublin as being the place where I was utterly a stranger, and remained there till my four years ended), I went as an army-surgeon half over the world. The first time I ever set foot in England again, was not many weeks before I saw, in the ball-room of the Cedars, that little sweet face of yours. The same face in which, two days ago, I read the look of love which stirs a man's heart to the very core. In a moment it obliterated the resolutions—conflicts—sufferings of twenty years, and restored me to a man's right and privilege of loving, wooing, marrying.—Shall we ever be married?

By the time you read this, if ever you do read it, that question will have been answered. It can do you no harm if for one little minute I

A Life for a Life

think of you as my wife; no longer friend, child, mistress, but *my wife*.

Think of all that would have been implied by that name. Think of coming home, and of all that home would have been—however humble—to me who never had a home in my whole life. Think of all I would have tried to make it to you. Think of sitting by my fireside, knowing that you were the only one required to make it happy and bright; that, good and pleasant, and dear as many others might be—the only absolute necessity to each of us was one another.

Then, the years that would have followed, in which we never had to say good-bye, in which our two hearts would daily lie open, clear and plain, never to have a doubt or a secret any more.

Then—if we should not always be only two!—I think of you as my wife—the mother of my children—

I was unable to conclude this last night. Now I only add a line before going into the town to gain information about—about this person: by whom his body was found, and where buried; with that intent I have already been searching the cathedral burying-ground; but there is no sign of graves there, all is smooth green turf; with the dew upon it glittering like a sheet of diamonds in the bright spring morning.

It reminded me of you—this being your hour for rising, you early bird, you little methodical girl. You may at this moment be out on the terrace, looking up to the hill-top, or down towards your favourite cedar-trees, with that sunshiny spring morning face of yours.

Pray for me, my love, my wife, my Theodora.

I have found his grave at last.

"In memory of Henry Johnston, only son of the Reverend William Henry Johnston, of Rockmount, Surrey: who met his death by an accident near this town, and was buried here. Born May 19, 1806. Died November 19, 1836."

Farewell, Theodora.

Chapter 26

HER STORY

Many, many weeks, months indeed have gone by since I opened this my journal. Can I bear the sight of it even now? Yes; I think I can.

I have been sitting ever so long at the open window, in my old attitude, elbow on the sill; only with a difference that seems to come natural now, when no one is by. It is such a comfort to sit with my lips on my ring. I asked him to give me a ring, and he did so. Oh! Max, Max, Max!

Great and miserable changes have befallen us, and now Max and I are not going to be married. Penelope's marriage also has been temporarily postponed, for the same reason, though I implored her not to tell it to Francis, unless he should make very particular inquiries, or be exceedingly angry at the delay. He was not. Nor did we judge it well to inform Lisabel. Therefore, papa, Penelope and I, keep our own secret.

Now that it is over, the agony of it smothered up, and all at Rockmount goes on as heretofore, I sometimes wonder, do strangers, or intimates, Mrs. Granton for instance, suspect anything? Or is ours, awful as it seems, no special and peculiar lot? Many another family may have its own lamentable secret, the burthen of which each member has to bear, and carry in society a cheerful countenance, even as this of mine.

Mrs. Granton said yesterday, mine was "a cheerful countenance." If so, I am glad. Two things only could really have broken my heart— his ceasing to love me, and his changing so in *himself*; not in his circumstances, that I could no longer worthily love him. By "him," I mean, of course Max. Max Urquhart, my betrothed husband, whom henceforward I can never regard in any other light.

How blue the hills are, how bright the moors! So they ought to be, for it is near midsummer. By this day fortnight—Penelope's marriage-day—we shall have plenty of roses. All the better; I would not like it to be a dull wedding, though so quiet; only the Trehernes and Mrs. Granton as guests, and me for the solitary bridesmaid.

"Your last appearance I hope, Dora, in that capacity," laughed the dear old lady.

"'Thrice a bridesmaid, ne'er a bride,' which couldn't be thought of you know. No need to speak—I guess why your wedding isn't talked about yet.—The old story, man's pride, and woman's patience. Never mind. Nobody knows anything but me, and I shall keep a quiet tongue in the matter. Least said is soonest mended. All will come right soon, when the Doctor is a little better off in the world."

I let her suppose so. It is of little moment what she or anybody thinks, so that it is nothing ill of him.

"Thrice a bridesmaid, never a bride." Even so. Yet, would I change lots with our bride Penelope, or any other bride? No.

Now that my mind has settled to its usual level; has had time to view things calmly, to satisfy itself that nothing could have been done different from what has been done; I may, at last, be able to detail these events. For both Max's sake and my own, it seems best to do it, unless I could make up my mind to destroy my whole journal. An unfinished record is worse than none. During our lifetimes we shall both preserve our secret; but many a chance brings dark things to light; and I have my Max's honour to guard, as well as my own.

This afternoon, papa being out driving, and Penelope gone to town to seek for a maid, whom the Governor's lady will require to take out with her—they sail a month hence—I shall seize the opportunity to write down what has befallen Max and me.

My own poor Max! But my lips are on his ring; this hand is as safely kept for him as when he first held it in his breast.

Let me turn back a page, and see where it was I left off writing my journal.

I did so; and it was more than I could bear at the time. I have had to take another day for this relation, and even now it is bitter enough to recall the feelings with which I put my pen by, so long ago, waiting for Max to come in "at any minute."

A Life for a Life

I waited ten days; not unhappily, though the last two were somewhat anxious, but it was simply lest anything might have gone wrong with him or his affairs. As for his neglecting or "treating me ill," as Penelope suggested, such a thought never entered my head. How could he treat me ill?—he loved me.

The tenth day, which was the end of the term he had named for his journey, I of course fully expected him. I knew if by any human power it could be managed, I should see him; he never would break his word. I rested on his love as surely as in waking from that long sick swoon I had rested on his breast. I knew he would be tender over me, and not let me suffer one more hour's suspense or pain that he could possibly avoid.

It may here seem strange that I had never asked Max where he was going, nor anything of the business he was going upon. Well, that was his secret, the last secret that was ever to be between us; so I chose not to interfere with it, but to wait his time. Also, I did not fret much about it, whatever it was. He loved me. People who have been hungry for love, and never had it all their lives, can understand the utterly satisfied contentment of this one feeling—Max loved me.

At dusk, after staying in all day, I went out, partly because Penelope wished it, and partly for health's sake. I never lost a chance of getting strong now. My sister and I walked alone silently, each thinking of her own affairs, when, at a turn in the road which led, not from the camp, but from the moorlands, she cried out, "I do believe there is Doctor Urquhart."

If he had not heard his name, I think he would have passed us without knowing us. And the face that met mine, when he looked up—I never shall forget it to my dying day.

It made me shrink back for a minute, and then I said—

"Oh! Max, have you been ill?"

"I do not know. Yes—possibly."

"When did you come back?"

"I forget—oh! four days ago."

A Life for a Life

"Were you coming to Rockmount?"

"Rockmount?—oh! no." He shuddered, and dropped my hand.

"Doctor Urquhart seems in a very uncertain frame of mind," said Penelope, severely, from the other side the road. "We had better leave him. Come, Dora."

She carried me off, almost forcibly. She was exceedingly displeased. Four days, and never to have come or written! She said it was slighting me and insulting the family.

"A man, too, of whose antecedents and connections we knew nothing. He may be a mere adventurer—a penniless Scotch adventurer; Francis always said he was."

"Francis is—" But I could not stay to speak of him, or to reply to Penelope's bitter words. All I thought was how to get back to Max, and entreat him to tell me what had happened. He would tell *me*. He loved *me*. So, without any feeling of "proper pride," as Penelope called it, I writhed myself out of her grasp, ran back to Dr. Urquhart, and took possession of his arm, my arm, which I had a right to.

"Is that you, Theodora?"

"Yes, it is I." And then I said, I wanted him to go home with me, and tell me what had happened.

"Better not; better go home with your sister."

"I had rather stay here. I mean to stay here."

He stopped, took both my hands, and forced a smile:—

"You are the determined little lady you always were; but you do not know what you are saying. You had better go and leave me."

I was sure then some great misery was approaching us. I tried to read it in his face. "Do you—" did he still love me; I was about to ask, but there was no need. So my answer, too, was brief and plain.

"I never will leave you as long as I live."

Then I ran back to Penelope, and told her I should walk home with Dr. Urquhart; he had something to say to me. She tried anger and authority. Both failed. If we had been summer lovers it might have been different, but now in his trouble I seemed to feel Max's right to me and my love, as I had never done before. Penelope might have lectured for everlasting, and I should only have listened, and then gone back to Max's side. As I did.

His arm pressed mine close; he did not say a second time, "Leave me."

"Now, Max, I want to hear."

No answer.

"You know there is something, and we shall never be quite happy till it is told. Say it outright; whatever it is, I shall not mind."

No answer.

"Is it something very terrible?"

"Yes."

"Something that might come between and part us?"

"Yes."

I trembled, though not much, having so strong a belief in the impossibility of parting. Yet there must have been an expression I hardly intended in the cry "Oh, Max, tell me," for he again stopped suddenly, and seemed to forget himself in looking at and thinking of me.

"Stay, Theodora,—you have something to tell *me* first. Are you better? Have you been growing stronger daily? You are sure?"

"Quite sure. Now—tell me."

A Life for a Life

He tried to speak once or twice, vainly. At last he said—

"I—I wrote you a letter."

"I never got it."

"No; I did not mean you should until my death. But my mind has changed. You shall have it now. I have carried it about with me, on the chance of meeting you, these four days. I wanted to give it to you—and—to look at you. Oh, my child, my child."

After a little while, he gave me the letter, begging me not to open it till I was alone at night.

"And if it should shock you—break your heart?"

"Nothing will break my heart."

"You are right, it is too pure and good. God will not suffer it to be broken. Now, goodbye."

For we had reached the gate of Rockmount. It had never struck me before that I had to bid him adieu here, that he did not mean to go in with me to dinner; and when he refused, I felt it very much. His only answer was, for the second time, "that I did not know what I was saying."

It was now nearly dark, and so misty that I could hardly breathe. Dr. Urquhart insisted on my going in immediately, tied my veil close under my chin, and then hastily untied it.

"Love, do you love me?"

He has told me afterwards, he forgot then for the time being every circumstance that was likely to part us; everything in the whole world but me. And I trust I was not the only one who felt that it is those alone who, loving as we did, are everything to one another, who have most strength to part.

When I came indoors, the first person I met was papa, looking quite bright and pleased; and his first question was—

A Life for a Life

"Where is Doctor Urquhart? Penelope said Doctor Urquhart was coming here."

I hardly know what was done during that evening, or whether they blamed Max or not. All my care was how best to keep his secret, and literally to obey him concerning it.

Of course I never named his letter, nor made any attempt to read it till I had bidden good night to them all, and smiled at Penelope's grumbling over my long candles and my large fire, "as if I meant to sit up all night." Yes, I had taken all these precautions in a quiet, solemn kind of way, for I did not know what was before me, and I must not fall ill if I could help. I was Max's own personal property.

How cross she was that night, poor Penelope! It was the last time she has ever scolded me.

For some things, Penelope has felt this more than any one could, except papa, for she is the only one of us who has a clear recollection of Harry.

Now, his name is written, and I can tell it—the awful secret I learned from Max's letter, which no one except me must ever read.

My Max killed Harry. Not intentionally—when he was out of himself and hardly accountable for what he did; in a passion of boyish fury, roused by great cruelty and wrong; but—he killed him. My brother's death, which we believed to be accidental, was by Max's hand.

I write this down calmly now; but it was awful at the time. I think I must have read on mechanically, expecting something sad, and about Harry likewise; I soon guessed that bad man at Salisbury must have been poor Harry—but I never guessed anything near the truth till I came to the words "I *murdered* him."

To suppose one feels a great blow acutely at the instant is a mistake—it stuns rather than wounds. Especially when it comes in a letter, read in quiet and alone, as I read Max's letter that night. And—as I remember afterwards seeing in some book, and thinking how true it was—it is strange how soon a great misery grows familiar. Waking up from the first few minutes of total bewilderment, I seemed to have been aware all these twenty years that my Max killed Harry.

O Harry, my brother, whom I never knew—no more than any stranger in the street, and the faint memory of whom was mixed with an indefinite something of wickedness, anguish, and disgrace to us all, if I felt not as I ought, then or afterwards, forgive me. If, though your sister, I thought less of you dead than of my living Max—my poor, poor Max, who had borne this awful burthen for twenty years—Harry, forgive me!

Well, I knew it—as an absolute fact and certainty—though as one often feels with great personal misfortunes, at first I could not realise it. Gradually I became fully conscious what an overwhelming horror it was, and what a fearful retributive justice had fallen upon papa and us all.

For there were some things I had not myself known till this spring, when Penelope, in the fulness of her heart at leaving us, talked to me a good deal of old childish days, and especially about Harry.

He was a spoiled child. His father never said him nay in anything—never, from the time when he sat at table, in his own ornamental chair, and drank champagne out of his own particular glass, lisping toasts that were the great amusement of everybody. He never knew what contradiction was, till, at nineteen, he fell in love, and wanted to get married, and would have succeeded, for they eloped (as I believe papa and Harry's mother had done), but papa prevented them in time. The girl, some village lass, but she might have had a heart nevertheless, broke it, and died. Then Harry went all wrong.

Penelope remembers how, at times, a shabby, dissipated man used to meet us children out walking, and kiss us and the nursery-maids all round, saying he was our brother Harry. Also, how he used to lie in wait for papa coming out of church, follow him into his library, where, after fearful scenes of quarrelling, Harry would go away jauntily, laughing to us, and bowing to mamma, who always showed him out and shut the door upon him with a face as white as a sheet.

My sister also remembers papa's being suddenly called away from home for a day or two, and, on his return, our being all put into mourning, and told that it was for brother Harry, whom we must never speak of any more. And once, when she was saying her geography lesson, and wanted to go and ask papa some questions about Stonehenge and Salisbury, mamma stopped her, saying she must take care never to mention these places to papa, for that poor Harry—she called him so now—had died miserably by an accident, and been buried at Salisbury.

She died the same year, and soon afterwards we came to Rockmount, living handsomely upon grandfather's money, and proud that we had already begun to call ourselves Johnston. Oh, me, what wicked falsehoods poor Harry told about his "family." Him we never again named; not one of our neighbours here ever knew that we had a brother.

The first shock over, hour after hour of that long night I sat, trying by any means to recall him to mind, my father's son, my own flesh and blood—at least by the half-blood—to pity him, to feel as I ought concerning his death, and the one who caused it. But do as I would, my thoughts went back to Max—as they might have done, even had he not been my own *Max*—*out* of deep compassion for one who, not being a premeditated and hardened criminal, had suffered for twenty years the penalty of this single crime.

It was such, I knew. I did not attempt to palliate it, or justify him. Though poor Harry was worthless, and Max is—what he is—that did not alter the question. I believe, even then, I did not disguise from myself the truth—that my Max had committed, not a fault, but an actual crime. But I called him *my* Max still. It was the only word that saved me, or I might, as he feared, have "broken my heart."

The whole history of that dreadful night, there is no need I should tell to any human being; even Max himself will never know it. God knows it, and that is enough. By my own strength, I never should have kept my life or reason till the morning.

But it was necessary, and it was better far that I should have gone through this anguish alone, guided by no outer influence, and sustained only by that Strength which always comes in seasons like these.

I seem, while stretched on the rack of those long night hours, to have been led by some supernatural instinct into the utmost depths of human and divine justice, human and divine love, in search of *the right*. At last I saw it, clung to it, and have found it my rock of hope ever since.

When the house below began to stir, I put out my candle, and stood watching the dawn creep over the grey moor-lands, just as on the morning when we had sat up all night with my father—Max and I. How fond my father was of him—my poor, poor father!

The horrible conflict and confusion of mind came back. I felt as if right and wrong were inextricably mixed together, laying me under a sort of moral paralysis, out of which the only escape was madness. Then out of the deeps I cried unto Thee: O Thou whose infinite justice includes also infinite forgiveness; and Thou heardest me.

"When the wicked man turneth away from his wickedness that he hath committed, and doeth that which is lawful and right, he shall save his soul alive."

I remembered these words: and unto Thee I trusted my Max's soul.

It was daylight now, and the little birds began waking up, one by one, until they broke into a perfect chorus of chirping and singing. I thought, was ever grief like this of mine? Yes—one grief would have been worse—if, this sunny summer morning, I knew he had ceased to love me, and I to believe in him—if I had lost him—never either in this world or the next, to find him more.

After a little, I thought if I could only go to sleep, though but for half-an-hour—it would be well. So I undressed and laid myself down, with Max's letter tight hidden in my hands.

Sleep came; but it ended in dreadful dreams, out of which I awoke, screaming, to see Penelope standing by my bedside, with my breakfast.

Now, I had already laid my plans—to tell my father all. For he must be told. No other alternative presented itself to me as possible—nor, I knew, would it to Max. When two people are thoroughly one, each guesses instinctively the other's mind; in most things always in all great things, for one faith and love includes also one sense of right. I was as sure as I was of my existence that Max meant my father to be told. Not even to make me happy would he have deceived me—and not even that we might be married, would he consent that we should deceive my father.

Thus, that my father must be told, and that I must tell him, was a matter settled and clear—but I never considered about how far must be explained to any one else, till I saw Penelope stand there with her familiar household face, half cross, half alarmed.

"Why, child, what on earth is the matter? Here are you, staring as if you were out of your senses—and there is Doctor Urquhart, who has been haunting the place like a ghost ever since daylight. I declare, I'll send for him and give him a piece of my mind."

"Don't, don't," I gasped, and all the horror returned—vivid as daylight makes any new anguish. Penelope soothed me—with the motherliness that had come over her since I was ill, and the gentleness that had grown up in her since she had been happy, and Francis loving. My miserable heart yearned to her, a woman like myself—a good woman, too, though I did not appreciate her once, when I was young and foolish, and had never known care, as she had. How it came out I cannot tell—I have never regretted it—nor did Max, for I think it saved my heart from breaking—but I then and there told my sister Penelope our dreadful story.

I see her still, sitting on the bed, listening with blanched face, gazing, not at me, but at the opposite wall. She made no outcry of grief or horror against Max. She took all in a subdued, quiet way, which I had not expected would have been Penelope's passion of bearing a great grief. She hardly said anything, till I cried with a bitter cry—

"Now I want Max. Let me rise and go down, for I must see Max."

Then we two women looked at one another pitifully, and my sister, my happy sister who was to be married in a fortnight, took me in her arms, sobbing,

"Oh, Dora, my poor, poor child."

All this seems years upon years ago, and I can relate it calmly enough, till I call to mind that sob of Penelope's.

Well, what happened next? I remember, Penelope came in when I was dressing, and told me, in her ordinary manner, that papa wished her to drive with him to the Cedars this morning.

"Shall I go, Dora?"

"Yes."

"Perhaps you will see *him* in our absence."

"I intend so."

She turned, then came back and kissed me. I suppose she thought this meeting between Max and me would be an eternal farewell.

The carriage had scarcely driven off when I received a message that Dr. Urquhart was in the parlour.

Harry—Harry, twenty years dead—my own brother killed by my husband! Let me acknowledge. Had I known this *before* he was my betrothed husband, chosen open-eyed, with all my judgment, my conscience, and my soul, loved, not merely because he loved me, but because I loved him, honoured him, and trusted him, so that even marriage could scarcely make us more entirely one than we were already—had I been aware of this before, I might not, indeed I think I never should have loved him. Nature would have instinctively prevented me. But now it was too late. I loved him, and I could not unlove him: Nature herself forbade the sacrifice. It would have been like tearing my heart out of my bosom; he was half myself—and maimed of him, I should never have been my right self afterwards. Nor would he. Two living lives to be blasted for one that was taken unwittingly twenty years ago! Could it—ought it so to be?

The rest of the world are free to be their own judges in the matter; but God and my conscience are mine.

I went downstairs steadfastly, with my mind all clear. Even to the last minute, with my hand on the parlour-door, my heart—where all throbs of happy love seemed to have been long, long forgotten—my still heart prayed.

Max was standing by the fire—he turned round. He, and the whole sunshiny room swam before my eyes for an instant,—then I called up my strength and touched him. He was trembling all over.

"Max, sit down." He sat down.

I knelt by him. I clasped his hands close, but still he sat as if he had been a stone. At last he muttered—

"I wanted to see you, just once more, to know how you bore it—to be sure I had not killed you also—oh, it is horrible, horrible!"

I said it was horrible—but that we would be able to bear it.

"We?"

"Yes—we."

"You cannot mean *that*?"

"I do. I have thought it all over, and I do."

Holding me at arm's length, his eyes questioned my inmost soul.

"Tell me the truth. It is not pity—not merely pity, Theodora?"

"Ah, no, no!"

Without another word—the first crisis was past—everything which made our misery a divided misery.—He opened his arms and took me once more into my own place—where alone I ever really rested, or wish to rest until I die.

Max had been very ill, he told me, for days, and now seemed both in body and mind as feeble as a child. For me, my childishness or girlishness, with its ignorance and weakness, was gone for evermore.

I have thought since, that in all women's deepest loves, be they ever so full of reverence, there enters sometimes much of the motherly element, even as on this day I felt as if I were somehow or other in charge of Max, and a great deal older than he. I fetched a glass of water, and made him drink it—bathed his poor temples and wiped them with my handkerchief—persuaded him to lean back quietly and not speak another word for ever so long. But more than once, and while his head lay on my shoulder, I thought of his mother, my mother who might have been—and how, though she had left him so many years, she must, if she knew of all he had suffered, be glad to know there was at last one woman found who would, did Heaven permit, watch over him through life, with the double love of both wife and mother, and who, in any case, would be faithful to him till death.

Faithful till death. Yes,—I here renewed that vow, and had Harry himself come and stood before me, I should have done the same. Look you, any one who after my death may read this;—there are two kinds of love, one, eager only to get its desire, careless of all risks and costs, in defiance almost of heaven and earth; the other, which in its most desperate longing has strength to say, "If it be right and for our good—if it be according to the will of God." This only, I think, is the true and consecrated love, which therefore is able to be faithful till death.

Max and I never once spoke about whether or not we should be married—we left all that in higher hands. We only felt we should always be true to one another—and that, being what we were, and loving as we did, God Himself could not will that any human will or human justice should put us asunder.

This being clear, we set ourselves to meet what was before us. I told him poor Harry's history, so far as I knew it myself; afterwards we began to consider how best the truth could he broken to my father.

And here let me confess something, which Max has long forgiven, but which I can yet hardly forgive myself. Max said, "And when your father is told, he shall decide what next is to be."

"How do you mean?" I cried.

"If he requires atonement, he must have it, even at the hands of the law."

Then, for the first time, it struck me that, though Max was safe so long as he made no confession, for the peculiar circumstances of

A Life for a Life

Harry's death left no other evidence against him, still, this confession once public (and it was, for had I not told Penelope?), his reputation, liberty, life itself, were in the hands of my sister and my father. A horror as of death fell upon me. I clung to him who was my all in this world, dearer to me than father, mother, brother, or sister; and I urged that we should both, then and there, fly—escape together anywhere, to the very ends of the earth, out of reach of justice and my father.

I must have been almost beside myself before I thought of such a thing. I hardly knew all it implied, until Max gravely put me from him.

"It cannot be you who says this. Not Theodora."

And suddenly, as unconnected and even incongruous things will flash across one in times like these, I called to mind the scene in my favourite play, when, the alternative being life or honour, the woman says to her lover, *"No, die!"* Little I dreamed of ever having to say to my Max almost the same words.

I said them, kneeling by him, and imploring his pardon for having wished him to do such a thing even for his safety and my happiness.

"We could not have been happy, child," he said, smoothing my hair, with a sad fond smile. "You do not know what it is to have a secret weighing like lead upon your soul. Mine feels lighter now than it has done for years. Let us decide: what hour to-night shall I come here and tell your father?"

Saying this, Max turned white to the very lips, but still he comforted me.

"Do not be afraid, my child. I am not afraid. Nothing can be worse than what has been—to me. I was a coward once, but then I was only a boy, hardly able to distinguish right from wrong. Now I see that it would have been better to have told the whole truth at once, and taken all the punishment. It might not have been death, or if it were, I could but have died."

"Max, Max!"

A Life for a Life

"Hush!" and he closed my lips so that they could not moan. "The truth is better than life, better even than a good name. When your father knows the truth, all else will be clear. I shall abide by his decision, whatever it be; he has a right to it. Theodora," his voice faltered, "make him understand, some day, that if I had married you, he never should have wanted a son,—your poor father."

These were almost the last words Max said on this, the last hour that we were together by ourselves. For minutes and minutes he held me in his arms, silently; and I shut my eyes, and felt, as if in a dream, the sunshine and the flower-scents, and the loud singing of the two canaries in Penelope's green-house. Then, with one kiss, he put me down softly from my place, and left me alone.

I have been alone ever since; God only knows *how* alone.

The rest I cannot tell to-day.

A Life for a Life

Chapter 27

HIS STORY

This is the last, probably, of those "letters never sent," which may reach you one day; when or how, we know not. All that is, is best.

You say you think it advisable that there should be an accurate written record of all that passed between your family and myself on the final day of parting, in order that no further conduct of mine may be misconstrued or misjudged. Be it so. My good name is worth preserving; for it must never be any disgrace to you that Max Urquhart loved you.

Since this record is to be minute and literal, perhaps it will be better I should give it impersonally, as a statement rather than a letter.

On February 9th, 1857, I went to Rockmount, to see Theodora Johnston, for the first time after she was aware that I had, long ago, taken the life of her half-brother, Henry Johnston, not intentionally, but in a fit of drunken rage. I came, simply to look at her dear face once more, and to ask her in what way her father would best bear the shock of this confession of mine, before I took the second step of surrendering myself to justice, or of making atonement in any other way that Mr. Johnston might choose. To him and his family my life was owed, and I left them to dispose of it or of me in any manner they thought best.

With these intentions, I went to Theodora. I knew her well. I felt sure she would pity me, that she would not refuse me her forgiveness, before our eternal separation; that though the blood upon my hands was half her own, she would not judge me the less justly, or mercifully, or Christianly. As to a Christian woman, I came to her—as I had come once before, in a question of conscience; also, as to the woman who had been my friend, with all the rights and honours of that name, before she became to me anything more and dearer. And I was thankful that the lesser tie had been included in the greater, so that both need not be entirely swept away and disannulled

I found not only my friend, upon whom, above all others. I could depend, but my own, my love, the woman above all women who was mine; who, loving me before this blow fell, clung to me still, and believing that God Himself had joined us together, suffered nothing to put us asunder.

How she made me comprehend this I shall not relate, as it concerns ourselves alone. When at last I knelt by her and kissed her blessed hands—my saint! and yet all woman, and all my own—I felt that my sin was covered, that the All-merciful had had mercy upon me. That while, all these years, I had followed miserably my own method of atonement, denying myself all life's joys, and cloaking myself with every possible ray of righteousness I could find, He had suddenly led me by another way, sending this child's love, first to comfort and then to smite me, that, being utterly bruised, broken, and humbled, I might be made whole.

Now, for the first time, I felt like a man to whom there is a possibility of being made whole. Her father might hunt me to death, the law might lay hold on me, the fair reputation under which I had shielded myself might be torn and scattered to the winds. But for all that I was safe, I was myself; the true Max Urquhart, a grievous sinner; yet no longer unforgiven or hopeless.

"I came not to call the righteous, but SINNERS to repentance."

That line struck home. Oh, that I could strike it home to every miserable heart as it went to mine. Oh! that I could carry into the utmost corners of the earth the message, the gospel which Dallas believed in, the only one which has power enough for the redemption of this sorrowful world—the gospel of the forgiveness and remission of sins.

While she talked to me—this my saint, Theodora—Dallas himself might have spoken, apostle-like, through her lips. She said, when I listened in wonder to the clearness of some of her arguments, that she hardly knew how they had come into her mind, they seemed to come of themselves; but they were there, and she was *sure* they were true. She was sure, she added, reverently, that if the Christ of Nazareth were to pass by Rock-mount door this day, the only word He would say unto me, after all I had done, would be "Thy sins are forgiven thee—rise up and walk."

A Life for a Life

And I did so. I went out of the house an altered man. My burthen of years had been lifted off me for ever and ever. I understood something of what is meant by being "born again." I could dimly guess at what they must have felt who sat at the Divine feet, clothed and in their right mind, or who, across the sunny plains of Galilee, leaped, and walked, and ran, praising God.

I crossed the moorland, walking erect, with eyes fixed on the blue sky, my heart tender and young as a child's. I even stopped, child-like, to pluck a stray primrose under a tree in a lane, which had peeped out, as if it wished to investigate how soon spring would come. It seemed to me so pretty—I might never have seen a primrose since I was a boy.

Let me relate the entire truth—she wishes it. Strange as it may appear, though hour by hour brought nearer the time when I had fixed to be at Rockmount, to confess unto a father that I had been the slayer of his only son—still that day was not an unhappy day. I spent it chiefly out of doors on the moorlands, near a wayside public-house, where I had lodged some nights, drinking in large draughts of the beauty of this external world, and feeling even outer life sweet, though nothing to that renewed life which I now should never lose again. Never—even if I had to go next day to prison and trial, and stand before the world a convicted homicide. Nay, I believe I could have mounted the scaffold amidst those gaping thousands that were once my terror, and die peacefully in spite of them, feeling no longer either guilty or afraid.

So much for myself, which will explain a good deal that followed in the interview which I have now to relate.

Theodora had wished to save me by herself explaining all to her father; but I would not allow this, and at length she yielded. However, things fell out differently from both our intentions: he learned it first from his daughter Penelope. The moment I entered his study I was certain Mr. Johnston knew.

Let no sinner, however healed, deceive himself that his wound will never smart again. He is not instantly made a new man of, whole and sound: he must grow gradually, even through many a returning pang, into health and cure. If any one thinks I could stand in the presence of that old man without an anguish sharp as death, which made me for the moment wish I had never been born, he is mistaken.

But alleviations came. The first was to see the old man sitting there alive and well though evidently fully aware of the truth, and having been so for some time, for his countenance was composed, his tea was placed beside him on the table, and there was an open Bible before him, in which he had been reading. His voice, too, had nothing unnatural or alarming in it, as, without looking at me, he bade the maidservant "give Doctor Urquhart a chair, and say, if any one interrupted, that we were particularly engaged." So the door was shut upon us, leaving us face to face.

But it was not long before he raised his eyes to me. It is enough, once in a lifetime, to have borne such a look.

"Mr. Johnston,"—but he shut his ears.

"Do not speak," he said; "what you have come to tell me I know already. My daughter told me this morning. And I have been trying ever since to find out what my Church says to the shedder of blood; what she would teach a father to say to the murderer of his child. My Harry, my only son! And you murdered him!"

Let the words which followed be sacred. If in some degree they were unjust, and overstepped the truth, let me not dare to murmur. I believe the curses he heaped upon me in his own words and those of the Holy Book, will not come, for its other and diviner words, which his daughter taught me, stand as a shield between me and him. I repeated them to myself in my silence, and so I was able to endure.

When he paused and commanded me to speak, I answered only a few words—namely, that I was here to offer my life for his son's life; that he might do with me what he would.

"Which means, that I should give you up to justice, have you tried, condemned, executed. You, Doctor Urquhart, whom the world thinks so well of. I might live to see you hanged."

His eyes glared, his whole frame was convulsed. I entreated him to calm himself; for his own health's sake, and the sake of his children.

A Life for a Life

"Yes, I will. Old as I am, this shall not kill me. I will live to exact retribution. My boy, my poor murdered Harry—murdered—murdered."

He kept repeating and dwelling on the word, till at length I said—

"If you know the whole truth, you must be aware that I had no intention to murder him."

"What, you extenuate? You wish to escape? But you shall not. I will have you arrested now, in this very house."

"Be it so, then."

And I sat down.

So, the end had come. Life, and all its hopes, all its work, were over for me. I saw, as in a second of time, everything that was coming—the trial, the conviction, the newspaper clatter over my name, my ill deeds exaggerated, my good deeds pointed at with the finger of scorn, which perhaps was the keenest agony of all—save one.

"Theodora!"

Whether I uttered her name, or only thought it, I cannot tell. However, it brought her. I felt she was in the room, though she stood by her sister's side, and did not approach me.

Again, I repeat, let no man say that sin does not bring its wages, which *must* be paid. Whosoever doubts it, I would he could sit as I sat, watching the faces of father and daughters, and thinking of the dead face which lay against my knee, that midnight, on Salisbury Plain.

"Children," I heard Mr. Johnston saying, "I have sent for you to be my witnesses in what I am about to do. Not out of personal revenge—which were unbecoming a clergyman—but because God and man exact retribution for blood. There is the man who murdered Harry. Though he were the best friend I ever had, though I esteemed him ever so much, which I did,—still, discovering this, I must have retribution.

A Life for a Life

"How, father?" Not *her* voice, but her sister's.

Let me do full justice to Penelope Johnston. Though it was she who told my secret to her father, she did it out of no malice. As I afterwards learned, chance led their conversation into such a channel that she could only escape betraying the truth by a direct lie. And with all her harshnesses, the prominent feature of her character is its truthfulness, or rather its abhorrence of falsehood. Nay, her fierce scorn of any kind of duplicity is such, that she confounds the crime with the criminal, and, once deceived, never can forgive,—as in the matter of Lydia Cartwright, my acquaintance with which gave me this insight into Miss Johnston's peculiarity.

Thus, though it fell to her lot to betray my confession, I doubt not she did so with most literal accuracy; acting towards me neither as a friend nor foe, but simply as a relater of facts. Nor was there any personal enmity towards me in her question to her father.

It startled him a little.

"How did you say? By the law, I conclude. There is no other way."

"And if so, what will be the result? I mean what will be done to him?"

"I cannot tell—how should I?"

"Perhaps I can; for I have thought over and studied the question all day," answered Miss Johnston, still in the same cold, clear, impartial voice. "He will be tried, of course. I find from your 'Taylor on Evidence,' father, that a man can be tried and convicted, solely on his own confession. But in this case, there being no corroborating proof; and all having happened so long ago, it will scarcely prove a capital crime. I believe no jury would give a stronger verdict than manslaughter. He will be imprisoned, or transported beyond seas; where, with his good character, he will soon work his liberty, and start afresh in another country, in spite of us. This, I think, is the common-sense view of the matter."

Astonished as Mr. Johnston looked, he made no reply. His daughter continued—

"And for this, you and we shall have the credit of having had arrested in our own house, a man who threw himself on our mercy, who, though he concealed, never denied his guilt; who never deceived us in any way. The moment he discovered the whole truth, dreadful as it was, he never shirked it, nor hid it from us; but told us outright, risking all the consequences. A man, too, against whom, in his whole life, we can prove but this one crime."

"What, do you take his part?"

"No," she said; "I wish he had died before he set foot in this house—for I remember Harry. But I see also that after all this lapse of years Harry is not the only person whom we ought to remember."

"I remember nothing but the words of this Book," cried the old man, letting his hand drop heavily upon it. "'Whoso sheddeth man's blood, by man shall his blood be shed.' What have you to say for yourself; *murderer*?"

All this time, faithful to her promise to me, she had not interfered—she, my love, who loved me; but when she heard him call me *that*, she shivered all over, and looked towards me. A pitiful, entreating look, but, thank God, there was no doubt in it—not the shadow of change. It nerved me to reply, what I will here record, by her desire and for her sake.

"Mr. Johnston, I have this to say. It is written,—'Whoso hateth his brother is a murderer,' and in that sense, I am one,—for I did hate him at the time; but I never meant to kill him—and the moment afterwards I would have given my life for his. If now, my death could restore him to you, alive again, how willingly I would die."

"Die, and face your Maker? an unpardoned man-slayer, a lost soul?"

"Whether I live or die," said I humbly, "I trust my soul is not lost. I have been very guilty; but I believe in One who brought to every sinner on earth the gospel of repentance and remission of sins."

At this, burst out the anathema—not merely of the father, but the clergyman,—who mingled the Jewish doctrine of retributive vengeance during this life with the Christian belief of rewards and punishments after death, and confounded the Mosaic gehenna with

A Life for a Life

the Calvinistic hell. I will not record all this—it was very terrible; but he only spoke as he believed, and as many earnest Christians do believe. I think, in all humility, that the Master Himself preached a different gospel.

I saw it, shining out of her eyes—my angel of peace and pardon. O Thou, from whom all love comes, was it impious if the love of this Thy creature towards one so wretched, should come to me like an assurance of Thine?

At length her father ceased speaking—took up a pen and began hastily writing. Miss Johnston went and looked over his shoulder.

"Papa, if that is a warrant you are making out, better think twice about it; for, as a magistrate, you cannot retract. Should you send Doctor Urquhart to trial, you must be prepared for the whole truth to come out. He must tell it; or, if he calls Dora and me as witnesses—she having already his written confession in full—we must."

"You must tell—what?"

"The provocation Doctor Urquhart received—how Harry enticed him, a lad of nineteen, to drink—made him mad, and taunted him. Everything will be made public—how Harry was so degraded that from the hour of his death we were thankful to forget that he had ever existed—how he died as he had lived—a boaster, a coward, spunging upon any one from whom he could get money, using his talents only to his shame, devoid of one spark of honesty, honour, and generosity. It is shocking to have to say this of one's own brother; but, father, you know it is the truth—and, as such, it must be told."

Amazed—I listened to her—this eldest sister, who, I knew, disliked me.

Her father seemed equally surprised,—until, at length, her arguments apparently struck him with uneasiness.

"Have you any motive in arguing thus?" said he, hurriedly and not without agitation; "why do you do it, Penelope?"

A Life for a Life

"A little, on my own account, though the great scandal and publicity will not much affect Francis and me—we shall soon be out of England. But for the family's sake,—for Harry's sake,—when all his wickednesses and our miseries have been safely covered up these twenty years—consider, father!"

She stung him deeper than she knew. I had guessed it before, when I was almost a stranger to him—but now the whole history of that old man's life was betrayed in one groan, which burst from the very depth of the father's soul.

"Eli—the priest of the Lord—his sons made themselves vile and he restrained them not. Therefore they died in one day, both of them. It was the will of the Lord."

The respectful silence which ensued, no one dared to break.

He broke it himself at last, pointing to the door. "Go! murderer, or man-slayer, or whatever you are, you must go free. Moreover, I must have your promise—no, your oath—that the secret you have kept so long, you will now keep for ever."

"Sir," I said; but he stopped me fiercely.

"No hesitations—no explanations—I will have none and give none. As you said, your life is mine—to do with it as I choose. Better you should go unpunished, than that I and mine should be disgraced. Obey me. Promise."

I did.

Thus, in another and still stranger way, my resolutions were broken, my fate was decided for me, and I have to keep this secret unconfessed to the end.

"Now, go. Put half the earth between us if you can—only go."

Again I turned to obey. Blind obedience seemed the only duty left me. I might even have quitted the house, with a feeling of total irresponsibility and indifference to all things, had it not been for a low cry which I heard, as in a dream.

A Life for a Life

So did her father. "Dora—I had forgotten. There was some sort of fancy between you and Dora. Daughter, bid him farewell, and let him go."

Then she said—my love said, in her own soft, distinct voice, "No, papa, I never mean to bid him farewell—that is, finally—never as long as I live."

Her father and sister were both so astounded that at first they did not interrupt her, but let her speak on.

"I belonged to Max before all this happened. If it had happened a year hence, when I was his wife, it would not have broken our marriage. It ought not now. When any two people are to one another what we are, they are as good as married; and they have no right to part, no more than man and wife have, unless either grows wicked, or both change. I never mean to part from Max Urquhart."

She spoke meekly, standing with hands folded and head drooping; but as still and steadfast as a rock. My darling —my darling!

Steadfast! She had need to be. What she bore during the next few minutes she would not wish me to repeat, I feel sure. She knows it, and so do I. She knows also that every stab with which I then saw her wounded for my sake, is counted in my heart, as a debt to be paid one day, if between those who love there can be any debts at all. She says not. Yet, if ever she is my wife.—People talk of dying for a woman's sake—but to live—live for her with the whole of one's being— to work for her, to sustain and cheer her—to fill her daily existence with tenderness and care—if ever she is my wife, she will find out what I mean.

After saying all he well could say, Mr. Johnston asked her how she dared think of me—me, laden with her brother's blood and her father's curse.

She turned deadly pale, but never faltered: "The curse causeless shall not come," she said, "for the blood upon his hand, whether it were Harry's or a stranger's, makes no difference; it is washed out. He has repented long ago. If God has forgiven him, and helped him to be what he is, and lead the life he has led all these years, why should I not forgive him? And if I forgive, why not love him, and if I love him, why break my promise, and refuse to marry him?"

"Do you mean, then, to marry him?" said her sister.

"Some day—if he wishes it—yes!"

From this time I myself hardly remember what passed; I can only see her standing there, her sweet face white as death, making no moan, and answering nothing to any accusations that were heaped upon her, except when she was commanded to give me up, entirely and for ever and ever.

"I cannot, father. I have no right to do it. I belong to him; he is my husband."

At last, Miss Johnston said to me—rather gently than not, for her, "I think, Doctor Urquhart, you had better go."

My love looked towards me, and afterwards at her poor father; she too said, "Yes, Max, go."

And then they wanted her to promise she would never see me nor write to me; but she refused.

"Father, I will not marry him for ever so long, if you choose—but I cannot forsake him. I must write to him. I am his very own, and he has only me. Oh, papa, think of yourself and my mother." And she sobbed at his knees.

He must have thought of Harry's mother, not hers, for this exclamation only hardened him.

Then Theodora rose, and gave me her little hand.—"It can hold firm, you will find. You have my promise. But whether or no, it would have been all the same. No love is worth having that could not, with or without a promise, keep true till death. You may trust me. Now, good-bye. Good-bye, my Max."

With that one clasp of the hand, that one look into her fond, faithful eyes, we parted. I have never seen her since.

A Life for a Life

This statement, which is as accurate as I can make it, except in the case of those voluntary omissions which I believe you yourself would have desired, I here seal up, to be delivered to you with those other letters in case I should die while you are still Theodora Johnston.

I have also made my will, leaving you all my effects, and appointing you my sole executrix; putting you, in short, in exactly the same position as if you had been my wife. This is best, in order that by no chance should the secret ooze out through any guesses of any person not connected with your family; also because I think it is what you would wish yourself. You said truly, I have only you.

Another word, which I do not name in my ordinary letters, lest I might grieve you by what may prove to be only a fancy of mine.

Sometimes, in the hard work of this my life here, I begin to feel that I am no longer a young man, and that the reaction after the great strain, mental and bodily, of the last few months, has left me not so strong as I used to be. Not that I think I am about to die,—far from it. I have a good constitution, which has worn well yet, and may wear on for some time, though not for ever, and I am nearly fifteen years older than you.

It is very possible that before any change can come, I may leave you, never a wife, and yet a widow. Possible, among the numerous fatalities of life, that we may never be married—ever even see one another again.

Sometimes, when I see two young people married and happy, taking it all as a matter of course, scarcely even recognising it as happiness—just like Mr. and Mrs. Treherne, who hunted me out lately, and insisted on my visiting them— I think of you and me, and it seems very bitter, and I look on the future with less faith than fear. It might not be so if I could see you now and then—but oftentimes this absence feels like death.

Theodora, if I should die before we are married, without any chance of writing down my last words, take them here.

No, they will not come. I can but crush my lips upon this paper—only thy name, not thee, and call thee "my love, my love!"

Remember, I loved thee—all my soul was full of the love of thee. It made life happy, earth beautiful, and heaven nearer. It was with me day and night, in work or rest—as much a part of me as the hand I write with, or the breath I draw. I never thought of myself; but of "us." I never prayed but I prayed for two. Love, my love, so many miles away—Oh, my God, why not grant me a little happiness before I die!

Yet, as once I wrote before, and as she says always in all things, *Thy will be done.*

Chapter 28

HER STORY

Friday night.

My Dear Max, —You have had your Dominical letter, as you call it, so regularly, that you must know all our doings at Rockmount almost as well as ourselves. If I write foolishly, and tell you all sorts of trivial things, perhaps some of them twice over, it is just because there is nothing else to tell. But, trivial or not, I have a feeling that you like to hear it—you care for everything that concerns me.

So, first, in obedience to orders, I am quite well, even though my handwriting is "not so pretty as it used to be." Do not fancy the hand shakes, or is nervous or uncertain. Not a bit of it. I am never nervous, nor weak either—now. Sometimes, perhaps, being only a woman after all, I feel things a little more keenly than I ought to feel; and then, not being good at concealment, at least not with you, this fact peeps out in my letters. For the home-life has its cares, and I feel very weary sometimes—and then, I have not you to rest upon— visibly, that is—though in my heart I do always. But I am quite well, Max, and quite content. Do not doubt it. He who has led us through this furnace of affliction, will lead us safely to the end.

You will be glad to hear that papa is every day less and less cold to me—poor papa! Last Sunday, he even walked home from church with me, talking about general subjects, like his old self, almost. Penelope has been always good and kind.

You ask if they ever name you? No.

Life at Rockmount moves slowly, even in the midst of marriage preparations. Penelope is getting a large store of wedding presents. Mrs. Granton brought a beautiful one last night from her son Colin.

I was glad you had that long friendly letter from Colin Granton— glad also that, his mother having let out the secret about you and me, he was generous enough to tell you himself that other secret, which I never told. Well, your guess was right; it was so. But I could not help it; I did not know it.—For me—how could any girl, feeling as I then

A Life for a Life

did towards you, feel anything towards any other man but the merest kindliness? — That is all: we will never say another word about it; except that I wish you always to be specially kind to Colin, and to do him good whenever you can — he was very good to me.

Life at Rockmount, as I said, is dull. I rise sometimes, go through the day, and go to bed at night, wondering what I have been doing during all these hours. And I do not always sleep soundly, though so tired. Perhaps it is partly the idea of Penelope's going away so soon; far away, across the sea, with no one to hove her and take care of her, save Francis.

Understand, this is not with any pitying of my sister for what is a natural and even a happy hot, which no woman need complain of; but simply because Francis is Francis — accustomed to think only of himself, and for himself. It may be different when he is married.

He was staying with us here a week; during which I noticed him more closely than in his former fly-away visits. When one lives in the house with a person — a dull house too, like ours, how wonderfully odds and ends of character "crop out," as the geologists say. Do you remember the weeks when you were almost continually in our house? Francis had what we used to call "the Doctor's room." He was pleasant and agreeable enough, when it pleased him to be so; but, for all that, I used to say to myself twenty times a day, "My dear Max!"

This merely implies that by a happy dispensation of Providence, I, Theodora Johnston, have not the least desire to appropriate my sister's husband, or, indeed, either of my sisters' husbands.

By-the-bye, in a letter from Augustus to papa, which reached me through Penelope, he names his visit to you. I am glad — glad he should show you such honour and affection, and that they all should see it. Do not give up the Trehernes; go there sometimes — for my sake. There is no reason why you should not. Papa knows it; he also knows I write to you — but he never says a word, one way or other. We must wait — wait and hope — or rather, trust. As you say, the difference between young and old people is, the one hopes, the other trusts.

I seem, from your description, to have a clear idea of the gaol, and the long, barren breezy flat amidst which it lies, with the sea in the distance. I often sit and think of the view outside, and of the dreary inside, where you spend so many hours; the corridors, the exercise-yards, and the cells; also your own two rooms, which you say are almost as silent and solitary, except when you come in and find my letter waiting you. I wish it was me!—pardon grammar—but I wish it was me—this living me. Would you be glad to see me? Ah, I know!

Look! I am not going to write about ourselves—it is not good for us. We know it all; we know our hearts are nigh breaking sometimes—mine is. But it shall not. We will live and wait.

What was I telling you about?—oh, Francis. Well, Francis spent a whole week at Rockmount, by papa's special desire, that they might discuss business arrangements, and that he might see a little more of his intended son-in-law than he has done of late years. Business was soon despatched—papa gives none of us any money during his lifetime; what will come to us afterwards we have never thought of inquiring. Francis did, though—which somewhat hurt Penelope—but he accounted for it by his being so "poor." A relative phrase; why, I should think £500 a year, certain, a mine of riches—and all to be spent upon himself. But as he says, a single man has so many inevitable expenses, especially when he lives in society, and is the nephew of Sir William Treherne, of Treherne Court. All "circumstances"! Poor Francis; whatever goes wrong he is sure to put between himself and blame the shield of "circumstances." Now, if I were a man, I would fight the world barefronted, anyhow. One would but be killed at last.

Is it wrong of me to write to you so freely about Francis? I hope not. All mine are yours, and yours mine; you know their faults and virtues as well as I do, and will judge them equally, as we ought to judge those who, whatever they are, are permanently our own. I have tried hard, this time, to make a real brother of Francis Charteris; and he is, for many things, exceedingly likeable—nay, lovable. I see, sometimes, clearly enough, the strange charm which has made Penelope so fond of him all these years. Whether, besides loving him, she can trust him—can look on his face and feel that he would not deceive her for the world—can believe every line he writes, and every word he utters, and know that whatever he does, he will do simply from his sense of right, no meaner motive interfering—oh,

Max, I would give much to be certain Penelope had this sort of love for her future husband!

Well, they have chosen their lot, and must make the best of one another. Everybody must, you know.

Heigho! what a homily I am giving you, instead of this week's history, as usual—from Saturday to Saturday.

The first few days there really was nothing to tell. Francis and Penelope took walks together, paid visits, or sat in the parlour talking—not banishing me, however, as they used to do when they were young. On Wednesday, Francis went up to London for the day, and brought back that important article, the wedding-ring. He tried it on at supper-time, with a diamond keeper, which he said would be just the thing for "the Governor's lady."

"Say wife at once," grumbled I, and complained of the modern fashion of slurring over that word, the dearest and sacredest in the language.

"Wife, then," whispered Francis, holding the ring on my sister's finger, and kissing it.

Tears started to Penelope's eyes; in her agitation she looked almost like a girl again, I thought; so infinitely happy. But Francis, never happy, muttered bitterly some regret for the past, some wish that they had been married years ago. Why were they not? It was partly his fault, I am sure.

The day after this he left, not to return till he comes to take her away finally. In the meanwhile, he will have enough to do, paying his adieux to his grand friends, and his bills to his tradespeople, prior to closing his bachelor establishment for ever and aye—how glad he must be.

He seemed glad, as if with a sense of relief that all was settled, and no room left for hesitation. It costs Francis such a world of trouble to make up his own mind—which trouble Penelope will save him for the future. He took leave of her with great tenderness, calling her "his good, faithful girl," and vowing—which one would think was quite unnecessary under the circumstances—to be faithful to her all the days of his life.

That night, when she came into my room, Penelope sat a long time on my bed talking; chiefly of old days, when she and Francis were boy and girl together—how handsome he was, and how clever—till she seemed almost to forget the long interval between. Well, they are both of an age—time runs equally with each; she is at least no more altered than he.

Here, I ought to tell you something, referring to that which, as we agreed, we are best not speaking of; even between ourselves. It is all over and done—cover it over, and let it heal.

My dear Max, Penelope confessed a thing, for which I am very sorry, but it cannot be helped now.

I told you they never name you here. Not usually, but she did that night. Just as she was leaving me, she exclaimed, suddenly—

"Dora, I have broken my promise—Francis knows about Doctor Urquhart."

"What!" I cried.

"Don't be terrified—not the whole. Merely that he wanted to marry you, but that papa found out he had done something wrong in his youth, and so forbade you to think of him."

I asked her, was she sure no more had escaped her? Not that I feared much; Penelope is literally accurate, and scrupulously straightforward in all her words and ways. But still, Francis being a little less so than she, might have questioned her.

"So he did, and I refused point-blank to tell him, saying it would be a breach of trust. He was very angry; jealous, I think," and she smiled, "till I informed him that it was not my own secret—all my own secrets I had invariably told him, as he me. At which, he said, 'Yes, of course,' and the matter ended. Are you annoyed? Do you doubt Francis's honour?"

A Life for a Life

No. For all that, I have felt anxious, and I cannot choose but tell Max; partly because he has a right to all my anxieties, and also, that he may guard against any possibility of harm. None is likely to come though; we will not be afraid.

Augustus, in his letter, says how highly he hears you spoken of in Liverpool already; how your duties at the gaol are the least of your work, and that whatever you do, or wherever you go, you leave a good influence behind you. These were his very words. I was proud, though I knew it all before.

He says you are looking thin, as if you were overworked. Max, my Max, take care. Give all due energy to the work you have to do, but remember me likewise; remember what is mine. I think, perhaps, you take too long walks between the town and the gaol, and that maybe, the prisoners themselves get far better and more regular meals than the doctor does. See to this, if you please, Dr. Urquhart.

Tell me more about those poor prisoners, in whom you take so strong an interest—your spiritual as well as medical hospital. And give me a clearer notion of your doings in the town, your practice and schemes, your gratis patients, dispensaries, and so on. Also, Augustus said you were employed in drawing up reports and statistics about reformatories, and on the general question now so much discussed,—What is to be done with our criminal classes? How busy you must be! Cannot I help you? Send me your MSS. to copy. Give me some work to do.

Max, do you remember our talk by the pond-side, when the sun was setting, and the hills looked so still, and soft, and blue? I was there the other day and thought it all over. Yes, I could have been happy, even in the solitary life we both then looked forward to, but it is better to belong to you as I do now.

God bless you and keep you safe!

Yours,

Theodora.

P.S.—I leave a blank page to fill up after Penelope and I come home. We are going into town together early to-morrow, to inquire about the character of the lady's-maid that is to be taken abroad, but we shall be back long before post-time. However, I have written all this overnight to make sure.

Sunday.

P.S.—You will have missed your Sunday letter to-day, which vexes me sore. But it is the first time you have ever looked for a letter and "wanted" it, and I trust it will be the last. Ah! now I understand a little of what Penelope must have felt, looking day after day for Francis's letters, which never came; how every morning before post-time she would go about the house as blithe as a lark, and afterwards turn cross and disagreeable, and her face would settle into the sharp, hard-set expression, which made her look so old even then. Poor Penelope! if she could have trusted him the while, it might have been otherwise—men's ways and lives are so different from women's—but it is this love without perfect trust which has been the sting of Penelope's existence.

I try to remember this when she makes me feel angry with her, as she did on Saturday. It was through her fault you missed your Sunday letter.

You know I always post them myself, in the town; our village post-office would soon set all the neighbours chattering about you and me. And besides, it is pleasant to walk through the quiet lanes we both know well with Max's letter in my hand, and think that it will be in his hand to-morrow. For this I generally choose the time when papa rests before dinner, with one or other of us reading to him, and Penelope has hitherto, without saying anything, always taken my place and set me free on a Saturday. A kindness I felt more than I expressed, many a time. But to-day she was unkind; shut herself up in her room the instant we returned from town; then papa called me and detained me till after post-time.

So you lost your letter; a small thing, you will say, and this was a foolish girl to vex herself so much about it. Especially as she can make it longer and more interesting by details of our adventures in town yesterday.

It was not altogether a pleasant day, for something happened about the servant which I am sure annoyed Penelope; nay, she being over-tired and over-exerted already, this new vexation, whatever it was, made her quite ill for the time, though she would not allow it, and when I ventured to question, bade me sharply, "let her alone." You know Penelope's ways, and may have seen them reflected in me sometimes. I am afraid, Max, that, however good we may be (of course!) we are not exactly what would be termed "an amiable family."

We were amiable when we started, however; my sister and I went up to town quite merrily. I am merry sometimes, in spite of all things. You see, to have every one that belongs to one happy and prosperous, is a great element in one's personal content. Other people's troubles weigh heavily, because we never know exactly how they will bear them, and because, at best, we can only sit by and watch them suffer, so little help being possible after all. But our own troubles we can always bear.

You will understand all I mean by "our own." I am often very sad for you, Max; but never afraid for you, never in doubt about you, not for an instant. There is no sting even in my saddest thought concerning you. I trust you, I feel certain that whatever you do, you will do right; that all you have to endure will be borne nobly and bravely. Thus, I may grieve over your griefs, but never over you. My love of you, like my faith in you, is above all grieving. Forgive this long digression; to-day is Sunday, the best day in all the week, and my day for thinking most of you.

To return. Penelope and I were both merry, as we started by the very earliest train, in the soft May morning; we had so much business to get through. You can't understand it, of course, so I omit it, only confiding to you our last crowning achievement—the dress. It is white *moire antique*; Dr. Urquhart has not the slightest idea what that is, but no matter; and it has lace flounces, half a yard deep, and it is altogether a most splendid affair. But the Governor's lady—I beg my own pardon—the Governor's wife, must be magnificent, you know.

It was the mantua-maker, a great West-end personage employed by the grand family to whom, by Francis's advice, Lydia Cartwright was sent, some years ago (by-the-bye, I met Mrs. Cartwright to-day, who asked after you, and sent her duty, and wished you would know that she had heard from Lydia),—this mantua-maker it was who recommended the lady's-maid, Sarah Enfield, who had once been a workwoman of her own. We saw the person, who seemed a decent young woman, but delicate-looking; said her health was injured with the long hours of millinery-work, and that she should have died, she thought, if a friend of hers, a kind young woman, had not taken her in and helped her. She was lodging with this friend now.

On the whole, Sarah Enfield sufficiently pleased us to make my sister decide on engaging her, if only Francis could see her first. We sent a message to his lodgings, and were considerably surprised to have the answer that he was not at home, and had not been for three weeks; indeed, he hardly ever was at home. After some annoyance, Penelope resolved to make her decision without him.

Hardly ever at home! What a lively life Francis must lead: I wonder he does not grow weary of it. Once, he half owned he was, but added, "that he must float with the stream—it was too late now—he could not stop himself." Penelope will, though.

As we drove through the Park, to the address Sarah Enfield had given us—somewhere about Kensington—Penelope wishing to see the girl once again and engage her—my sister observed, in answer to my remark, that Francis must have many invitations.

"Of course he has. It shows how much he is liked and respected. It will be the same abroad. We shall gather round us the very best society in the island. Still, he will find it a great change from London."

I wonder, is she at all afraid of it, or suspects that he once was? that he shrank from being thrown altogether upon his wife's society—like the Frenchman who declined marrying a lady he had long visited because "where should he spend his evenings?" O me! what a heartbreaking thing to feel that one's husband needed somewhere to spend his evenings.

We drove past Holland Park—what a bonnie place it is (as you would say); how full the trees were of green leaves and birds. I don't know where we went next—I hardly know anything of London, thank goodness!—but it was a pretty, quiet neighbourhood, where we had the greatest difficulty in finding the house we wanted, and at last had recourse to the post-office.

A Life for a Life

The post-mistress—who was rather grim—"knew the place, that is, the name of the party as lived there—which was all she cared to know. She called herself Mrs. Chaytor, or Chater, or something like it," which we decided must be Sarah Enfield's charitable friend, and accordingly drove thither.

It was a small house, a mere cottage, set in a pleasant little garden, through the palings of which I saw, walking about, a young woman with a child in her arms. She had on a straw hat with a deep lace fall that hid her face, but her figure was very graceful, and she was extremely well dressed. Nevertheless, she looked not exactly "the lady." Also, hearing the gate-bell, she called out, "'Arriet," in no lady's voice.

Penelope glanced at her, and then sharply at me.

"I wonder—" she began; but stopped—told me to remain in the carriage while she went in, and she would fetch me if she wanted me.

But she did not. Indeed, she hardly stayed two minutes. I saw the young woman run hastily in-doors, leaving her child—such a pretty boy! screaming after his "mammy,"—and Penelope came back, her face the colour of scarlet.

"What? Is it a mistake?" I asked.

"No—yes," and she gave the order to drive on.

Again I inquired if anything were the matter, and was answered, "Nothing—nothing that I could understand." After which she sat with her veil down, cogitating; till, all of a sudden, she sprang up as if some one had given her a stab at her heart. I was quite terrified, but she again told me it was nothing, and bade me "let her alone." Which, as you know, is the only thing one can do with my sister Penelope.

But at the railway-station we met some people we knew, and she was forced to talk; so that by the time we reached Rockmount she seemed to have got over her annoyance, whatever it was, concerning Sarah Enfield, and was herself again. That is, herself in one of those moods when, whether her ailment be mental or physical, the sole chance of its passing away is, as she says, "to leave her alone."

I do not say this is not trying—doubly so now, when, just as she is leaving, I seem to understand my sister better and love her more than ever I did in my life. But I have learned at last not to break my heart over the peculiarities of those I care for; but try to bear with them as they must with mine, of which I have no lack, goodness knows!

I saw a letter to Francis in the post-bag this morning, so I hope she has relieved her mind by giving him the explanation which she refused to me. It must have been some deception practised on her by this Sarah Enfield, and Penelope never forgives the smallest deceit.

She was either too much tired or too much annoyed to appear again yesterday, so papa and I spent the afternoon and evening alone. But she went to church with us, as usual, to-day—looking pale and tired—the ill mood—"the little black dog on her shoulder," as we used to call it, not having quite vanished.

Also, I noticed an absent expression in her eyes, and her voice in the responses was less regular than usual. Perhaps she was thinking this would almost be her last Sunday of sitting in the old pew, and looking up to papa's white hair, and her heart being fuller, her lips were more silent than usual.

You will not mind my writing so much about my sister Penelope? You like me to talk to you of what is about me, and uppermost in my thoughts, which is herself at present. She has been very good to me, and Max loves every one whom I love, and every one who loves me.

I shall have your letter to-morrow morning. Good night!

Theodora.

Chapter 29

HIS STORY

My Dear Theodora,—This is a line extra, written on receipt of yours, which was most welcome. I feared something had gone wrong with my little methodical girl.

Do not keep strictly to your Dominical letter just now—write any day that you can. Tell me everything that is happening to you—you must, and ought. Nothing must occur to you or yours that I do not know. You are mine.

Your last letter I do not answer in detail till the next shall come: not exactly from press of business; I would make time if I had it not; but from various other reasons, which you shall have by-and-by.

Give me, if you remember it, the address of the person with whom Sarah Enfield is lodging. I suspect she is a woman of whom, by the desire of her nearest relative, I have been in search of for some time. But, should you have forgotten, do not trouble your sister about this. I will find out all I wish to learn some other way. Never apologise for, or hesitate at, writing to me about your family— all that is yours is mine. Keep your heart up about your sister Penelope: she is a good woman, and all that befalls her will be for her good. Love her, and be patient with her continually. All your love for her and the rest takes nothing from what is mine, but adds thereto.

Let me hear soon what is passing at Rockmount. I cannot come to you, and help you—would I could! My love! My love!

Max Urquhart.

There is little or nothing to say of myself this week, and what there was you heard yesterday.

A Life for a Life

Chapter 30

HER STORY

My Dear Max,—I write this in the middle of the night; there has been no chance for me during the day; nor, indeed, at all—until now. To-night, for the first time, Penelope has fallen asleep. I have taken the opportunity of stealing into the next room, to comfort—and you.

My dear Max! Oh, if you knew! oh, if I could but come to you for one minute's rest, one minute's love!—There—I will not cry any more. It is much to be able to write to you; and blessed, infinitely blessed to know you are—what you are.

Max, I have been weak, wicked of late; afraid of absence, which tries me sore, because I am not strong, and cannot stand up by myself as I used to do; afraid of death, which might tear you from me, or me from you, leaving the other to go mourning upon earth for ever. Now I feel that absence is nothing—death itself nothing, compared to one loss—that which has befallen my sister, Penelope.

You may have heard of it, even in these few days—ill news spreads fast. Tell me what you hear; for we wish to save my sister as much as we can. To our friends generally, I have merely written that, "from unforeseen differences," the marriage is broken off. Mr. Charteris may give what reasons he likes at Treherne Court. We will not try to injure him with his uncle.

I have just crept in to look at Penelope; she is asleep still, and has never stirred. She looks so old—like a woman of fifty, almost. No wonder. Think—ten years—all her youth to be crushed out at once. I wonder, will it kill her? It would me.

I wanted to ask you—do you think, medically, there is any present danger in her state? She lies quiet enough; taking little notice of me or anybody—with her eyes shut during the daytime, and open, wide-staring, all night long. What ought I to do with her? There is only me, you know. If you fear anything, send me a telegram at once. Do not wait to write.

A Life for a Life

But, that you may the better judge her state, I ought just to give you full particulars, beginning where my last letter ended.

That "little black dog on her shoulder," which I spoke of so lightly!—God forgive me! also for leaving her the whole of that Sunday afternoon with her door locked, and the room still as death; yet never once knocking to ask, "Penelope, how are you?"

On Sunday night, the curate came to supper, and papa sent me to summon her; she came downstairs, took her place at table, and conversed. I did not notice her much, except that she moved about in a stupid, stunned-like fashion, which caused papa to remark more than once, "Penelope, I think you are half asleep." She never answered.

Another night, and the half of another day, she must have spent in the same manner. And I let her do it without inquiry! Shall I ever forgive myself?

In the afternoon of Monday, I was sitting at work, busy finishing her embroidered marriage handkerchief, alone in the sunshiny parlour, thinking of my letter, which you would have received at last; also thinking it was rather wicked of my happy sister to sulk for two whole days, because of a small disappointment about a servant—if such it were. I had almost determined to shake her out of her ridiculous reserve, by asking boldly what was the matter, and giving her a thorough scolding if I dared; when the door opened, and in walked Francis Charteris.

Heartily glad to see him, in the hope his coming might set Penelope right again, I jumped up and shook hands cordially. Nor till afterwards did I remember how much this seemed to surprise and relieve him.

"Oh, then, all is right!" said he. "I feared, from Penelope's letter, that she was a little annoyed with me. Nothing new that, you know."

"Something did annoy her, I suspect," and I was about to blurt out as much as I knew or guessed of the foolish mystery about Sarah Enfield, but some instinct stopped me. "You and Penelope had better settle your own affairs," said I, laughing. "I'll go and fetch her."

"Thank you." He threw himself down on the velvet arm-chair—his favourite lounge in our house for the last ten years. His handsome profile turned up against the light, his fingers lazily tapping the arm of the chair, a trick he had from his boyhood,—this is my last impression of Francis—as *our* Francis Charteris.

I had to call outside Penelope's door three times, "Francis is here," "Francis is waiting," "Francis wants to speak to you," before she answered or appeared; and then, without taking the slightest notice of me, she walked slowly downstairs, holding by the wall as she went.

So, I thought, it is Francis who has vexed her after all, and determined to leave them to fight it out and make it up again—this, which would be the last of their many lovers' quarrels. Ah! it was.

Half-an-hour afterwards, papa sent for me to the study, and there I saw Francis Charteris standing, exactly where you once stood—you see, I am not afraid of remembering it myself or of reminding you. No, my Max! Our griefs are nothing, nothing!

Penelope also was present, standing by my father, who said, looking round at us with a troubled, bewildered air:—

"Dora, what is all this? Your sister comes here and tells me she will not marry Francis. Francis rushes in after her, and says, I hardly can make out what. Children, why do you vex me so? Why cannot you leave an old man in peace?"

Penelope answered:—"Father, you shall be left in peace, if you will only confirm what I have said to that—that gentleman, and send him out of my sight."

Francis laughed:—"To be called back again presently. You know you will do it, as soon as you have come to your right senses, Penelope. You will never disgrace us in the eyes of the world—set everybody gossiping about our affairs for such a trifle."

My sister made him no answer. There was less even of anger than contempt—utter, measureless contempt—in the way she just lifted up her eyes and looked at him—looked him over from head to heel, and turned again to her father.

"Papa, make him understand—I cannot—that I wish all this ended; I wish never to see his face again."

"Why?" said papa, in great perplexity.

"He knows why."

Papa and I both turned to Francis, whose careless manner changed a little: he grew red and uncomfortable. "She may tell if she chooses; I lay no embargo of silence upon her. I have made all the explanations possible, and if she will not receive them, I cannot help it. The thing is done, and cannot be undone. I have begged her pardon, and made all sorts of promises for the future—no man can do more."

He said this sullenly, and yet as if he wished to make friends with her, but Penelope seemed scarcely even to hear.

"Papa," she repeated, still in the same stony voice, "I wish you would end this scene; it is killing me. Tell him, will you, that I have burned all his letters, every one. Insist on his returning mine. His presents are all tied up in a parcel in my room, except this; will you give it back to him?"

She took off her ring, a small common turquoise which Francis had given her when he was young and poor, and laid it on the table. Francis snatched it up, handled it a minute, and then threw it violently into the fire.

"Bear witness, Mr. Johnston, and you too, Dora, that it is Penelope, not I, who breaks our engagement. I would have fulfilled it honourably—I would have married her."

"Would you?" cried Penelope, with flashing eyes, "no—not that last degradation—no!"

"I would have married her," Francis continued, "and made her a good husband too. Her reason for refusing me is puerile—perfectly puerile. No woman of sense, who knows anything of the world, would urge it for a moment. Nor man either, unless he was your favourite—who, I believe, is at the bottom of this, who, for all you know, may be doing exactly as I have done—Doctor Urquhart."

A Life for a Life

Papa started and said hastily, "Confine yourself to the subject on hand, Francis. Of what is this that my daughter accuses you? Tell me, and let me judge."

Francis hesitated, and then said, "Send away these girls, and you shall hear."

Suddenly, it flashed upon me *what* it was. How the intuition came, how little things, before unnoticed, seemed to rise and put themselves together, including Saturday's story—and the shudder that ran through Penelope from head to foot, when on Sunday morning old Mrs. Cartwright curtsied to her at the church-door—all this I cannot account for, but I seemed to know as well as if I had been told everything. I need not explain, for evidently you know it also, and it is so dreadful, so unspeakably dreadful.

Oh, Max, for the first minute or so, I felt as if the whole world were crumbling from under my feet—as I could trust nobody, believe in nobody—until I remembered you. My dear Max, my own dear Max! Ah, wretched Penelope!

I took her hand as she stood, but she twisted it out of mine again. I listened mechanically to Francis, as he again began rapidly and eagerly to exculpate himself to my father.

"She may tell you all, if she likes. I have done no worse than hundreds do in my position, and under my unfortunate circumstances, and the world forgives them, and women too. How could I help it? I was too poor to marry. And before I married I meant to do every one justice—I meant—"

Penelope covered her ears. Her face was so ghastly, that papa himself said, "I think, Francis, explanations are idle. You had better defer them and go."

"I will take you at your word," he replied haughtily. "If you or she think better of it, or of me, I shall be at any time ready to fulfil my engagement—honourably, as a gentleman should. Good-bye; will you not shake hands with me, Penelope?"

He walked up to her, trying apparently to carry things off with a high air, but he was not strong enough, or hardened enough. At sight of my sister sitting there, for she had sank down at last, with a face like a corpse, only it had not the peace of the dead, Francis trembled.

"Forgive me, if I have done you any harm. It was all the result of circumstances. Perhaps, if you had been a little less rigid—had scolded me less and studied me more—But you could not help your nature, nor I mine. Good-bye, Penelope."

She sat, impassive; even when with a sort of involuntary tenderness, he seized and kissed her hand; but the instant he was gone—fairly gone—with the door shut upon him and his horse clattering down the road—I heard it plainly—Penelope started up with a cry of "Francis—Francis!"—Oh, the anguish of it!—I can hear it now.

But it was not this Francis she called after—I was sure of that—I saw it in her eyes. It was the Francis of ten years ago—the Francis she had loved—now as utterly dead and buried, as if she had seen the stone laid over him, and his body left to sleep in the grave.

Dead and buried—dead and buried. Do you know, I sometimes wish it were so; that she had been left, peacefully widowed—knowing his soul was safe with God. I thought, when papa and I—papa who that night kissed me, for the first time since one night you know—sat by Penelope's bed, watching her—"If Francis had only died!"

After she was quiet, and I had persuaded papa to go to rest, he sent for me and desired me to read a psalm, as I used to do when he was ill—you remember? When it was ended, he asked me, had I any idea what Francis had done that Penelope could not pardon?

I told him, difficult and painful as it was to do it, all I suspected—indeed, felt sure of. For was it not the truth?— the only answer I could give. For the same reason I write of these terrible things to you without any false delicacy—they are the truth, and they must be told.

Papa lay for some time, thinking deeply. At last he said:—

"My dear, you are no longer a child, and I may speak to you plainly. I am an old man, and your mother is dead. I wish she were with us now, she might help us: for she was a good woman, Dora. Do you think—take time to consider the question—that your sister is acting right?"

I said, "quite right."

"Yet, I thought you held that doctrine, 'the greater the sinner the greater the saint'; and believed every crime a man can commit may be repented, atoned, and pardoned?"

"Yes, father; but Francis has never either repented or atoned."

No; and therefore I feel certain my sister is right. Ay, even putting aside the other fact, that the discovery of his long years of deception must have so withered up her love,—scorched it at the root, as with a stroke of lightning—that even if she pitied him, she must also despise. Fancy, despising one's *husband!*

Besides, she is not the only one wronged. Sometimes, even sitting by my sister's bedside, I see the vision of that pretty young creature—she was so pretty and innocent when she first came to live at Rockmount,—with her boy in her arms; and my heart feels like to burst with indignation and shame, and a kind of shuddering horror at the wickedness of the world—yet with a strange feeling of unutterable pity lying at the depth of all.

Max, tell me what you think—you who are so much the wiser of us two; but I think that even if she wished it still, my sister *ought not* to marry Francis Charteris.

Ah me! papa said truly I was no longer a child. I feel hardly even a girl, but quite an old woman—familiar with all sorts of sad and wicked things, as if the freshness and innocence had gone out of life, and were nowhere to be found.

Except when I turn to you, and lean my poor sick heart against you—as I do now. Max, comfort me!

You will, I know, write immediately you receive this. If you could have come—but that is impossible.

Augustus you will probably see, if you have not done so already—for he already looks upon you as the friend of the family, though in no other light as yet; which is best. Papa wrote to Sir William, I believe; he said he considered some explanation a duty, on his daughter's account; further than this, he wishes the matter kept quiet. Not to disgrace Francis, I thought; but papa told me one-half the world would hardly consider it any disgrace at all. Can this be so? Is it indeed such a wicked, wicked world?

—Here my letter was stopped by hearing a sort of cry in Penelope's room. I ran in, and found her sitting up in her bed, her eyes starting, and every limb convulsed. Seeing me, she cried out—

"Bring a light;—I was dreaming. But it's not true. Where is Francis?"

I made no reply, and she slowly sank down in her bed again. Recollection had come.

"I should not have gone to sleep. Why did you let me? Or why cannot you put me to sleep for ever and ever, and ever and ever?" repeating the word many times. "Dora!" and my sister fixed her piteous eyes on my face, "I should be so glad to die. Why won't you kill me?"

I burst into tears.

Max, you will understand the total helplessness one feels in the presence of an irremediable grief like this: how consolation seems cruel, and reasoning vain. "Miserable comforters are ye all," said Job to his three friends; and a miserable comforter I felt to this my sister, whom it had pleased the Almighty to smite so sore, until I remembered that He who smites can heal.

I lay down outside the bed, put my arm over her, and remained thus for a long time, not saying a single word—that is, not with my lips. And since our weakness is often our best strength, and when we wholly relinquish a thing, it is given back to us many a time in double measure, so, possibly, those helpless tears of mine did Penelope more good than the wisest of words.

She lay watching me—saying more than once—

"I did not know you cared so much for me, Dora."

It then came into my mind, that as wrecked people cling to the smallest spar, if, instead of her conviction that in losing Francis she had lost her all, I could by any means make Penelope feel that there were others to cling to, others who loved her dearly, and whom she ought to try and live for still—it might save her. So, acting on the impulse, I told my sister how good I thought her, and how wicked I myself had been for not long since discovering her goodness. How, when at last I learned to appreciate her, and to understand what a sorely-tried life hers had been, there came not only respect, but love. Thorough sisterly love; such as people do not necessarily feel even for their own flesh and blood, but never, I doubt, except to them. (Save, that in some inexplicable way, fondly reflected, I have something of the same sort of love for your brother Dallas.)

Afterwards, she lying still and listening, I tried to make my sister understand what I had myself felt when she came to my bedside and comforted me that morning, months ago, when I was so wretched; how no wretchedness of loss can be altogether unendurable, so long as it does not strike at the household peace, but leaves the sufferer a little love to rest upon at home.

And at length I persuaded her to promise that, since it made both papa and me so very miserable to see her thus,—and papa was an old man, too, we might not have him with us many years—she would, for our sakes, try to rouse herself, and see if life were not tolerable for a little longer.

"Yes," she answered, closing her heavy eyes, and folding her hands in a pitiful kind of patience, very strange in our quick, irritable Penelope. "Yes—just a little longer. Still, I think I shall soon die. I believe it will kill me."

I did not contradict her, but I called to mind your words, that, Penelope, being a good woman, all would happen to her for good. Also, it is usually not the good people who are killed by grief: while others take it as God's vengeance, or as the work of blind chance, they receive it humbly as God's chastisement, live on, and endure. I do not think my sister will die—whatever she may think or desire just now. Besides, we have only to deal with the present, for how can we look forward a single day? How little we expected all this only a week ago?

A Life for a Life

It seems strange that Francis could have deceived us for so long; years, it must have been; but we have lived so retired, and were such a simple family for many things. How far Penelope thinks we know—papa and I—I cannot guess: she is totally silent on the subject of Francis. Except in that one outcry, when she was still only half awake, she has never mentioned his name.

There was one thing more I wanted to tell you, Max; you know I tell you everything.

Just as I was leaving my sister, she, noticing I was not undressed, asked me if I had been sitting up all night, and reproached me for doing so.

I said, "I was not weary; that I had been quietly occupying myself in the next room."

"Reading?"

"No."

"What were you doing?" with sharp suspicion.

I answered without disguise—

"I was writing to Max."

"Max who?—Oh, I had forgotten his name."

She turned from me, and lay with her face to the wall, then said—

"Do you believe in him?"

"Yes, I do."

"You had better not. You will live to repent it. Child, mark my words. There may be good women—one or two, perhaps—but there is not a single good man in the whole world."

My heart rose to my lips; but deeds speak louder than words. I did not attempt to defend you. Besides, no wonder she should think thus.

Again she said, "Dora, tell Doctor Urquhart he was innocent comparatively; and that I say so. He only killed Harry's body, but those who deceive us are the death of one's soul. Nay," and by her expression I felt sure it was not herself and her own wrongs my sister was thinking of—"there are those who destroy both body and soul."

I made no answer; I only covered her up, kissed her, and left her; knowing that in one sense I did not leave her either forsaken or alone.

And now, I must leave you too, Max; being very weary in body, though my mind is comforted and refreshed; ay, ever since I began this letter. So many of your good words have come back to me while I wrote—words which you have let fall at odd times, long ago, even when we were mere acquaintances. You did not think I should remember them? I do, every one.

This is a great blow, no doubt. The hand of Providence has been heavy upon us and our house, lately. But I think we shall be able to bear it. One always has courage to bear a sorrow which shows its naked face, free from suspense or concealment; stands visibly in the midst of the home, and has to be met and lived down patiently, by every member therein.

You once said that we often live to see the reason of affliction; how all the events of life hang so wonderfully together, that afterwards we can frequently trace the chain of events, and see in humble faith and awe, that out of each one has been evolved the other, and that everything, bad and good, must necessarily have happened exactly as it did. Thus, I begin to see—you will not be hurt, Max?—how well it was, on some accounts, that we were not married, that I should still be living at home with my sister; and that, after all she knows, and she only, of what has happened to me this year, she cannot reject any comfort I may be able to offer her on the ground that I myself know nothing of sorrow.

A Life for a Life

As for me personally, do not fear; I have *you*. You once feared that a great anguish would break my heart: but it did not. Nothing in this world will ever do that—while I have *you*.

Max, kiss me—in thought, I mean—as friends kiss friends who are starting on a long and painful journey, of which they see no end, yet are not afraid. Nor am I. Good-bye, my Max.

Yours, only and always,

Theodora Johnston.

A Life for a Life

Chapter 31

HIS STORY

My Dear Theodora,—You will have received my letters regularly; nor am I much surprised that they have not been answered. I have heard, from time to time, in other ways, all particulars of your sister's illness and of you. Mrs. Granton says you keep up well, but I know that, could I see it now, it would be the same little pale face which used to come stealing to me from your father's bedside, last year.

If I ask you to write, my love, believe it is from no doubt of you, or jealousy of any of your home-duties; but because I am wearying for a sight of your handwriting, and an assurance from yourself that you are not failing in health, the only thing in which I have any fear of your failing.

To answer a passage in your last, which I have hitherto let be, there was so much besides to write to you about—the passage concerning friends parting from friends. At first I interpreted it that in your sadness of spirit and hopelessness of the future, you wished me to sink back into my old place, and be only your friend. It was then no time to argue the point, nor would it have made any difference in my letters, either way; but now let me say two words concerning it.

My child, when a man loves a woman, before he tries to win her, he will have, if he loves unselfishly and generously, many a doubt concerning both her and himself. In fact, as I once read somewhere, "When a man truly loves a woman, he would not marry her upon any account, unless he was quite certain he was the best person she could possibly marry." But as soon as she loves him, and he knows it, and is certain that, however unworthy he may be, or however many faults she may possess—I never told you you were an angel, did I, little lady?—they have cast their lot together, chosen one another, as your Church says, "for better, for worse,"—then the face of things is entirely changed. He has his rights, close and strong as no other human being can have with regard to her—she has herself given them to him—and if he has any manliness in him he never will let them go, but hold her fast for ever and ever.

A Life for a Life

My dear Theodora, I have not the slightest intention of again subsiding into your friend. I am your lover and your betrothed husband. I will wait for you any number of years, till you have fulfilled all your duties, and no earthly rights have power to separate us longer. But in the meantime I hold fast to *my* rights. Everything that lover or future husband can be to you, I must be. And when I see you, for I am determined to see you at intervals, do not suppose that it will be a friend's kiss—if there be such a thing—that—But I have said enough—it is not easy for me to express myself on this wise.

My love, this letter is partly to consult you on a matter which is somewhat on my mind. With any but you I might hesitate; but I know your mind almost as I know my own, and can speak to you, as I hope I always shall—frankly and freely as a husband would to his wife.

About your sister Penelope and her great sorrow I have already written fully. Of her ultimate recovery, mentally as well as bodily, I have little doubt: she has in her the foundations of all endurance—a true upright nature and a religious mind. The first blow over, a certain little girl whom I know will be to her a saving angel; as she has been to others I could name. Fear not, therefore—"Fear God, and have no other fear": you will bring your sister safe to land.

But, you are aware, Penelope is not the only person who has been shipwrecked.

I should not intrude this side of the subject at present, did I not feel it to be in some degree a duty, and one that, from certain information that has reached me, will not bear deferring. The more so, because my occupation here ties my own hands so much. You and I do not live for ourselves, you know—nor indeed wholly for one another. I want you to help me, Theodora.

In my last, I informed you how the story of Lydia Cartwright came to my knowledge, and how, beside her father's coffin, I was entreated by her old mother to find her out, and bring her home if possible. I had then no idea who the "gentleman" was, but afterwards was led to suspect it might be a friend of Mr. Charteris. To assure myself, I one day put some questions to him—point-blank, I believe, for I abhor diplomacy, nor had I any suspicion of him personally. In the answer, he gave me a point-blank and insulting denial of any knowledge on the subject.

When the whole truth came out, I was in doubt what to do consistent with my promise to the poor girl's mother. Finally, I made inquiries; but heard that the Kensington cottage had been sold up, and the inmates removed. I then got the address of Sarah Enfield—that is, I commissioned my old friend, Mrs. Ansdell, to get it, and sent it to Mrs. Cartwright, without either advice or explanation, except that it was that of a person who knew Lydia. Are you aware that Lydia has more than once written to her mother, sometimes enclosing money, saying she was well and happy, but nothing more?

I this morning heard that the old woman, immediately on receiving my letter, shut up her cottage, leaving the key with a neighbour, and disappeared. But she may come back, and not alone; I hope, most earnestly, it will not be alone. And therefore I write, partly to prepare you for this chance, that you may contrive to keep your sister from any unnecessary pain, and also from another reason.

You may not know it,—and it is a hard thing to have to enlighten my innocent love, but your father is quite right; Lydia's story is by no means rare, nor is it regarded in the world as we view it. There are very few—especially among the set to which Mr. Charteris belonged—who either profess or practise the Christian doctrine, that our bodies also are the temples of the Holy Spirit,—that a man's life should be as pure as a woman's, otherwise no woman, however she may pity, can, or ought to respect him, or to marry him. This, it appears to me, is the Christian principle of love and marriage— the only one by which the one can be made sacred, and the other "honourable to all." I have tried, invariably, in every way to set this forth; nor do I hesitate to write of it to my wife that will be—whom it is my blessing to have united with me in every work which my conscience once compelled as atonement and my heart now offers in humblest thanksgiving.

But enough of myself.

While this principle, of total purity being essential for both man and woman, cannot be too sternly upheld, there is also another side to the subject, analogous to one of which you and I have often spoken. You will find it in the seventh chapter of Luke and eighth of John:

written, I conclude, to be not only read, but acted up to by all Christians who desire to have in them "the mind of Christ."

Now, my child, you see what I mean—how the saving command, *"Go and sin no more,"* applies to this sin also.

You know much more of what Lydia Cartwright used to be than I do; but it takes long for any one error to corrupt the entire character; and her remembrance of her mother, as well as her charity to Sarah Enfield, imply that there must be much good left in the girl still. She is young. Nor have I heard of her ever falling lower than this once. But she may fall; since, from what I know of Mr. Charteris's present circumstances, she must now, with her child, be left completely destitute. It is not the first similar case, by many, that I have had to do with; but my love never can have met with the like before. Is she afraid? does she hesitate to hold out her pure right hand to a poor creature who never can be an innocent girl again; who also, from the over-severity of Rockmount, may have been let slip a little too readily, and so gone wrong?

If you do hesitate, say so; it will not be unnatural nor surprising. If you do not, this is what I want: being myself so placed that though I feel the thing ought to be done, there seems no way of doing it, except through you. Should the Cartwrights reappear in the village, persuade your father not altogether to set his face against them, or have them expelled the neighbourhood. They must leave—it is essential for your sister that they should; but the old woman is very poor. Do not have them driven away in such a manner as will place no alternative between sin and starvation. Besides, there is the child—how a man can ever desert his own child I—but I will not enter into that part of the subject. This a strange "love" letter; but I write it without hesitation—my love will understand.

You will like to hear something of me; but there is little to tell. The life of a gaol surgeon is not unlike that of a horse in a mill; and, for some things, nearly as hopeless; best fitted, perhaps, for the old and the blind. I have to shut my eyes to so much that I cannot remedy, and take patiently so much to fight against which would be like knocking down the Pyramids of Egypt with one's head as a battering-ram, that sometimes my courage fails.

A Life for a Life

This great prison is, you know, a model of its kind, on the solitary, sanitary, and moral improvement system; excellent, no doubt, compared with that which preceded it. The prisoners are numerous, and as soon as many of them get out they take the greatest pains to get in again; such are the comforts of gaol life contrasted with that outside. Yet they seem to me often like a herd of brute beasts, fed and stalled by rule in the manner best to preserve their health, and keep them from injuring their neighbours; their bodies well looked after, but their souls—they might scarcely have any! They are simply Nos. 1, 2, 3, and so on, with nothing of human individuality or responsibility about them. Even their faces grow to the same pattern, dull, fat, clean, and stolid. During the exercising hour, I sometimes stand and watch them, each pacing his small bricked circle, and rarely catch one countenance which has a ray of expression or intelligence.

Good as many of its results are, I have my doubts as to this solitary system; but they are expressed on paper in the MS. you asked for, my kind little lady! so I will not repeat them here.

Yet it will be a change of thought from your sister's sickroom for you to think of me in mine—not a sick-room though, thank God! This is a most healthy region: the sea-wind sweeps round the prison-walls, and shakes the roses in the governor's garden till one can hardly believe it is so dreary a place inside. Dreary enough sometimes to make one believe in that reformer who offered to convert some depraved region into a perfect Utopia, provided the males above the age of fourteen were all summarily hanged.

Do you smile, my love, at this compliment to your sex at the expense of mine? Yet I see wretches here, whom I cannot hardly believe share the same common womanhood as my Theodora. Think over carefully what I asked you about Lydia Cartwright; it is seldom suddenly, but step by step, that this degradation comes. And at every step there is hope; at least, such is my experience.

Do not suppose, from this description, that I am disheartened at my work here; besides rules and regulations, there is still much room for personal influence, especially in hospital. When a man is sick or dying, unconsciously his heart is humanised—he thinks of God. From this simple cause, my calling has a great advantage over all others; and it is much to have physical agencies on one's side, as I do not get them in the streets and towns. To-day, looking up from a clean, tidy, airy cell, where the occupant had at least a chance of learning to read if he chose; and, seeing through the window the patch of bright blue sky, fresh and pure as ever sky was, I thought of two lines you once repeated to me out of your dear head, so full of poetry:-

> "God's in His heaven;
> All's right with the world."

Yesterday I had a holiday. I took the railway to Treherne Court, wishing to learn something of Rockmount. You said it was your desire I should visit your brother-in-law and sister sometimes.

They seemed very happy—so much as to be quite independent of visitors, but they received me warmly, and I gained tidings of you. They escorted me back as far as the park-gates, where I left them standing, talking and laughing together, a very picture of youth and fortune, and handsome looks; a picture suited to the place, with its grand ancestral trees branched down to the ground; its green slopes, and its herds of deer racing about—while the turrets of the magnificent house which they call "home," shone whitely in the distance.

You see I am taking a leaf out of your book, growing poetical and descriptive; but this brief contrast to my daily life made the impression particularly strong.

You need have no anxiety for your youngest sister; she looked in excellent health and spirits. The late sad events do not seem to have affected her. She merely observed, "She was glad it was over, she never liked Francis much. Penelope must come to Treherne Court for change, and no doubt she would soon make a far better marriage." Her husband said, "He and his father had been both grieved and annoyed—indeed, Sir William had quite disowned his nephew—such ungentlemanly conduct was a disgrace to the family." And then Treherne spoke about his own happiness—how his father and Lady Augusta perfectly adored his wife, and how the hope and pride of the family were centred in her, with more to the same purport. Truly this young couple have their cup brimming over with life and its joys.

A Life for a Life

My love, good-bye; which means only "God be with thee!" nor in any way implies "farewell."—Write soon. Your words are, as the Good Book expresses it, "sweeter than honey and the honeycomb," to me unworthy.

Max Urquhart.

I should add, though you would almost take it for granted, that in all you do concerning Mrs. Cartwright or her daughter, I wish you to do nothing without your father's knowledge and consent.

Chapter 32

HER STORY

Another bright, dazzlingly bright summer morning, on which I begin writing to my dear Max. This seems the longest-lasting, loveliest summer I ever knew, outside the house. Within, all goes on much in the same way, which you know.

My moors are growing all purple, Max; I never remember the heather so rich and abundant; I wish you could see it! Sometimes I want you so! If you had given me up, or were to do so now, from hopelessness, pride, or any other reason, what would become of me! Max, hold me fast. Do not let me go.

You never do. I can see how you carry me in your heart continually; and how you are for ever considering how you can help me and mine. And if it were not become so natural to feel this, so sweet to depend upon you, and accept everything from you without even saying "Thank you," I might begin to express "gratitude"; but the word would make you smile.

I amused you once, I remember, by an indignant disclaimer of obligations between such as ourselves; how everything given and received ought to be free as air, and how you ought to take me as readily if I were heiress to ten thousand a year, as I would you if you were the Duke of Northumberland. No, Max; those are not these sort of things that give me, towards you, the feeling of "gratitude," — it is the goodness, the thoughtfulness, the tender love and care. I don't mean to insult your sex by saying no man ever loved like you; but few men love in that special way, which alone could have satisfied a restless, irritable girl like me, who finds in you perfect trust and perfect rest.

If not allowed to be grateful on my own account, I may be in behalf of my sister Penelope.

After thus long following out your orders, medical and mental, I begin to notice a slight change in Penelope. She no longer lies in bed late, on the plea that it shortens the day; nor is she difficult to persuade in going out. Further than the garden she will not stir; but there I get her to creep up and down for a little while daily. Lately, she has begun to notice her flowers, especially a white moss-rose, which she took great pride in, and which never flowered until this summer. Yesterday, its first bud opened,—she stopped and examined it.

"Somebody has been mindful of this—who was it?"

I said, the gardener and myself together.

"Thank you." She called John—showed him what a good bloom it was, and consulted how they should manage to get the plant to flower again next year. She can then look forward to "next year."

You say, that as "while there is life there is hope," with the body; so, while one ray of hope is discernible, the soul is alive. To save souls alive, that is your special calling. It seems as if you yourself had been led through deep waters of despair, in order that you might personally understand how those feel who are drowning, and therefore know best how to help them. And lately, you have in this way done more than you know of. Shall I tell you? You will not be displeased.

Max—hitherto, nobody but me has seen a line of your letters. I could not bear it. I am as jealous over them as any old miser; it has vexed me even to see a stray hand fingering them, before they reach mine. Yet, this week I actually read out loud two pages of one of them to Penelope! This was how it came about.

I was sitting by her sofa, supposing her asleep. I had been very miserable that morning: tried much in several ways, and I took out your letter to comfort me. It told me of so many miseries, to which my own are nothing, and among which you live continually, yet are always so patient and tender over mine. I said to myself—"how good he is!" and two large tears came with a great splash upon the paper, before I was aware. Very foolish, you know, but I could not help it. And, wiping my eyes, I saw Penelope's wide open, watching me.

"Has Doctor Urquhart been writing anything to wound you?" said she, slowly and bitterly.

I eagerly disclaimed this.

"Is he ill?"

"Oh no, thank God!"

"Why, then, were you crying?"

Why, indeed? But what could I say except the truth, that they were not tears of pain, but because you were so good, and I was so proud of you? I forgot what arrows these words must have been into my sister's heart. No wonder she spoke as she did, spoke out fiercely, and yet with a certain solemnity.

"Dora Johnston, you will reap what you sow, and I shall not pity you. Make to yourself an idol, and God will strike it down. *Thou shalt have none other gods but me.*' Remember Who says that, and tremble."

I should have trembled, Max, had I *not* remembered. I said to my sister, as gently as I could, "that I made no idols; that I knew all your faults, and you mine, and we loved one another in spite of them, but we did not worship one another—only God. That if it were His will we should part, I believed we could part. And—" here I could not say any more for tears.

Penelope looked sorry.

"I remember you preaching that doctrine once, child, but—" she started up violently—"can't you give me something to amuse me? Read me a bit of that—that nonsense. Of all amusing things in this world, there is nothing like a love-letter. But don't believe them, Dora,"—she grasped my hand hard—"they are every one of them lies."

I said that I could not judge, never having received a "love-letter" in all my life, and hoped earnestly I never might.

"No love-letters? What does he write to you about, then?"

I told her in a general way. I would not see her half-satirical, half-incredulous smile. It did not last very long. Soon, though she turned away and shut her eyes, I felt sure she was both listening and thinking.

"Doctor Urquhart cannot have an easy or pleasant life," she observed, "but he does not deserve it. No man does."

"Or woman either," said I, as gently as I could.

Penelope bade me hold my tongue; preaching was my father's business, not mine, that is, if reasoning were of any avail.

I asked, did she think it was not?

"I think nothing about nothing. I want to smother thought. Child, can't you talk a little? Or stay, read me some of Doctor Urquhart's letters; they are not love-letters, so you can have no objection."

It went hard, Max, indeed it did! till I considered — perhaps, to hear of people more miserable than herself, more wicked than Francis, might not do harm but good to my poor Penelope.

So I was brave enough to take out my letter and read from it (with reservations now and then, of course), about your daily work and the people concerned therein; all that interests me so much, and makes me feel happier and prouder than any mere "love-letter" written to or about myself. Penelope was interested too, both in the gaol and the hospital matters. They touched that practical, benevolent, energetic half of her, which till lately has made her papa's right hand in the parish. I saw her large black eyes brightening up, till an unfortunate name, upon which I fell unawares, changed all.

Max, I am sure she had heard of Tom Turton. Francis knew him. When I stopped with some excuse, she bade me go on, so I was obliged to finish the miserable history. She then asked —

"Is Turton dead?"

I said, "No," and referred to the postscript where you say that both yourself and his poor old ruined father hope Tom Turton may yet live to amend his ways.

Penelope muttered—

"He never will. Better he died."

I said Dr. Urquhart did not think so.

She shook her head impatiently, exclaiming she was tired, and wished to hear no more, and so fell into one of her long, sullen silences, which sometimes last for hours.

I wonder whether, among the many cruel things she must lie thinking about, she ever thinks, as I do often, what has become of Francis?

Sometimes, puzzling over how best to deal with her, I have tried to imagine myself in her place, and consider what would have been my own feelings towards Francis now. The sharpest and most prominent would be the ever-abiding sense of his degradation,—he who was so dear, united to the constant terror of his sinking lower and lower to any depth of crime or shame. To think of him as a bad man, a sinner against heaven, would be tenfold worse than any sin or cruelty against me.

Therefore, whether or not her love for him has died out, I cannot help thinking there must be times when Penelope would give anything for tidings of Francis Charteris. I wish you would find out whether he has left England, and then perhaps in some way or other I may let Penelope understand that he is safe away—possibly to begin a new and better life, in a new world.

A new and better life. This phrase—Penelope might call it our "cant," yet what we solemnly believe in is surely not cant—brings me to something I have to tell you this week. For some reasons I am glad it did not occur until this week, that I might have time for consideration.

Max, if you remember, when you made to me that request about Lydia Cartwright, I merely answered "that I would endeavour to do

A Life for a Life

as you wished"; as, indeed, I always would, feeling that my duty to you, even in the matter of "obedience," has already begun. I mean to obey, you see, but would rather do it with my heart, as well as my conscience. So, hardly knowing what to say to you, I just said this, and no more.

My life has been so still, so safely shut up from the outside world, that there are many subjects I have never even thought about, and this was one. After the first great shock concerning Francis, I put it aside, hoping to forget it. When you revived it, I was at first startled; then I tried to ponder it over carefully, so as to come to a right judgment and be enabled to act in every way as became not only myself, Theodora Johnston, but—let me not be ashamed to say it—Theodora, Max Urquhart's wife.

By-and-by, all became clear to me. My dear Max, I do not hesitate; I am not afraid. I have been only waiting opportunity; which at length came.

Last Sunday I overheard my class—Penelope's that was, you know—whispering something among themselves, and trying to hide it from me; when I put the question direct, the answer was:—

"Please, Miss, Mrs. Cartwright and Lydia have come home." I felt myself grow hot as fire—I do now, in telling you. Only it must be borne—it must be told.

Also another thing, which one of the bigger girls let out, with many titters, and never a blush,—they had brought a child with them.

Oh, Max, the horror of shame and repulsion, and then the perfect anguish of pity that came over me! These girls of our parish, Lydia was one of them; if they had been taught better; if I had tried to teach them, instead of all these years studying or dreaming, thinking wholly of myself and caring not a straw about my fellow-creatures. Oh, Max—would that my life had been more like yours!

It shall be henceforth. Going home through the village, with the sun shining on the cottages, of whose inmates I know no more than of the New Zealand savages,—on the group of ragged girls who were growing up at our very door, no one knows how, and no one cares—I made a vow to myself. I that have been so blessed—I that am so happy—yes, Max, happy! I will work with all my strength, while it is day. You will help me. And you will never love me the less for anything I feel—or do.

I was going that very afternoon, to walk direct to Mrs. Cartwright's, when I remembered your charge, that nothing should be attempted without my father's knowledge and consent.

I took the opportunity when he and I were sitting alone together—Penelope gone to bed. He was saying she looked better. He thought she might begin visiting in the district soon, if she were properly persuaded. At least she might take a stroll round the village. He should ask her to-morrow.

"Don't, papa. Oh, pray don't!"—and then I was obliged to tell him the reason why. I had to put it very plainly before he understood—he forgets things now sometimes.

"Starving, did you say?—Mrs. Cartwright, Lydia, and the child?—What child?"

"Francis's."

Then he comprehended,—and, oh, Max, had I been the girl I was a few months ago, I should have sunk to the earth with the shame he said I ought to feel at even alluding to such things. But I would not stop to consider this, or to defend myself; the matter concerned not me, but Lydia. I asked papa if he did not remember Lydia?

She came to us, Max, when she was only fourteen, though, being well-grown and handsome, she looked older;—a pleasant, willing, affectionate creature, only she had "no head," or it was half-turned by the admiration her beauty gained, not merely among her own class, but all our visitors. I remember Francis saying once—oh, how angry Penelope was about it—that Lydia was so naturally elegant she could be made a lady of in no time, if a man liked to take her, educate and marry her. Would he had done it! spite of all broken vows to Penelope. I think my sister herself might have forgiven him, if he had only honestly fallen in love with poor Lydia, and married her.

These things I tried to recall to papa's mind, but he angrily bade me be silent.

"I cannot," I said, "because, if we had taken better care of the girl, this might never have happened. When I think of her—her pleasant ways about the house—how she used to go singing over her work of mornings—poor innocent young thing—oh, papa! papa!"

"Dora," he said, eyeing me closely; "what change has come over you of late?"

I said, I did not know, unless it was that which must come over people who have been very unhappy—the wish to save other people as much happiness as they can.

"Explain yourself. I do not understand." When he did, he said abruptly,—

"Stop. It was well you waited to consult with me. If your own delicacy does not teach you better, I must. My daughter—the daughter of the clergyman of the parish—cannot possibly be allowed to interfere with these profligates."

My heart sunk like lead

"But you, papa? They are here; you, as the rector, must do something. What shall you do?"

He thought a little.

"I shall forbid them the church and the sacrament; omit them from my charities; and take every lawful means to get them out of the neighbourhood. This, for my family's sake, and the parish's—that they may carry their corruption elsewhere."

"But they may not be wholly corrupt. And the child—that innocent, unfortunate child!"

"Silence, Dora. It is written, *The seed of evil-doers shall never be renowned*. The sinless must suffer with the guilty; there is no hope for either."

"Oh, papa," I cried, in an agony, "Christ did not say so. He said, *'Go, and sin no more.'*"

Was I wrong? If I was, I suffered for it. What followed was very hard to bear.

Max, if ever I am yours, altogether in your power, I wonder, will you ever give me those sort of bitter, cruel words? Words which people, living under the same roof think nothing of using—mean nothing by them—yet they cut sharp, like swords. The flesh closes up after them—but oh, they bleed—they bleed! Dear Max, reprove me as you will, however much, but let it be in love, not in anger or sarcasm. Sometimes people drop carelessly, by quiet firesides, and with a good-night kiss following, as papa gave to me, words which leave a scar for years.

Next day, I was just about to write and ask you to find some other plan for helping the Cartwrights, since we neither of us would choose to persist in one duty at the expense of another—when papa called me to take a walk with him.

Is it not strange, the way in which good angels seem to take up the thread of our dropped hopes and endeavours, and wind them up for us, we see not how, till it is all done? Never was I more surprised than when papa, stopping to lean on my arm, and catch the warm, pleasant wind that came over the moors, said suddenly

"Dora, what could possess you to talk to me as you did last night? And why, if you had any definite scheme in your head, did you relinquish it so easily?"

"Papa, you forbade it."

"So, even when differing from your father, you consider it right to obey him?"

"Yes,—except—"

"Say it out, child."

"Except in the case of any duty which I felt to be not less sacred than the one I owe to my father."

A Life for a Life

He made no reply.

Walking on, we passed Mrs. Cartwright's cottage. It was quiet and silent, the door open, but the window-shutter half closed, and there was no smoke from the chimney. I saw papa turn round and look. At last he said:—

"What did you mean by telling me they were 'starving'?"

I answered the direct, entire truth. I was bold, for it was your mind as well as my own I was speaking out, and I knew it was right. I pleaded chiefly for the child—it was easiest to think of it, the little creature I had seen laughing and crowing in the garden at Kensington. It seemed such a dreadful thing for that helpless baby to die of want, or live to turn out a reprobate.

"Think, papa," I cried, "if that poor little soul had been our own flesh and blood—if you were Francis's father, and this had been your grandchild!"

To my sorrow, I had forgotten for the time a part of poor Harry's story—the beginning of it: you shall know it some day—it is all past now. But papa remembered it. He faltered as he walked—at last he sat down on a tree by the roadside, and said, "He must go home."

Yet still, either by accident or design, he took the way by the lane where is Mrs. Cartwright's cottage. At the gate of it a little ragged urchin was poking a rosy face through the bars; and, seeing papa, this small fellow gave a shout of delight, tottered out, and caught hold of his coat, calling him "Daddy." He started—I thought he would have fallen, he trembled so: my poor old father.

When I lifted the little thing out of his way, I too started. It is strange always to see a face you know revived in a child's face—in this instance it was shocking—pitiful. My first thought was, we never must let Penelope come past this way. I was carrying the boy off—I well knew where, when papa called me.

"Stop. Not alone—not without your father."

A Life for a Life

It was but a few steps, and we stood on the door-sill of Mrs. Cartwright's cottage. The old woman snatched up the child, and I heard her whisper something about "Run—Lyddy—run away."

But Lydia, if that white, thin creature huddled up in the corner were she, never attempted to move.

Papa walked up to her.

"Young woman, are you Lydia Cartwright, and is this your child?"

"Have you been meddling with him? You'd better not! I say, Franky, what have they been doing to mother's Franky?"

She caught at him, and hugged him close, as mothers do. And when the boy, evidently both attracted and puzzled by papa's height and gentlemanly clothes tried to get back to him, and again call him "Daddy," she said angrily, "No, no, 'tis not your daddy. They're no friends o' yours. I wish they were out of the place, Franky, boy."

"You wish us away. No wonder. Are you not ashamed to look us in the face—my daughter and me?"

But papa might have said ever so much more, without her heeding. The child having settled himself on her lap, playing with the ragged counterpane that wrapped her instead of a shawl, Lydia seemed to care for nothing. She lay back with her eyes shut, still and white. We may be sure of one thing—she has preferred to starve.

"Dunnot be too hard upon her, sir," begged the old woman. "Dunnot, please, Miss Dora. She bean't a lady like you, and he were such a fine coaxing young gentleman. It's he that's most to blame."

My father said sternly, "Has she left him, or been deserted by him—I mean Mr. Francis Charteris?"

"Mother," screamed Lydia, "what's that? What have they come for? Do they know anything about him?"

She did not, then.

A Life for a Life

"Be quiet, my lass," said the mother, soothingly, but it was of no use.

"Miss Dora," cried the girl, creeping to me, and speaking in the same sort of childish pitiful tone in which she used to come and beg Lisabel and me to intercede for her when she had annoyed Penelope, "do, Miss Dora, tell me. I don't want to see him, I only want to hear. I've heard nothing since he sent me a letter from prison, saying I was to take my things and the baby's and go. I don't know what's become of him, no more than the dead. And, miss, he's that boy's father—miss—please——"

She tried to go down to her knees, but fell prone on the floor. Max, who would have thought, the day before, that this day I should have been sitting with Lydia Cartwright's head on my lap, trying to bring her back to this miserable life of hers; that papa would have stood by and seen me do it, without a word of blame!

"It's the hunger," cried the mother. "You see, she isn't used to it now; he always kept her like a lady."

Papa turned and walked out of the cottage. I afterwards found out that he had bought the loaf at the baker's shop down the village, and got the bottle of wine from his private cupboard in the vestry. He returned with both—one in each pocket—then, sitting down on a chair, cut the bread and poured out the wine, and fed these three himself with his own hands. My dear father!

Nor did he draw back when, as she recovered, the first word that came to the wretched girl's lips was "Francis."

"Mother, beg them to tell me about him. I'll do him no harm, indeed I won't, neither him nor them. Is he married? Or," with a sudden gasp, "is he dead? I've thought sometimes he must be, or he never would have left the child and me. He was always fond of us, wasn't he, Franky?"

I told her, to the best of my knowledge, Mr. Charteris was living, but what had become of him we could none of us guess. We never saw him now.

Here, looking wistfully at me, Lydia seemed suddenly to remember old times, to become conscious of what she used to be, and what she was now. Also, in a vague sort of way, of how guilty she had been towards her mistress and our family. How long or how deep the feeling was I cannot judge, but she certainly did feel. She hung her head, and tried to draw herself away from my arm.

"I'd rather not trouble you, Miss Dora, thank you."

I said it was no trouble, she had better lie still till she felt stronger.

"You don't mean that. Not such as me."

I told her she must know she had done very wrong, but if she was sorry for it, I was sorry for her, and we would help her, if we could, to an honest livelihood.

"What, and the child too?"

I looked towards papa; he answered distinctly, but sternly, "Principally for the sake of the child."

Lydia began to sob. She attempted no exculpation—expressed no penitence—just lay and sobbed like a child. She is hardly more even yet—only nineteen, I believe. So we sat—papa as silent as we, resting on his stick, with his eyes fixed on the cottage floor, till Lydia turned to me with a sort of fright.

"What would Miss Johnston say if she knew?" I wondered, indeed, what my sister would say.

And here, Max—you will hardly credit it, nobody would, if it were an incident in a book—something occurred which, even now, seems hardly possible—as if I must have dreamed it all.

Through the open cottage door a lady walked right in, looked at us all, including the child, who stopped in his munching of bread to stare at her with wide-open blue eyes—Francis's eyes; and that lady was my sister Penelope.

She walked in and walked out again, before we had our wits about us sufficiently to speak to her, and when I rose and ran after her, she had slipped away somehow, so that I could not find her. How she came to take this notion into her head, after being for weeks shut up indoors;—whether she discovered that the Cartwrights had returned, and came here in anger, or else, prompted by some restless instinct, to have another look at Francis's child—none of us can guess; nor have we ever dared to inquire.

When we got home, she was lying in her usual place on the sofa, as if she wanted us not to notice that she had been out at all. Still, by papa's desire, I spoke to her frankly—told her the circumstances of our visit to the two women—the destitution in which we found them; and how they should be got away from the village as soon as possible.

She made no answer whatever, but lay absorbed, as it were—hardly moving, except an occasional nervous twitch, all afternoon and evening, until I called her in to prayers, which were shorter than usual—papa being very tired. He only read the Collect, and repeated the Lord's Prayer, in which, among the voices that followed his, I distinguished, with surprise, Penelope's. It had a steadiness and sweetness such as I never heard before. And when—the servants being gone—she went up to papa, and kissed him, the change in her manner was something almost startling.

"Father, when shall you want me in the district again?" said she.

"My dear girl!"

"Because I am quite ready to go. I have been ill, and it has made me unmindful of many things; but I am better now. Papa, I will try and be a good daughter to you. I have nobody but you."

She spoke quietly and softly, bending her head upon his grey hairs. He kissed and blessed her. She kissed me, too, as she passed, and then went away to bed, without any more explanation.

But from that time—and it is now three days ago—Penelope has resumed her usual place in the household—taken up all her old duties, and even her old pleasures; for I saw her in her green-house this morning. When she called me, in something of the former quick, imperative voice, to look at an air-plant that was just coming into flower, I could not see it for tears.

A Life for a Life

Nevertheless, there is in her a difference. Not her serious, almost elderly-looking face, nor her manner, which has lost its sharpness, and is so gentle sometimes that when she gives her orders the servants actually stare—but the marvellous composure which is evident in her whole demeanour; the bearing of a person who, having gone through that sharp agony which either kills or cures, is henceforth settled in mind and circumstances, to feel no more any strong emotion, but go through life placidly and patiently, without much further change, to the end. The sort of woman that nuns are made of—or Sœurs de la Charité; or Protestant lay-sisters, of whom every village has some; and almost every family owns at least one, She will, to all appearance, be our one—our elder sister, to be regarded with reverence unspeakable, and be made as happy as we possibly can. Max, I am learning to think with hope and without pain, of the future of my sister Penelope.

One word more, and this long letter ends.

Yesterday, papa and I walking on the moor, met Mrs. Cartwright, and learned full particulars of Lydia. From your direction, her mother found her out, in a sort of fever, brought on by want. Of course, everything had been taken from the Kensington cottage for Francis's debts. She was turned out with only the clothes she wore. But you know all this already, through Mrs. Ansdell.

Mrs. Cartwright is sure it was you who sent Mrs. Ansdell to them, and that the money they received week by week, in their worst distress, came from you. She said so to papa, while we stood talking.

"For it was just like our doctor, sir,—as is kind to poor and rich—I'm sure he used to look at you, sir, as if he'd do anything in the world for you—as many's the time, I've seed him a-sitting by your bedside when you was ill. If there ever was a man living as did good to every poor soul as came in his way—it be Doctor Urquhart."

Papa said nothing.

After the old woman had gone, he asked if I had any plans about Lydia Cartwright.

I had one, which we must consult about when she is better,—whether she might not, with her good education, be made one of the schoolmistresses that you say, go from cell to cell, instructing the female prisoners in these model gaols. But I hesitated to start this project to papa—so told him I must think the matter over.

"You are growing quite a thinking woman, Dora; who taught you, who put it into your mind to act as you do?—you, who were such a thoughtless girl;—speak out, I want to know?"

I told him—naming the name of my dear Max; the first time it has ever passed my lips in my father's hearing, since that day. It was received in silence.

Some time after, stopping suddenly, papa said to me, "Dora, some day, I know you will go and marry Doctor Urquhart."

What could I say? Deny it, deny Max—my love, and my husband? or tell my father what was not true? Either was impossible.

So we walked on, avoiding conversation until we came to our own churchyard, where we went in and sat in the porch, sheltering from the noon-heat, which papa feels more than he used to do. When he took my arm to walk home, his anger had vanished, he spoke even with a sort of melancholy.

"I don't know how it is, my dear, but the world is altering fast. People preach strange doctrines, and act in strange ways, such as were never thought of when I was young. It may be for good or for evil—I shall find out by-and-by. I was dreaming of your mother last night; you are growing very like her, child." Then suddenly, "Only wait till I am dead, and you will be free, Theodora."

My heart felt bursting; oh, Max, you do not mind me telling you these things? What should I do if I could not thus open my heart to you?"

Yet it is not altogether with grief or without hope, that I have thought over what then passed between papa and me. He knows you—knows too that neither you nor I have ever deceived him in anything. He was fond of you once; I think sometimes he misses you still, in little things wherein you used to pay him attention, less like a friend than a son.

A Life for a Life

Now, Max, do not think I am grieving—do not imagine I have cause to grieve. They are as kind to me as ever they can be. My home is as happy as any home could be made, except one, which, whether we shall ever find or not, God knows. In quiet evenings such as this, when, after a rainy day, it has just cleared up in time for the sun to go down, and he is going down peacefully in amber glory, with the trees standing up so purple and still, and the moorlands lying bright, and the hills distinct even to their very last faint rim—in such evenings as this, Max, when I want you and cannot find you, but have to learn to sit still by myself, as now, I learn to think also of the meeting which has no farewell, of the rest that comes to all in time, of the eternal home, We shall reach that—some day.

Your faithful,

Theodora.

Chapter 33

HIS STORY

Treherne Court,

Sunday night.

My Dear Theodora,—The answer to my telegram has just arrived, and I find it is your sister whom we are to expect, not you. I shall meet her myself by the night train, Treherne being quite incapable; indeed, he will hardly stir from the corridor that leads to his wife's room.

You will have heard already that the heir so ardently looked for has only lived a few hours. Lady Augusta's letters, which she gave me to address, and I took care to post myself, would have assured you of your sister's safety, though it was long doubtful. It will comfort you to know that she is in excellent care, both her medical attendants being known to me professionally, and Lady Augusta being a real mother to her, in tenderness and anxiety.

You will wonder how I came here. It was by accident—taking a Saturday holiday, which is advisable now and then; and Treherne's mother detained me, as being the only person who had any control over her son. Poor fellow! he was almost out of his mind. He never had any trouble before, and he knows not how to bear it. He trembled in terror—thus coming face to face with that messenger of God who puts an end to all merely mortal joys—was paralysed at the fear of losing his blessings, which, numerous as they are, are all of this world. My love, whom I thought to have seen to-night, but shall not see—for how long?—things are more equally balanced than we suppose.

You will be sorry about the little one. Treherne seems indifferent; his whole thought being, naturally, his wife; but Sir William is grievously disappointed. A son too—and he had planned bonfires, and bell-ringings, and rejoicings all over the estate. When he stood looking at the little white lump of clay, which is the only occupant of the grand nursery, prepared for the heir of Treherne Court, I heard the old man sigh as if for a great misfortune.

You will think it none, since your sister lives. Be quite content about her—which is easy for me to say, when I know how long and anxious the days will seem at Rockmount. It might have been better, for some things, if you, rather than Miss Johnston, had come to take charge of your sister during her recovery; but, maybe, all is well as it is. Tomorrow I shall leave this great house, with its many happinesses, which have run so near a chance of being overthrown, and go back to my own solitary life, in which nothing of personal interest ever visits me but Theodora's letters.

There were two things I intended to tell you in my Sunday letter; shall I say them still? for the more things you have to think about the better, and one of them was my reason for suggesting your presence here, rather than your eldest sister's.—(Do not imagine though, your coming was urged by me wholly for other people's sakes. The sight of you—just for a few hours—one hour—People talk of water in the desert— the thought of a green field to those who have been months at sea—well, that is what a glimpse of your little face would be to me. But I cannot get it—and I must not moan.)

What was I writing about? oh, to bid you tell Mrs. Cartwright from me that her daughter is well in health and doing well. After her two months' probation here, the governor, to whom alone I communicated her history (names omitted), pronounces her quite fitted for the situation. And she will be formally appointed thereto. This is a great satisfaction to me—as she was selected solely on my recommendation, backed by Mrs. Ansdell's letter. Say also to the old woman, that I trust she receives regularly the money her daughter sends her through me; which indeed is the only time I ever see Lydia alone. But I meet her often in the wards, as she goes from cell to cell, teaching the female prisoners; and it is good to see her sweet grave looks, her decent dress and mien, and her unexpressible humility and gentleness towards everybody.— She puts me in mind of words you know—which in another sense, other hearts than poor Lydia's might often feel—that those love most to whom most has been forgiven.

Hinting this, though not in reference to her, in a conversation with the governor, he observed, rather coldly, "He had heard it said Doctor Urquhart held peculiar opinions upon crime and punishment—that, in fact, he was a little too charitable."

I sighed—thinking that of all men, Dr. Urquhart was the one who had the most reason to be charitable: and the governor fixed his eyes upon me somewhat unpleasantly. Any one running counter, as I do, to several popular prejudices, is sure not to be without enemies. I should be sorry, though, to have displeased so honest a man, and one whom, widely as we differ in some things, is always safe to deal with, from his possessing that rare quality—justice.

You see, I go on writing to you of my matters—just as I should talk to you if you sat by my side now, with your hand in mine, and your head here. (So you found two grey hairs in those long locks of yours last week. Never mind, love. To me you will be always young.)

I write as I hope to talk to you one day. I never was among those who believe that a man should keep all his cares secret from his wife. If she is a true wife, she will soon read them on his face, or the effect of them; he had better tell them out and have them over. I have learned many things since I found my Theodora: among the rest is, that when a man marries, or loves with the hope of marrying, let him have been ever so reserved, his whole nature opens out—he becomes another creature; in degree towards everybody, but most of all to her he has chosen. How altered I am—you would smile to see, were my little lady to compare these long letters with the brief, businesslike productions which have heretofore borne the signature "Max Urquhart."

I prize my name a little. It has been honourable for a number of years. My father was proud of it, and Dallas. Do you like it? Will you like it when—if——No, let me trust in heaven, and say, when you bear it?

Those papers of mine which you saw mentioned in the Times—I am glad Mr. Johnston read them; or at least you suppose he did. I believe they are doing good, and that my name is becoming pretty well known in connection with them, especially in this town. A provincial reputation has its advantages; it is more undoubted—more complete. In London, a man may shirk and hide; his nearest acquaintance can scarcely know him thoroughly; but in the provinces it is different. There, if he has a flaw in him, either as to his antecedents, his character, or conduct, be sure scandal will find it out; for she has every opportunity. Also, public opinion is at once stricter and more narrow-minded in a place like this than in a great metropolis. I am glad to be earning a good name here, in this honest, hard-working, commercial district, where my fortunes are apparently cast; and where, having been a "rolling stone" all my life, I mean to settle and "gather moss," if I can. Moss to make a little nest soft and warm for—my love knows who.

Writing this, about the impossibility of keeping anything secret in a town like this, reminds me of something which I was in doubt about telling you or not: finally, I have decided that I will tell you. Your sister being absent, will make things easier for you. You will not have need to use any of those concealments which must be so painful in a home. Nevertheless, I do think Miss Johnston ought to be kept ignorant of the fact that I believe, nay, am almost certain, Mr. Francis Charteris is at this present time living in Liverpool.

No wonder that all my inquiries about him in London failed. He has just been discharged from this very gaol. It is more than likely he was arrested for liabilities long owing, or contracted after his last fruitless visit to his uncle, Sir William. I could easily find out, but hardly consider it delicate to make inquiries, as I did not, you know, after the debtor—whom a turnkey here reported to have said he knew me. Debtors are not criminals by law—their ward is justly held private. I never visit any of them unless they come into hospital.

Therefore my meeting with Mr. Charteris was purely accidental. Nor do I believe he recognised me—I had stepped aside into the warder's room. The two other discharged debtors passed through the entrance-gate and quitted the gaol immediately; but he lingered, desiring a car to be sent for—and inquiring where one could get handsome and comfortable lodgings in this horrid Liverpool. He hated a commercial town.

You will ask, woman-like, how he looked? Ill and worn, with something of the shabby, "poor gentleman" aspect, with which we here are only too familiar. I overheard the turnkey joking with the carman about taking him to "handsome rooms." Also, there was about him an ominous air of what we in Scotland call the "down-draught"; a term, the full meaning of which you probably do not understand—I trust you never may.

You will see by its date how many days ago the first part of this letter was written. I kept it back till the cruel suspense of your sister's sudden relapse was ended—thinking it a pity your mind should be

A Life for a Life

burthened with any additional care. You have had, in the meantime, the daily bulletin from Treherne Court—the daily line from me.

How are you, my child?—for you have forgotten to say. Any roses out on your poor cheeks? Look in the glass and tell me. I must know, or I must come and see. Remember, your life is part of mine, now.

Mrs. Treherne is convalescent—as you know. I saw her on Monday for the first time. She is changed, certainly; it will be long before she is anything like the Lisabel Johnston of my recollection, full of health and physical enjoyment. But do not grieve. Sometimes, to have gone near the gates of death, and returned, hallows the whole future life. I thought, as I left her, lying contentedly on her sofa, with her hand in her husband's, who sits watching as if truly she were given back to him from the grave, that it may be good for those two to have been so nearly parted. It may teach them, according to a line you once repeated to me (you see, though I am not poetical, I remember all your bits of poetry), to

> "Hold every mortal joy
> With a loose hand,"

since nothing finite is safe, unless overshadowed by the belief in, and the glory of, the Infinite.

My dearest—my best of every earthly thing—whom to be parted from temporarily, as now, often makes me feel as if half myself were wanting—whom to lose out of this world would be a loss irremediable, and to leave behind in it would be the sharpest sting of death—better, I have sometimes thought, of late—better be you and I than Treherne and Lisabel.

In all these letters I have scarcely mentioned Penelope—you see I am learning to name your sisters as if mine. She, however, has treated me almost like a stranger in the few times we happened to meet—until last Monday.

I had left the happy group in the library—Treherne, tearing himself from his wife's sofa—honest fellow! to follow me to the door—where he wrung my hand, and said, with a sob like a school-boy, that he had never been so happy in his life before, and he hoped he was thankful for it. Your eldest sister, who sat in the window sewing—

her figure put me somewhat in mind of you, little lady—bade me good-bye—she was going back to Rockmount in a few days.

I quitted them, and walked alone across the park, where the chestnut-trees—you remember them—are beginning, not only to change, but to fall; thinking how fast the years go, and how little there is in them of positive joy. Wrong—this!—and I know it; but, my love, I sin sorely at times. I nearly forgot a small patient I have at the lodge-gates, who is slipping so gradually, but surely, poor wee man! into the world where he will be a child for ever. After sitting with him half-an-hour, I came out better.

A lady was waiting outside the lodge gates. When I saw who it was, I meant to bow and pass on, but Miss Johnston called me. From her face, I dreaded it was some ill news about you.

Your sister is a good woman and a kind.

She said to me, when her explanations had set my mind at ease—

"Doctor Urquhart, I believe you are a man to be trusted. Dora trusts you. Dora once said, you would be just, even to your enemies."

I answered, I hoped it was something more than justice that we owed even to our enemies.

"That is not the question," she said sharply; "I spoke only of justice. I would not do an injustice to the meanest thing—-the vilest wretch that crawls."

"No."

She went on—

"I have not liked you, Doctor Urquhart: nor do I know if my feelings are altered now—but I respect you. Therefore, you are the only person of whom I can ask a favour. It is a secret. Will you keep it so?"

"Except from Theodora."

"You are right. Have no secrets from Theodora. For her sake, and your own—for your whole life's peace—never, even in the lightest thing, deceive that poor child!"

Her voice sharpened, her black eyes glittered a moment, and then she shrank back into her usual self. I see exactly the sort of woman, which, as you say, she will grow into—sister Penelope—aunt Penelope. Every one belonging to her must try, henceforth, to spare her every possible pang.

After a few moments, I begged her to say what I could do for her.

"Read this letter, and tell me if you think it is true."

It was addressed to Sir William Treherne; the last humble appeal of a broken-down man; the signature "Francis Charteris."

I tried my best to disguise the emotion which Miss Johnston herself did not show, and returned the letter, merely inquiring if Sir William had answered it.

"No. He will not. He disbelieves the facts."

"Do you, also?"

"I cannot say. The—the writer was not always accurate in his statements."

Women are, in some things, stronger and harder than men. I doubt if any man could have spoken as steadily as your sister did at this minute. While I explained to her, as I thought it right to do, though with the manner of one talking of a stranger to a stranger, the present position of Mr. Charteris, she replied not a syllable. Only passing a felled tree—she suddenly sank down upon it, and sat motionless.

"What is he to do?" she said, at last.

I replied that the Insolvent Court could free him from his debts, and grant him protection from further imprisonment; that though thus sunk in circumstances, a Government situation was hardly to be hoped for, still there were in Liverpool, clerk-ships and mercantile opportunities, in which any person so well educated as he, might begin the world again—health permitting.

"His health was never good—has it failed him?"

" I fear so."

Your sister turned away. She sat—we both sat—for some time, so still that a bright-eyed squirrel came and peeped at us, stole a nut a few yards oft and scuttled away with it to Mrs. Squirrel and the little ones up in a tall sycamore hard by.

I begged Miss Johnston to let me see the address once more, and I would pay a visit, friendly or medical, as the case might allow, to Mr. Charteris, on my way home to-night.

"Thank you, Doctor Urquhart."

I then rose and took leave, time being short.

"Stay, one word if you please. In that visit, you will of course say, if inquired, that you learned the address from Treherne Court. You will name no other names?"

"Certainly not."

"But afterwards, you will write to me?"

"I will."

We shook hands, and I left her sitting there on the dead tree. I went on, wondering if anything would result from this curious combination of accidents: also, whether a woman's love, if cut off at the root, even like this tree, could be actually killed, so that nothing could revive it again. What think you, Theodora?

But this trick of moralising, caught from you, shall not be indulged. There is only time for the relation of bare facts.

A Life for a Life

The train brought me to the opposite shore of our river, not half a mile's walk from Mr. Charteris's lodgings. They seemed "handsome lodgings" as he said—a tall new house, one of the many which, only half-built, or half-inhabited, make this Birkenhead such a dreary place. But it is improving, year by year—I sometimes think it may be quite a busy and cheerful spot by the time I take a house here, as I intend. You will like a hilltop, and a view of the sea.

I asked for Mr. Charteris, and stumbled up the half-lighted stairs, into the wholly dark drawing-room.

"Who the devil's there?"

He was in hiding, you must remember, as indeed I ought to have done, and so taken the precaution first to send up my name—but I was afraid of non-admittance.

When the gas was lit, his pale, unshaven, sallow countenance, his state of apparent illness and weakness, made me cease to regret having gained entrance, under any circumstances. Recognising me, he muttered some apology.

"I was asleep—I usually do sleep after dinner." Then recovering his confused faculties, he asked with some *hauteur*, "To what may I attribute the pleasure of seeing Doctor Urquhart? Are you, like myself, a mere bird of passage, or a resident in Liverpool?"

"I am surgeon of—gaol."

"Indeed, I was not aware. A good appointment, I hope? And what gaol did you say?"

I named it again, and left the subject. If he chose to wrap himself in that thin cloak of deception, it was no business of mine to tear it off. Besides, one pities a ruined man's most petty pride.

But it was an awkward position. You know how haughty Mr. Charteris can be; you know also that unlucky peculiarity in me, call it Scotch shyness, cautiousness, or what you please, my little English girl must cure it, if she can. Whether or not it was my fault, I soon felt that this visit was turning out a complete failure, We conversed in the civillest manner, though somewhat disjointedly, on politics, the climate and trade of Liverpool, etc., but of Mr. Charteris and his real condition, I learned no more than if I were meeting him at a London dinner-party, or a supper with poor Tom Turton—who is dead, as you know. Mr. Charteris did not, it seems, and his startled exclamation at hearing the fact was the only natural expression during my whole visit. Which, after a few rather broad hints, I took the opportunity of a letter's being brought in, to terminate.

Not, however, with any intention on my side of its being a final one. The figure of this wretched-looking invalid, though he would not own to illness—men seldom will—lying in the solitary, fireless lodging-house parlour, where there was no indication of food, and a strong smell of opium—followed me all the way to the jetty, suggesting plan after plan concerning him.

You cannot think how pretty even our dull river looks of a night, with its two long lines of lighted shores, and other lights scattered between in all directions, every vessel's rigging bearing one. And to-night, above all things, was a large bright moon, sailing up over innumerable white clouds, into the clear dark zenith, converting the town of Liverpool into a fairy city, and the muddy Mersey into a pleasant river, crossed by a pathway of silver—such as one always looks at with a kind of hope that it would lead to "some bright isle of rest." There was a song to that effect popular when Dallas and I were boys.

As the boat moved off, I settled myself to enjoy the brief seven minutes of crossing—thinking, if I had but the little face by me looking up into the moonlight she is so fond of, the little hand to keep warm in mine!

And now, Theodora, I come to something which you must use your own judgment about telling your sister Penelope.

Half-way across, I was attracted by the peculiar manner of a passenger, who had leaped on the boat just as we were shoved off, and now stood still as a carved figure, staring down into the foamy track of the paddle-wheels. He was so absorbed that he did not notice me, but I recognised him at once, and an ugly suspicion entered my mind.

A Life for a Life

In my time I have had opportunities of witnessing, stage by stage, that disease—call it dyspepsia, hypochondriasis, or what you will—it has all names and all forms—which is peculiar to our present state of high civilisation, where the mind and the body seem cultivated into perpetual warfare one with the other. This state—some people put poetical names upon it—but we doctors know that it is at least as much physical as mental, and that many a poor misanthrope, who loathes himself and the world, is merely an unfortunate victim of stomach and nerves, whom rest, natural living, and an easy mind would soon make a man again. But that does not remove the pitifulness and danger of the case. While the man is what he is, he is little better than a monomaniac.

If I had not seen him before, the expression of his countenance, as he stood looking down into the river, would have been enough to convince me how necessary it was to keep a strict watch over Mr. Charteris.

When the rush of passengers to the gangway made our side of the boat nearly deserted, he sprang up the steps of the paddle-box, and there stood.

I once saw a man commit suicide. It was one of ours, returning from the Crimea. He had been drinking hard, and was put under restraint, for fear of delirium tremens; but when he was thought recovered, one day, at broad noon, in sight of all hands, he suddenly jumped overboard. I caught sight of his face as he did so—it was exactly the expression of Francis Charteris.

Perhaps, in any case, you had better never repeat the whole of this to your sister.

Not till after a considerable struggle did I pull him down to the safe deck once more. There he stood breathless.

"You were not surely going to drown yourself, Mr. Charteris?"

"I was. And I will."

"Try,—and I shall call the police to prevent your making such an ass of yourself."

It was no time to choose words, and in this sort of disease the best preventive one can use, next to a firm, imperative will, is ridicule. He answered nothing—but gazed at me in simple astonishment, while I took his arm and led him out of the boat and across the landing-stage.

"I beg your pardon for using such strong language, but a man must be an ass indeed who contemplates such a thing;—here, too, of all places. To be fished up out of this dirty river like a dead rat, for the entertainment of the crowd; to make a capital case at the magistrate's court to-morrow, and a first-rate paragraph in the Liverpool Mercury,—'Attempted Suicide of a Gentleman.' Or, if you really succeeded, which I doubt, to be 'Found Drowned,'—a mere body, drifted ashore with cocoanut husks and cabbages at Waterloo, or brought in as I once saw at these very stairs, one of the many poor fools who do this here yearly. They had picked him up eight miles higher up the river, and so brought him down, lashed behind a rowing-boat, floating face upwards"—

"Ah!"

I felt Charteris shudder.

You will too, my love, so I will repeat no more of what I said to him. But these ghastly pictures were the strongest arguments available with such a man. What was the use of talking to him of God, and life, and immortality? he had told me he believed in none of these things. But he believed in death—the epicurean's view of it—"to lie in cold obstruction and to rot." I thought, and still think, that it was best to use any lawful means to keep him from repeating the attempt. Best to save the man first, and preach to him afterwards.

He and I walked up and down the streets of Liverpool almost in silence, except when he darted into the first chemist's shop he saw to procure opium.

"Don't hinder me," he said imploringly, "it is the only thing that keeps me alive."

Then I walked him about once more, till his pace flagged, his limbs tottered, he became thoroughly passive and exhausted. I called a car, and expressed my determination to see him safe home.

A Life for a Life

"Home! No, no, I must not go there." And the poor fellow summoned all his faculties, in order to speak rationally. "You see, a gentleman in my unpleasant circumstances—in short, could you recommend any place—a quiet, out-of-the-way place, where—where I could hide?"

I had suspected things were thus. And now, if I lost sight of him even for twenty-four hours, he might be lost permanently. He was in that critical state, when the next step, if it were not to a prison, might be into a lunatic asylum.

It was not difficult to persuade him that the last place where creditors would search for a debtor would be inside a gaol, nor to convey him, half-stupefied as he was, into my own rooms, and leave him fast asleep on my bed.

Yet, even now, I cannot account for the influence I so soon gained, and kept; except that any person in his seven senses always has power over another nearly out of them, and to a sick man there is no autocrat like the doctor.

Now for his present condition. The day following, I removed him to a country lodging, where an old woman I know will look after him. The place is humble enough, but they are honest people. He may lie safe there till some portion of health returns; his rent, etc.—my prudent little lady will be sure to be asking after my "circumstances"—well, love, his rent for the next month at least I can easily afford to pay. The present is provided for—as to his future, Heaven only knows.

I wrote, according to promise, to your sister Penelope, explaining where Mr. Charteris was, his state of health, and the position of his affairs; also, my advice, which he neither assents to nor declines, that, as soon as his health will permit, he should surrender himself in London, go through the Insolvent Court, and start anew in life. A hard life at best, since, whatever situation he may obtain, it will take years to free him from all his liabilities.

Miss Johnston's answer I received this morning. It was merely an envelope containing a bank-note of £20, Sir William's gift, possibly; I told her he had better be made aware of his nephew's abject state,—or do you suppose it is from herself? I thought beyond your quarterly allowance, you had none of you much ready money? If there is anything I ought to know before applying this sum to the use of Mr. Charteris, you will, of course, tell me?

I have been to see him this afternoon. It is a poor room he lies in, but clean and quiet. He will not stir out of it; it was with difficulty I persuaded him to have the window opened, so that we might enjoy the still autumn sunshine, the church-bells, and the little robin's song. Turning back to the sickly drawn face, buried in the sofa-pillows, my heart smote me with a heavy doubt as to what was to be the end of Francis Charteris.

Yet I do not think he will die; but he will be months, years in recovering, even if he is ever his old self again—bodily, I mean—whether his inner self is undergoing any change, I have small means of judging. The best thing for him, both mentally and physically, would be a fond, good woman's constant care; but that he cannot have.

I need scarcely say, I have taken every precaution that he should never see nor hear anything of Lydia; nor she of him. He has never named her, nor any one; past and future seem alike swept out of his mind; he only lives in the miserable present, a helpless, hopeless, exacting invalid. Not on any account would I have Lydia Cartwright see him now. If I judge her countenance rightly, she is just the girl to do exactly what you women are so prone to—forgive everything, sacrifice everything, and go back to the old love. Ah! Theodora, what am I that I should dare to speak thus lightly of women's love, women's forgiveness?

I am glad Mr. Johnston allows you occasionally to see Mrs. Cartwright and the child, and that the little fellow is so well cared for by his grandmother. If, with his father's face, he inherits his father's temperament, the nervously sensitive organisation of a modern "gentleman," as opposed to the healthy animalism of a working man, life will be an uphill road to that poor boy.

His mother's heart aches after him sorely at times, as I can plainly perceive. Yesterday, I saw her stand watching the line of female convicts—those with infants—as one after the other they filed out, each with her baby in her arms, and passed into the exercising-ground. Afterwards, I watched her slip into one of the empty cells, fold up a child's cap that had been left lying about, and look at it wistfully, as if she almost envied the forlorn occupant of that dreary nook, where, at least, the mother had her child with her continually. Poor Lydia! she may have been a girl of weak will, easily led astray, but I am convinced that the only thing which led her astray must have been, and will always be, her affections.

Perhaps, as the grandmother cannot write, it would be a comfort to Lydia, if your next letter enabled me to give to her a fuller account of the welfare of little Frank. I wonder, does his father ever think of him? or of the poor mother? He was "always kind to them," you tell me she declared; possibly fond of them, so far as a selfish man can be. But how can such an one as he understand what it must be to be a *father!*

My love, I must cease writing now. It is midnight, and I have to take as much sleep as I can; my work is very hard just at present; but happy work, because through it I look forward to a future.

Your father's brief message of thanks for my telegram about Mr. Treherne was kind. Will you acknowledge it in the way you consider would be most pleasing—that is, least unpleasing, to him, from me?

And now, farewell—farewell, my only darling.

Max Urquhart.

P.S.—After the fashion of a lady's letter, though not, I trust, with the most important fact therein. Though I re-open my letter to inform you of it, lest you might learn it in some other way, I consider it of very slight moment, and only name it because these sort of small unpleasantnesses have a habit of growing like snow-balls, every yard they roll.

Our chaplain has just shown me in this morning's paper a paragraph about myself, not complimentary, and decidedly ill-natured. It hardly took me by surprise; I have of late occasionally caught stray comments, not very flattering, on myself and my proceedings, but they troubled me little. I know that a man in my position, with aims far beyond his present circumstances, with opinions too obstinate and manners too blunt to get these aims carried out, as many do, by the aid of other and more influential people, such a man must have enemies.

Be not afraid, love—mine are few; and be sure I have given them no cause for animosity. True, I have contradicted some, and not many men can stand contradiction—but I have wronged no man to my knowledge. My conscience is clear. So they may spread what absurd reports or innuendoes they will—I shall live it all down.

My spirit seems to have had a douche-bath this morning, cold, but salutary. This tangible annoyance will brace me out of a little feeble-heartedness that has been growing over me of late; so be content, my Theodora.

I send you the newspaper paragraph. Read it, and burn it. Is Penelope come home? I need scarcely observe that only herself and you are acquainted, or will be, with any of the circumstances I have related with respect to Mr. Charteris.

Chapter 34

HER STORY

A fourth Monday, and my letter has not come. Oh, Max, Max!—You are not ill, I know; for Augustus saw you on Saturday. Why were you in such haste to slip away from him? He himself even noticed it.

For me, had I not then heard of your well-being, I should have disquieted myself sorely. Three weeks—twenty-one days—it is a long time to go about as if there were a stone lying in the corner of one's heart, or a thorn piercing it. One may not acknowledge this: one's reason, or better, one's love, may often quite argue it down; yet it is there. This morning, when the little postman went whistling past Rockmount gate, I turned almost sick with fear.

Understand me—not with one sort of fear. Faithlessness or forgetfulness are—Well, with you they are—simply impossible! But you are my Max; anything happening to you happens to me; nothing can hurt you without hurting me. Do you feel this as I do? if so, surely, under any circumstances, you would write.

Forgive! I meant not to blame you; we never ought to blame what we cannot understand. Besides, all this suspense may end to-morrow. Max does not intend to wound me; Max loves me.

Just now, sitting quiet, I seemed to hear you saying: "My little lady," as distinctly as if you were close at hand, and had called me. Yet it is a year since I have heard the sound of your voice, or seen your face.

Augustus says, of late you have turned quite grey. Never mind, Max! I like silver locks. An old man I knew used to say, "At the root of every grey hair is a cell of wisdom." How will you be able to bear with the foolishness of this me? Yet, all the better for you. I know you would soon be ten years younger—looks and all—if, after your hard work, you had a home to come back to, and—and *me*.

See how conceited we grow! See the demoralising result of having been for a whole year loved and cared for; of knowing ourselves, for the first time in our lives, first object to somebody!

A Life for a Life

There now, I can laugh again; and so I may begin and write my letter. It shall not be a sad or complaining letter, if I can help it.

Spring is coming on fast. I never remember such a March. Bud of chestnuts bursting, blackbirds singing, primroses out in the lane, a cloud of snowy wind-flowers gleaming through the trees of my favourite wood, concerning which, you remember, we had our celebrated battle about blue-bells and hyacinths. They are putting out their leaves already; there will be such quantities this year. How I should like to show you my bank of—ahem! *blue-bells!*

Mischievous still, you perceive. Obstinate, likewise; almost as obstinate as—you.

Augustus hints at some "unpleasant business" you have been engaged in lately. I conclude some controversy, in which you have had to "hold your own" more firmly than usual. Or new "enemies,"—business foes only of course, about which you told me I must never grieve, as they were unavoidable. I do not grieve; you will live down any passing animosity. It will be all smooth sailing by-and-by. But in the meantime, why not tell me? I am not a child—and—I am to be your wife, Max.

Ah, now the thorn is out, the one little sting of pain. It isn't this child you were fond of, this ignorant, foolish, naughty child, it is your wife, whom you yourself chose, to whom you yourself gave her place and her rights, who comes to you with her heart full of love and says, "Max, tell me!"

Now, no more of this, for I have much to tell you—I tell *you* everything.

You know how quietly this winter has slipped away with us at Rockmount; how, from the time Penelope returned, she and I seemed to begin our lives anew together, in one sense beginning almost as little children, living entirely in the present; content with each day's work and each day's pleasure,—and it was wonderful how many small pleasures we found—never allowing ourselves either to dwell on the future or revert to the past. Except when by your desire. I told my sister of Francis's having passed through the Insolvent Court, and how you were hoping to obtain for him a situation as corresponding clerk. Poor Francis! all his grand German and Spanish to have sunk down to the writing of a merchant's business-letters, in a musty Liverpool office! Will he ever bear it? Well, except this time, and once afterwards, his name has never been mentioned, either by Penelope or me. The second time happened thus—I did not tell you then, I will now. When our Christmas bills came in—our private ones, my sister had no money to meet them. I soon guessed that—as, from your letter, I had already guessed where her half-yearly allowance had gone. I was perplexed, for though she now confides to me nearly everything of her daily concerns, she has never told me *that*. Yet she must have known I knew—that you would be sure to tell me.

At last, one morning, as I was passing the door of her room, shecalled me in.

She was standing before a chest-of-drawers, which, I had noticed, she always kept locked. But to-day the top drawer was open, and out of a small jewel-case that lay on it, she had taken a string of pearls.

"You remember this?"

Ah, yes! But Penelope looked steadily at it; so, of course, did I.

"Have you any idea, Dora, what it is worth, or how much William gave for it?"

I knew: for Lisabel had told me herself, in the days when we were all racking our brains to find out suitable marriage presents for the governor's lady.

"Do you think it would be wrong, or that the Trehernes would be annoyed, if I sold it?"

"Sold it!"

"I have no money—and my bills must be paid. It is not dishonest to sell what is one's own, though it may be somewhat painful."

I could say nothing. The pain was keen—even to me. She then reminded me how Mrs. Granton had once admired these pearls, saying, when Colin married she should like to give her daughter-in-law just such another necklace.

A Life for a Life

"If she would buy it now—if you would not mind asking her—"

"No, no!"

"Thank you, Dora."

She replaced the necklace in its case, and gave it into my hand. I was slipping out of the room, when she said—

"One moment, child. There was something more I wished to say to you. Look here."

She unlocked drawer after drawer. There lay, carefully arranged, all her wedding clothes, even to the white silk dress, the wreath, and veil. Everything was put away in Penelope's own tidy, over-particular fashion, wrapped in silver paper, or smoothly folded, with sprigs of lavender between. She must have done it leisurely and orderly, after her peculiar habit, which made us, when she was only a girl of seventeen, tease Penelope by calling her "old maid!"

Even now, she paused more than once, to refold or rearrange something—tenderly, as one would arrange the clothes of a person who was dead—then closed and locked every drawer, putting the key, not on her household-bunch, but in a corner of her desk.

"I should not like anything touched in my lifetime, but, should I die—not that this is likely; I believe I shall live to be an old woman—still, should I die, you will know where these things are. Do with them exactly what you think best. And if money is wanted for—" She stopped, and then, for the first time, I heard her pronounce his name, distinctly and steadily, like any other name, "for Francis Charteris, or any one belonging to him—sell them. You will promise?"

I promised.

Mrs. Granton, dear soul! asked no questions, but took the necklace, and gave me the money, which I brought to my sister. She received it without a word.

After this, all went on as heretofore; and though sometimes I have felt her eye upon me when I was opening your letters, as if she

A Life for a Life

fancied there might be something to hear, still, since there never was anything, I thought it best to take no notice. But, Max, I wished often, and wish now, that you would tell me if there is any special reason why, for so many weeks, you have never mentioned Francis?

I was telling you about Penelope. She has fallen into her old busy ways—busier than ever, indeed. She looks well too, "quite herself again," as Mrs. Granton whispered to me, one morning when—wonderful event—I had persuaded my sister that we ought to drive over to lunch at the Cedars, and admire all the preparations for the reception of Mrs. Colin, next month.

"I would not have liked to ask her," added the good old lady; "but since she did come, I am glad. The sight of my young folk's happiness will not pain her? She has really got over her trouble, you think?"

"Yes, yes," I said hastily, for Penelope was coming up the green-house walk. Yet when I observed her, it seemed not herself but a new self—such as is only born of sorrow which smiled out of her poor thin face, made her move softly, speak affectionately, and listen patiently to all the countless details about "my Colin" and "my daughter Emily" (bless the dear old lady, I hope she will find her a real daughter). And though most of the way home we were both more silent than usual, something in Penelope's countenance made me, not sad or anxious, but inly awed, marvelling at its exceeding peace. A peace such as I could have imagined in those who had brought all their earthly possessions and laid them at the Apostles' feet; or holier still, and therefore happier,—who had left all, taken up their cross, and followed *him*. Him who through His life and death taught the perfection of all sacrifice, self-sacrifice.

I may write thus, Max, may I not? It is like talking to myself, talking to you.

It was on this very drive home that something happened, which I am going to relate as literally as I can, for I think you ought to know it. It will make you love my sister as I love her, which is saying a good deal.

Watching her, I almost—forgive, dear Max!—but I almost forgot my letter to you, safely written overnight, to be posted on our way home from the Cedars, till Penelope thought of a village post-office we had just passed.

"Don't vex yourself child," she said, "you shall cross the moor again; you will be quite in time; and I will drive round, and meet you just beyond the ponds."

And, in my hurry, I utterly forgot that cottage you know, which she has never yet been near, nor is aware who live in it. Not till I had posted my letter, did I call to mind that she would be passing Mrs. Cartwright's very door!

However, it was too late to alter plans, so I resolved not to fret about it. And, somehow, the spring feeling came over me; the smell of furze-blossoms, and of green leaves budding; the vague sense as if some new blessing were coming with the coming year. And, though I had not Max with me, to admire my one stray violet that I found, and listen to my lark—the first, singing up in his white cloud, still I thought of you, and I loved you! With a love that, I think, those only feel who have suffered, and suffered together: a love that, though it may have known a few pains, has never, thank God, known a single doubt. And so you did not feel so very far away.

Then I walked on as fast as I could, to meet the pony-carriage, which I saw crawling along the road round the turn-past the very cottage. My heart beat so! But Penelope drove quietly on, looking straight before her. She would have driven by in a minute; when, right across the road, in front of the pony, after a dog or something, I saw run a child.

How I got to the spot I hardly know; how the child escaped I know still less; it was almost a miracle. But there stood Penelope, with the little fellow in her arms. He was unhurt—not even frightened.

I took him from her—she was still too bewildered to observe him much—besides, a child alters so in six months. "He is all right, you see. Run away, little man."

"Stop! there is his mother to be thought of" said Penelope; "where does he live? whose child is he?"

Before I could answer, the grandmother ran out, calling—"Franky—Franky."

It was all over. No concealment was possible.

I made my sister sit down by the roadside, and there, with her head on my shoulder, she sat till her deadly paleness passed away, and two tears slowly rose and rolled down her cheeks; but she said nothing.

Again I impressed upon her what a great comfort it was that the boy had escaped without one scratch; for there he stood, having once more got away from his granny, staring at us, finger in mouth, with intense curiosity and enjoyment.

"Off with you!" I cried more than once. But he kept his ground; and when I rose to put him away—my sister held me.

Often I have noticed, that in her harshest days Penelope never disliked nor was disliked by children. She had a sort of instinct for them. They rarely vexed her, as we, or her servants, or her big scholars always unhappily contrived to do. And she could always manage them, from the squalling baby that she stopped to pat at a cottage door, to the raggedest young scamp in the village, whom she would pick up after a pitched battle, give a good scolding to, then hear all his tribulations, dry his dirty face, and send him away with a broad grin upon it, such as was upon Franky's now.

He came nearer, and put his brown little paws upon Penelope's silk gown.

"The pony," she muttered; "Dora, go and see after the pony."

But when I was gone, and she thought herself unseen, I saw her coax the little lad to her side, to her arms, hold him there and kiss him;—oh! Max, I can't write of it; I could not tell it to anybody but you.

After keeping away as long as was practicable, I returned, to find Franky gone, and my sister walking slowly up and down; her veil was down, but her voice and step had their usual "old-maidish" quietness,—if I dared without a sob at the heart, even think that word concerning our Penelope!

Leaving her to get into the carriage, I just ran into the cottage to tell Mrs. Cartwright what had happened, and assured her that the child had received no possible harm; when, who should I see sitting over the fire but the last person I ever expected to see in that place!

Did you know it?—was it by your advice he came?—what could be his motive in coming? or was it done merely for a whim—just like Francis Charteris?

Anywhere else I believe I could not have recognised him. Not from his shabbiness; even in rags Francis would be something of the gentleman; but from his utterly broken-down appearance, his look of hopeless indifference, settled discontent; the air of a man who has tried all things and found them vanity.

Seeing me, he instinctively set down the child, who clung to his knees, screaming loudly to "Daddy."

Francis blushed violently, and then laughed. "The brat owns me, you see; he has not forgotten me—likes me also a little, which cannot be said for most people. Heyday, no getting rid of him? Come along then, young man; I must e'en make the best of you."

Franky, nothing loath, clambered up, hugged him smotheringly round the neck, and broke into his own triumphant "Ha! ha! he!"—His father turned and kissed him.

Then, somehow, I felt as if it were easier to speak to Francis Charteris. Only a word or two—inquiries about his health—how long he had left Liverpool—and whether he meant to return.

"Of course. Only a day's holiday. A horse in a mill—that is what I am now. Nothing for it but to grind on to the end of the chapter—eh, Franky my boy?"

"Ha! ha! he!" screamed the child, with another delighted hug.

"He seems fond of you," I said.

"Oh yes; he always was." Francis sighed. I am sure, nature was tugging hard at the selfish, pleasure-loving heart. And pity—I know it was not wrong, Max!—was pulling sore at mine.

A Life for a Life

I said I had heard of his illness in the winter, and was glad to find him so much recovered:—how long had he been about again?

"How long? Indeed I forget. I am so apt to forget things now. Except"—he added bitterly—"the clerk's stool and the office window with the spider-webs over it—and the thirty shillings a week. That's my income, Dora—I beg your pardon, Miss Dora,—I forgot I was no longer a gentleman, but a clerk at thirty shillings a week."

I said I did not see why that should make him less of a gentleman; and, broken-down as he was,—sitting crouching over the fire with his sickly cheek pressed against that rosy one,—I fancied I saw something of the man—the honest, true man—flash across the forlorn aspect of poor Francis Charteris.

I would have liked to stay and talk with him, and said so, but my sister was outside.

"Is she? will she be coming in here?"—And he shrank nervously into his corner. "I have been so ill, you know."

He need not be afraid, I told him—we should have driven off in two minutes. There was not the slightest chance of their meeting—in all human probability he would never meet her more.

"Never more!"

I had not thought to see him so much affected.

"You were right, Dora, I never did deserve Penelope—yet there is something I should like to have said to her. Stop, hold back the curtain—she cannot see me sitting here?" So, as she drove slowly past, Francis watched her; I felt more than glad—proud that he should see the face which he had known blooming and young, and which would never be either the one or the other again in this world, and that he should see how peaceful and good it was.

"She is altered strangely."

I asked, in momentary fear, did he think her looking out of health?

"Oh no—it is not that. I hardly know what it is;" then, as with a sudden impulse, "I must go and speak to Penelope."

And before I could hinder him, he was at the carriage side. No fear of a "scene." They met—O Max, can any two people so meet who have been lovers for ten years!

It might have been that the emotion of the last few minutes left her in that state when no occurrence seemed unexpected or strange—but Penelope, when she saw him, only gave a slight start;—and then looked at him, straight in the face, for a minute or so.

"I am sorry to see that you have been ill."

That one sentence must have struck him, as it did me, with the full conviction of how they met—as Penelope and Francis no more—merely Miss Johnston and Mr. Charteris.

"I have been ill," he said, at last. "Almost at death's door. I should have died, but for Doctor Urquhart and—one other person, whose name I discovered by accident. I beg to thank her for her charity."

He blushed scarlet in pronouncing the word. My sister tried to speak, but he stopped her.

"Needless to deny."

"I never deny what is true," said Penelope gravely. "I only did what I considered right, and what I would have done for any person whom I had known so many years. Nor would I have done it at all, but that your uncle refused."

"I had rather owe it to you—twenty times over!" he cried. "Nay—you shall not be annoyed with gratitude—I came but to own my debt—to say, if I live, I will repay it; if I die—"

She looked keenly at him:—"You will not die."

"Why not? What have I to live for—a ruined, disappointed, disgraced man? No, no—my chance is over for this world, and I do not care how soon I get out of it."

"I would rather hear of your living worthily in it."

"Too late, too late."

"Indeed it is not too late."

Penelope's voice was very earnest, and had a slight falter that startled even me. No wonder it misled Francis—he who never had a particularly low opinion of himself, and who for so many years had been fully aware of a fact—which, I once heard Max say, ought always to make a man humble rather than vain—how deeply a fond woman had loved him.

"How do you mean?" he asked eagerly.

"'That you have no cause for all this despair. You are a young man still; your health may improve; you are free from debt, and have enough to live upon. Whatever disagreeables your position has, it is a beginning—you may rise. A long and prosperous career may lie before you yet—I hope so."

"Do you?"

Max, I trembled. For he looked at her as he used to look when they were young. And it seems so hard to believe that love ever can die out. I thought, what if this exceeding calmness of my sister's should be only the cloak which pride puts on to hide intolerable pain?—But I was mistaken. And now I marvel, not that he, but that I—who know my sister as a sister ought—could for an instant have seen in those soft sad eyes anything beyond what her words expressed—the more plainly, as they were such extremely kind and gentle words.

Francis came closer, and said something in a low voice, of which I caught only the last sentence,—"Penelope, will you trust me again?"

I would have slipped away—-but my sister detained me; tightly her fingers closed on mine; but she answered Francis composedly:

"I do not quite comprehend you."

"Will you forgive and forget? will you marry me?"

"Francis!" I exclaimed indignantly; but Penelope put her hand upon my mouth.

"That is right. Don't listen to Dora—she always hated me. Listen to me. Penelope, you shall make me anything you choose; you would be the saving of me—that is, if you could put up with such a broken, sickly, ill-tempered wretch."

"Poor Francis!" and she just touched him with her hand. He caught it and kept it. Then Penelope seemed to wake up as out of a dream.

"You must not," she said hurriedly; "you must not hold my hand."

"Why not?"

"Because I do not love you any more."

It was so; he could not doubt it. The vainest man alive must, I think, have discerned at once that my sister spoke out of neither caprice nor revenge, but in simple sadness of truth. Francis must have felt almost by instinct that, whether broken or not, the heart so long his, was his no longer—the love was gone.

Whether the mere knowledge of this made his own revive, or whether finding himself in the old familiar places—this walk was a favourite walk of theirs—the whole feeling returned in a measure, I cannot tell; I do not like to judge. But I am certain that, for the time, Francis suffered acutely.

"Do you hate me, then?" said he at length.

"No; on the contrary, I feel very kindly towards you. There is nothing in the world I would not do for you."

"Except marry me?"

"Even so."

"Well, well; perhaps you are right. I, a poor clerk, with neither health, nor income, nor prospects—"

He stopped, and no wonder, before the rebuke of my sister's eyes.

"Francis, you know you are not speaking as you think. You know I have given you my true reason, and my only one. If we were engaged still, in outward form, I should say exactly the same, for a broken promise is less wicked than a deceitful vow. One should not marry—one ought not—when one has ceased to love."

Francis made her no reply. The sense of all he had lost, now that he had lost it, seemed to come upon him heavily, overwhelmingly. His first words were the saddest and humblest I ever heard from Francis Charteris.

"I deserve it all. No wonder you will never forgive me."

Penelope smiled—a very mournful smile.

"At your old habit of jumping at conclusions! Indeed, I have forgiven you long ago. Perhaps, had I been less faulty myself, I might have had more influence over you. But all was as it was to be, I suppose; and it is over now. Do not let us revive it."

She sighed, and sat silent for a few moments, looking absently across the moorland; then with a sort of wistful tenderness—the tenderness which, one clearly saw, for ever prevents and excludes love—on Francis.

"I know not how it is, Francis, but you seem to me Francis no longer—quite another person. I cannot tell how the love has gone, but it is gone; as completely as if it had never existed. Sometimes I was afraid if I saw you it might come back again; but I have seen you, and it is not there. It never can return again any more."

"And so, from henceforth, I am no more to you than any stranger in the street?"

"I did not say that—it would not be true. Nothing you do will ever be indifferent to me. If you do wrong—oh, Francis, it hurts me so! it will hurt me to the day of my death. I care little for your being very prosperous, or very happy; possibly no one is happy; but I want you to be good. We were young together, and I was very proud of you:— let me be proud of you again as we grow old."

"And yet you will not marry me?"

"No, for I do not love you; and never could again, no more than I could love another woman's husband. Francis," speaking almost in a whisper, "you know as well as I do, that there is one person, and only one, whom you ought to marry."

He shrank back, and for the second time—the first being when I found him with his boy in his arms—Francis turned scarlet with honest shame.

"Is it you—is it Penelope Johnston who can say this?"

"It is Penelope Johnston."

"And you say it to me?"

"To you."

"You think it would be right?"

"I do."

There were long pauses between each of these questions, but my sister's answers were unhesitating. The grave decision of them seemed to smite home—home to the very heart of Francis Charteris. When his confusion and surprise abated, he stood with eyes cast down, deeply pondering.

"Poor little soul!" he muttered. "So fond of me, too—fond and faithful. She would be faithful to me to the end of my days."

"I believe she would," answered Penelope.

Here arose a piteous outcry of "Daddy, Daddy!" and little Franky, bursting from the cottage, came and threw himself in a perfect paroxysm of joy upon his father. Then I understood clearly how a good and religious woman like our Penelope could not possibly have continued loving, or thought of marrying, Francis Charteris, any more than if, as she said, he had been another woman's husband.

"Dora, pray don't take the child away. Let him remain with his father."

And from her tone, Francis himself must have felt—if further confirmation were needed—that now and henceforth Penelope Johnston could never view him in any other light than as Franky's father.

He submitted—it always was a relief to Francis to have things decided for him. Besides, he seemed really fond of the boy. To see how patiently he let Franky clamber up him, and finally mount on his shoulder, riding astride, and making a bridle of his hair, gave one a kindly feeling, nay, a sort of respect, for this poor sick man whom his child comforted; and who, however erring he had been, was now, nor was ashamed to be, a father.

"You don't hate me, Franky," he said, with a sudden kiss upon the fondling face. "You owe me no grudge, though you might, poor little scamp! You are not a bit ashamed of me; and, by God!" (it was more a vow than an oath) "I'll never be ashamed of you."

"I trust in God you never will," said Penelope solemnly.

And then, with that peculiar softness of voice which I now notice whenever she speaks of or to children, she said a few words, the substance of which I remember Lisabel and myself quizzing her for, years ago, irritating her with the old joke about old bachelors' wives and old maids' children—namely, that those who are childless, and know they will die so, often see more clearly and feel more deeply, than parents themselves, the heavy responsibilities of parenthood.

Not that she said this exactly, but you could read it in her eyes, as in a few simple words she praised Franky's beauty, hinted what a solemn thing it was to own such a son, and, if properly brought up, what a comfort he might grow.

Francis listened with a reverence that was beyond all love, and a humility touching to see. I, too, silently observing them both, could not help hearkening even with a sort of awe to every word that fell from the lips of my sister Penelope. All the while hearing, in a vague fashion, the last evening song of my lark, as he went up merrily into his cloud,—just as I have watched him, or rather his progenitors, numberless times; when, along this very road, I used to lag behind Francis and Penelope, wondering what on earth they were talking about, and how queer it was that they never noticed anything or anybody except one another.

Heigho! how times change!

But no sighing: I could not sigh, I did not. My heart was full, Max, but not with pain. For I am learning to understand what you often said, what I suppose we shall see clearly in the next life if not in this—that the only permanent pain on earth is sin. And, looking in my sister's dear face, I felt how blessed, above all mere happiness, is the peace of those who have suffered and overcome suffering, who have been sinned against and have forgiven.

After this, when Franky, tired out, dropped suddenly asleep, as children do, his father and Penelope talked a good while, she inquiring, in her sensible, practical way, about his circumstances and prospects; he answering, candidly and apparently truthfully, without any hesitation, anger, or pride; every now and then looking down, at the least movement of the pretty, sleepy face; while a soft expression, quite new in Francis Charteris, brightened his own. There was even a degree of cheerfulness and hope in his manner, as he said, in reply to some suggestion of my sister's—

"Then you think, as Doctor Urquhart did, that my life is worth preserving—that I may turn out not such a bad man after all!"

"How could a man be anything but a good man, who really felt what it is to be the father of a child?"

Francis replied nothing, but he held his little son closer to his breast. Who knows but that the pretty boy may be heaven's messenger to save the father's soul?

You see, Max, I still like, in my old moralising habit, to "justify the ways of God to men," to try and perceive the use of pain, the reason of punishment; and to feel, not only by faith, but experience, that, dark as are the ways of Infinite Mercy, they are all safe ways. *"All things work together for good to them that love* HIM."

And so, watching these two, talking so quietly and friendly together, I thought how glad my Max would be; I remembered all my Max had done—Penelope knows it now; I told her that night. And, sad and anxious as I am about you and many things, there came over my heart one of those sudden sunshiny refts of peace, when we feel that whether or not all is happy, all is well.

Francis walked along by the pony-carriage for a quarter of a mile, or more.

"I must turn now. This little man ought to have been in his bed an hour or more: he always used to be. His mother"—Francis stopped—"I beg your pardon." Then, hugging the boy in a sudden passion of remorse, he said, "Penelope, if you want your revenge, take this. You cannot tell what a man feels, who, when the heyday of youth is gone, longs for a home, a virtuous home, yet knows that he never can offer or receive unblemished honour with his wife—never give his lawful name to his first-born."

This was the sole allusion made openly to what both tacitly understood was to be, and which you, as well as we, will agree is the best thing that can be, under the circumstances.

And here I have to say to you, both from my sister and myself, that if Francis desires to make Lydia Cartwright his wife, and she is willing, tell them both that if she will come direct from the gaol to Rockmount, we will receive her kindly, provide everything suitable for her (since Francis must be very poor, and they will have to begin housekeeping on the humblest scale), and take care that she is married in comfort and credit. Also, say that former things shall never be remembered against her, but that she shall be treated henceforward with the respect due to Francis's wife; in some things, poor loving soul! a better wife than he deserves.

So he left us. Whether in this world he and Penelope will ever meet again, who knows? He seemed to have a foreboding that they never will, for, in parting, he asked, hesitatingly, if she would shake hands?

She did so, looking earnestly at him,—her first love, who, had he been true to himself and to her, might have been her love for ever. Then I saw her eyes wander down to the little head which nestled on his shoulder.

A Life for a Life

"Will you kiss my boy, Penelope?"

My sister leaned over and touched Franky's forehead with her lips.

"God bless him! God bless you all!"

These were her last words, and however long both may live, I have a conviction that they will be her last words—to Francis Charteris.

He went back to the cottage; and through the rosy spring twilight, with a strangely solemn feeling, as if we were entering upon a new spring in another world, Penelope and I drove home.

And now, Max, I have told you all about these. About myself—No, I'll not try to deceive you; God knows how true my heart is, and how sharp and sore is this pain.

Dear Max, write to me;—if there is any trouble, I can bear it; any wrong—supposing Max could do me wrong—I'll forgive. I fear nothing, and nothing has power to grieve me, so long as you hold me fast, as I hold you.

Your faithful

Theodora.

P. S. —A wonderful, wonderful thing—it only happened last night. It hardly feels real yet.

Max, last night, after I had done reading, papa mentioned your name of his own accord.

He said, Penelope, in asking his leave, as we thought it right to do before we sent that message to Lydia, had told him the whole story about your goodness to Francis. He then inquired abruptly how long it was since I had seen Dr. Urquhart.

I told him never since that day in the library—now a year ago.

"And when do you expect to see him?"

"I do not know." And all the bitterness of parting—the terrors lest life's infinite chances should make this parting perpetual—the murmurs that will rise, why hundreds and thousands who care little for one another should be always together, whilst we—we—O Max! it all broke out in a sob, "Papa, papa, how *can* I know?"

My father looked at me as if he would read me through.

"You are a good girl and an honourable. He is honourable too. He would never persuade a child to disobey her father."

"No, never!"

"Tell him,"—and papa turned his head away, but he did say it, I could not mistake, "tell Doctor Urquhart if he likes to come over to Rockmount for one day only, I shall not see him, but you may."

Max, come. Only for one day of holiday rest. It would do you good. There are green leaves in the garden, and sunshine and larks in the moorland, and—there is me. Come!

Chapter 35

HIS STORY

My Dear Theodora,—I did not write, because I could not. In some states of mind nothing seems possible to a man but silence. Forgive me, my love, my comfort and joy.

I have suffered much, but it is over now, at least the suspense of it; and I can tell you all, with the calmness that I myself now feel. You are right; we love one another; we need not be afraid of any tribulation.

Before entering on my affairs, let me answer your letter—all but its last word, "Come!" My other self, my better conscience, will herself answer that.

The substance of what you tell me, I already know. Francis Charteris came to me on Sunday week, and asked for Lydia. They were married two days after—I gave the bride away. Since then I have drunk tea with them at his lodging, which, poor as it is, has already the cheerful comfort of a home with a woman in it, and that woman a wife.

I left them—Mr. Charteris sitting by the fire with his boy on his knee; he seems passionately fond of the little scapegrace, who is, as you said, his very picture. But more than once I caught his eyes following Lydia with a wistful, grateful tenderness.

"The most sensible, practical girl imaginable," he said, during her momentary absence from the room; "and she knows all my ways, and is so patient with them. 'A poor wench,' as Shakespeare hath it. 'A poor wench, sir, but mine own?'"

For her, she busied herself about house matters, humble and silent, except when her husband spoke to her, and then her whole face brightened. Poor Lydia! None familiar with her story are likely to see much of her again; Mr. Charteris seems to wish, and for very natural reasons, that they should begin the world entirely afresh; but we may fairly believe one thing concerning her as concerning another

A Life for a Life

poor sinner,—"*Her sins, which were many, are forgiven, for she loved much.*"

After I returned from them, I found your letter. It made me cease to feel what I have often felt of late, as if hope were knocking at every door except mine.

I told you once, never to be ashamed of showing me that you love me. Do not be; such love is a woman's glory, and a man's salvation.

Let me now say what is to be said about myself, beginning at the beginning.

I mentioned to you once that I had here a good many enemies, but that I should soon live them down; which, for some time, I hoped and believed, and still believe that it would have been so, under ordinary circumstances. I have ever held that truth is stronger than falsehood, that an honest man has but to sit still, let the storm blow over, and bide his time. It does not shake this doctrine that things have fallen out differently with me.

For some time I had seen the cloud gathering; caught evil reports flying about; noticed that in society or in public meetings, now and then an acquaintance gave me the "cold shoulder." Also, what troubled me more, for it was a hindrance felt daily, my influence and authority in the gaol did not seem quite what they used to be. I met no tangible affront, certainly, and all was tolerably smooth sailing, till I had to find fault, and then, as you know, a feather will show which way the wind blows!

It was a new experience, for, at the worst of times, in camp or hospital, my poor fellows always loved me—I found it hard.

More scurrilous newspaper paragraphs, the last and least obnoxious of which I sent you lest you might hear of it in some other way, followed those proceedings of mine concerning reformatories. Two articles—the titles, "Physician, heal thyself," and "Set a thief to catch a thief," will give you an idea of their tenor—went so far as to be actionable libels. Several persons here, our chaplain especially, urged me to take legal proceedings in defence of my character, but I declined.

A Life for a Life

One day, arguing the point, the chaplain pressed me for my reasons, which I gave him, and will give you, for I have since had only too much occasion to remember them literally.

I said I had always had an instinctive dislike and dread of the law; that a man was good for little if he could not defend himself by any better weapons than the verdict of an ignorant jury, and a specious, sometimes lying, barrister's tongue.

The old clergyman, alarmed, "hoped I was not a duellist," at which I only smiled. It never occurred to me to take the trouble of denying any such ridiculous purpose. I knew not how, when once the ball is set rolling against a man, his lightest words are made to gather weight and meaning, his very looks are brought in judgment upon him. It is the way of the world.

You see I can moralise, a sign that I am recovering myself; I think, with the relief of telling all out to you.

"But," reasoned the chaplain, "when a man is innocent, why should he not declare it? Why sit tamely under calumny? It is unwise,—nay, unsafe. You are almost a stranger here, and we in the provinces like to find out everything about everybody. If I might suggest," and he apologised for what he called the friendly impertinence, "why not be a little less modest, a little more free with your personal history, which must have been a remarkable one, and let some friend, in a quiet, delicate way, see that the truth is as widely disseminated as the slander? If you will trust me—"

"I could not choose a better pleader," said I gratefully; "but it is impossible."

"How so? A man like you can have nothing to dread—nothing to conceal."

I said again, all I could find words to say—

"It is impossible."

He urged no more, but I soon felt painfully certain that some involuntary distrust lurked in the good man's mind, and though he continued the same to me in all our business relations, a cloud came over our private intercourse, which was never removed.

About this time another incident occurred. You know I have a little friend here, the governor's motherless daughter, a bonnie wee child whom I meet in the garden sometimes, where we water her flowers, and have long chats about birds, beasts, and the wonders of foreign parts. I even have given a present or two to this, my child-sweetheart. Are you jealous? She has your eyes!

Well, one day when I called Lucy, she came to me slowly, with a shy, sad countenance; and I found out after some pains, that her nurse had desired her not to play with Dr. Urquhart again, because he was "naughty."

Dr. Urquhart smilingly inquired what he had done.

The child hesitated.

"Nurse does not exactly know, but she says it is something very wicked—as wicked as anything done by the bad people in here. But it isn't true—tell Lucy it isn't true?"

It was hard to put aside the little loving face, but I saw the nurse coming. Not an ill-meaning body, but one whom I knew for as arrant a gossip as any about this place. Her comments on myself troubled me little; I concluded it was but the result of that newspaper tattle, against which I was gradually growing hardened; nevertheless, I thought it best just to say that I had heard with much surprise what she had been telling Miss Lucy.

"Children and fools speak truth," said the woman saucily.

"Then you ought to be the more careful that children always hear the truth." And I insisted upon her repeating all the ridiculous tales she had been circulating about me.

When, with difficulty, I got the facts out of her, they were not what I expected, but these: Somebody in the gaol had told somebody else how Dr. Urquhart had been in former days such an abandoned character, that still his evil conscience always drove him among criminals; made him haunt gaols, prisons, reformatories, and take an interest in every form of vice. Nay, people had heard me say—and truly they might!—*à propos* to a late hanging at Kirkdale—that I had sympathy even for a murderer.

I listened—you will imagine how—to all this.

For an instant I was overwhelmed; I felt as if God had forsaken me; as if His mercy were a delusion; His punishments never-ending; His justice never satisfied. Despite my promise to your father, I might, in some fatal way, have betrayed myself, even on the spot, had I not heard the little girl saying, with a sob, almost—poor pet!—

"For shame, nurse! Doctor Urquhart isn't a wicked man; Lucy loves him."

And I remembered you.

"My child," I said, in a whisper, "we are all wicked; but we may all be forgiven; I trust God has forgiven me"; and I walked away without another word.

But since then I have thought it best to avoid the governor's garden; and it has cost me more pain than you would imagine—the contriving always to pass at a distance, so as to get only a nod and smile, which cannot harm her, from little Lucy.

About this time—it might be two or three days after, for out of work-hours I little noticed how time passed—an unpleasant circumstance occurred with Lucy's father.

I must have told you of him; for he is a remarkable man— young still, and well-looking; with manners like his features, hard as iron, though delicate and polished as steel. He seems born to be the ruler of criminals. Brutality, meanness, or injustice would be impossible to him. Likewise, another thing—mercy.

It was on this point that he and I had our difference.

We met in the east ward, when he pointed out to me, in passing, the announcement on the centre slate of "a boy to be whipped."

A Life for a Life

It seems ridiculous, but the words sickened me. For I knew the boy, knew also his offence; and that such a punishment would be the first step towards converting a mere headstrong lad, sent here for a street row, into a hardened ruffian. I pleaded for him strongly.

The governor listened—polite, but inflexible.

I went on speaking with unusual warmth; you know my horror of these floggings; you know, too, my opinion on the system of punishment, viewed as mere punishment, with no ulterior aim at reformation. I believe it is only our blinded human interpretation of things spiritual, which transforms the immutable law that evil is its own avenger and that the wrath of God against sin must be as everlasting as His pity for sinners—into the doctrine of eternal torment, the worm that dieth not, and the fire that is never quenched.

The governor heard all I had to say; then, politely always, regretted that it was impossible either to grant my request, or release me from my duty.

"There is, however, one course which I may suggest to Doctor Urquhart, considering his very peculiar opinions, and his known sympathy with criminals. Do you not think, it might be more agreeable to you to resign?"

The words were nothing; but as he fixed on me that keen eye, which, he boasts, can, without need of judge or jury, detect a man's guilt or innocence, I felt convinced that with him too my good name was gone. It was no longer a battle with mere side-winds of slander—the storm had begun.

I might have sunk like a coward, if there were only myself to be crushed under it. As it was, I looked the governor in the face.

"Have you any special motive for this suggestion?"

"I have stated it."

"Then allow me to state, that whatever my opinions may be, so long as my services are useful here, I have not the slightest wish or intention of resigning."

A Life for a Life

He bowed, and we parted.

The boy was flogged. I said to him, "Bear it; better confess,"—as he had done—"confess and be punished now. It will then be over." And I hope, by the grateful look of the poor young wretch, that with the pain, the punishment was over; that my pity helped him to endure it, so that it did not harden him, but, with a little help, he may become an honest lad yet.

When I left him in his cell, I rather envied him.

It now became necessary to look to my own affairs, and discover if possible all that report alleged against me—false or true—as well as the originator of these statements. Him I at last by the merest chance discovered.

My little lady, with her quick, warm feelings, must learn to forgive, as I have long ago forgiven. It was Mr. Francis Charteris.

I believe still, it was less from malice premeditated, than from a mere propensity for talking, and that looseness and inaccuracy of speech which he always had—that he, when idling away his time in the debtors' ward of this gaol, repeated, probably with extempore additions, what your sister Penelope once mentioned to him concerning me—namely, that I was once about to be married, when the lady's father discovered a crime I had committed in my youth—whether dishonesty, duelling, seduction, or what, he could not say—but it was something absolutely unpardonable by an honourable man, and the marriage was forbidden. On this, all the reports against me had been grounded.

After hearing this story, which one of the turnkeys whose children were down with fever, told me while watching by their bedside, begging my pardon for doing it, honest man! I went and took a long walk down the Waterloo shore, to calm myself and consider my position. For I knew it was in vain to struggle any more. I was ruined.

An innocent man might have fought on; how any one, with a clear conscience, is ever conquered by slander, or afraid of it, I cannot understand. With a clean heart, and truth on his tongue, a man ought to be as bold as a lion. I should have been; but—My love, you know.

This Waterloo shore has always been a favourite haunt of mine. You once said you should like to live by the sea; and I have never heard the ripple of the tide without thinking of you—never seen the little children playing about and digging on the sands without thinking—God help me! if one keeps silence, it is not because one does not feel the knife. "Who would have thought the old man had so much blood in him?"

Let me stop. I will not pain you, my love, more than I can help. Besides, as I told you, the worst of my suffering is ended.

I believe I must have sat till nightfall among the sandhills by the shore. For years to come, if I live so long, I shall see as clear and also as unreal as a painting—that level sea-line, along which moved the small white silent ships, and the steamers, with their humming paddle-wheels and their trailing thread of smoke, dropping one after the other into what some one of your favourite poets, my child, calls "the under world." There seemed a great weight on my head—a weariness all over me. I did not feel anything much, after the first half-hour, except a longing to see your little face once again, and then, if it were God's will, to lie down and die, somewhere near you, quietly, giving no trouble to you or to any one any more. You will remember, I was not in my usual health, and had had extra hard work, for some little time.

Well, my dear one, this is enough about myself, that day. I went home and fell into harness as usual; there was nothing to be done but to wait till the storm burst, and I wished for many reasons to retain my situation at the gaol as long as possible.

But it was a difficult time; rising to each day's duty, with total uncertainty of what might happen before night: and, duty done, struggling against a depression such as I have not known for these many years. In the midst of it came your dear letters—cheerful, loving, contented—unwontedly contented they seemed to me. I could not answer them, for to have written in a false strain was impossible, and to tell you everything seemed equally so. I said to myself, "No, poor child! she will learn all soon enough. Let her be happy while she can."

A Life for a Life

I was wrong; I was unjust to you and to myself. From the hour you gave me your love, I owed it to us both to give you my full confidence, as much as if you were my wife. I had no right to wound your dear heart by keeping back from it any sorrows of mine. Forgive me, and forgive something else, which, I now see, was crueller still. Theodora, I wished many times that you were free; that I had never bound you to my hard lot, but kept silence and left you to forget me, to love some one else better than me—pardon, pardon!

For I was once actually on the point of writing to you, saying this, when I remembered something you had said long ago,—that whether or no we were ever married you were glad we had been betrothed—that so far we might always be a help and comfort to one another. For, you added, when I was blaming myself and talking as men do of "honour," and "pride"—to have left you free when you were not free, would have given you all the cares of love, with neither its rights, nor duties, nor sweetnesses; and this might—you did not say it would—but it might have broken your heart.

So in my bitter strait I trusted that pure heart, whose instinct, I felt, was truer than all my wisdom. I did not write the letter, but at the same time, as I have told you, it was impossible to write any other, even a single line.

Your last letter came. Happily, it reached me the very morning when the crisis, which I had been for weeks expecting, occurred. I had it in my pocket all the time I stood in that room before those men,—but I had best relate from the beginning.

You are aware that any complaints respecting the officers of this gaol, or questions concerning its internal management, are laid before the visiting justices. Thus, after the governor's hint, on every board day, I prepared myself for a summons. At length it came; ostensibly for a very trivial matter—some relaxation of discipline which I had ordered and been counteracted in. But my conduct had never been called into question before, and I knew what it implied. The very form of it—"The governor's compliments, and he requests Doctor Urquhart's attendance in the board-room";—instead of "Doctor, come up to my room and talk the matter over," was sufficient indication of what was impending.

A Life for a Life

I found present, besides the governor and chaplain, an unusual number of magistrates. These, who are not always or necessarily gentlemen, stared at me as if I had been some strange beast, all the time I was giving my brief evidence about the breach of regulations complained of. It was soon settled, for I had been careful to keep within the letter of the law, and I made a motion to take leave, when one of the justices requested me to "wait a bit, they hadn't done with me yet."

These sort of men, low-born—not that that is any disgrace, but a glory, unless accompanied with a low nature—and "dressed in a little brief authority," one often meets with here; I was well used to deal with them, and to their dealings with the like of me—a poor professional, whose annual income was little more than they would expend, carelessly, upon one of their splendid "feeds." But, until lately, among my co-mates in office, I had been both friendly and popular. Now, they took their tone from the rest, and even the governor and the chaplain preserved towards me a rigid silence. You do not know our old mess phrase of being "sent to Coventry." If you did, you would understand how those ten minutes that, according to my orders, I sat aloof from the board, while other business was proceeding, were not the pleasantest possible.

Men amongst men grow hard, are liable to evil passions, fits of pride, hatred, and revenge, that are probably unfamiliar to you sweet women. It was well I had your letter in my pocket. Besides, there is something in coming to the crisis of a great misfortune which braces up a man's nerves to meet it. So, when the governor, turning round in his always courteous tone, said the board requested a few minutes' conversation with me, I could rise and stand steady, to meet whatever shape of hard fortune lay before me.

The governor, like most men of non-intrusive but iron will, who have both temper and feelings perfectly under control, has a very strong influence wherever he goes. It was he who opened and carried on with me, what he politely termed, a "little conversation."

"These difficulties," continued he, after referring to the dismissed complaint of my straining the rules of the gaol to their utmost limit, from my "sympathy with criminals," "these unpleasantnesses, Doctor Urquhart, will, I fear, be always occurring. Have you reconsidered the hint I gave to you, some little time ago?"

I answered that it was rarely my habit to take hints; I preferred having all things spoken right out.

"Such candour is creditable, though not always possible or advisable. I should have been exceedingly glad if you had saved me from what I feel to be my duty, however painful, namely, to repeat my private suggestion publicly."

"You mean that I should tender my resignation?"

"Excuse my saying—and the board agrees with me—that such a step seems desirable, for many reasons."

I waited, and then asked for those reasons.

"Doctor Urquhart must surely be aware of them."

A man is not bound to rush madly into his ruin. I determined to die fighting, at any rate. I said, addressing the board—

"Gentlemen, I am not aware of having conducted myself in any manner that unfits me for being surgeon to this gaol. Any slight differences between the governor and myself are mere matters of opinion, which signify little, so long as neither trenches on the other's authority, and both are amenable to the regulations of the establishment. If you have any cause of complaint against me, state it, reprove or dismiss me, it is your right; but no one has a right without just grounds to request me to resign."

The governor, even - through that handsome, impassive, masked countenance of his, looked annoyed. For an instant his hard manner dropped into the old friendliness, even as when, in the first few weeks after his wife's death, he and I used to sit playing chess together of evenings, with little Lucy between us.

"Doctor, why will you misapprehend me? It is for your own sake that I wish, before the matter is opened up further, you should resign your post."

After a moment's consideration, I requested him to explain himself more clearly.

A Life for a Life

One of the magistrates here cried out with a laugh—"Come, come, Doctor, no shamming. You are the town's talk." And another suggested that "Brown had better mind his p's and q's; there were such things as actions for libel."

I replied if the gentlemen referred to the scurrilous allegations against me which had appeared in print, they might speak without fear; I had no intention of prosecuting for libel. This silenced them a moment, and then the first magistrate said—

"Give a dog a bad name and hang him; but surely, Doctor, you can't be aware what a very bad name you have somehow got in these parts, or you would have been more eager to draw your neck out of the halter in time. Why, bless my soul, man alive, do you know what folk make you out to be?"

"This discussion is growing foreign to the matter in hand," interrupted the governor, who I felt had never taken his sharp eyes off me. "The question is merely this: that any officer in authority among criminals must of necessity bear an unblemished character. Neither in the establishment nor out of it ought people to be able to say of him that—that——"

"Say it out, sir."

"—That there were circumstances in his former life which would not bear inspection, and that merely accident drew the line between himself and the convicts he was bent on re-forming."

"Hear, hear!" said a justice, who had long thwarted me in my schemes; having a conscientious objection to reforming everybody—including himself.

"Nay," said the governor. "I did not give this as a fact,—only a report. These reports have come to such a height, that they must either be proved or denied. And therefore I wished, before any public inquiry became necessary—unless, indeed, Doctor Urquhart will consent to the explanatory self-defence which he definitely refused Mr. Thorley—"

And they both looked anxiously at me—these two whom I have always found honest, honourable men, and who were once my friends, or at least friendly' associates—the chaplain and the governor.

Theodora, no one need ever dread lest the doctrine of total forgiveness should make guilt no burthen, and repentance pleasant and easy. There are some consequences of sin which must haunt a sinner to the day of his death.

It might have been one minute or ten, that I stood motionless, feeling as if I could have given up life and all its blessings without a pang, to be able to face those men with a clear conscience, and say, "It is all a lie. I am innocent."

Then, for my salvation, came the thought—it seemed spoken into my ear, the voice half like Dallas's, half like yours—"If God hath forgiven thee, why be afraid of men?" And I said, humbly enough—yet, I trust, without any cringing or abjectness of fear—that I wished, before taking any further step, to hear the whole of the statements current against myself, and how far they were credited by the gentlemen before me.

The accusation, I was informed, stood thus: floating rumours having accumulated into a substantive form—terribly near the truth! that I had, in my youth, either here or abroad, committed some crime which rendered me amenable to the laws of my country; and though, by some trick of law, I had escaped justice, the ban upon me was such, that only by the wandering life which I myself had owned to having led, could I escape the fury of public opinion. The impression against me was now so strong, in the gaol and out of it, that the governor would not engage even by his own authority to preserve mine unless I furnished him with an immediate, explicit denial to this charge. Which, he was pleased to say, if it had not been so widely spread, so mysterious in its origin, and so oddly corroborated by accidental admissions on my part, he should have treated as simply ridiculous.

"And now," he added, apparently re-assured by the composure with which I had listened, "I have only to ask you to deny it, point-blank, before the board and myself."

I asked, what must I deny?

A Life for a Life

"Why, if the accusations were not too ludicrous to express, just state that you are neither forger, burglar, nor body-snatcher; that you never either killed a man (unprofessionally, of course, if we may be excused the joke)—for professional purposes, or shot him irregularly in a duel, or waylaid him with pistols behind a hedge."

"Am I supposed to have committed all these crimes?"

"Such is the gullibility of the public; you really are," said the governor, smiling.

On the indignant impulse of the moment, I denied them each and all, upon my honour as a gentleman; until, feeling the old chaplain cordially grip my hand, I was roused into a full consciousness of where and what I was, and what, either by word or implication, I had been asserting.

Somebody said, "Give him air; no wonder he feels it, poor fellow!" And so, after a little, I gathered up my faculties, and saw the board sitting waiting; and the governor with pen and ink before him.

"This painful business will soon be settled, Doctor," said he cheerfully. "Just answer a question or two, which, as a matter of form, I will put in writing, and then, if you will do me the honour to dine with me to-day, we can consult how best to make the statement public; without of course compromising your dignity. To begin. You hereby make declaration that you were never in gaol? never tried at any assizes? have never committed any act which rendered you liable to prosecution under our criminal law?"

He ran the words off carelessly, and paused for my answer. When none came, he looked up, his own penetrative, suspicious look.

"Perhaps I did not express myself clearly?" And he slightly changed the form of the sentence. "Now, what shall I write, Doctor Urquhart?"

If I could then and there have made full confession, and gone out of that room an arrested prisoner, it would have been, so far as regarded myself, a relief unutterable, a mercy beyond all mercies. But I had to remember your father. The governor laid down his pen.

A Life for a Life

"This looks, to say the least, rather strange."

"Doctor," cried one of the board, "you must be mad to hold your tongue and let your character go to the dogs in this way."

Alas, I was not mad; I saw all that was vanishing from me—inevitably, irredeemably—my good name, my chance of earning a livelihood, my sweet hope of a home and a wife. And I might save everything, and keep my promise to your father also, by just one little lie.

Would you have had me utter it? No, love; I know you would rather have had me die.

The sensation was like dying, for one minute, and then it passed away. I looked steadily at my accusers; for accusation, at all events strong suspicion, was in every countenance now; and told them that though I had not perpetrated a single one of the atrocious crimes laid to my charge, still the events of my life had been peculiar; and circumstances left me no option but the course I had hitherto pursued, namely, total silence. That if my good character were strong enough to sustain me through it, I would willingly retain my post at the gaol, and weather the storm as I best could. If this course were impossible—

"It is impossible," said the governor decisively.

"Then I have no alternative but to tender my resignation."

It was accepted at once.

I went out from the board-room a disgraced man, with a stain upon my character which will last for life, and follow me wherever I plant my foot. The honest Urquhart name, which my father bore, and Dallas—which I ought to have given stainless to my wife, and left—if I could leave nothing else—to my children—ay, it was gone. Gone, for ever and ever.

I stole up into my own rooms, and laid myself down on my bed, as motionless as if it had been my coffin.

Fear not, my love; one sin was saved me, perhaps by your letter of that morning. The wretchedest, most hopeless, most guilty of men would never dare to pray for death so long as he knew that a good woman loved him.

When daylight failed, I bestirred myself, lit my lamp, and began to make a few preparations and arrangements about my rooms—it being clear that, wherever I went, I must quit this place as soon as possible.

My mind was almost made up as to the course I ought to pursue; and that of itself calmed me. I was soon able to sit down, and begin this letter to you; but got no further than the first three words, which, often as I have written them, look as new, strange, and precious as ever: *"My dear Theodora."* Dear,—God knows how infinitely! and mine—altogether and everlastingly mine. I felt this, even now. In the resolution I had made, no doubts shook me with respect to you; for you would bid me to do exactly what conscience urged—ay, even if you differed from me. You said once, with your arms round my neck, and your sweet eyes looking up steadfastly in mine:—"Max, whatever happens, always do what you think to be right, without reference to me. I would love you all the better for doing it, even if you broke my heart."

I was pondering thus, planning how best to tell you of things so sore; when there came a knock to my room-door. Expecting no one but a servant, I said "Come in," and did not even look up—for every creature in the gaol must be familiar with my disgrace by this time.

"Doctor Urquhart, do I intrude?"

It was the chaplain.

Theodora, if I have ever in my letters implied a word against him—for the narrowness and formality of his religious belief sometimes annoyed and were a hindrance to me—remember it not. Set down his name, the Reverend James Thorley, on the list of those whom I wish to be kept always in your tender memory, as those whom I sincerely honoured, and who have been most kind to me of all my friends.

A Life for a Life

The old man spoke with great hesitation, and when I thanked him for coming, replied in the manner which I had many a time heard him use in convict cells:—

"I came, sir, because I felt it to be my duty."

"Mr. Thorley, whatever was your motive, I respect it, and thank you."

And we remained silent—both standing—for he declined my offer of a chair. Noticing my preparations, he said, with some agitation, "Am I hindering your plans for departure? Are you afraid of the law?"

He seemed relieved; then, after a long examining look at me, quite broke down.

"O Doctor, Doctor, what a terrible thing this is! who would have believed it of you!"

It was very bitter, Theodora.

When he saw that I attempted neither answer nor defence, the chaplain continued sternly:—"I come here, sir, not to pry into your secrets, but to fulfil my duty as a minister of God; to urge you to make confession, not unto me, but unto Him whom you have offended, whose eye you cannot escape, and whose justice sooner or later will bring you to punishment. But perhaps," seeing I bore with composure these and many similar arguments; alas, they were only too familiar! "perhaps I am labouring under a strange mistake? You do not look guilty, and I could as soon have believed in my own son's being a criminal, as you. For God's sake break this reserve, and tell me all."

"It is not possible."

There was a long pause, and then the old man said, sighing:—

"Well, I will urge no more. Your sin, whatever it be, rests between you and the Judge of sinners. You say the law has no hold over you?"

"I said I was not afraid of the law."

"Therefore, it must have been a moral, rather than a legal crime, if crime it was." And again I had to bear that searching look, so dreadful because it was so eager and kind. "On my soul, Doctor Urquhart, I believe you to be entirely innocent."

"Sir," I cried out, and stopped; then asked him "if he did not believe it possible for a man to have sinned and yet repented?"

Mr. Thorley started back—so greatly shocked that I perceived at once what an implication I had made. But it was too late now; nor, perhaps, would I have had it otherwise.

"As a clergyman—I—I——" He paused. "'*If a man sin a sin which is not unto death,*'—You know the rest. '*And there is a sin which is unto death; I do not say that he shall pray for it.*' But never that we shall *not* pray for it."

And falling down on his knees beside me, the old chaplain repeated in a broken voice:—

"*Remember not the sins of my youth nor my transgressions; according to thy mercy, think thou upon me, O Lord, for thy goodness.*' Not ours, which is but filthy rags; for *Thy* goodness, through Jesus Christ, O Lord."

"Amen."

Mr. Thorley rose, took the chair I gave him, and we sat silent. Presently he asked me if I had any plans? Had I considered what exceeding difficulty I should find in establishing myself anywhere professionally, after what had happened this day?

I said, I was fully aware that, so far as my future prospects were concerned, I was a ruined man.

"And yet you take it so calmly?"

"Ay."

A Life for a Life

"Doctor," said he, after again watching me, "you must either be innocent, or your error must have been caused by strong temptation, and long ago retrieved. I will never believe but that you are now as honourable and worthy a man as any living."

"Thank you."

An uncontrollable weakness came over me; Mr. Thorley, too, was much affected.

"I'll tell you what it is, my dear fellow," said he, as he wrung my hand, "you must start afresh in some other part of the world. You are no older than my son-in-law was when he married and went to Canada, in your own profession too. By the way, I have an idea."

The idea was worthy of this excellent man, and of his behaviour to me. He explained that his son-in-law, a physician in good practice, wanted a partner—some one from the old country, if possible.

"If you went out, with an introduction from me, he would be sure to like you, and all might be settled in no time. Besides, you Scotch hang together so—my son-in-law is a Fife man—and did you not say you were born or educated at St. Andrews? The very thing!"

And he urged me to start by next Saturday's American mail.

A sharp struggle went on within my mind. Mr. Thorley evidently thought it sprang from another cause, and, with much delicacy, gave me to understand that in the promised introduction, he did not consider there was the slightest necessity to state more than that I had been an army surgeon, and was his valued friend; that no reports against me were likely to reach the far Canadian settlement, whither I should carry both to his son-in-law and the world at large, a perfectly unknown and unblemished name.

If I had ever wavered, this decided me. The hope must go. So I let it go, in all probability, for ever.

Was I right? I can hear you say, "Yes, Max."

In bidding the chaplain farewell, I tried to explain to him, that in this generous offer he had given to me more than he guessed—faith not only in heaven, but in mankind, and strength to do without shrinking what I am bound to do—trusting that there are other good Christians in this world besides himself who dare believe that a man may sin and yet repent— that the stigma even of an absolute crime is not hopeless, nor eternal.

His own opinion concerning my present conduct, or the facts of my past history, I did not seek; it was of little moment; he will shortly learn all.

My love, I have resolved, as the only thing possible to my future peace, the one thing exacted by the laws of God and man—to do what I ought to have done twenty years ago—to deliver myself up to justice.

Now I have told you; but I cannot tell you the infinite calm which this resolution has brought to me. To be free; to lay down this living load of lies, which has hung about me for twenty years; to speak the whole truth before God and man—confess all, and take my punishment—my love, my love, if you knew what the thought of this is to me, you would neither tremble nor weep, but rather rejoice!

My Theodora, I take you in my arms, I hold you to my heart, and love you with a love that is dearer than life and stronger than death, and I ask you to let me do this.

In the enclosed letter to your father, I have, after relating all the circumstances of which I here inform you, implored him to release me from a pledge which I ought never to have given. Never, for it was putting the fear of man before the fear of God: it was binding myself to an eternal hypocrisy, an inward gnawing of shame, which paralysed my very soul. I must escape it; you must try to release me from it,—my love, who loves me better than herself, better than myself, I mean this poor worthless self, battered and old, which I have often thought was more fit to go down into the grave than live to be my dear girl's husband. Forgive me if I wound you. By the intolerable agony of this hour, I feel that the sacrifice is just and right.

You must help me, you must urge your father to set me free. Tell him—indeed I have told him—that he need dread no disgrace to the family, or to him who is no more. I shall state nothing of Henry

A Life for a Life

Johnston excepting his name, and my own confession will be sufficient and sole evidence against me.

As to the possible result of my trial, I have not overlooked it. It was just, if only for my dear love's sake, that I should gain some idea of the chances against me. Little as I understand of the law, and especially English law, it seems to me very unlikely that the verdict will be wilful murder, nor shall I plead guilty to that. God and my own conscience are witness that I did *not* commit murder, but unpremeditated manslaughter.

The punishment for this is, I believe, sometimes transportation, sometimes imprisonment for a long term of years. If it were death—which perhaps it might as well be to a man of my age, I must face it. The remainder of my days, be they few or many, must be spent in peace.

If I do not hear within two days' post from Rockmount, I shall conclude your father makes no opposition to my determination, and go at once to surrender myself at Salisbury. *You* need not write; it might compromise you; it would be almost a relief to me to hear nothing of or from you, until all was over.

And now farewell. My personal effects here I leave in charge of the chaplain, with a sealed envelope, containing the name and address of the friend to whom they are to be sent in case of my death, or any other emergency. This is yourself. In my will, I have given you, as near as the law allows, every right that you would have had as my wife.

My wife—my wife in the sight of God, farewell! That is, until such time as I dare write again. Take good care of yourself—be patient and have hope. In whatever he commands—he is too just a man to command an injustice—obey your father.

Forget me not—but you never will. If I could have seen you once more, have felt you close to my heart—but perhaps it is better as it is.

Only a week's suspense for you, and it will be over. Let us trust in God; and farewell! Remember how I loved you, my child!

Max Urquhart.

A Life for a Life

Chapter 36

HIS STORY

My Dear Theodora,—By this time you will have known all. Thank God, it is over. My dear, dear love—my own faithful girl—it is over!

When I was brought back to prison to-night, I found your letters; but I had heard of you the day before, from Colin Granton. Do not regret the chance which made Mr. Johnston detain my letter to you, instead of forwarding it at once to the Cedars. These sort of things never seem to me as accidental; all was for good. In any case, I could not have done otherwise than I did; but it would have been painful to have done it in direct opposition to your father. The only thing I regret is, that my poor child should have had the shock of first seeing these hard tidings of my surrender to the magistrate, and my public confession, in a newspaper.

Granton told me how you bore it. Tell him I shall remember gratefully, all my life, his goodness to you, and his leaving his young wife—(whom he dearly loves, I can see) to come to me, here. Nor was he my only friend; do not think I was either contemned or forsaken. Sir William Treherne and several others offered any amount of bail for me; but it was better I should remain in prison, during the few days between my committal and the assizes. I needed quiet and solitude.

Therefore, my love, I dared not have seen you, even had you immediately come to me. You have acted in all things as my dear girl was sure to act, wise, thoughtful, self-controlled, and oh! how infinitely loving.

I had to stop here for want of daylight—but they have now brought me my allowance of candle—slender enough, so I must make haste. I wish you to have this full account as soon as possible after the brief telegram which I know Mr. Granton sent you, the instant my trial was over. A trial, however, it was not—in my ignorance of law, I imagined much that never happened. What did happen, I will here set down.

A Life for a Life

You must not expect me to give many details; my head was rather confused, and my health has been a good deal shaken, though do not take heed of anything Granton may tell you about me or my looks. I shall recover now.

Fortunately, the four days of imprisonment gave me time to recover myself in a measure, and I was able to write out the statement I meant to read at my trial. I preferred reading it, lest any physical weakness might make me confused or inaccurate. You see I took all rational precautions for my own safety. I was as just to myself as I would have been to another man. This for your sake, and also for the sake of those now dead, upon whose fair name I have brought the first blot.

But I must not think of that—it is too late. What best becomes me is humility, and gratitude to God and man. Had I known in my wretched youth, when, absorbed in terror of human justice, I forgot justice divine, had I but known there were so many merciful hearts in this world!

After Colin Granton left me last night, I slept quietly, for I felt quiet and at rest. Oh the peace of an unburdened conscience, the freedom of a soul at ease—which, the whole truth being told, has no longer anything to dread, and is prepared for everything!

I rose calm and refreshed, and could see through my cell-window that it was a lovely spring morning. I was glad my Theodora did not know what particular day of the assizes was fixed for my trial. It would make things a little easier for her.

It was noon before the case came on: a long time to wait.

Do not suppose me braver than I was. When I found myself standing in the prisoner's dock, the whole mass of staring faces seemed to whirl round and round before my eyes. I felt sick and cold; I had lost more strength than I thought. Everything present melted away into a sort of dream through which I fancied I heard you speaking, but could not distinguish any words; except these, the soft, still tenderness of which haunted me as freshly as if they had been only just uttered:

"My dear Max! my dear Max!"

A Life for a Life

By this I perceived that my mind was wandering, and must be recalled; so I forced myself to look round at the judge, jury, witness-box—in the which was one person sitting with his white head resting on his hand. I felt who it was.

Did you know your father was subpoenaed here? If so, what a day this must have been for my poor child! Think not, though, that the sight of him added to my suffering. I had no fear of him or of anything now. Even public shame was less terrible than I thought; those scores of inquisitive eyes hardly stabbed so deep as in days past did many a kind look of your father's, many a loving glance of yours.

The formalities of the court began, but I scarcely listened to them. They seemed to me of little consequence. As I said to Granton when he urged me to employ counsel, a man who only wants to speak the truth can surely manage to do it, in spite of the incumbrances of the law.

It came to an end—the long, unintelligible indictment—and my first clear perception of my position was the judge's question:—

"How say you, prisoner at the bar, guilty, or not guilty?"

I pleaded "guilty," as a matter of course. The judge asked several questions, and held a long discussion with the counsel for the crown, on what he termed "this very remarkable case," the purport of it was, I believe, to ascertain my sanity; and whether any corroboration of my confession could be obtained. It could not. All possible witnesses were long since dead, except your father.

He still kept his position, neither turning towards me, nor yet from me,—neither compassionate nor revengeful, but sternly composed; as if his long sorrows had obtained their solemn satisfaction, and even though the end was thus, he felt relieved that it had come. As if he, like me, had learned to submit that our course should be shaped for us rather than by us; being taught that even in this world's events, the God of Truth will be justified before men; will prove that those who, under any pretence, disguise or deny the truth, live not unto Him, but unto the father of lies.

A Life for a Life

Is it not strange, that then and there I should have been calm enough to think of these things? Ay, and should calmly write of them now? But as I have told you, in a great crisis my mind always recovers its balance and becomes quiet. Besides, sickness makes us both clear-sighted and far-sighted wonderfully so, sometimes.

Do not suppose from this admission, that my health is gone or going; but, simply that I am, as I see in the looking-glass, a somewhat older and feebler man than my dear love remembers me a year ago. But I must hasten on.

The plea of guilty being recorded, no trial was necessary; the judge had only to pass sentence. I was asked whether, by counsel or otherwise, I wished to say anything in my own defence? And then I rose and told the whole truth.

Do not grieve for me, Theodora? The truth is never really terrible. What makes it so is the fear of man, and that was over with me; the torment of guilty shame, and that was gone too. I have had many a moment of far sharper anguish, more grinding humiliation than this, when I stood up and publicly confessed the sin of my youth, with the years of suffering which had followed—dare I say expiated it?

There is a sense in which no sin ever can be expiated, except in One Blessed Way;—yet, in so far as man can atone to man, I believed I had atoned for mine; I had tried to give a life for a life, morally speaking; nay, I had given it. But it was not enough; it could not be. Nothing less than the truth was required from me—and I here offered it. Thus, in one short half-hour, the burthen of a lifetime was laid down for ever.

The judge—he was not unmoved, so they told me afterwards—said he must take time to consider the sentence. Had the prisoner any witnesses as to character?

Several came forward. Among the rest, the good old chaplain, who had travelled all night from Liverpool, in order, he said, just to shake hands with me to-day—which he did, in open court—God bless him!

There was also Colonel Turton; with Colin Granton—who had never left me since daylight this morning—but they all held back when they saw rise and come forward, as if with the intention of being sworn, your father.

Have no fear, my love, for his health. I watched him closely all this day. He bore it well—it will have no ill result, I feel sure. From my observation of him, I should say that a great and salutary change had come over him, both body and mind, and that he is as likely to enjoy a green old age as any one I know.

When he spoke, his voice was as steady and clear as before his accident it used to be in the pulpit.

"My lords and gentlemen, I was subpoenaed to this trial. Not being called upon to give evidence, I wish to make a statement upon oath."

There must have been a "sensation in the court," as newspapers say, for I saw Granton look anxiously at me. But I had no fears. Your father, whatever he had to say, was sure to speak the truth, not a syllable more or less, and the truth was all I wanted.

The judge here interfered, observing that there being no trial, he could receive no legal evidence against the prisoner.

"Nor have I any such evidence to give: I wish only for justice. My lord, may I speak?"

Assent was given.

Your father's words were brief and formal; but you will imagine how they fell on one ear at least.

"My name is William Henry Johnston, clerk, of Rockmount, Surrey. Henry Johnston, who—died—on the night of November 19th, 1836, was my only son. I know the prisoner at the bar. I knew him for some time before he was aware whose father I was, or I had any suspicion that my son came to his death in any other way than by accident."

"Was your first discovery of these painful facts by the prisoner's present confession?"

"No, my lord." Your father hesitated, but only momentarily. "He told me the whole story, himself a year ago, under circumstances that would have induced most men to conceal it for ever."

The judge inquired why was not this confession made public at once?

"Because I was afraid. I did not wish to make my family history a byword and a scandal. I exacted a promise that the secret should be kept inviolate. This promise he has broken—but I blame him not. It ought never to have been made."

"Certainly not. It was thwarting the purposes of justice and of the law."

"My lord, I am an old man, and a clergyman; I know nothing about the law; but I know it was a wrong act to bind any man's conscience to live a perpetual lie."

Your father was here asked if he had anything more to say?

"A word only. In the prisoner's confession, he has, out of delicacy to me, omitted three facts, which weigh materially in extenuation of his crime. When he committed it he was only nineteen, and my son was thirty. He was drunk, and my son, who led an irregular life, had made him so, and afterwards taunted him, more than a youth of nineteen was likely to bear. Such was his statement to me, and knowing his character and my son's, I have little doubt of its perfect accuracy."

The judge looked up for his notes. "You seem, sir, strange to say, to be not unfavourable towards the prisoner."

"I am just towards the prisoner. I wish to be, even though he has on his hands the blood of my only son."

After the pause which followed, the judge said—

"Mr. Johnston:—the Court respects your feelings, and regrets to detain you longer or put you to any additional pain. But it may materially aid the decision of this very peculiar case, if you will answer another question. You are aware that, all other evidence being wanting, the prisoner can only be judged by his own confession. Do you believe, on your oath, that this confession is true?"

"I do. I am bound to say from my intimate knowledge of the prisoner, that I believe him to be now, whatever he may have been in his youth, a man of sterling honour and unblemished life; one who would not tell a lie to save himself from the scaffold."

"The Court is satisfied."

But before he sat down, your father turned, and, for the first time that day, he and I were face to face.

"I am a clergyman, as I said, and I never was in a court of justice before. Is it illegal for me to address a few words to the prisoner?"

Whether it was or not, nobody interrupted him.

"Doctor Urquhart," he said, speaking loud enough for every one to hear, "what your sentence may be I know not, or whether you and I shall ever meet again until the day of judgment. If not, I believe that if we are to be forgiven our debts according as we forgive our debtors, I shall have to forgive you then. I prefer to do it now, while we are in the flesh, and it may comfort your soul. I, Henry Johnston's father, declare publicly that I believe what you did was done in the heat of youth, and has ever since been bitterly repented of. May God pardon you, even as I do this day."

I did not see your father afterwards. He quitted the court directly after sentence was given—three months' imprisonment—the judge making a long speech previously; but I heard not a syllable. I heard nothing but your father's words—saw no one except himself; sitting there below me, with his hands crossed on his stick, and a stream of sunshine falling across his white hairs—Theodora—Theodora—I cannot write—it is impossible.

Granton got admission to me for a minute, after I was taken back to prison. He told me that the "hard labour" was remitted, that there had been application made for commutation of the three months into one, but the judge declined. If I wished, a new application should be made to the Home Secretary.

No, my love, suffer him not to do it. Let nothing more be done. I had rather abide my full term of punishment. It is only too easy.

Do not grieve for me. Trust me, my child, many a peer puts on his robes with a heavier heart than I put on this felon's dress, which shocked Granton so much that he is sure to tell you of it. Never mind it—my clothes are not me, are they, little lady? Who was the man that wrote—

> "Stone walls do not a prison make,
> Nor iron bars a cage,
> Minds innocent—"

Am I innocent? No, but I am forgiven, as I believe, before God and man. And are not all the glories of heaven preparing, not for sinless but for pardoned souls?

Therefore, I am at peace. This first night of my imprisonment is, for some things, as happy to me as that which I have often imagined to myself; when I should bring you home for the first time to my own fireside.

Not even that thought, and the rush of thoughts that came with it, are able to shake me out of this feeling of unutterable rest: so perfect that it seems strange to imagine I shall ever go out of this cell to begin afresh the turmoil of the world—as strange as that the dead should wish to return again to life and its cares. But this as God wills.

My love, good night. Granton will give you any further particulars. Talk to him freely—it will be his good heart's best reward. His happy, busy life, which is now begun, may have been made all the brighter for the momentary cloud which taught him that Providence oftentimes blesses us in better ways than by giving us exactly the thing we desired. He told me when we parted, which was the only allusion he made to the past—that though Mrs. Colin was "the dearest little woman in all the world," he should always adore as "something between a saint and an angel," Miss Dora.

Is she my saint and angel? Perhaps—if she were not likewise the woman of my love.

A Life for a Life

What is she doing now, I wonder? Probably vanishing, lamp in hand, as I have often watched her, up the stair into her own wee room—where she shuts the door and remembers me.

Yes, remember me—but not with pain. Believe that I am happy—that whatever now befalls me, I shall always be happy.

Tell your father—

No, tell him nothing. He surely knows all. Or he will know it—when, this life having passed away like a vapour, he and I stand together before the One God—who is also the Redeemer of sinners.

Write to me, but do not come and see me. Hitherto, your name has been kept clear out of everything; it must he still, at any sacrifice to both of us. I count on this from you. You know, you once said, laughing, you had already taken in your heart the marriage vow of "obedience," if I chose to exact it.

I never did, but I do now. Unless I send for you—which I solemnly promise to do if illness or any other cause makes it necessary—obey me, your husband: do not come and see me.

Three months will pass quickly. Then? But let us not look forward.

My love, good night.

Max Urquhart.

A Life for a Life

Chapter 37

HER STORY

Max says I am to write an end to my journal, tie it up with his letters and mine, fasten a stone to it, and drop it over the ship's bulwarks into this blue, blue sea.—That is, either he threatened me or I him—I forget which, with such a solemn termination; but I doubt if we shall ever have courage to do it. It would feel something like dropping a little child into this "wild and wandering grave," as a poor mother on board had to do yesterday.

"But I shall see him again," she sobbed, as I was helping her to sew the little white body up in its hammock. "The good God will take care of him and let me find him again, even out of the deep sea. I cannot lose him; I loved him so."

And thus, I believe, no perfect love, or the record of it, in heart or in word, can ever be lost. So it is of small matter to Max and me, whether this, our true love's history, sinks down into the bottom of the ocean; to sleep there—as we almost expected we should do yesterday, there was such a storm; or is sealed up and preserved for the benefit of—of our great-grandchildren.

Ah! that poor mother and her dead child!

—Max here crept down into the berth to look for me—and I returned with him and left him resting comfortably on the quarter-deck, promising not to stir for a whole hour. I have to take care of him still; but, as I told him, the sea winds are bringing some of its natural brownness back to his dear old face:—and I shall not consider him "interesting" any more.

During the three months that Max was in prison, I never saw him. Indeed, we never once met from the day we said good-bye in my father's presence, till the day that—But I will continue my story systematically.

All those three months Max was ill; not dangerously—for he said so, and I could believe him. It would have gone very hard with me if I could not have relied on him in this, as in everything. Nevertheless, it was a bitter time, and now I almost wonder how I bore it. Now, when I am ready and willing for everything, except the one thing, which, thank God, I shall never have to bear again—separation.

The day before he came out of prison, Max wrote to me a long and serious letter. Hitherto, both our letters had been filled up with trivialities, such as might amuse him and cheer me; we deferred all plans till he was better. My private thoughts, if I had any, were not clear even to myself, until Max's letter.

It was a very sad letter. Three months' confinement in one cell, with one hour's daily walk round a circle in a walled yard—prisoner's labour, for he took to making mats, saying it amused him; prisoner's rules and fare—no wonder that towards the end even his brave heart gave way.

He broke down utterly. Otherwise he never would have written to me as he did—bidding me farewell, *me!* At first I was startled and shocked: then I laid down the letter and smiled—a very sad sort of smile of course, but still it was a smile. The idea that Max and I could part, or desire to do so, under any human circumstances, seemed one of those amusingly impossible things that one would never stop to argue in the least, either with one's self or any other person. That we loved one another, and therefore some day should probably be married, but that anyhow we belonged to one another till death, were facts at once as simple, natural, and immutable, as that the sun stood in the heavens or that the grass was green.

I wrote back to Max that night.

Not that I did it in any hurry, or impulse of sudden feeling. I took many hours to consider both what I should say, and in what form I should put it. Also, I had doubts whether it would not be best for him, if he accepted the generous offer of Mr. Thorley's son-in-law, made with full knowledge of all circumstances, to go first to America alone. But, think how I would, my thoughts all returned and settled in the same track, in which was written one clear truth; that after God and the right—which means all claims of justice and conscience—the first duty of any two who love truly is towards one another.

A Life for a Life

I have thought since, that if this truth were plainer seen and more firmly held, by those whom it concerns—many false notions about honour, pride, self-respect, would slip off; many uneasy doubts and divided duties would be set at rest; there would be less fear of the world and more of God, the only righteous fear. People would believe more simply in His ordinance, instituted "from the beginning"—not the mere outward ceremony of a wedding; but the love which draws together man and woman, until it makes them complete in one another, in the mystical marriage union, which, once perfect, should never be disannulled. And if this union begins, as I think it does, from the very hour each feels certain of the other's love—surely, as I said to Max—to talk about giving one another up, whether from poverty, delay, altered circumstances, or compulsion of friends, anything in short except changed love, or lost honour—like poor Penelope and Francis—was about as foolish and wrong as attempting to annul a marriage. Indeed, I have seen many a marriage that might have been broken with far less unholiness than a real troth plight, such as was this of ours.

After a little more "preaching" (a bad habit that I fear is growing upon me, save that Max merely laughs at it, or when he does not laugh he actually listens!), I ended my letter by the earnest advice that he should go and settle in Canada, and go at once; but that he must remember he had to take with him one trifling encumbrance—me.

When the words were written, the deed done, I was a little startled at myself. It looked so exceedingly like my making *him* an offer of marriage! But then—good-bye, foolish doubt! good-bye, contemptible shame! Those few tears that burned my cheeks after the letter was gone, were the only tears of the sort that I ever shed—that Max will ever suffer me to shed. Max loves me!

His letter in reply I shall not give—not a line of it. It was only *for me*.

So that being settled, the next thing to consider was how matters could be brought about, without delay either. For, with Max's letter, I got one from his good friend Mrs. Ansdell, at whose house in London he had gone to lodge. Her son had followed his two sisters—they were a consumptive family—leaving her a poor old childless widow now. She was very fond of my dear Max, which made her quick-sighted concerning him, and so she wrote as she did, delicately, but sufficiently plainly, to me, whom she said he had told

A Life for a Life

her was, in case of any sudden calamity, to be sent for as "his dearest friend."

My dear Max! Now, we smile at these sad forebodings; we believe we shall both live to see a good old age. But if I had known that we should only be married a year, a month, a week,—if I had been certain he would die in my arms the very same day—I should still have done exactly what I did.

In one sense, his illness made my path easier. He had need of me, vital, instant need, and no one else had. Also, he was so weak that even his will had left him; he could neither reason nor resist. He just wrote, "You are my conscience; do as you will, only do right." And then, as Mrs. Ansdell afterwards told me, he lay for days and days, calm, patient; waiting, he says, for another angel than Theodora.

Well—we smile now, at these days, as I said; thank God, we can smile; but it would not do to live them over again.

Max refused to let me come to see him at Mrs. Ansdell's, until my father had been informed of all our plans. But papa went on in his daily life, now so active and cheerful; he did not seem to remember anything concerning Dr. Urquhart and me. For two whole days did I follow him about, watching an opportunity, but it never came. The first person who learned my secret was Penelope.

How many a time, in these strange summers to come, shall I call to mind that soft English summer night, under the honeysuckle bush,—Penelope and I sitting at our work; she talking the while of Lisabel's new hope, and considering which of us two should best be spared to go and take care of her in her trial.

"Or, indeed, papa might almost be left alone, for a week or two. He would hardly miss us—he is so well. I should not wonder, if, like grandfather, whom you don't remember, Dora,—he lived to be ninety years old."

"I hope he may; I hope he may!"

And I burst out sobbing; then, hanging about my sister's neck, I told her all.

"Oh!" I cried, for my tongue seemed unloosed, and I was not afraid of speaking to her, nor even of hurting her—if now she could be hurt by the personal sorrows that mine recalled to her mind. "Oh, Penelope, don't you think it would be right? Papa does not want me—nobody wants me. Or if they did—"

I stopped. Penelope said, meditatively—"*A man shall leave his father and his mother and cleave unto his wife.*"

"And equally, a woman ought to cleave unto her husband. I mean to ask my father's consent to my going with Max to Canada."

"Ah! that's sudden, child.," And by her start of pain I felt how untruly I had spoken, and how keenly I must have wounded my sister in saying, "Nobody wanted me" at home.

Home, where I lived for nearly twenty-seven years, all of which now seem such happy years. "God do so unto me and more also," as the old Hebrews used to say, if ever I forget Rockmount, my peaceful maiden-home!

It looked so pretty that night, with the sunset colouring its old walls, and its terrace-walk, where papa was walking to and fro, bareheaded, the rosy light falling like a glory upon his long white hair. To think of him thus pacing his garden, year after year, each year growing older and feebler, and I never seeing him, perhaps never hearing from him; either not coming back at all, or returning after a lapse of years to find nothing left to me but my father's grave!

The conflict was very terrible; nor would Max himself have wished it less. They who do not love their own flesh and blood, with whom they have lived ever since they were born, how can they know what any love is?

We heard papa call us—"Come in, you girls! The sun is down, and the dews are falling."

Penelope put her hand softly on my head.

"Hush, child, hush! Steal into your own room and quiet yourself. I will go and explain things to your father."

A Life for a Life

I was sure she must have done it in the best and gentlest way; Penelope does everything so wisely and gently now; but when she came to look for me, I knew, before she said a word, that it had been done in vain.

"Dora, you must go yourself and reason with him. But take heed what you say and what you do. There is hardly a man on this earth for whom it is worth forsaking a happy home and a good father."

And truly, if I had ever had the least doubt of Max, or of our love for one another; if I had not felt as it were already married to him, who had no tie in the whole wide world but me—I never could have nerved myself to say what I did say to my father. If, in the slightest word, it was unjust, unloving or undutiful—may God forgive me, for I never meant it! My heart was breaking almost—but I only wanted to hold fast to the right, as I saw it, and as, so seeing it, I could not but act.

"So, I understand you wish to leave your father?"

"Papa!—papa!"

"Do not argue the point I thought that folly was all over now. It must be over. Be a good girl, and forget it. There!"

I suppose I must have turned very white, for I felt him take hold of me, and press me into a chair beside him. But it would not do to let my strength go.

"Papa, I want your consent to my marriage with Doctor Urquhart. He would come and ask you himself; but he is too ill. We have waited a long time, and suffered much. He is not young, and I feel old—quite old myself, sometimes. Do not part us any more."

This was, as near as I can recollect, what I said—said very quietly and humbly, I know it was; for my father seemed neither surprised nor angry; but he sat there as hard as a stone, repeating only, "It *must* be over."

"Why?"

He answered by one word:—"*Harry.*"

"No other reason?"

"None."

Then I dared to speak out plain, even to my father. "Papa, you said, publicly, you had forgiven him for the death of Harry."

"But I never said I should forget."

"Ay, there it is!" I cried out bitterly. "People say they forgive, but they cannot forget. It would go hard with some of us if the just God dealt with us in like manner."

"You are profane."

"No! only I am not afraid to bring God's truth into all the circumstances of life, and to judge them by it. I believe,—if Christ came into the world to forgive sinners, we ought to forgive them too."

Thus far I said—not thinking it just towards Max that I should plead merely for pity to be shown to him or to me who loved him; but because it was the right and the truth, and as such, both for Max's honour and mine, I strove to put it clearly before my father. And then I gave way, pleading only as a daughter with her father, that he should blot out the past, and not for the sake of one long dead and gone break the heart of his living child.

"Harry would not wish it—I am sure he would not. If Harry has gone where he, too, may find mercy for his many sins, I know that he has long ago forgiven my dear Max."

My father, muttering something about "strange theology," sat thoughtful. It was some time before he spoke again.

"There is one point of the subject you omit entirely. What will the world say? I, a clergyman, to sanction the marriage of my daughter with the man who took the life of my son? It is not possible."

Then I grew bold:—"So, it is not the law of God, or justice, or nature, that keeps us asunder—but the world? Father, you have no right to part Max and me for fear of the world."

When it was said, I repented myself of this. But it was too late. All his former hardness returned as he said:—

"I am aware that I have no legal right to forbid your marriage. You are of age: you may act, as you have all along acted, in defiance of your father."

"Never in defiance, nor even in secret disobedience;" and I reminded him how all things had been carried on—open and plain—from first to last; how patiently we had waited, and how, if Max were well and prosperous, I might still have said, "We will wait a little longer." Now— —

"Well, and now?"

I went down on my very knees, and with tears and sobs besought my father to let me be Max's wife.

It was in vain.

"Good night: go to your bed, Dora, and weary me no more."

I rose, certain now that the time was come when I must choose between two duties—between father and husband; the one to whom I owed existence, the other to whose influence I owed everything that had made me a girl worth living, or worth loving. Such crises do come to poor souls!—God guide them, for He only can.

"Good night, father"—my lips felt dry and stiff—it was scarcely my own voice that I heard, "I will wait—there are still a few days."

He turned suddenly upon me. "What are you planning? Tell the truth."

"I meant to do so." And then, briefly,—for each word came out with pain, as if it were a last breath,—I explained that Dr. Urquhart would have to leave for Canada in a month—that, if we had gained my

A Life for a Life

father's consent, we intended to be married in three weeks, remain a week in England, and then sail.

"And what if I do not give my consent?'

I stopped a moment, and then strength came.

"I must be Max's wife still. God gave us to one another, and God only shall put us asunder."

After that, I remember nothing till I found myself lying in my own bed with Penelope beside me.

No words can tell how good my sister Penelope was to me in the three weeks that followed. She helped me in all my marriage preparations; few and small, for I had little or no money except what I might have asked papa for, and I would not have done that—not for worlds! Max's wife would have come to him almost as poor as Griseldis, had not Penelope one day taken me to those locked-up drawers of hers.

"Are you afraid of ill-luck with these things? No? Then choose whatever you want, and may you have health and happiness to wear them, my dear."

And so—with a little more stitching—for I had a sort of superstition that I should like to be married in one new white gown, which my sister and I made between us—we finished and packed the small wardrobe which was all the marriage portion poor Theodora Johnston could bring to her husband.

My father must have been well aware of our preparations, for we did not attempt to hide them; the household knew only that Miss Dora was "going a journey," but he knew better—that she was going to leave him and her old home, perhaps for evermore. Yet he said nothing. Sometimes I caught him looking earnestly at me—at the poor face which I saw in the looking-glass—growing daily more white and heavy-eyed—yet he said nothing.

Penelope told me when, hearing me fall, she had run into the library that night, he bade her "take the child away, and say she must not speak to him on this subject any more." I obeyed. I behaved all through those three weeks as if each day had been like the innumerable other days that I had sat at my father's table, walked and talked by his side, if not the best loved, at least as well loved as any of his daughters. But it was an ordeal such as even to remember gives one a shiver of pain, wondering how one bore it.

During the daytime I was quiet enough, being so busy, and, as I said, Penelope was very good to me; but at night I used to lie awake, seeing, with open eyes, strange figures about the room—especially my mother, or some one I fancied was she. I would often talk to her, asking her if I were acting right or wrong, and whether all that I did for Max she would not have once done for my father? then rouse myself with a start, and a dread that my wits were going, or that some heavy illness was approaching me, and if so, what would become of Max?

At length arrived the last day—the day before my marriage

It was not to be here, of course; but in some London church, near Mrs. Ansdell's, who was to meet me herself at the railway-station early the same morning, and remain with me till I was Dr. Urquhart's wife. I could have no other friend; Penelope and I agreed that it was best not to risk my father's displeasure by asking for her to go to my marriage. So, without sister or father, or any of my own kin, I was to start on my sad wedding-morning—quite alone.

During the week, I had taken an opportunity to drive over to the Cedars, shake hands with Colin and his wife, and give his dear old mother one long kiss, which she did not know was a good-bye. Otherwise I bade farewell to no one. My last walk through the village was amidst a deluge of August rain, in which my moorlands vanished, all mist and gloom. A heavy, heavy night: it will be long before the weight of it is lifted off my remembrance.

And yet I knew I was doing right, and, if needed, would do it all over again. Every human love has its sacrifices and its anguishes, as well as its joys—the one great love of life has often most of all. Therefore, let those beware who enter upon it lightly, or selfishly, or without having counted its full cost.

"I do not know if we shall be happy," said I to Penelope, when she was cheering me with a future that may never come—"I only know that Max and I have cast our lots together, and that we shall love one another to the end."

And in that strong love armed, I lived—otherwise, many times that day, it would have seemed easier to have died.

When I went, as usual, to bid papa good night, I could hardly stand. He looked at me suspiciously.

"Good night, my dear. By-the-bye, Dora, I shall want you to drive me to the Cedars to-morrow."

"I—I—Penelope will do it." And I fell on his breast with a pitiful cry. "Only bid me good-bye! Only say 'God bless you,' just once, father."

He breathed hard. "I thought so. Is it to be to-morrow?"

"Yes."

"Where?"

I told him.

For a few minutes papa let me lie where I was; patting my shoulder softly, as one does a sobbing child—then, still gently, he put me away from him.

"We had better end this, Dora; I cannot bear it. Kiss me. Good-bye."

"And not one blessing? Papa, papa!"

My father rose, and laid his hand solemnly on my head:-

"You have been a dutiful girl to me, in all things save this, and a good daughter makes a good wife. Farewell—wherever you go,—God bless you!"

And as he closed the library-door upon me I thought I had taken my last look of my dear father.

A Life for a Life

It was only six o'clock in the morning when Penelope took me to the station. Nobody saw us—nobody knew. The man at the railway stopped us, and talked to Penelope for full two minutes about his wife's illness—two whole minutes out of our last five.

—My sister would not bid me good-bye—being determined, she said, to see me again, either in London or Liverpool, before we sailed. She had kept me up wonderfully, and her last kiss was almost cheerful, or she made it seem so. I can still see her—very pale, for she had been up since daylight, but otherwise quiet and tearless, pacing the solitary platform—our two long shadows gliding together before us, in the early morning sun. And I see her, even to the last minute, standing with her hand on the carriage-door—smiling.

"Give Doctor Urquhart my love—tell him, I know he will take care of you. And child"—turning round once again with her "practical" look that I knew so well—"remember, I have written 'Miss Johnston,' on your boxes. Afterwards, be sure that you alter the name. Good-bye,—nonsense, it is not really good-bye."

Ay, but it was. For how many, many years?

In that dark, gloomy, London church, which a thundery mist made darker and stiller—I first saw again my dear Max.

Mrs. Ansdell said, lest I should be startled and shocked, that it was only the sight of me which overcame him; that he was really better. And so when, after the first few minutes, he asked me, hesitatingly, "if I did not find him much altered?" I answered boldly, "No! that I should soon get accustomed to his grey hair; besides, I never remembered him either particularly handsome or particularly young." At which he smiled—and then I knew again my own Max! and all things ceased to feel so mournfully strange.

We went into one of the far pews, and Max tried on my ring. How his hands shook! so much that all my trembling passed away, and a great calm came over me. Yes—I had done right. He had nobody but me.

So we sat, side by side, neither of us speaking a word, until the pew-opener came to say the clergyman was ready.

A Life for a Life

There were several other couples waiting to be married at the same time—who had bridesmaids, and friends, and fathers. We three walked up and took our places—there was no one to pay heed to us. I saw the verger whisper something to Max—to which he answered "Yes," and the old man came and stood behind Mrs. Ansdell and me. A few other folk were dotted about in the pews, but I only noticed them as moving figures, and distinguished none.

The service began—which I—indeed we both—had last heard at Lisabel's wedding—in our pretty church, all flower-adorned, she looking so handsome and happy, with her sisters near her, and her father to give her away. For a moment I felt very desolate: and hearing a pew-door open and a footstep come slowly up the aisle, I trembled with a vague fear that something might happen, something which even at the last moment might part Max and me.

But it did not; I heard him repeat the solemn promises—how dare any one make them lightly, or break them afterwards! to *"love, comfort, honour and keep me, in sickness and in health, and, forsaking all other, keep me only unto him, so long as we both should live."* And I felt that I also, out of the entire trust I had in him, and the great love I bore him, could cheerfully forsake all other, father, sisters, kindred, and friends, for him. They were very dear to me, and would be always: but he was part of myself,—my husband.

And here let me relate a strange thing—so unexpected that Max and I shall always feel it as a special blessing from heaven to crown all our pain and send us forth on our new life in peace and joy. When in the service came the question:—"Who giveth this woman," etc.—there was no answer, and the silence went like a stab to my heart. The minister, thinking there was some mistake, repeated it again:—"Who giveth this woman to be married to this man?"

"I do."

It was not a stranger's voice, but my dear father's.

My husband had asked me where I should best like to go for our marriage journey. I said, to St. Andrews. Max grew much better there. He seemed better from the very hour, when, papa having remained with us till our train started, we were for the first time left alone by our two selves. An expression ungrammatical enough to be

A Life for a Life

quite worthy, Max would say, of his little lady, but people who are married will understand what it means.—We did, I think, as we sat still, my head on his shoulder and my hand between both his, watching the fields, trees, hills, and dales, fly past like changing shadows; never talking at all, nor thinking much, except—the glad thought came in spite of all the bitterness of these good-byes—that there was one good-bye which never need be said again. We were married.

I was delighted with St. Andrews. We shall always talk of our four days there, so dream-like at the time, yet afterwards become clear in remembrance down to the minutest particulars. The sweetness of them will last us through many a working hour, many an hour of care—such as we know must come, in ours as in all human lives. We are not afraid: we are together.

Our last day in St. Andrews was Sunday, and Max took me to his own Presbyterian church, in which he and his brother were brought up, and of which Dallas was to have been a minister. From his many wanderings it so happened that my husband had not heard the Scotch service for many years, and he was much affected by it. I too—when, reading together the psalms at the end of his Bible, he showed me, silently, the name written in it—Dallas Urquhart.

The psalm—I shall long remember it, with the tune it was sung to—which was strange to me, but Max knew it well of old, and it had been a particular favourite with Dallas. Surely if spirit, freed from flesh, be everywhere, or, if permitted, can go anywhere that it desires,—not very far from us two, as we sat singing that Sunday, must have been our brother Dallas.

> "How lovely is thy dwelling-place,
> O Lord of hosts, to me!—
> The tabernacles of thy grace
> How pleasant, Lord, they be!
> My thirsty soul longs vehemently
> Yea, faints, thy courts to see
> My very heart and flesh cry out,
> O living God, for thee. . .
>
> Blest are they, in thy house who dwell,
> Who ever give thee praise;

A Life for a Life

> Blest is the man whose strength thou art,
> In whose heart are thy ways:
> Who, passing thorough Baca's vale,
> Therein do dig up wells:
> Also the rain that falleth down
> The pools with water fills.
> Thus they from strength unwearied go
> Still forward unto strength:
> Until in Zion they appear
> Before the Lord at length."

Amen! So, when this life is ended, may we appear, even there still together,—my husband and I!

Contrary to our plans, we did not see Rockmount again, nor Penelope, nor my dear father. It was thought best not, especially as in a few years at latest, we hope, God willing, to visit them all again, or perhaps even to settle in England.

After a single day spent at Treherne Court, Augustus went with us one sunshiny morning on board the American steamer, which lay so peacefully in the middle of the Mersey—just as if she were to lie there for ever, instead of sailing, and we with her—in one little half-hour. Sailing far away, far away, to a home we knew not, leaving the old familiar faces and the old familiar land.

It seemed doubly precious now, and beautiful; even the sandy flats, that Max had so often told me about, along the Mersey shore. I saw him look thoughtfully towards them, after pointing out to me the places he knew, and where his former work had lain.

"That is all over now," he said, half sadly. "Nothing has happened as I planned, or hoped, or—"

"Or feared."

"No. My dear wife, no! Yet all has been for good. All is very good. I shall find new work in a new country."

"And I too?"

Max smiled. "Yes, she too. We'll work together, my little lady!"

The half-hour was soon over—the few last words soon said. But I did not at all realise that we were away, till I saw Augustus wave us good-bye, and heard the sudden boom of our farewell gun as the *Europa* slipped off her mail-tender, and went steaming seaward alone—fast, oh! so fast.

The sound of that gun, it must have nearly broken many a heart, many a time! I think it would have broken mine, had I not, standing, close-clasped, by my husband's side, looked up in his dear face, and read, as he in mine, that to us thus together, everywhere was Home.